About The Aut

C000258774

W J Stockdale studied English at Oxfc
bemusement of his tutors. He always dreamed of making a career
out of writing, but thankfully his understanding wife supports
him to do it anyway. He lives in Oxford, and when he's not writing,
he can be encountered either plotting his next Big Trip Abroad,
or cycling about the beautiful English countryside.

He is also partial to a slice of cake and a cup of tea.

PRAISE FOR WHERE INNOCENCE ENDS

Shortlisted for the Caledonia Novel Award
"A pacy, exciting tale which has been assiduously researched."
Caledonia Novel Award

*"A spell-binding tale that transports the reader into the 1800's.
This historical adventure has a style reminiscent of classic
novelist Charles Dickens. The prose is intricate and the
characterization vivid. Scenes are described with cinematic
detail."*
Clive Cussler Adventure Writers' Competition

*"A splendid romp – balls, fighting, politics, pirates, love
lost, buckles swashed and do derringed. A modern-day CS
Forester."*
Simon Conway

Where Innocence Ends

The Victor Winter Saga, Volume 1

WJ Stockdale

MORAG PUBLISHING

Copyright © 2022 WJ Stockdale All rights reserved

The characters and events portrayed in this book are fictitious.
Any similarity to real persons, living or dead, is coincidental and
not intended by the author.

No part of this book may be reproduced, or stored in a retrieval
system, or transmitted in any form or by any means, electronic,
mechanical, photocopying, recording, or otherwise, without
express written permission of the publisher.

ISBN 978-1-7391614-1-5

First Edition

For Lisa, and the next adventure

Every life is a march from innocence,
through temptation, to virtue or vice.

Lyman Abbott

I

Sir Godfrey Ramsay preferred the idea of a son to the reality. From my first recollections, he met any display of independence with an animosity designed to scare me into silence. I was not the son he had hoped for. So I learned to censor myself – to play the part he had cast me for. But still I disappointed him. Because I was not his son.

I was found wrapped in blankets at the gates of the small village church in Wrakeley, Hertfordshire. They said the frost that morning was so thick as to crunch underfoot, and had any more than my nose been exposed to the elements, I should not have survived. But I did. I always do.

I was found by Sir Godfrey's groundskeeper as he made his way to the house through the treacle-black pre-dawn. They said it was a miracle old Jack saw me at all – not used to looking more than a few feet ahead, and certainly not before the sun had come up. Maybe it was the pull of his faith, gained at sea in the face of a storm which shipwrecked him and drowned his crew.

Jack had told me the story enough times as he stoked the fire in my nursery. There was something in the thrill of the escape which bore retelling, even as it terrified me. To a young child brought up in the safety of a wealthy patron's care, the sea was an unimaginable thing: huge and powerful, tempting and fickle.

Whatever it was – whatever fate you choose to place your faith in, old Jack picked me up and carried me with him to his work that morning. As he sat in the kitchen, sipping his tea, I was passed from scullery maid, to housemaid, to cook, as the household awoke and took an interest in what the groundskeeper had brought in. Curious faces looked in as I stared out, oblivious to the change in fortune occurring around me: driftwood carried by the current.

Mrs Hobbs, the housekeeper, soon got wind of what was going on, and would doubtless have had me taken back out to the cemetery to join its other residents had Mr Oakes, the steward, not intervened. Mr Oakes was closer than anyone to Sir Godfrey, and to the bemusement of the staff, insisted on taking me straight before the master of the house. It was there, still wrapped in blankets, nose still red from the night's ordeal, that my fate was decided. And for years to come I knew nothing of the conversation that ensued.

Sir Godfrey Ramsay, as I would later learn, was a man of considerable means: a London gentleman who had expanded upon his father's vision, building an empire which stretched around the globe. He had a fortune and a reputation of the utmost respectability. He was, in the eyes of all society, a success.

Yet for all this, there was one sphere in which he was lacking. Lady Ramsay lay where I had been found that very morning. An elegant Portuguese lady, and the daughter of a wealthy merchant herself, her health had begun to fail in London, and she had moved permanently to Wrakeley on the doctor's advice. However, the infection had taken hold of her by then, and whilst she extended her stay in the country, she all too soon passed from this life.

Sir Godfrey's short experience of marriage had left him without an heir, and had plunged the household into a period of mourning for which it seemed there could be no cure. He had become prone to bouts of depression and flights of passion, and whilst Mr Oakes had been confident in his purpose as he made his way to his master's study that day, he wavered on the threshold. He saw Sir Godfrey stood at the window behind his writing desk, hand wrapped around his chin. Before him the sickly winter sun bled through the mist rising off the front lawn, and it was evident he was lost in his thoughts – thoughts which inevitably tended towards bitterness and regret. Mr Oakes shifted uneasily in the doorway, and cleared his throat.

'Sir – I'm sorry to trouble you so early in the day, but the groundskeeper came to the house this morning with an unusual offering.'

2

Sir Godfrey did not turn, merely gesturing with his hand. 'I'm not in the mood for staff issues this morning, Oakes. Take care of it, whatever it is.'

'Very good sir... Only – this offering may be of particular interest to you, sir.'

Mr Oakes had stepped within the room now, and as his master turned, an irritable scowl on his face, he thought to close the door behind him.

'Oakes...' Sir Godfrey never finished his sentence, presumably intended to remind his steward of his station, and send him scurrying from the room. At that moment, he saw me for the first time – though he cannot have seen more than blankets and a nose. Mr Oakes took his opportunity to explain.

'I didn't wish to be presumptuous, sir. But since the terrible loss of Lady Ramsay, and how it left this house...'

Sir Godfrey raised his hand for silence, his eyes never leaving the bundle in his steward's arms. As if a sudden movement might startle this apparition from existence, he walked with exaggerated care around his desk and towards me. Mr Oakes searched his master's face for a sign of his mood, but found it inscrutable. His eyes had narrowed, his brow furrowed and his mouth was set halfway between a smile and a sneer. He stared as if he were interrogating the new arrival through telepathy.

The silence which had been commanded now stretched out. The solemn faces of ancestors looked down upon the scene from their places on the wall, forming a ghostly magisterium, joining their living family in judgement. The mist on the hills outside the windows still cloaked the land in a soft silver shroud, encasing the familiar within the strange, and seemingly drawing the possibility of the other world closer to our own. With these thoughts Mr Oakes once again shifted uneasily but said nothing, allowing Sir Godfrey the time to reconcile himself to this most unexpected turn of events –

perhaps drawing strength from the assembly looking down on him. Finally, he lifted his gaze and spoke.

'Oakes – what are the circumstances which have led to this child being in front of me? Recount all that you know.'

And so he told the story, as it in turn had been recounted to him by Jack. When he had finished, Sir Godfrey looked once more at me, and had only one further question.

'And you say there were no other persons to be seen?'

'None, sir. Very much abandoned to the charity of the parish.'

'Little blighter shouldn't have lasted the night. There's plenty a soused sailor frozen solid along the Wapping wall this morning.'

'Indeed sir. The frost is thick on the lawn.'

'And yet he clung on. You have to admire the tenacity.'

Sir Godfrey's gaze moved past his steward, settling on the portrait of his wife.

'Oakes – I'm not a religious man, as you know. Dear Catherine took God from me when she went. But there is a strange sense of providence about this child. He's made it from her doorstep to mine... perhaps he deserves a chance at life. I want him cleaned up and cared for. Let's see what fate has given us today.'

And so it was that on January 5th, in the year of our Lord 1804, I was taken into his household.

II

I was raised as something of a curiosity at Wrakeley: an experiment never quite successful enough for the outside world. I longed for friendship and for a family to be tied to – but the boys who worked on the estate made it clear that I was not welcome, being neither one of them nor one of their masters.

Before I had learnt to avoid the stables, I was chased from them, with horse dung and cries of 'half-caste' flying at my back. If I ventured below stairs I would find conversations strangely cut short amongst the maids, and dark looks cast in my direction, whilst Mr Oakes would scold me for finding me there. Meanwhile Sir Godfrey himself was frequently away on business for long periods, monitoring my progress only through the reports of my tutors. It was a solitary existence, but preferable to the curtailed one from which Sir Godfrey had rescued me.

I was very conscious of his benevolence, and the occasional pang of loneliness was a small price to pay for being kept warm, safe, fed, clothed, and on occasion, humoured. In return I applied myself fully to my studies, eager to earn the approval of my patron, and to become the son he lacked. I was certain that if he would only allow me to accompany him to London, and to learn his trade, I would be his most loyal apprentice.

Every year, we observed my birthday together on 5th January, and every year Sir Godfrey would ask me what I desired. Only then would I venture to speak my true feelings to him, and ask to join him in London. At first he laughed. Later, he scowled. But on my tenth birthday, he laughed once more:

'I thought you would say this, Victor, and you make me very happy. Desire can be a fickle thing, especially to a young man: I did not wish to force you down my path – especially if your tutors did not believe you capable. I have waited to see what you might make of yourself, and I have sometimes taken your persistence poorly, when it has verged on insolence: indulgence does not come naturally to me. But believe me when I say I could not want anything more for you. Your tutors are satisfied that you have potential, and so I have made the necessary provisions. You and I will travel to London together tomorrow, and I shall show you everything!'

After ten years, this was my release from the quiet oppression of Wrakeley. This was escape and adventure – and the promise alone was enough to stop me sleeping that night. My mind raced with thoughts of London: of bustling streets, monuments, the mighty Thames, and a multitude of other fancies I only half understood, yet dreamt into wild significance. A single, happy thought dominated them all, however: I would no longer be alone.

We took up residence in Sir Godfrey's house in St James's Square. My reception in London could not have been more different to Wrakeley. Here I was greeted as a celebrity. Mrs Robson, Mrs Hobbs' successor as housekeeper, explained that the London staff had 'heard a great deal' about me, and had long wondered when they might finally meet me. After so many years of being 'Sir Godfrey's unwanted orphan' (though never once to my face), it seemed impossible that anyone might be interested to meet me – but I was overjoyed nonetheless. A still greater fuss was made on account of it having been my birthday, and the very next day I was taken by Mr Oakes to Sir Godfrey's tailor on Pall Mall, where I was measured for a new set of clothes. Sir Godfrey explained: 'If you're to accompany me, you must look the part, my boy. Can't have you at my side looking halfway to threadbare! Tongues will wag. People will think business is on the wane. And between you and me, thanks to our new trade with Russia, it couldn't be better!'

Here again, the nature of my welcome was wholly unexpected. I felt like an imposter as I followed Mr Oakes into Harding and Howell's: the silks, velvets and lace, draped elegantly over counters and against walls, flaunted opulence beyond anything I had seen. There was nothing to compare with this in Wrakeley. A shop assistant hurried over and greeted us warmly. Mr Oakes bade him spare no expense to clothe me, and when I emerged from the shop some time later I left behind a small armada of workers creating new jackets, breeches, and shirts, as well as stockings, handkerchiefs, bow ties, cravats, a hat, and a fine pair of gloves. Although slightly bewildered, I began to feel a strange new sense of confidence. As I looked about the shop, I saw other gentlemen and ladies in similarly fine attire, and dared to imagine myself passing for their equal.

It was therefore with great excitement that I awaited delivery of my new finery and, once dressed for the occasion, we set out across London. Despite the cold, the streets were far from empty. Leaving St James's in our coach, we passed small groups of well-dressed folk making their way along The Strand, wrapped up against the elements.

We rattled along wide streets, past newspaper sellers and flower girls singing to sell their wares, and costermongers pushing produce carts along pavements. I stared out at buildings I had only seen in pictures, suddenly made real before me: Somerset House, St Mary le Strand, and then St Clement Danes, before passing through the gateway at Temple Bar and entering the City. At once the streets grew narrower, the old City stoically different from its upstart Westminster rival. Approaching Ludgate Hill the streets closed in still further, like an elderly relative, leaning over inquisitively, but threatening to topple down onto us at any moment.

At the same time the press of people swelled from a constant trickle to a flood. At the crossroads our driver slowed the coach to a crawl to negotiate the whirlpool which had gathered there, and though the delay exasperated Sir Godfrey, I could not hide my fascination with the sights, sounds and smells now all around me. Animal and human rubbed shoulders as horse competed with pedestrian for the right of way, while dogs, cats and other creatures threaded under and in-between the travellers. Other carriages barged slowly through the throng, the drivers shouting themselves hoarse to clear the road from the incessant waves of traffic. I turned to ask my patron what the cause of this sudden swell might be.

'Look to your left, Victor, and you will see for yourself.'

And sure enough, craning my neck out of the carriage, a patch-work quilt of canvas stretched away down the intersecting street. The noise from the tumult swirled, cry consuming cry, single words chewed together and swallowed, but soon I discerned voices:

'Half a quire of paper for a penny!'

'Grapes! Tuppence a pound of grapes!'

'Sold again! Penny a pound! Get your potatoes here!'

'Three pair a ha'penny – bootlaces!'

The Fleet Street Market. A seething mass of people selling and buying, shouting out their offers, from paper to fruit to laces. Amongst them I could see women with thick shawls, bustling through the crowds with baskets on their arms, stopping at stalls to assess the wares. A quick press of an onion between two fingers, or the weighing of a sheaf of paper. And others: a knife-sharpener had set his stones down against a frontage, and stood on a box, alternately advertising for business, and turning to deliver his services. A few yards on, a basket weaver picked out her likely customers, offering to sell a better or bigger basket for a lower price than the ones draped on everyone around her.

And then I saw more. My eye was drawn to someone nearby moving with unusual speed, weaving his way through unseen gaps like only the dogs and cats had seemed able. I wondered what his business might be, until it was bawled across the scene:

'Stop! Thief!'

A shiver ran through the crowd, as if it were one being – connected in mind and body. Heads turned, searching for the culprit – but he was practised at his trade, and had already disappeared from view. I felt a pang of guilt, knowing I had taken pleasure in the episode – a colourful part of a colourful scene, the like of which I should never have seen in Wrakeley village, where the market sellers knew all their customers by name, and never had to vie with one another for their favour.

A great cry from our own carriage drew my attention back, and we surged forward, free of the swirl. With my head still thrust out of the window, I caught a glimpse of an enormous dome and colonnaded frontage directly before us: St Paul's cathedral. This was a spectacle of a different sort, but no less captivating. The sheer scale of it was breath-taking. Surely as grand as anything in Paris or Rome. London claimed to be the city at the centre of the world, and here was the centre of that city.

'A fine building, Victor. Soaring and strong. Does it impress you?' asked Sir Godfrey.

'Indeed it does, sir! I have never seen the like!'

'I am sure Christopher Wren would be satisfied with your reaction. A cathedral fit for London. But make no mistake, my boy – these monuments are not built on charity and goodwill. There is a reason they find a home here. London has money. Money made from trade. Even in Wren's day the East India Company was bringing back silks and satins from the Orient. From Harding and Howell's, to the scoundrels flogging their wares behind us, the English market is insatiable for goods. We live in momentous times. Bonaparte tried to break us with the sword, but Nelson saw to that ambition. Then he tried to break our economy. He knew we were nothing without our trade. He thought he could block our markets. But our markets are everywhere! Wherever you go in this world, you will find an English outpost, with local traders beating a path to its door. They know that the Frenchman or the American is like to turn on his own country-man at any moment – let alone a foreigner. Trade with them only when you must, and on favourable terms. But a trade agreement with an Englishman? That is one which will endure, and bring prosperity to both parties.

'You will see today that Ramsay's is built on its reputation. Integrity. Without that, we are nothing. A few guineas made on a dishonest agreement will end with a loss. You don't have to trick people to make money. You have to understand them – a much trickier prospect. And it starts with the books. Here we are!'

The carriage drew to a halt, and the footman sprang to open the door and place a step for us to descend.

'This is our main office, Victor. You'll find not a coffee bean, nor a tea leaf, nor a yard of cloth here. The real secret to business is administration. And this is where it occurs!'

I stepped out of the carriage and looked upon the centre of the Ramsay empire. A featureless brick building of three storeys stared dourly back at me. Two large sash windows stood either side of a white door. Above the door, a sign read 'Ramsay's Importers & Exporters'.

We walked inside, into a dark room with desks either side of a central corridor, and were greeted by a short, wiry man with large round glasses and a stoop. Sir Godfrey introduced him as Mr Crisp, the chief accountant of the company. Mr Crisp leant forward, and shook my hand in what I forever after took to be the manner of a man not used to activity, nor society.

'Victor', said Sir Godfrey. 'I require five minutes of Mr Crisp's time.'

He did not excuse himself, nor ask me to leave, and so we remained in the corridor while they conducted their business. Mr Crisp spoke precisely and in short sentences. There was a dryness to his language: no incidental observation, no reference to his own views. Everything was based in recorded fact, almost as if he were reading from one of his ledgers. Seventy-three barrels of Portuguese port, unloaded yesterday from the London docks. Part of a shipment of cinnamon from Ceylon, unloaded from an Indiaman three days past, customs duty paid, and now sitting in the company's warehouse. A full shipment of silks from Surat, expected in the next three days. Sir Godfrey asked to examine the books, and they removed themselves to a desk. My attention wandered and I began to examine my surroundings.

The room was panelled with a rich, dark hardwood, and the floor carpeted in a thick burgundy pile. At the end of the corridor, facing the door, a longcase clock with an elaborately carved body marked out the passing seconds of time with a monotonous tock. The desks were arrayed in rows to my left and right as in a classroom, all facing the front of the office, while behind them sat a cohort of clerks, busily scratching their records onto the lined paper of their books. The sound of quills and of the clock was somehow amplified by the absence of any other, save the muttering of Mr Crisp and Sir Godfrey, absorbed in their record-checking. Not one of the clerks seemed in the least interested or disturbed by our presence. Their eyes remained fixed directly in front of them. On the walls hung two large oil paintings of ocean-going vessels battling towering seas. Masts and rigging jutted perilously out into the foam and the hulls seemed on the verge of toppling into the waves.

Leaning forward, I could see sailors in tarpaulin jackets rushing frantically across the decks, tying away ropes, as the waters stood poised above their heads. The paintings were full of fury and danger, with disaster looming only a moment away. I could not for the life of me draw the link between this tomb of ambition, and the energy and adventure of the pictures. I glanced down at a clerk's work, the better to appreciate the skill behind this vocation – but what I saw did nothing to change my opinion. The books were divided into columns and rows spread across every page. Down the left were listed strange creations such as 'Rattan', and 'Sac Saturni', whilst alongside them were a mass of numbers and more numbers, some presumably quantities, some prices, but most beyond meaning – and certainly giving me no desire to learn more. I had studied hard all through my childhood, determined to learn and to be of value to Sir Godfrey and his business. But if this was the secret to business, I was happy for it to stay a secret.

A familiar hand clapped over my shoulder. 'Learning the dark art of the books?'

I turned and looked up into the beaming face of my patron, fresh from examining books of his own.

'I'm pleased you take my counsel so readily. Yes indeed – this is where Ramsay's undercuts the competition and outsmarts its rivals. Detail, detail, detail, my boy. Organisation, planning, accuracy. We are not the only merchants in London. Not by a long chalk! So why do we prosper? How do we attract custom? Because we plan and we organise better than anyone else. This office is testament to that. Why do you think I keep our clerks in such luxury?'

I had wondered the very same thing. It seemed odd that a company which prided itself on economy and efficiency should keep such opulent offices for its clerks.

'I cannot tell, Sir Godfrey. What is the reason?'

'Perception, Victor!' he declared with a broad smile which suggested he was not wholly disappointed in my response. 'When I bring prospective clients here, they see a company which values its administration above all. If I place an order for one hundred tons of saltpetre, I want to know I'll get one hundred tons – not ninety-five. And I shall want the finest saltpetre. Not the sludge the French use. I'll want Indian. One hundred percent Indian. Uncut, unspoiled, dry as a bone. One look around these offices, one look at these books, will tell me that not a grain will go unaccounted for. Not one mile of that saltpetre's journey will be unknown – and I shall load my rifle with confidence.'

He paused, pleased with his lesson – and I saw his logic. But the pictures continued to exert their hold over me. If the true nature of my patron's work was not the adventure and excitement I saw in them, then perhaps I had been mistaken. Perhaps the future *I* wanted was not the future *he* wanted. Try as I might, I could not appreciate the precision of the books like I appreciated the daring of the sailors on those ships. My gaze lingered one last time on the painting nearest me.

He sighed, and now I knew I had disappointed him. 'Those paintings are part of the story too, of course. What we do here is the key – but it does not capture the imagination of the Romantics. And for better or worse, we are in the age of Romance. Men read Wordsworth and Coleridge in the clubs. It's even rumoured Carlton House has a copy of Childe Harold. I suppose I too once indulged these fancies – so I put these paintings on the walls.' For just a moment he seemed lost in a reverie, staring beyond the painting, before his eyes returned to me. 'But I grew up, Victor – as we all must, and put away childish things. These are our ships. This is the other part of the business. This is what you want to see, isn't it?!'

I conceded a small nod. 'I would be interested, Sir Godfrey, to see the other part of the business as well.'

His eyes narrowed in disapproval, but for a moment I saw the glimmer of a smile. 'Very well. We shall visit Mr Crawshaw at the docks, and I shall attempt to improve your opinion of this work over the course of our journey!'

So it was that at the age of just ten, I was shown what he described as 'the keys to the kingdom'. And the kingdom of Sir Godfrey Ramsay was a bountiful land. He had had the good fortune to be born into his father's wealth, but had nonetheless invested wisely and at times remarkably. He saw trends where others saw chance events. He saw markets where others saw merely customers.

As it stood now, he ran a mill and dyeing works in Manchester, and owned a small armada of vessels which traded his and other people's goods around the world. Diversity, he told me, was the key to weathering fickle markets. Sir Godfrey bought tea from the East India Company and sold it in England. He took raw cotton from the fields of the United States, and processed it in his mills. What he could not use, he sold on to competitors for a healthy profit. He sold sugar cane and rum from the Caribbean to the Americans. He transported coffee from Java to the cafés of England and, when the war was over, he would be the first to supply it to Europe once more. In spite of the war, somehow he still managed to supply French perfumes to the British aristocracy - though I was told not to ask how. But at the centre of it all was cloth. Everyone in the world wanted Manchester cloth, and Sir Godfrey was happy to provide it. Using the latest machines, he could offer it at a price his competitors could not match, and still make a profit.

Everything he did, he did with a sizeable margin, and through a network of contacts which spread across the British Empire and beyond. His presence in every major locale in the world allowed him to seize new opportunities wherever they might occur, from the vacuum in the spice trade, caused by the collapse of the Dutch East India Company, through the re-opening of the Russian ports, to the burgeoning opium markets of China.

When our carriage reached the London docks I realised I had barely noticed the city passing by, so intent had I been on digesting every word he uttered. The docks could not have been more different to the head office. In front of us a long brick perimeter wall led away in both directions and disappeared around corners. It was at least twelve feet high, yet above it a forest of masts, naked but for their bright flags, soared forth. Closer to us, and hard against the wall in places, vast, solid warehouses competed with the masts for their space in the sky. Around the gates gathered a mob of labourers – hopeful dock-workers, sailors, street sweepers, and costermongers of all sorts – all set on making their livings from the world within, while customs men patrolled, regulating their entrance to that world. And their constant vigilance was needed, with the ragged urchins who seemed to appear from every corner and alley, sniping and searching for just one opportunity to pass unnoticed into the riches on offer within. With a smart tongue and a brandish of the whip, our driver pushed his way through this mob, and with a rather more measured tongue and the brandishing of papers by Sir Godfrey, we passed the customs men and into the docks themselves.

The first thing that struck me inside the walls was the noise. The air was filled with calls, whistles, alarms and the crashes and bangs of scores of sacks, crates, barrels and pallets. Wagons clattered up and down all sides of the quay, horse-shoes and wheels ringing on stone. Chains clanked as they slowly worked their heavy loads down, then rattled as they were released and flew back up. Seagulls screeched as they circled above, eyeing the riches as greedily as the urchins beyond the wall. Dockers called to each other as they passed goods from deck to shore, while customs men shouted as they instructed the impounding or release of goods. Here a quartermaster marked up his ledger as provisions were taken on board his vessel; there a captain watched carefully as his cargo was unloaded down a gangplank.

Our carriage barrelled unerringly through the maelstrom, past a long row of identical brick warehouses which buzzed with activity. Looking up at their windows I saw cranes laden with cargo dotted amongst them. An army of workers of all hues busied themselves either lifting goods to the upper floors, or lowering them down, to rest on wagons or in stacks on the cobblestones. Amongst them, birds swooped and dived, pausing to investigate a sack left unattended on the cobbles, before scattering like flies as the owner appeared from a doorway, foul-mouthed and threatening violence. Street-sweepers moved between the wagons, clearing the horse-droppings away from the cargoes.

The smell was at once overpowering and yet impossible to capture. It was a mixture of so many different scents, unnaturally brought together from the furthest reaches of the empire. The familiar tang of horse dung mixed with pepper and cinnamon, tea and coffee, and then, becoming all-consuming, the dominant flavour of tobacco. The carriage drew to a halt, and Sir Godfrey stepped from the door.

'Here we are, Victor!' he said, gesturing grandly with both arms at buildings I could not see in front of the carriage, but which I could nevertheless smell. 'This is what all the numbers mean. This is the reality.'

I stepped eagerly from my seat, and turned to look with him at the tobacco dock. Here the warehouses were squat, unlike those we had passed before. The smell was everywhere and unmistakeable. On the far side of the carriage, three ships sat moored together against the quay. From the nearest, a steady stream of labourers carried crate after crate down the gangplank and in through the open doors of the nearest warehouse. Several officers stood watching the work, ensuring that having survived a journey of thousands of miles, the goods did not suddenly disappear in their final furlong, whether by mishap or design. The officer nearest the warehouse entrance recognised my patron and marched over.

'Sir Godfrey,' he declared smartly, with a deferential nod.

'Mr Crawshaw. Good day!'

'Two merchants arrived this morning from Virginia, sir.'

'Tonnage?'

'One thousand, three hundred and twelve all told, sir.'

'Excellent. And the warehouse?'

'Plenty of space, sir. Though I dare say they won't be here long. Clients are desperate for a consignment. The feud with the Americans has caused quite a shortage. We'll be able to command a handsome price.'

'Excellent, excellent. And the captains?'

'Both reports on my desk, sir, and both currently supervising unloading.'

'I should like to speak with the senior captain. And I should like to introduce my ward, Victor Winter.'

Mr Crawshaw shifted his attention at my introduction, and gave me an equally smart nod. I immediately felt a warmth for this efficient and energetic man, who had not hesitated in treating me as an equal.

'Victor has met Mr Crisp at the main office, Mr Crawshaw, but has expressed a stronger interest in the business you oversee.' A wry smile crept over Sir Godfrey's face, just as I felt mine turning a deep crimson.

'Is that so, sir? Well I'm sure we could use an extra pair of hands on the ropes!'

Mr Crawshaw returned the smile, before Sir Godfrey continued:

'Please send the captain to your office immediately. This war with France is coming to an end, and we must be poised to take full advantage. I need information!'

'Very good, sir.'

'Victor – I should like you to come with me. Perhaps hearing a little of the sea-faring life may do some good.'

Mr Crawshaw's office was spartan but practical. It was the office of a man who spent more time in the warehouse or out on the quay than immured behind a desk. But if I had thought the smell of tobacco was strong on the quay, it was nothing compared to the smell in the building. It permeated the walls like damp, climbing up the brickwork from floor to floor, and oozing out into the air of the

17

office. Sir Godfrey and the captain seemed immune to the flavour – but to me it was overwhelming, and I soon found myself in the grip of a vicious headache, such that I was able only to concentrate in waves on the conversation at hand. The captain was well-built, though not portly and, despite his recent arrival, he presented himself immaculately. His coat was without blemish or crease, and whilst not flamboyant, it showed understated good taste. He was clean-shaven and his hair carefully combed and parted. This was a man who took pride in his bearing even after a long voyage. His deep blue eyes fixed with an intensity on my patron, and I imagined at that moment that there could be no finer calling in life than to be such an adventurer, officer, and leader of men.

'Captain. Welcome home. I am keen to know how the war goes in North America, and to know any news of the war on the continent. Perchance you have encountered some Royal Navy ships on blockade duty these past few days?'

'Good day, Sir Godfrey.' The voice was clipped and precise, which I thought to be in perfect keeping with his appearance. 'I would that the weather here were more like Virginia, sir. I cannot recall a winter so severe. But I am grateful for the fire you have provided. As to the progress of the wars, we may all rest easy. The Americans retreated from Canada through November. Our navy remains in control of the seas, and allows our shipping to pass, while blockading theirs. The war is a distraction, if you will permit me sir, from the real business to our east. France is on its knees, and the allied armies press toward Paris itself. We met a Royal Navy brig in the channel three days ago whose captain confirmed the situation. Wellington himself says the war will be over by April.'

Sir Godfrey leant back in his chair.

'As soon as that? Arrangements will have to be made. Now, tell me about your journey...'

The tobacco reached with wispish fingers into my head, and squeezed. I felt my attention ebb. After what seemed an age, the captain was dismissed and, having written some instructions in a letter, Sir Godfrey led me out of the office to the blessed relief of the quayside once more. All my interest in the bustle of the docks was now replaced with the desire to breathe fresh air and, happily, having passed the letter to Mr Crawshaw, Sir Godfrey ushered me back into our carriage for our return to St James's Square.

'Well, Victor. What did you make of that?'

I wrestled to overcome my nausea, if only to make it clear that I wished never to be engaged as a clerk in my life.

'That was most interesting, sir. The docks are a fascinating and vibrant place.'

'Indeed they are, my boy. Indeed they are. They are the hub of London. And London is the hub of the world. So there is nothing one cannot learn at the docks. Did you note the letter I passed to Mr Crawshaw?'

'I did, sir. Might I ask what it contained?'

'Ever inquisitive, are you not?! Your curiosity does you credit. That letter has instructed Mr Crawshaw to begin preparations for a fleet of vessels filled with our goods to cross the channel. We have an opportunity here to make a name for ourselves. Paris has been closed off from the world for years. We shall be the ones to reopen the door. We may have only two months – and we must ensure that our first consignment is a cornucopia of luxury, garnered from all around the world. Mr Crawshaw has a busy few weeks ahead of him!'

Sir Godfrey's enthusiasm was clear even through my suffering, and so I made a show of sharing it as we returned home. Despite the cold of the carriage, it was still a great relief to be out of the thick miasma, and my health improved further when I was installed in the library with a roaring fire, where I passed the remainder of the day engrossed in tales of adventure on the seas.

III

The weather in London grew colder. The canal in St James's park froze over, and pavements sprouted lethal patches of ice. Accompanying Sir Godfrey on his walk one morning, we saw floes making their aimless, spinning passage down the Thames. A crowd might have gathered to look, had it not been so cold. Instead, Sir Godfrey paused mid-stride, then turned and hurried home, almost dragging me behind him. Even as I recovered my breath in the entrance hall, he scribbled a note and dispatched a courier to deliver it to Mr Crawshaw.

Three days later, I awoke to the news that the river had stopped. The servants gossiped in the corridors. There would be a spectacle, they said. I begged Sir Godfrey to indulge me, and let us observe the phenomenon. He was sceptical, but acquiesced in spite of Mrs Robson's protestations.

'The very idea!' she muttered, dressing me in my warmest overclothes. 'You'll catch your death out there, Master Winter.'

There was a curious expression on my patron's face as we walked along the Strand to the waterfront. It was not one I had seen before, and I wondered if this might be the face of a serious man hiding his excitement. The idea amused me. It was hard to imagine a man as worldly as Sir Godfrey excited by anything. But as we emerged onto the riverbank by Blackfriars Bridge, it was I who betrayed my excitement.

'Look, Sir Godfrey!' I exclaimed, squeezing his hand. 'The river is frozen! Frozen solid!'

And so it was. Yet this was not at all the strangest thing about the scene. For below us, on the busiest waterway in the world, was now an armada of tents.

Bright and tawdry flags flew from every pole and line, enticing the public towards the goods on sale. Boar and chicken roasted on spits, men served ale from barrels, and entertainers moved amongst the crowds, some juggling, some chanting, some tumbling. There were Indians in turbans and thick furs banging drums. A group of Africans huddled together, cloaked in the bright skins of strange animals, singing bewitching melodies while their leader entreated passers-by for a coin. Short, powerful men with sheepskin hats and waistcoats performed a bizarre, squatting and kicking dance in a circle, shouting encouragement to each other as they went. Games of all sorts were underway across the ice, sending more men sliding on their behinds as they competed, from skittles to aunt sally to football. And everywhere, dotted amongst the tents and the people, were braziers. Fires on the Thames. It did not seem possible, yet there they were.

I proceeded eagerly onto the ice, pulling my chaperone with me. The footing was uncertain, and more than once I was saved from a sudden fall by his firm grasp. But I persevered, my sense of adventure undiminished.

'Stay close, Victor,' he warned. 'I don't wish to lose you in the crowd.'

And with that we plunged into the spectacle, pausing to sample the entertainments. Traders called out for our attention from within their murky stalls, but Sir Godfrey would stop only long enough to look before moving on, he now pulling me forward.

'Vagabonds and confidence tricksters all,' he declared as we shuffled along. 'This lady will promise to tell your fortune simply to send you to a certain address where an associate will slice you up and take your wallet.'

I peered into the tent in question and saw the shadowy form of a woman with dark features, long hair and bright robes, sitting at a table covered with cards. I longed to enter and learn more, but instead we walked on.

We passed several more tents, offering similar mysteries, all of which Sir Godfrey was equally dismissive. However, as we approached a large tent with a crowd of men spilling out, and loud singing coming from within, he slowed. On the side of the tent was daubed 'The City of Moscow', and it occurred to me that perhaps today London was indeed as cold as the Russian capital.

'Now, don't you find that curious?'

In truth I found everything around me curious at that moment, but before I could reply, he continued. 'That is Captain Horwell, and there next to him is my friend George Danvers. I dare say those men around them are several of Captain Horwell's crew. What do you think they are doing here?'

'Might they be enjoying the spectacle, sir, much like us?'

'I am here in my role as patron, indulging my ward's interest in a rare spectacle. I doubt very much that Captain Horwell and Mr Danvers there have a similar arrangement. Mr Danvers also keeps an office at the London docks – and I have seen him there in close conversation with Captain Horwell on many occasions. But never out of that office. What do you think might draw them out from their usual rendezvous?'

Once again I was aware that my patron expected a specific answer – and once again I felt the frustration of knowing I disappointed him.

'Not sure? Let's ask them, shall we? There's nothing like a pot of ale to get tongues wagging.' And he stepped forward into the gloom of the tent, pulling me in his wake.

As my eyes grew accustomed to the dark, it became clear that whatever business brought Captain Horwell and Mr Danvers together here, it was not happy. Their heads hung down over their pots, and they spoke in low, morose mutters which conveyed their mood more clearly than any words.

This mood seemed to pass by my patron completely unnoticed, as he strode to their table and cheerily began his interview.

'George! Captain Horwell. I did not expect to find you here. What news from the docks? I trust all is well?'

Mr Danvers gave Sir Godfrey a tired and withering look which suggested he did not appreciate the interruption. I wondered if we were at all welcome at the table.

'Hello, Sir Godfrey,' he drawled. 'Do join us, won't you?'

Despite his invitation neither he nor his colleague made any attempt to make space for us.

Now, at last, it seemed Sir Godfrey sensed the mood.

'Tell me all, Captain Horwell. Or must I piece it together from your crew?'

'I'd wager you've already done most of the piecing, Sir Godfrey. And it's as you would surmise. The docks are frozen. Just like here. Frozen solid. Froze up last night. Must be upward of forty boats marooned there. We were due out this morning with a full cargo of cloth bound for Stockholm. God knows when we'll get out now.'

'Or if,' added Mr Danvers, lifting his pot.

'If?'

'Aye - if,' confirmed Captain Horwell. 'The timbers were creaking something dreadful last night. The ice ain't got nowhere to go – so it squeezes the ships all round. When it starts melting, the boats will either sink or swim – and that's the first we'll know about it. No one even knows yet whether Lloyd's will foot the bill.'

'Good Lord. I am sorry. I had my concerns – but I confess I thought I was overly cautious. Was the cargo...'

'...Lord Elsfield's? Wasn't it just,' interjected Mr Danvers. 'And he'll know by now, no doubt. And he'll be looking to vent his spleen on us. Who knows. Maybe the ice will break underneath us and save him the trouble. Or maybe it will break under *him*.'

'I am sure Lord Elsfield will appreciate the unique circumstances that have caused his inconvenience, George.'

Mr Danvers, pot to his mouth, snorted loudly. He wiped the spilled ale from his face with a handkerchief before looking up directly into Sir Godfrey's eyes. 'Now I don't believe that any more than you do, Sir Godfrey. His Lordship is many things, but forgiving is not one of them. Captain Horwell and I will waste no time in removing ourselves from London just as soon as we are able to. There'll be no work for us here for a while.'

Sir Godfrey's eyes narrowed, and I thought he was about to offer some hope to the miserable pair. But after a pause, he merely said:

'Gentlemen, it is the worst luck.'

He turned and ushered me to lead out of the tent, but then a thought seemed to strike him, and he turned back to the table.

'You know – Archangel is keeping me very busy these days.'

This time it was Captain Horwell who responded: 'You'll excuse us for not congratulating you on your success, Sir Godfrey.'

There was a moment's silence. The atmosphere had been unwelcoming when we entered; now it was uncomfortable. Two swarthy men with unkempt beards and large, rough-hewn hands turned from their business at the bar and peered enquiringly at Captain Horwell. My patron seemed once again not to notice however, instead stepping closer to the table.

'If you are bent on leaving London, gentlemen... I would urge you to visit my operation in Russia.'

A change came over the face of Mr Danvers, and his words came slowly and with the strangest of tones – as if his mind had wandered far from the tent: 'You know – odd as it may sound, I've become quite fond of this recent climate. I've a mind to find a place where a man can sit in a tent on a river all year round. Captain Horwell – don't you think there's merit in that?'

'Aye - I suppose if one knew who to talk to in such a place – and one were able to secure letters of good standing and an introduction...'

Smiles crept round the corners of all three men's eyes. Mr Danvers pushed a pot of ale towards Sir Godfrey.

'I think I'll drink to that, Sir Godfrey.'

'Your good health, gentlemen. Please pay your respects to Mr Crawshaw at your earliest convenience. You will find him most accommodating.'

We stayed only long enough for Sir Godfrey to take one last swig of his pot, but in that time the atmosphere in the tent changed completely. Low mutterings were replaced with excitable chatter. The men at the bar were now laughing heartily with each other – though even their laughter remained unsettling to me. Sir Godfrey raised his hat to his friends and took me by the hand as we departed.

'Never miss an opportunity to do a friend a service, Victor. We all need friends.'

'Is that what you did in there, sir?'

'Those unfortunate men will have lost a considerable amount to this weather. Lord Elsfield too, I don't doubt – but he can better afford it. I offered to find them employment in Russia for a while. Until their copybook is wiped clean here in England.'

I pondered this wisdom carefully, turning it in my mind like the Rosetta stone while we wandered onwards through the city of tents. His ambition for me weighed heavily. He had indulged me in bringing me here, and I hoped that I might at last be earning his trust – maybe even his affection. But I was also conscious of every lesson he passed down to me, and the expectation that came with it. I dared not disappoint him. I now paid little attention to the entertainments we passed, trying instead to manufacture a question which would impress him. But as we passed through a thicket of people, my eyes were drawn to a sight which utterly dissolved my purpose.

My feet forgot themselves and stood still. My mouth dropped open, and my arm seemed to stretch out before me of its own accord, pointing across the river in sheer amazement. A great grey creature the size of a house was walking alongside the bridge. It seemed to move slowly – ponderously – and yet each step was the length of a bench, so that its handlers had to run to stay alongside, yelping and prodding at its sides to direct it towards the fair.

I had seen pictures of such a thing before, but never expected to see one here in London – much less walking on the surface of the Thames. Its skin hung down like loosened leather from its belly, its giant ears flapped gently in the sharp air, and with its trunk it seemed to sense and smell all around it – like a dog with a telescopic nose. Its languid pace and desiccated skin gave the impression of great age, whilst the eyes, constantly moving like the trunk, suggested an inquisitive, intelligent mind behind.

On its side and legs I could now make out writing, and saw that the handlers were taking payment in exchange for a paintbrush, and the chance to daub a slogan upon the beast. It seemed a tawdry purpose for such a magnificent creature.

'Incredible, is it not?' The observation was clearly aimed at me – yet I did not recognise the voice nor, on turning, its owner. I turned back to the spectacle, and he continued nonetheless.

'It's called an elephant. Loxodonta africana. Largest animal on terra firma. The ancient Greeks used to ride into battle on them. I'm told there are millions in the jungles and plains of Africa. Great armies of them, roaming ceaselessly across the continent. They have no natural predators. They simply wander.'

It seemed too wonderful to be true: in this modern world, a species which roamed the earth without threat, and without servitude. I gazed in awe, and with something approaching envy, at the great beast which was now before me.

'I cannot imagine what it would be like. To see a great herd on the move.'

'If you cannot imagine it, then you must see it for yourself, young sir. Don't take *my* word for it!'

His excitement was infectious, and I looked now with a renewed interest at the stranger. His piercing dark eyes stared back at me – I could feel their intensity like a burning slow match on my skin. Above the eyes was a fine black top hat and a heavy brow; beneath, a wide, grinning mouth with gleaming teeth. He seemed a similar age to Sir Godfrey. A fob watch chain snaked out from his waistcoat and buried itself in the breast pocket of his coat. The coat's inner lining was rich burgundy, with laurels interwoven around repeating coats of arms. A large cloak was fastened around his neck, and covered his back and shoulders. His attire and the power of his presence left me in no doubt that here was a man of import.

'Victor. There you are! What on earth did you think...' Sir Godfrey's voice, suddenly urgent and then silent, and I realised with a start that I had been without him since being transfixed by the elephant. Between the animal and the stranger, I had been utterly bewitched.

'Godfrey! What a surprise to see you here! I would not have thought these fripperies your thing at all.' The stranger's voice, jovial and full of life, addressing my patron like an old friend.

'Andrew.'

'Do I take it that you know my new friend here?' He gestured to me as I stood with a look of utter bewilderment on my face.

Sir Godfrey drew in a deep breath, and composed himself.

'Victor, I have the honour to introduce Lord Elsfield.'

'Andrew, please!' A flamboyant bow, removing his top hat and sweeping it under his body. 'I presume I have the pleasure to address Sir Godfrey's new business partner?'

I blushed at the flattery.

'Victor is my apprentice, Andrew. He came to me as an orphan and I have raised him at Wrakeley. He is showing a commendable interest in my operations, so he now resides with me in London, the better to understand the business.'

'Good Lord, Godfrey! You are a dark horse! A child all this time and never a word?'

'As you know Andrew, I prefer to keep business and my personal affairs separate.'

'Indeed you do – but even so I must admire the extent of your partitioning. You are full of surprises, sir.'

'As indeed are you,' replied Sir Godfrey, with a tone I could not quite place.

'One tries not to be a bore, Godfrey! Speaking of which – have you seen the elephant of the ice?! Truly a spectacle to remember. The magic of Africa walking before us on the waters of the Thames.'

Sir Godfrey made a curt nod of acknowledgement.

'I was just marvelling with young Victor here at the sight.' He turned back to me, his broad grin still firmly in place. 'Did you know that in many cultures an elephant is considered a bringer of good fortune? If you look, you can see that people have written wishes onto its legs. Would you like to make a wish on the elephant, Victor?'

It seemed a wonderful idea. All notion of debasing the creature was swept away in my excitement. To touch the skin of an elephant from Africa. The very words conjured emotions and images I could not express. To connect with something so alien – so otherworldly. To *feel* its mystery – its majesty. The largest animal on the earth. To share in its magic – if only for a moment. I found myself mimicking Lord Elsfield's beaming smile, my eyes widening.

'I would, my Lord. I absolutely would!'

'Well we must ask Sir Godfrey's permission, of course. He knows what's best, does he not?'

Together we turned to look at my patron with pleading faces. Sir Godfrey did not seem to share our sense of wonder, appearing altogether more circumspect. However, his narrowed eyes opened, and his clenched jaw softened under our joint assault.

'Very well, Victor. But let's be quick about it. I'm sure Lord Elsfield here has better things to do than indulging young boys.'

I nodded, only half listening, and hurried away with Sir Godfrey and my new friend.

The elephant up close was even more awe-inspiring, towering above me, trunk still wandering as its legs were kept in place by its handlers. My paint brush quivered for a moment as I considered what to write on its bristly skin.

'What will you wish for, young Victor?' asked Lord Elsfield, appearing almost mischievous with his eyebrows raised and that infectious smile still glued to his face.

'I do not know, my Lord.'

'Well – make it from the heart. No good wishing with your head.'

I pondered his advice, certain it was not what Sir Godfrey, standing alongside with a distinct look of disapproval, would have said. I looked upwards at the magical beast above me. Africa. Adventure. These were the jumbled words which forced their way out onto the living canvas. I did not even know their meaning, but caught up in the excitement of the moment, I imbued them with all of the half-imagined aspirations of a ten-year-old boy. Beaming with hope, I handed the brush back to Sir Godfrey, who turned to return it to a handler.

At that moment, something struck me in the belly with such force that I folded over, fighting just for air. Large hands gripped my sides, and in an instant I was lifted from the ice, and slung like a sack of coal over a shoulder. Eyes watering, lungs failing, utterly disoriented, I tried to shout an alarm – but all that came forth was a hoarse whisper.

I was helpless – unable even to raise my head to see. All I knew was the pungent smell of tobacco emanating from every stitch of the rough tweed I bounced against, and the rasp of heavy breathing as my assailant broke into a run, weaving through the distracted crowd.

Slowly recovering, I saw before me the rags he wore over his shoes. Another moment and the horizon came into view, and the crowd, thinning behind us. We had emerged into a clearing, surrounded by only the backs of tents – but still our pace did not slow. With a rising panic I realised: I was being kidnapped. I began to struggle, drawing a string of threats and curses such as I had never heard. His voice was deep and guttural – the voice of a man accustomed to doing harm. But weighed against his threats was the fear that my life, and all that I held dear, was disappearing behind me. I drew breath and, twisting towards his ear, screamed for help with every ounce of energy I could muster. The effect was immediate.

With a roar of dismay and a violent spasm I was thrown from his shoulder and flung down onto the ice so that, for the second time in as many minutes, the breath was knocked out of me. Towering over me now, his face contorted with rage: brow knotted and mouth working furiously to find its words. His hands clenched into fists by his sides and his chest heaved as he screamed back at me.

'You filthy, stinking, whoreson...'

He never finished his sentence. As I lay crumpled at his feet, a figure appeared behind him and clamped a hand on his shoulder. As he spun round, a blurred fist flew at his jaw and knocked him straight to the ice beside me. His vanquisher stood where he had moments before, but instead of rage, there was a look of grim determination on his face. Sir Godfrey had found me.

His head flicked from my fallen assailant to me, and his expression softened instantly.

'Are you hurt, my boy?'

'No, sir,' I replied, finding that sheer terror had somehow deadened the pain in my belly.

'Good. Stay still a moment. This vermin and I are going to have words.'

He moved with his familiar purposefulness, but his eyes gleamed with a ferocity I hadn't seen before. He laid a firm hand on the man, and lifted him, dazed and weak, to his feet.

'You're quite the Hector, aren't you – preying on small children? They must be very proud of you in your rookery.'

Sir Godfrey spoke softly, but with such menace that I too felt it, refracted from its target onto me. His captive was of average height and well-built, with a face which spoke of countless brawls and crimes. Yet squirm as he might, he could not break my patron's grasp. Sir Godfrey had always been the master of his environment. I had believed his environment to be the coffee house and Stock Exchange. But even here he projected his authority, so that all three of us understood that the fight was over.

It was then that I saw the others. Two accomplices, also with feet bound in rags, approaching past the tents with silent steps. Sir Godfrey's back was to them, interrogating his captive, and he had not a hope of seeing or hearing them until they were upon him. Without thinking, I shouted a warning. Both accomplices flinched and their heads twitched towards me. Sir Godfrey turned, and saw his stalkers. A cackle rose up from the man in his grasp. We were trapped and outnumbered, and the danger I had thought to be passed was now more real than ever.

Barely had the cackle finished echoing around the banks of the frozen river than it was ended, Sir Godfrey launching his elbow smartly into his captive's nose. He crumpled to the ground, blood flowing bright crimson onto the white ice before me, and I felt bile burn at the top of my throat.

The two remaining men now looked less sure of themselves. They approached slowly, while Sir Godfrey stood between them and me like a guardian colossus. No-one spoke. The only sound was the wind, whistling across the ice.

Sir Godfrey crouched down into a pugilist's pose, hands balled into fists, arms extended before him. The master of Wrakeley Park was transformed. He looked every inch the fighter, and I wondered whether this was a ruse, or whether there was a whole part of him that I somehow did not know. A kick backwards with his heel caught the fallen man once more in the face. There was a low groan, but little movement from him. The sudden violence of it caused his two friends to hesitate again though, and that was to be their downfall.

As they looked to each other for reassurance, Sir Godfrey flew at them, and though his target twisted to deflect the coming blow he was too slow. A right fist, carrying the full weight of Sir Godfrey's skidding frame, connected with his mouth. He fell backwards and, as Sir Godfrey struggled to balance, the man's torso landed on his wayward knee. There was a cry of anguish and then only silence, as he lay sprawled on the ground. Sir Godfrey, however, was now sprawled alongside him, the poise of the pugilist replaced by animal panic, scrambling to regain his feet while the last accomplice closed on him. A right boot struck his face as he rose, and though he recoiled and wavered, he withstood the blow and raised his arms to repulse further attacks.

A swinging left fist destined for his face and a right aimed at his midriff were stoutly defended and then, his balance regained, Sir Godfrey counter-attacked. There was a quick sidestep, and then a right fist sailing towards an unprotected lower back. The back arched up with the impact, and in an instant Sir Godfrey's left soared upwards to meet the jaw.

From the opening cackle to this coup de grace, the battle could not have lasted thirty seconds. Yet three grown men now lay on the ice before my patron – a man of business and letters. A man who prized administration above all, and whose experience of violence went no further than seasonal hunts, where the pull of a trigger or flash of a crop was the sum of the activity.

A very different man now stood before me – a man who caused me to question everything I knew. I had been raised by Sir Godfrey's household – and I now realised I had seen him only through their eyes. My emotions swung wildly between fear and rapture as I imagined what unknown adventures he might be involved in.

My patron returned to the prone body of his first victim. He knelt down beside him, reached into his inside jacket, and retrieved a crude wallet.

'Let us see if we can learn anything about our unwelcome guests, Victor,' he said.

At that moment, I caught a glimpse of movement and, turning, saw the second assailant rising groggily to his feet. His right hand reached into his jacket, and emerged clutching a gleaming knife. My mouth dropped open in horror. Fighting with fists was one matter – but fists were no match for a blade.

In a single stride the man was within striking distance of my patron, whose back remained turned to him. The warning cry was formed on my lips, when the crack of a gunshot rang across the ice. Everything stopped for a moment. Sir Godfrey, the assailant, and my scream – caught in my throat and lost in shock. And then time resumed. All heads turned to follow the sound. A man with a fine top hat and a long dark cloak swept back over his shoulders stood sideways to us, between two tents. His right arm was extended straight out, and at its end he grasped a pistol with a smoking barrel. His left hand sat at his waist, holding a second pistol, and as we watched he took a step forward, dropping his right arm and raising his left to level the unfired gun at the assailant. He did this slowly and deliberately, leaving us in no doubt that here was a marksman who missed only when he chose to. The assailant did not wait to find out. He dropped his knife to the ice and skidded away, all thought of revenge scattered by the steady arm and long, glinting barrel.

Still the hero of the scene held his stance, and with it the moment itself, gun still pointing where the danger had been. Then, calmly, he withdrew his left arm into his cloak, replacing the pistol in his belt. The spell was broken. A smile spread across his face as he strode towards us, and I suddenly recognised my new acquaintance, the ebullient Lord Elsfield. I recovered my wits, my voice and my limbs, and half leapt, half stumbled to reach Sir Godfrey and throw my arms around him.

I was at a loss for what to say, but here, in the centre of London, surrounded by humanity, I knew I had nearly lost a family for a second time. The realisation broke over me like a wave and overwhelmed me. I was in tears, attached by some animal force to the person who had now saved my life not once, but twice. It was to this strange spectacle that Lord Elsfield presented himself, still smiling, and with his hands now placed on his hips.

'My dear friend. What terrible scrapes you find yourself in!'

My patron said nothing in response, merely grimacing as he rose and I released my grip on him. He put his hand to the cheek which had taken the impact of the boot.

'Are you hurt, my good fellow? That was quite a blow you received.'

'No,' he replied, checking himself over before returning his hand to the cheek. 'Thanks to you, Andrew. It appears I owe you my life.'

'Not a bit of it, Godfrey. I did what any of us would have done. It was the raising of a hand and the pressure of a finger – no more.'

'Well, I'm glad you venture out with duelling pistols. Perhaps I might learn from your example.'

'Indeed you should! The streets of London are no place to be caught alone and unarmed. In a fair fight you certainly showed those vagabonds some English backbone. But you can't rely on gutter-types to fight fairly. But what am I saying,' he added, another broad smile forming across his face. 'You're not alone! Young Victor here is already into his teenage years, surely, and has the build of Jack Broughton himself.'

I was unsure who Jack Broughton might be, but blushed once again at the presumed compliment.

'Victor is but ten years old, Andrew, and hardly of an age to be fibbing foot pads and highwaymen.'

'Nonetheless, I can see he is already a valuable ally. Which reminds me, as one ally to another, there is a matter I wished to discuss with you, if I might?'

'You have me in your debt. Please: speak freely.'

With this, the two men began to walk away, leaving the few curious passers-by to investigate what had occurred, and whether help should be sought for those remaining prone on the ice. I followed behind, more eager now than ever to learn about the relationship between my patron and this dashing pistoleer.

'It has to do with this damned ice, Godfrey. This was one surprise no one saw coming. No one, except you, I understand.'

Sir Godfrey turned his head, and looked with narrowed eyes and a furrowed brow at his rescuer.

'You take an unusual interest in the details of my operation, Andrew.'

'Not at all! Rather, it is because the details of your operation are unusual that they attract my interest! I understand that you have not a single vessel on the Thames at the moment. When would you say that this was last the case? An operation the size of yours, with not one cargo in its home dock? I believe this could be a first!'

'I can hardly be accused of arranging the weather, Andrew. No amount of bribery or blackmail could manage that.'

'My dear fellow!' responded Lord Elsfield, with a chuckle and a hearty slap on my patron's back, 'Bribery and blackmail are certainly not your modus operandi! I would not dream of suggesting it. You misconstrue my meaning. No. I am merely complimenting you on your sagacity regarding the recent act of God.'

'Is that what Lloyd's is calling it?'

A sharp look now flashed from Lord Elsfield to my patron.

'Lloyd's will bow to the community. They stand to lose their position if they back away from this... event. That is worth far more to them than the claims they will foot.'

'I am glad to hear it. Many livelihoods depend on it.'

'Exactly, old friend, exactly. And that is precisely what I wished to speak with you about.'

'Go on...'

'I'm afraid my ships have not been as fortunate as yours. They were caught in the ice yesterday. Whether they will require repair or not when the ice melts is a matter for the shipyards. That loss will be covered, one way or the other. But there are commitments I have made. Contracts I have taken; employment I have given. As you know – time is money. People are depending on me for supply, for wages, for simple sustenance. In short, old friend, I need your ships.'

We were still some several yards from the riverbank, yet here my patron stopped, and with him Lord Elsfield.

'Surely you're not serious?'

'I would only take those currently empty out in the estuary. And I would of course reimburse you for their loan.'

'Andrew. You know as well as I do that an empty ship is not an idle ship. They have each and every one been repurposed. I am sorry. What you ask is impossible. It would in turn hamstring me and my operations. I would be happy, however, to send word to other ports that there is work to be found here with you. I am sure it would be a matter of days before Spanish, Portuguese, and Baltic vessels arrived.'

Lord Elsfield dismissed these words with a slow shake of his head.

'I'm afraid that won't do, old friend. The need is urgent. I cannot wait even a day. Come. These are the very situations for which our association was founded. The gunpowder still hangs in the air from where I saw off your attackers. This is a modest request.'

Sir Godfrey paused, looking thoughtfully into his companion's face, before replying.

'You and I have different views, it would seem, on the purpose of our association. I would not make demands on an associate which I knew to be damaging. Nor would I pretend it to be a small thing. I am truly sorry for your losses to the ice. You are not alone, and I am sure that your good name and business will not suffer as a result. I would advocate using the cold and the ice where your cargoes lie to sustain any perishable goods. I will send word to all my vessels that they are to advertise work with you at their next ports of call. I shall remain in your debt for your actions today, Andrew – and I shall repay it as I am able. I trust you can understand my stance. I would not begrudge you a similar one were our situations reversed.'

He did not allow Lord Elsfield to respond, but instead turned immediately to me, saying: 'Victor, please bid Lord Elsfield good day. We have had quite enough excitement. We are going home.'

I did as instructed to the now motionless Lord Elsfield and, taking my patron's outstretched hand, was hurried the last few yards to the safety of the riverbank without a backwards glance. The image of this intriguing man's face however, stayed with me. So dashing and animated at first, yet in response to our farewell, utterly dispassionate – as if drained of all energy by my patron's rebuttal.

We walked home at an uncomfortable pace. I wondered if it was an automatic response to our ordeal, or whether it might be in order to prevent the myriad questions which were already competing, confused and incomplete, in my mind. Regardless of the intent however,

I reached St James's out of breath, with the bruises from my own assaults now throbbing, and without a word having been uttered by either of us. We were greeted at the door by the comforting sight of Mr Oakes, and while he took our coats, I took my opportunity. I knew my questions would be unwelcome, but I could not remain silent.

'Sir Godfrey – who is Lord Elsfield?'

'No one with whom you would wish to associate.'

He replied without turning.

'But *you* do, sir. Who is he, and why do you not *wish* to associate with him?'

Still with his back to me, Sir Godfrey forced out a long sigh. His shoulders sank.

'Oakes. We will go to the library. We are not to be disturbed.'

'Very good, sir.'

Turning to me at last, he said: 'Come with me, Victor. It's time you saw a little more.'

The library was warm, thanks to Mr Oakes's roaring fire. Sir Godfrey bade me sit, while he remained standing. For minutes he said nothing, only pacing back and forth in front of the grate. I too remained silent, unsure of what explanation I might receive. Eventually, he spoke.

'Lord Elsfield and I are... business associates. We have worked... together... for a long time.' He paused, but I did not interject. His words came slowly and with something akin to pain written on his face. I did not wish to discourage him.

'We met at school, and both inherited the operations of our fathers. We saw from the beginning that it would be better to work together than against one another, as many market forces would have us do.

'Our association is not a formal one. It does not bear any legal force. Indeed, it does not bear any name. What we do is not illegal – you should understand that. But it is... unusual. We inform each other of our intentions, our interests, our needs. We then find ways to support each other whilst retaining our own interests. Over time our association has drawn in others. Businessmen whose interests overlap with our own, and who like us see the benefits of alliance over competition. We are now twelve in number. We share resources when practical. We pass information when possible. We discuss and agree who is the prime candidate for new contracts – particularly government contracts. And we use our influence to secure those contracts, without the distraction of competing bids.

'We are known to each other of course, but also to a select few others: our most trusted deputies and captains. Mr Oakes, for instance, understands the nature of The Association. We make ourselves known to these deputies by means of a signet ring, here,' he motioned to his ring – one which I had never before closely marked, but from which I now found myself unable to tear my eyes. A stag stood proudly engraved in the gold, face turned to the front and antlers raised to the sky. 'It is a symbol of the closest circle of trust. It indicates our mutual loyalty, given and required by all. My deputies understand this.'

I moved in my seat, a question forming on my lips. But Sir Godfrey halted it with the gesture of his hand:

'This raises your inevitable question: why then did I refuse help to Lord Elsfield today? Did I not counsel never to refuse help to a friend? And we should all be friends within The Association – that is why we speak to each other using only first names. I am afraid the answer is not straightforward. It is subtle – much like him. Outwardly The Association is strong, unbreakable, resolute. However, it is dependent on the equal and total honesty of all members. We are all human, Victor, and at times we all waver. I am not alone in suspecting that Lord Elsfield acts only in his own interests, to maintain his superiority over us all. Today's request seemed to me typical of this approach. I could not condone it – not at the price it would have cost me. I am a relatively cautious man. You may already have perceived this. When I see an opportunity, I prepare for it. When it comes to pass, I act upon it. But I do not do so on a whim. I rely on information rather than intuition. Today my caution has proved valuable. My vessels sit safely off the English coast, some with full cargoes, some soon to be filled with the cargoes which others now cannot transport. I have won this opportunity by opting to be cautious. The same option was available to the rest of The Association, when I informed them of my plans three days ago.

'On other occasions, my caution has caused me to miss opportunities which others, such as Lord Elsfield, have seized upon. At times I have infuriated and even enraged him – today being but a mild example. But at times he too has infuriated me with his lack of regard for proper procedure – for delicacy, or for the views of others. He is a risk-taker. He took a risk three days ago when he kept his vessels in harbour. He lost. He took a risk today in asking for my help. He knew it would not be likely to succeed. But he saw an opportunity as my rescuer, and he has ever been one to seize an opportunity, and to consider its merits later. I fear I was rather curt with him – but having known each other this long, we are adept at swiftly raising each other's ire. This contretemps will soon be forgotten as he searches for a more practical solution to his setback.'

I remained silent. My patron's world of books – of numbers scrawled into ledgers in darkened offices – was fast becoming a distant distraction. There was a world of intrigue, of subtlety and manoeuvre here. A world which utterly confused, and yet utterly enthralled me. And there was more. Even the dashing entrance of Lord Elsfield could not make me forget it.

'What happened today, Sir Godfrey? It all happened so quickly, I did not have time to think.'

'You were the target of some very evil men. They make a living from kidnapping the young and the defenceless. They would have thought either to ransom you or worse. I blame myself for not being more careful. I'm afraid in my distraction at the frost fair I neglected my duty as your patron and protector. I apologise. I will not let it happen again. You would be right to be angry with me.' With this, he took a stance immediately before me, hands clasped behind his back and head bowed.

I had never heard such words from my patron. From a man who had provided so much for me and asked for nothing in return. I could not imagine that he might be culpable for any neglect.

'Sir Godfrey – I do not know how I could be angry with you. I believe I was more fearful for *you* than I was for myself.'

'Is that so?! Well then, there must be some fire in you, Victor!' He approached me and put his hand on my shoulder, kneeling so that his eyes were now level with mine. 'It does you great credit that in a moment of danger you thought of others rather than yourself. We learn most about ourselves in these moments – when our minds may not be able to access their reason, and we must rely on our instincts instead. Your instincts are noble, Victor.'

I blushed at the praise, of which I felt entirely undeserving, having sat mute while he withstood multiple assaults. Nonetheless, my question had not been answered. He had missed my point and I was emboldened enough to press.

'But why did they single *us* out, sir? And how did you manage to overcome them? I have never seen the like before.'

He rose, resuming his pacing. 'Yes. I suppose I look just as vulnerable as the next fop! I wonder whether we stayed too long in that tent with the sailors. Those we spoke with are good fellows – but I would advise you in general to stay away from the rank and file. They make their livings any way they can, and in their current predicament they will resort to any means. More fool them for picking on me! No reason they should know, but I was quite the pugilist at school. Rarely tested outside the gymnasium, of course, but as I said – one reverts to instinct at these times, and I still train with the great John Jackson himself when I'm in town, to keep my eye in.'

There was a curious smile on his face as he said this – an expression which for once I recognised. It was guilt. An admission that he had allowed me to believe there was no more to him than met the eye. With all his talk of caution, I wondered what other secrets he might keep, and if he might not rather enjoy surprising people from time to time.

'I will confess that I have kept this enthusiasm of mine from you, Victor. The pugilistic art is not admired by all. Indeed, some consider it base, even barbaric behaviour. But to see it performed well is to know otherwise. Please know, however, that I have not and would never wilfully deceive you. I rather judged that a time might come when you might take an interest in it as a hobby. Today was not at all what I had in mind, but the time has indeed come for you to learn. I shall sleep easier at night knowing that you have some idea how to defend yourself, should it ever come to that. But do not let this detract from what I have already shown you of my business. Pugilism is a hobby, like hunting or fishing. Book-keeping may seem dull and dreary to you now, but it is the foundation of all business. Book-keeping, and information. Seek to know all that you can, value all the information you are given, and you will find opportunities where others do not, and see patterns where others see only chaos.'

He paused, appearing to consider his own words, as I fought in vain to contain my excitement at the promised tuition, nodding madly, like a pigeon faced with a platter of grain.

'I see I have quietened you. I hope that is a good sign. Our world is a muddled and confused sphere, Victor. We construct models and methods to order it, the better to move within it. But they are only models. The confusion is real. If I may offer you one last piece of advice – control it where you can, but accept the confusion where you cannot. You will not succeed in controlling it all. Not even the most brilliant men can do that. Today my lack of judgement put you in danger. That much I can and will control better.'

He said the last words almost as a promise to himself, and I wondered at his meaning.

IV

I did not have long to wonder. As the end of the long war with France grew closer, Sir Godfrey gathered all his resources in anticipation of the new Parisian markets. I began to understand more of his work. Scraps of information became vital clues to avoiding mishaps once across the channel. They came in many forms and from many sources, but were all sewn together to create an understanding of the challenges the expedition would face. What goods were most sought in Paris? What prices would they pay? Who would rule the toll gates surrounding the city, and how would we negotiate a fair price with that ruler?

I was permitted to watch the planning from the London offices, under oath to remain quiet and still amongst the silently scribbling clerks. Their morbid solemnity was, however, mercifully offset by regular trips to the docks, and the irrepressibly eager Mr Crawshaw. His attitude seemed at odds with the dispassion which my patron favoured, and I found myself warming to him immensely. I was therefore grateful that he was present at the quayside when Sir Godfrey announced that I was not part of his plans. He felt like an ally, and that gave me courage.

'The fall of Paris is imminent, Mr Crawshaw. It is time we moved the fleet to Dover. I should like you to accompany me overland, however. We will have much to discuss on the way.'

'Very good, sir – though I fear we may give Master Winter a fearful headache with all our talk of business.'

'Victor will not be accompanying us to Dover, Mr Crawshaw.'

I could not tell whether it was my look of surprise or Mr Crawshaw's which prompted his justification.

'Just six weeks ago I was given a stark reminder of my responsibilities to him...'

'...I heard of the affair, sir.'

'Once again my error of judgement nearly cost another's life. It was more than I could bear. I will not put him in danger again.'

'Sir Godfrey! My lessons have taught me to fight back.'

I surprised myself as I realised the strength of my conviction.

'Be quiet, Victor! This is not a discussion.'

'But what of my learning?! My apprenticeship?!'

'Your apprenticeship depends entirely upon your time spent with Mr Crisp and his clerks! Any time spent away from that office is time wasted!'

'I beg your pardon, sir...'

'...Not now, Crawshaw!'

'I have spent my *life* staring at books! I have begged you, for *years*, to let me come to London so that I could *see* the world – not hide from it!'

Sir Godfrey's face was puce. But though his mouth opened, no sound came out. He turned to Mr Crawshaw, who raised his eyebrows and shrugged. As the silence drew out, I felt my courage seeping away. Had I really just shouted at my patron? In public? When he spoke again, Sir Godfrey's voice was quiet and steely.

'A word in your office, if I may, Mr Crawshaw. Victor: you will wait outside.'

The wall dividing Mr Crawshaw's office was thick, and though I tried, I could not follow their conversation. I could tell their voices apart, however, and I recognised Sir Godfrey's tone. It was one I had received myself many times, and it did not invite response. Perhaps conversation was the wrong word.

Quite abruptly, the voices stopped, and a moment later, the two men stepped into view.

'Since you are adamant you are here to see the world, Victor, and since you are already so familiar with the world of books, Mr Crawshaw and I have come to an arrangement. He will escort you down to Dover personally. He will see that you stay out of harm's way. He will be entirely responsible for your safety – though I have reminded him that after a month of weekly pugilism lessons, you are now perfectly capable of looking after yourself.'

Though his tone remained, I scarcely noticed it. Sir Godfrey had relented. I would have my freedom. I looked to Mr Crawshaw, but he was locked sheepishly in my patron's gaze.

We travelled down to Dover the very next day in Sir Godfrey's coach. The two men talked incessantly of their plans, but far from causing the headache Mr Crawshaw had feared, I listened in awe. My patron had anticipated everything, and left no element to chance.

Transport was in short supply in war-ravaged France – particularly carts. But Sir Godfrey had been in contact with the Calais harbourmaster, and had commandeered an armada of barges to sail the cargo down to Paris on their canals.

'The roads will be awash with the detritus of war, my boy,' he told me, seemingly pleased with my curiosity. 'If it isn't fleeing French soldiers, abandoning their posts, it will be refugees or, worst of all, our own troops. They'll think nothing of looting a cargo train. So we must avoid giving them the invitation. I have obtained letters from London, granting our free passage. I have sent messages to key contacts along the canals, and paid them well to let us through unhindered. And I have employed a small security force to dissuade the more resolute would-be pirates. But water is our best friend. Soldiers and civilians alike will watch us pass but not think to swim to us.'

His plan seemed brilliant to me – and I marvelled at the elegant mind that had created it.

We reached our lodgings in Dover before nightfall, after a day of scheming which had restored my ardour to follow in Sir Godfrey's footsteps. It was a strangely subdued Mr Crawshaw who sat down opposite me in our room however.

'I'm glad you're here, Victor. You know, Sir Godfrey's glad too. He may insist he's your patron, not your father – but he cares deeply for you. He may not have planned for you to join us, but that doesn't mean he doesn't want you here.'

His words came falteringly, and I sensed his awkwardness infecting me. Yet there was a question I had longed to ask.

'Sir Godfrey told me he was once a Romantic, Mr Crawshaw. An adventurer. But he said he grew up. Does that happen to everyone? Will I put away childish things?'

Mr Crawshaw frowned and sighed.

'He did not "grow up", Victor. I should not speak ill of Sir Godfrey – he's a good and decent man – but he's lying to you, as he's lied to himself these many years. You may know this already – but Sir Godfrey has lost loved ones before. Lady Catherine was his world – and when she died, he blamed himself. Of course, there was no blame to be had. But grief can drive you to see things that aren't there.

'It was grief that changed him, not age. He's a more cautious man because of her – because of what happened to her. And so you see, he's cautious with you. He's torn between the Romantic he is, and the man of reason he believes he must be. In his heart he's your father. Why else did he take you in all those years ago? But in his head, he's your patron.'

'Sir Godfrey is *more* than a father to me. I want to do what he does – or *did*. I want to travel the world, create an empire... I want to defeat footpads and highwaymen using only my fists and my wits. I want to send ships to far flung places, and have them bring back exotic things. He's my hero... I want him to see me as more than an office clerk.'

'Victor. How can you think that? He sees you as so much more than a clerk.'

'Then why is that all he wants for me? All he trains me for? There is so much more to his work, but he does not trust me with anything more than a pen.'

'It's not trust in you he lacks: it's trust in the world. That's the price of the adventure you've described. Come down to the quay with me tomorrow. You'll learn much more there than in that office.'

His words gave me some comfort. He understood my frustrations. I smiled, and passed the night dreaming of my exploits as the captain of my ship, discovering new lands and winning fame and fortune wherever I went.

I was awoken by Mr Crawshaw in early morning gloom, and handed the first of many cups of tea. Our short walk down to the waterfront revealed a hive of activity, as sailors rushed about the decks and rigging of their vessels, making preparations for the voyage. Rowing boats scudded back and forth across the harbour, taking captains and officers to their commands. Seagulls swooped amongst them, searching for unguarded morsels, and issuing their shrill cries against the low cloud.

'Napoleon's abdicated,' he told me as we reached his station on the quay. 'We received word this morning. We should have safe passage now. We'll leave tomorrow, on the morning tide. Sir Godfrey would have gone today, if we weren't still loading.'

The war that had consumed Europe all my life was over. I nodded my understanding, still half asleep. A steward appeared and offered another mug of tea to each of us. I gratefully accepted and, between burying my face in its steaming warmth, scanned the panorama before me.

The scale of the expedition was monumental. It made the operations at the London dock look provincial. Over thirty ships, some owned by Sir Godfrey, others hired for the occasion, were arrayed within the broad sweep of the harbour. Much of their cargo was already aboard – but plenty still remained on wharves and in warehouses along the quay. Crates, sacks, barrels and chests, containing untold wonders to delight the war-weary French people. All through the day still more arrived by boat or by wagon, and were deposited awaiting final loading onto their ships. My chaperone never grew tired of my questions, and even seemed to take pleasure in my interest. I became more certain than ever that this was my calling.

As evening drew in, a high-spirited Sir Godfrey appeared, and suggested that we take dinner in The Ship Inn to toast the success of the enterprise. Mr Crawshaw politely declined, stating that he was honoured to be invited, but that there remained much to be done.

So it was that Sir Godfrey and I alone entered the establishment that night. We were seated at a table away from the noise of the main room, which was understandably animated given the news from France. Sir Godfrey had only just begun to pour the wine when a familiar voice nearby called out: 'Well, well, well! Sir Godfrey Ramsay! And his apprentice, Victor! How splendid to see you both.'

I turned with my patron to see a beaming Lord Elsfield crossing the floor to stop a few feet from our table, once again resplendent in a fine double-breasted navy jacket, an azure cravat, and buff-coloured breeches, all expertly tailored to his form.

'What brings you to Dover at this happy time my friends?' He asked, hands outstretched in a gesture of welcome.

'As you can well imagine, Andrew, we are here to exploit the new market.'

'Of course, of course! The wheels of commerce never stop, eh Godfrey?'

'Indeed.'

A moment's pause was prevented from becoming an uncomfortable silence by Lord Elsfield:

'Would you mind if I joined you for a drink Godfrey?'

'Not at all. Victor – please afford Lord Elsfield some room.'

I duly shuffled along in my booth.

'Wine, Andrew?'

'Absolutely.' He sat, and having carefully adjusted his clothes, reached for his now filled glass. 'Now then: you will sail for Calais on the morning tide, yes?'

Sir Godfrey inclined his head.

'And may I presume you have arranged terms with a local merchant there for the purchase of your shipment?'

'Indeed not, sir!' I broke in. 'Sir Godfrey has organised transport to Paris! Ours will be the first English convoy to reach Paris in a generation!'

Sir Godfrey's face remained inscrutable, while Lord Elsfield allowed himself a raised eyebrow.

'Is that so? You found a route to Paris, eh? You really are full of surprises. I am sure I could not have organised such an enterprise. I cannot begin to imagine the detail of your planning. Such determination. You will learn a lot from Sir Godfrey Ramsay, Victor.'

'I hope to, my Lord.'

'Oh Andrew, please! I am simply Andrew to my friends.'

I failed to conceal my delight at the notion of being on personal terms with a Lord of the realm.

'Yes – a master of elaborate planning, Godfrey. You always were. And I was ever grateful to be associated with you for that.'

'Our association has been of mutual benefit, Andrew.'

'Indeed it has! For it is difficult for a man immersed in detail to perceive the grander scale of things. There is no criticism in that. It is the way of the world. It is the reason a general does not command each and every platoon. There must be a stratagem, and there must be battlefield tactics.'

Sir Godfrey said nothing in response, yet I sensed his disapproval at being labelled a junior officer. Lord Elsfield appeared not to notice his mood, continuing:

'You know, I really owe you an apology, old friend. After you refused to help me with those ships during the freeze, I really was most vexed. I considered all sorts of childish revenges. It was in retrospect very poor of me. But then the most elegant solution presented itself! You don't mind if I share a confidence with you, do you? I feel sure I can trust Victor to keep a secret.'

The intrigue Lord Elsfield hinted at was too tempting. I nodded my agreement to his terms, not speaking for fear of interrupting. He glanced from me to Sir Godfrey and began: 'As you know, I was without means to transport goods for some weeks. And for an empire built on trade, this presented me with quite a problem. But a friend happened to pay me a visit during the freeze, and his complaint was this: he had bought Consols – government bonds, Victor – some years ago, at the point of Bonaparte's retreat from Moscow. He had expected that, together with the victories in the Peninsula Campaign, the war would swiftly reach its conclusion, and he would sell his bonds for a healthy return. He confessed that he had over-invested, and that he now found himself in immediate need of a profitable sale, or some other source of liquidity. He was rather alarmed that, with the American war now also occupying our forces, there was no such opportunity for profit in sight.

'Well, it occurred to me that here we are, my dear Godfrey, rushing around the world trading goods, while all the wealth one could wish for is located in a square mile of London. So why send ships to sea to gather it from far-flung lands? All one need do in this modern age is trade a few bonds or shares.'

I sensed that my patron was growing increasingly uncomfortable. He shifted in his seat and cleared his throat before reaching for his wine, but he did not interrupt.

'I must confess that I did not concoct my stratagem there and then. But by the morning I had sent a note to my friend telling him that his troubles were over. I had good information that the war would be finished in days, not weeks or months. In fact, so certain was I of this information, that I asked him to further invest in Consols on my behalf. A few thousand pounds was enough to restore his confidence, and to ensure I was in a position to benefit myself. I wonder, young Victor, if you are aware of the rather sensational events of last February 21st?'

I looked inquiringly between Lord Elsfield and my patron. Sir Godfrey responded on my behalf, with a weary voice.

'He is not – though I surmise you are about to introduce him to the frivolousness of the Stock Exchange.'

'Indeed I am! For it has proved an excellent resource.'

Sir Godfrey said nothing in further protest, but sat far back in his chair, exuding an air of disapproval.

'In the early hours of February 21st, my dear Victor, a man announcing himself as Colonel Du Bourg of the British Army walked into this very establishment and declared that he had that moment arrived from France. Though he professed to carry confidential military information, he left the owner in no doubt that his news was nothing less than the end of the war.'

He paused to let the statement resonate, and to take a sip of his wine before continuing.

'That same Colonel Du Bourg made haste to London, stopping at staging posts along the way where again he was careless enough to convey the content of his message to others. By the time he arrived in London, rumour was spreading. By the time the Stock Exchange opened, speculation was rife. The value of Consols rocketed as people reacted to the news, believing them now an excellent investment. Several people who were in a position to sell large quantities of these bonds made considerable sums. As you know, I had been fortunate enough to receive this information in advance, and having passed this information on to my friend, we both profited from the situation.'

Once again I looked between the two men, sure I had misunderstood something.

'But, Sir Godfrey, Lord Elsfield: the war did *not* end in February... You must forgive my ignorance my Lord.'

I felt foolish, impudent even, to be questioning such a man – but Lord Elsfield's face beamed brighter still.

'Quite right, Victor! Quite right! The information was false! The mysterious Colonel Du Bourg disappeared upon reaching London, never to be seen again. By the end of the day, with rumours unsubstantiated, the price of Consols had fallen once again. The window of opportunity had closed. But do you see, my friends?!' He looked now directly at Sir Godfrey. 'The veracity of the information did not matter. What mattered was that it was perceived to be true, and hence the market responded accordingly. What is truth but perception? This is the triumph of man over nature – over reality itself! This whole episode has opened my eyes, Godfrey. And I have you to thank for it!'

For the second time that day I marvelled at a mind capable of such complexity. I was sure I did not fully understand his story, but it was clear nonetheless that Lord Elsfield had turned simple information into success and riches. What was more, he had done so without needing an armada of vessels, or a company of sailors. Sir Godfrey's description of this man returned to my mind. He was indeed subtle. He was a risk-taker. And now I perceived his 'lack of regard for proper procedure'. But I wondered if this was to be scorned so readily. He bent the world to fit his needs. It was not Sir Godfrey's way, but it met with success.

It was Sir Godfrey, now sitting forward once more, who broke the silence of my reflection.

'I wonder if the Committee of the Stock Exchange would share your philosophy, Andrew.'

'Ha! As you know, Godfrey, they do not! They feel duped, Victor. They are even now hunting for a scapegoat. Someone to blame for the false information.'

'Indeed, they have published a list of persons under suspicion.'

'Yes they have, my friend. But is my name upon it?'

'It is not. But I would wager that your "friend's" is.'

'Quite so, quite so. That poor fellow Cochrane. He really is a good chap. Principled to a fault. I am sure nothing will come of it in any case. He's done no more than I.'

'As you say, Andrew.'

Silence fell. Sir Godfrey remained stoically sombre, while Lord Elsfield continued to sip his wine with an air of satisfaction.

'Perhaps you might seek me out on your return from Calais, Victor. I should like to hear the impression of one who has laid eyes on the Old Enemy for the first time.'

'Victor will not be making the crossing.'

'Oh really? I assumed...'

'Perhaps you assumed a ten-year-old boy could captain a ship? Or negotiate favourable terms in fluent French with the harbourmaster?'

'No need for that now, Godfrey. You have brought him to Dover – presumably to see the operation here. It is hardly a leap of the imagination or indeed faith to presume him capable of crossing the channel with you.'

'As you have already demonstrated this evening, my friend: your imagination is able to see things mine is not.'

The two looked at each other for a moment, motionless. Then Lord Elsfield rose abruptly to his feet.

'Well I shan't keep you from your supper, gentlemen. It was most pleasant to share your table. Godfrey: I apologise for any slight. Your ward is of course your responsibility and no-one else's. I believe even our own Lord Nelson was *eleven* when he went to sea on a man-of-war. Only stowaways get on board sooner than that.'

With a polite nod, he was gone, and we were left in a silence which neither Sir Godfrey or I seemed inclined to break.

For my part, Lord Elsfield's final words reverberated through my mind like a ship's bell through the fog. My journey to Dover had been proscribed – yet here I was, through protest and persuasion. Now the journey to Calais was placed beyond my reach – and I could not bear it. The smell of the sea permeated every alehouse and alleyway of this town – pressing its case on everyone within it. It penetrated the walls and the floors of the buildings, and even as I lay awake in bed that night it surrounded me. It was the smell of adventure. It was the smell of *freedom*. And I was intoxicated.

If a lord of the realm could not persuade my patron to take me any further, then another way must be sought. I would stow away. At first I recoiled from the thought, shocked at my own nerve. But like the bell, it returned and resounded. It became more real with every reverberation. I had watched the loading all day at Mr Crawshaw's side. No-one would question if they saw me there again at first light. My only challenge was to deceive Mr Crawshaw when we awoke. It pained me to do so, but I knew that he must either refuse to help me, and inform Sir Godfrey of my scheme, or else risk his livelihood and worse if he were caught smuggling me onto the ship.

And so, when Mr Crawshaw muttered a soft farewell to me in the darkness of the morning, I mumbled a response from the depths of my covers, and willed my excitement to conceal itself and not betray me. With the door closed behind his departure, I sprang to my feet. I had barely slept all night, yet I had rarely felt so alive – so aware of my surroundings. As I climbed from my window to the street below, my whole body seemed to tingle with anticipation. My ears heard every foot scuff and distant murmur, and my eyes penetrated every dark corner and doorway. Before a weary dockworker or patrolling wharf guard could step into view, I had disappeared from theirs. I reached the waterfront unseen and unheard, and it was the work of only a few moments to find a crate with a loose lid whose contents could be exchanged with my own. Within ten minutes I had swapped the safety and staleness of my predetermined existence for the excitement and adventure of the sea. I wondered how many of the clerks in Sir Godfrey's London office had stowed away aboard an armada bound for foreign lands. I smiled to myself, knowing that at last I was answering the call within me.

Voices grew louder around me, and a sudden lurch told me that my crate was being lifted and taken aboard. I heard the creak and groan of ship's timbers, and felt the thump as I was dropped into position. It was not long after that the bosun's calls resounded through my makeshift cabin, and the timbers changed their song as I imagined the sails being lashed into place and the hull gathering speed through the water. Again I allowed myself a secret smile. I was at sea. There was no turning back now.

The motion of the ship suddenly changed. From a gentle creep, it seemed to buck, and then to writhe like a nervous horse. Cooped up below decks in the semi-darkness, my stomach struggled to cope, and I felt the energy of the morning's excitement drain away. When I could bear it no longer, I gently lifted the lid of my crate, and peered out. Through the murk of the lower deck I saw dark shapes scuttling over the rows of cargo stacked around me. The other stowaways. Rats. I had not considered when I should show myself above decks – but there would be no point to my endeavour if I remained below for the entire voyage. These sinister companions simply forced the issue.

As I approached the forward hatch, the sounds of the ship found their way down to me, and my senses began to recover their edge. I stood there and drank it in. The slop of the waves against the hull; the hum of the rigging as the wind flew through it; the slap of the sails as they were unfurled and made fast. Even the overpowering smell of brine seemed to me daring and exotic. Suddenly the light from above was blotted out, and a strange voice called out:

'There you are! Cook's looking for you! Come on!'

In two lithe bounds the voice was dangling above me on the ladder, offering a hand to pull me up. In the spirit of adventure which had brought me this far, I took the hand and burst blinking into the sunlight of a crisp spring morning in the English Channel. Above me sailors ran up ratlines like monkeys, and crossed the yards as if ambling along the Serpentine. Ahead I saw the bowsprit of the ship and beyond it a dark green sea, mottled with a thousand crests, each rolling away for an eternity, meeting the grey-blue sky in a line of haze. I thought back to Old Jack at Wrakeley, and the stories he had told me of his days at sea. I hoped he would be proud of me, now on my own sea adventure. An officer on the quarterdeck called out a command and, turning instinctively to follow the noise, I saw the unmistakeable face of my patron behind him, deep in conversation with Mr Crawshaw.

Of all the ships I might have been delivered to, I had come to Sir Godfrey's. I froze. He must see me. For what seemed an age, I struggled and failed to tear my eyes from him, knowing that at any moment he would catch sight of me. A rough pull on my arm stirred me from my trance, and before I knew what was happening, I was being spirited away to the ship's galley, where a ruddy-faced cook handed me a steaming bucket of broth to carry to the forecastle. Back and forth I was sent, grateful for a task which gave me licence to be on deck, and to avoid closer scrutiny. As the hours passed, I became increasingly hopeful that I might avoid detection altogether. Calais came into view with a stirring of interest from all aboard, in spite of the officers' attempts to maintain discipline. The cook doused the galley fires and handed me over to a steward, who promptly pressed a bottle of wine into my hands and sent me into the captain's cabin. Before I even had time to register a protest, I was face to face with my patron once more. Stood around a large square table with the captain, Mr Crawshaw, and other officers, he glanced up on my entrance and immediately returned his gaze to the chart on the table.

Somehow, he had not recognised me. I felt my face burning crimson and scurried as quickly as I could away from the door. I was not quick enough. Sir Godfrey looked up a second time, and as he followed my movement, I saw the frown etched deeply into his brow. His eyes caught mine, and once again I found myself transfixed. For a moment neither of us moved or said a word. I was dimly aware of his colleagues slowly following his gaze, as a group of philosophers might gather to inspect a curio.

'Gentlemen, might I beg a moment's privacy before we resume? Mr Crawshaw: a word if I may.' Sir Godfrey's voice was an almost unrecognisable whisper, yet it commanded instant obedience. His eyes remained locked onto mine while the room emptied, forbidding my escape. The ship groaned and rocked – a living, feeling witness to the tribunal. It was the only voice in our dark, dank space, marking the lengthening seconds as the fear welled up within me. In the corner of my vision, Mr Crawshaw's head twitched restlessly from side to side.

'Mr Crawshaw. It would appear I did not make my instructions to you sufficiently clear.' Still he did not break his stare. 'I distinctly recall stating that Victor should remain in London. Yet I was prevailed upon to allow him to travel to Dover. Now he stands before me as we cross the Channel to France. Would you care to explain how this has happened?'

Only now, with the accusation laced like a bandage beneath the glove of his question, did he turn to look at his quartermaster.

The ship groaned again, but Mr Crawshaw offered no response. Sir Godfrey waited.

The silence was unbearable. 'He had no part in this!' I blurted.

Suddenly Sir Godfrey's voice was a roar. 'I did not ask for your lies!'

'I don't know, Sir Godfrey. I kept your ward close by all through my work yesterday, and bade him farewell in our lodging in Dover not three hours ago. I have been at your side ever since.'

'Am I supposed to believe that he has therefore earned his passage here without your assistance? That he somehow stole aboard without a soul noticing him? That he took up a position as ship's boy without anyone questioning his credentials?'

Again, Mr Crawshaw offered no response. I felt the guilt consume me. My urge for adventure, all youthful excitement and energy, had brought blame on a man who had only ever shown me kindness. In spite of Sir Godfrey's warning, I could not remain mute.

'This was my own doing, Sir Godfrey!'

A vicious glance turned my way, but I remained resolute.

'You have bade me study your operation with all my energy – the better to win your approval. Mr Crawshaw has offered limitless insight and patience for my questions. It may displease you, sir, but this study has only confirmed my desire to emulate your success – to adventure to foreign lands and build an empire. When I learnt I would not be allowed to sail with you, I was so disappointed, I took matters into my own hands. I spent all yesterday at the wharf. It was not difficult for me to conceive how to stow away unnoticed.'

I felt my resolve wavering. What started as a fiery protestation of innocence had collapsed into a smouldering apology, and I found my head hanging unbidden from my shoulders, ashamed of its body.

'Not difficult, was it? Not difficult to defy me? To put your own foolish notions above the wisdom and direction of your elders? I have heard enough. I do not blame you, Mr Crawshaw, for this boy's wilful disregard of authority. I have clearly become far too indulgent with him. I shall soon rectify my mistake! You will remain here, Victor. I warn you not to test my will further today. Mr Crawshaw: let us prepare for our arrival on deck. Bring the chart.'

He strode past me without a second glance, and I suddenly felt afraid and alone. I had sought adventure: now I longed only for home. Mr Crawshaw collected the chart, a pained expression buried in his brow. Cries drifted down to us from the masthead, and the ship began to heel as it swung to enter the harbour.

'You've pushed him too far, you know.' He rolled it up, placed it under his arm, and opened the door. 'He will forgive you, though.'

I was left to watch our triumphant arrival from the cabin window: once again the outsider; once again the misfit – neither cook's boy nor heir to the company.

V

Mr Crawshaw was mistaken. Sir Godfrey did not forgive me. I was sent to Manchester, to lodge with the mill master there, Mr Trenchard, and his family. I was tutored and, but for his occasional business visits and an annual Christmas return to Wrakeley, I saw no more of my former patron. It seemed that he had thought better of his experiment in philanthropy.

At times, I wondered if he had forgotten me altogether, so complete was the silence emanating from St James's Square and from Wrakeley. At fifteen however, as I made my annual departure from Wrakeley to renew my exile, Sir Godfrey surprised me. Handing me a letter for Mr Trenchard as we bade farewell, he offered a firm handshake and declared:

'You know, your time in Manchester has been a penance for me as much as for you. I brought you to London too soon. I know that now. You have always been ambitious, and I suppose I yielded to that ambition. You still had a great deal to learn. But much water has passed under the bridge since then, and I trust it has taught you forebearance. I hear only good news from Mr Trenchard. It is time for your advancement'.

It was not an apology – but nor was it without an affection which I had long since assumed to be absent. His words rattled around my head as I rattled north inside the carriage, with little else of note to accompany them. When I reached Manchester, Mr Trenchard revealed that Sir Godfrey's letter instructed him to take me as his apprentice, 'the better that Victor might understand the mill operation'.

And so for six months I followed Mr Trenchard, and learned first-hand how to run a complex business and manage teams of workers. I was determined to take the opportunity to regain Sir Godfrey's trust. Mr Trenchard informed me that since the end of the war, workers' wages had plummeted. Maintaining the morale of the workforce was therefore now his main focus – but towards the end of July he became concerned that the city was growing restless. He even suggested I might return to Wrakeley for my safety – but I persuaded him that Sir Godfrey was far too busy, and that he would not take kindly to having me foisted on him at the slightest sign of unrest in the provinces.

The following month, I accompanied Mr Trenchard to observe a public rally at St Peter's Field. His complaints of the political activism of the labourers intrigued me, and I took the opportunity to witness it first hand, the better to understand it. We joined a group of industrialists and magistrates in a house on the south-eastern corner of the field. The conversation amongst the party was universally condemning of the gathering, and in fear of the growing mass of people they watched. Indeed, looking behind our building I could see ranks of cavalry, infantry and even artillery arrayed, presumably to quell the anxieties of the peacekeepers.

The one oddity in our party was a young girl of a similar age to myself, chaperoned by a magistrate. She wore a simple white frock and shoes, with golden hair in ringlets which fell carelessly around her face. Her chaperone seemed ill at ease to be entrusted with her care, fidgeting nervously as he attempted both to fulfil his peacekeeping duties and to ensure her safety. Like me, she asked a succession of questions which made me wonder all the more about the reason for her presence. The thought formed my next question to Mr Trenchard, who responded: 'Ha! That would be Mr McNeil's daughter, Annabel. Poor man. She is the very definition of precocious. She will not leave a matter alone once she has decided to become interested in it. I understand she has taken an interest now in radical politics. Slavery; workers' rights; women's rights: I don't rightly know which is more fashionable. Perhaps we will learn today for ourselves!'

It was clear that Mr Trenchard set little store by radical politics. However, I found its champion in this room beguiling.

'And who is Mr McNeil, sir?'

He turned to me, perhaps sensing I required a full answer, rather than a desultory comment. His tone was conspiratorial.

'My apologies, Master Winter. Mr McNeil is the owner of the mill at Quarry Reach. A key competitor of ours. Very much known to Sir Godfrey. He is in London at present, and in his absence Miss McNeil has clearly enforced her will on her chaperone to attend this insult to our parliament. Ah! Thankyou, George.' This latter remark as a servant presented him with a glass of brandy to steady the nerves.

Once more Mr Trenchard had made his opinions plain without being invited, and I wondered that he seemed to have so little subtlety to his character, and yet commanded so great a workforce. I judged a small challenge to be in order.

'Mr Trenchard. Please tell me why you view this peaceful gathering as an insult to our parliament?'

I had raised my voice slightly louder than intended, and noted the turned heads of several of our party, magistrates and Miss McNeil included. Mr Trenchard wore the look of a man not used to being challenged, particularly not in public, and certainly not by a man so many years his junior. However, he remained unsure of my influence with Sir Godfrey, and responded in a civil fashion.

'It is an insult, Master Winter, to the established rule of law in this country. But most of all, it is an insult to the veterans of the wars we have so recently survived. These demonstrations are the product of the French Revolution, with its seditious, envious and murderous doctrines. Make no mistake: these people would gladly see us all under the guillotine, while they broke the machines in the factories that have made this nation the foremost power in the world. No reform is enough for this rabble. For it is not reform, but revolution that they truly seek. But fear not! We are here with our trusted peace-keepers, and we will not hesitate to do what must be done.' With this he raised his glass to the magistrates before him and drained it, before signalling George for a second.

I was not surprised that a mill master such as Mr Trenchard, and presumably many of the men in the room, viewed this rally with fear. It stood to reason that they would support a status quo which had put them into their current comfort, and raised them above the workers. However, I wondered how long peace could be maintained through the threat of the sabre and the rifle. My limited understanding of the French Revolution gave me to think that Britain had avoided a similar upheaval not through greater repression, but through greater dispensation. I voiced neither agreement nor disagreement with his opinion, but returned to surveying the scene from the window. The field, itself no more than three acres, was no longer visible beneath the gathered throng, and yet still more streamed from every side-street to join them. I had never seen so many people in one place. They must have numbered fifty thousand.

'Are you insulted by what you see?'

The whispered voice in my ear startled me, but I restrained the urge to turn. The register betrayed the owner.

'I confess I am not,' I replied, keeping my voice equally low. 'It strikes me that if we hold ourselves on this island as better than the French, then we must behave better. If there is a gathering of this scale, then there is a grievance. If there is a grievance, we should look to address it, not subdue it.'

'These are stirring words, Mr Winter.'

Her use of my name put an involuntary smile on my face. She had noticed me as I had noticed her.

'Miss McNeil, I believe?' I had not spoken with a girl of my age before, but I adopted what I hoped was a chivalrous tone, part-turning to her and offering a small bow. She reciprocated and, encouraged, I continued.

'Please do not presume me to be a radical such as Mr Hunt. I cannot advocate universal suffrage. What would our votes count for compared to the thousands below us today? Are we to allow our country to be guided by the whim of the masses? Who guides *their* votes but the likes of Mr Hunt himself? But there is much that can be done between the current state and that which he agitates for.'

'These sound like very liberal sentiments, Mr Winter.' There was a half-smile which danced delicately at the corner of her mouth.

'I confess I have not considered my politics, Miss McNeil – I say only what I see, and what I believe should be done. Do liberal politics offend you?'

'On the contrary. Whilst I could not presume to understand every nuance, I confess I cannot see the evil in some modicum of reform for the men and women who live in this country. The law calls the air of England too pure for a slave to breathe, yet here stand fifty thousand of our countrymen who are enslaved by the factories, and a government which works only to keep them in poverty. I believe this makes me a liberal.'

Her eloquence took me by surprise and for a moment there was a silence which I feared she would take as a sign of my disapproval.

'Your passion is infectious, Miss McNeil,' I responded, hoping to make amends. 'However, I fear our views are not shared in this room. Perhaps we would be wise to keep our sentiments to ourselves.'

'Oh I am well-versed in that art. My father does not condone liberal tendencies. He is of a mind with your Mr Trenchard.'

'Is that so? Then your temperance does you great credit.'

We remained close together and watched the crowd grow yet further. I found myself intrigued and even a little in awe of her strength of character and, beneath the simplicity of her dress and appearance, I saw great beauty in her. The silence now seemed to stand easily between us, and I felt a growing bond even though we exchanged no further words.

Around one o'clock a carriage bearing Mr Hunt and his entourage appeared at the edge of the gathering, and the crowd parted to allow him access to the stage like Moses commanding the Red Sea. One man wordlessly directing the will of so many was precisely the issue of which I had warned Miss McNeil – and of which the magistrates were also clearly sensible. There was a stirring within their group, and then dispatch riders were sent running from the building. Mr Trenchard appeared greatly agitated, exchanging hurried words with his colleagues and sending nervous glances in my direction. Excusing myself from Miss McNeil's company, I returned to his side.

'We're arresting him,' he declared with a strangely shrill tone and a tilt of the head at Mr Hunt, now standing on his stage surrounded by his sea of followers.

'How?!' I asked, incredulous not that such an order might be given, but that it might be executed, with such a mass of humanity between the order and its success. I could not imagine that the people, as well-spirited as they had been so far, would be complicit in the arrest of their champion.

'The warrant has been issued. The militia has been sent for, and I shall be joining it!'

'I was not aware you were a military man, Mr Trenchard.' Having by this time fortified his courage with several glasses of brandy, he did not detect the slight.

'I am a member of the Yeomanry, Master Winter, and it is my duty as a loyal subject of the crown to keep the peace and protect the realm.'

These were fine words from a man who had benefitted enormously from the favour of a wealthy master, and whose sole responsibility was to maintain the status quo. Here before him was a challenge to that responsibility, and now the magistrates had given him permission to put that challenge down with the sword. It was a blunt response from a blunt man, in a roomful of blunted, frightened men.

I had not lived as an adult through the years of war as they had, but I had learnt enough to know that using the sword on one's own countrymen rarely led to peace and prosperity. I thought to try a different tack.

'Are not some of these men here our own labourers and families, Mr Trenchard?'

'Undoubtedly they are, Master Winter. Makes my blood run cold, I can tell you, to think that they might cry for revolution today, and sit plotting in the mill tomorrow, all the while taking the work and the pay that is given them.'

'Indeed. But will they be appeased by the sight of you riding at them – at their friends and families? Will this cool their blood? Will they return to the mill tomorrow sedate and without malice?'

'Appease, Master Winter? Appease?! Why! They are fortunate to have work! There are as many again outside the mills, ready to take up the labour of those who find it underpaid, or 'demeaning', or against their 'politics'. No – there shall be no appeasing! There shall be a lesson. And I shall deliver it!'

Quite contrary to damping Mr Trenchard's ardour, I saw I had only stoked it. I turned away in frustration, to see McNeil, suddenly standing only feet away.

'I heard what you said.' She looked down at her wringing hands, knowing it had been a private conversation. 'It is not for me to say, but I believe you spoke well.'

I felt my cheeks redden. I had not spoken for her benefit, but was now moved to do so.

'I fear I have only made him more resolute.'

'He is drunk, Mr Winter. Drunken men cannot be reasoned with.'

Her frankness caught me off-guard, and I spoke almost without thinking: 'I shall go with him. Perhaps I can dissuade him from the saddle.'

Her blue eyes looked directly into mine, and there was such intensity in them, I felt that she looked into my very soul. I knew already there could be no retreat.

'You are very brave, Mr Winter. You are not like other men.'

With every word and every look now I felt more compelled to act. I returned to Mr Trenchard, now fumbling with a sorry-looking sabre and scabbard, attempting to attach it to his belt.

'Mr Trenchard. I should very much like to accompany you in your duty, sir.' Given his state, I thought to appeal to his sense of honour.

He paused, looking me up and down as if for the first time.

'You wish to join me in the throng do you, Master Winter?'

'I feel it is my duty as much as yours, sir, to protect the rule of law in our land... and to protect our families and friends.' I caught Miss McNeil's eye as I concluded.

'Very well then. George! Another horse for Master Winter here! And find him a sword!'

I will admit that I was scared. Courage had surged through me as I declared my intent, but it ebbed while we sat on our mounts, waiting for the Yeomanry to form. It was a unit in name alone, comprising shopkeepers and publicans rather than military men, and many of them had clearly taken Mr Trenchard's liquid approach to preparations. They were ill-trained, ill-disciplined and ill-at-ease in their formation. As we spurred forward, heads turned and voices were raised in alarm. The people pressed against us on all sides, even to our rear, cutting off our line of retreat. The field itself was so enclosed, and the attendance so great, that they had nowhere to go as we attempted to move through them. The sea of noise from a hundred thousand cries was all-engulfing, so that we could not even hear the man nearest us passing commands, ordering those about us to disperse. We were the enemy to these people. We came to deny them their right to be heard

– or even to speak. We were the slavers surrounded by the slaves, and the fear amongst us was palpable.

I could not say where it started, but somewhere in front of us, someone cracked. I saw the glint of a drawn blade, heard a shriek, and then the world turned to mayhem. The situation had been a powder-keg, and the Yeomanry was the spark. In an instant, every rider had drawn their blade. All around, the cries turned to screams, and the wave of noise crashed in upon us. Sabres rose and fell, horses reared and trampled, men with nowhere to flee raised their arms to shield themselves and their families. Women and children seemed to be everywhere, and everywhere there was the steel of the panicking Yeomanry, bright with the blood of the defenceless. I saw Mr Trenchard in front of me raise his sabre, rusty and dented, and cut down clumsily to his right. I did not see whether it struck flesh or not – but I could not stand idly by. I felt hands tugging at my boots, and knew that if I did not escape, I would be cast down into the crowd. I urged my mount forward against the tail of Mr Trenchard's. Unsheathing my sabre, I slapped its rump with the flat of the blade, and watched it immediately reared up in fright. Mr Trenchard issued a high-pitched scream and lurched for the neck of his horse, wrapping his arms tightly around to save himself from falling, while his sabre fell uselessly to the ground. As he fought to control his horse, I saw in front of him a woman and child, both dressed in white, cowering beneath its raised hooves. Acting on instinct, I spurred into harm's way, shielding them from the animal's flailing. It took all my strength to hold my mount steady while Mr Trenchard's bucked and struggled alongside it, but eventually he regained control and, with a wild-eyed glance at me, turned for the safety of the field's edge, and bolted.

I looked down at the terrified pair, still in danger of being trampled by the press all around them, and begged them to take my hand and ride to safety with me. There was no time for thinking in the maelstrom – only action. First the child was passed to me, and then the woman climbed up, and as steadily as I could, I guided my charges away from the massacre. The horse moved slowly with the load, but the field was clearing towards the edges and the going became easier. A bugle sounding behind made me look back, and there I saw more misery heaped on the crowd – for charging in now to rescue the floundering Yeomanry were the Hussars. The magistrates had ordered in the regular army against a peaceful rally. I saw an officer attempt to stay the madness, shaking a Yeoman and putting up his sword – but already too much blood had been spilled. Only yards away a horse reared, and a woman fell under its hooves. To my right a man was carried away by his friends, viscera spilling from a sabre slash across his middle. I turned away. The sight was sickening.

We reached the field's edge, close to the magistrates' position, and I halted my horse. The woman slid immediately from my saddle, and gestured to be given her child. I felt numb. Devoid of any words which could lend compassion to the scene.

'Winter.' I stuttered. 'Victor Winter.' The absurdity of introducing myself stung me even as I heard my words, yet I did not know what else to say.

'Elizabeth Gaunt, sir. You saved our lives, sir. Thank you.' And she turned and ran for safety.

I dismounted, not knowing whether I would find Mr Trenchard returned to his station, or whether he had fled further, all thought of duty vanquished. There was an eerie silence as I climbed the stairs of the house, yet when I emerged into the room I found it populated with almost its full contingent. Mr Trenchard was conspicuous by his absence, but arrayed against the windows, the magistrates watched the soldiers below hacking and thrusting to their command with anxious faces. Hasty notes were scribbled for further arrests, messengers were sent forth, but barely a word was spoken.

Miss McNeil joined me, bewildered, in the corner of the room.

'I do believe you saved those people's lives, Victor.'

The use of my Christian name shook me from my trance, and I turned to look at her, eyes burning once again with that inner passion.

'I... I didn't know what to do,' I muttered.

'You did what you could.'

'Madness. They just went mad. All of them.'

I felt a pressure on my hand. She squeezed. It was warm and tender and alive. My heart raced, yet this was not the beat of terror. Another emotion was rising within me – and it had taken me quite by surprise.

'I fear Mr Trenchard has forgotten himself,' she said, remarkably diplomatically. 'You would be best to remain here until the field is cleared.'

I nodded automatically, still struggling to take in her words, but seeing her eyes and feeling her hands on mine.

'When it is safe, you must come home with us. We shall send word to him.'

VI

It took several hours before the magistrates, cognisant of the blood on their hands, summoned up the courage to leave the scene. Even then, they were escorted to their homes by Hussars. Pockets of rioting had sprung up across Manchester as word of the events at St Peter's Field spread. There were rumours of almost a thousand casualties, and some said the country would be plunged into revolution. I was only dimly aware of these developments at the time, however. My bruised mind was still reliving the chaos of the massacre, surfacing only occasionally to recognise my feelings for Miss McNeil, which seemed to grow by the hour.

Her chaperone, a Mr Smythe, was every inch as cowardly as Mr Trenchard, and refused to release his escort from their guard duty. They remained with us at his house for a full day and a half, the agitated lieutenant making increasingly desperate pleas that it was not the job of the military to guard civil property or persons, except in a national emergency. Mr Smythe quite predictably insisted that a national emergency was indeed what we now faced, and that he did not wish to have to report that the lieutenant had abandoned his post. 'Justice of the Peace' can rarely have been so misapplied.

Miss McNeil told me of her father, a highly successful businessman like Sir Godfrey, and his work. She asked me every question she could conceive about life in London, and I answered her as best I could from my memory. She yearned to join her father there next season, she told me, and while I kept the nature of my exile from her, I could easily sympathise. Despite knowing it was unbecoming of her, she revealed her fascination with politics to me, and particularly with the reformist causes of Mr William Wilberforce. It was this, as Mr Trenchard had guessed, which had drawn her to St Peter's Field that day. She even spoke of a Manchester Female Reform Society, formed by activist women, with which she had sympathies.

72

I found her company electrifying. She was as passionate as she was beautiful and I soon realised that I was in love with her. When word was received from the recalcitrant Mr Trenchard that he was once more safely quartered at home, I felt a keen sadness that I must be taken from her company. I promised to write to her, and it was with hopes of a swift reunion that I returned to Mr Trenchard's care.

My hopes did not last long. When word of the Peterloo Massacre, as the press came to call it, reached London, Sir Godfrey came to Manchester. He met with me, and listened carefully to my re-telling of events. He was grateful, he told me, to have such a reliable source on which to base his decisions. His meeting with Mr Trenchard was swift, and his voice echoed throughout the corridors, leaving no-one in any doubt that Sir Godfrey had seen straight to the heart of the matter. I left the house with him that day, with no opportunity to take my leave of Miss McNeil. Mr Trenchard never worked for Ramsay's Importers & Exporters again. My apprenticeship in Manchester was at an end, and I did not know when or even if I would see Miss McNeil again.

Instead we returned to London, and I to the clerk's office. After years longing for a reconciliation with my patron and a return to the city, it felt cruelly ironic that now, having found companionship and contentment with Miss McNeil in Manchester, that wish was fulfilled. Sir Godfrey, finally, even seemed apologetic for my years of exile, muttering that he had allowed too much time to slip by, and that he had meant only to 'shock some sense into a boy with far too Romantic a view of the world'. Yet more irony that my encounter with Miss McNeil and my scrape with death had precipitated my restoration.

As if to salve a guilty conscience, he began to introduce me to his associates, and from time to time I would catch sight of a golden ring matching his. It was a tantalising reminder that beneath the stale air and ink and paper of the clerks' office that was my new prison, he quietly moved in powerful circles, spanning the globe with clandestine schemes.

Yet not once did he ask what I had learned in Manchester, or where my interests now lay. To him I was a project – not a person. While I was more sensible than ever of the second chance I had been afforded, I was also wary of my patron's caprices. If a boyish misdemeanour merited a five year exile, a second, adolescent transgression might well spell the end of my sponsorship. My second chance was never more than an ill-judged foray from disaster, and that knowledge weighed upon my mind.

My heart, however, remained fixed on the beguiling Miss McNeil, with whom I exchanged avid letters, describing to her the glimpses of London placed in front of me by my patron's work. Her replies resonated with me, bemoaning a sense of being incarcerated in her home while the world raced ever forward without her. We both spoke fondly of being reunited in the capital.

On turning eighteen, I was introduced to Almack's assembly rooms. Sir Godfrey pronounced the institution whimsical and self-involved – but allowed that it was the 'most principled and harmless of institutions with which a man of your years might become associated.' At the time, I found it utterly bewitching: the attention to detail – to etiquette, to the décor, to the dress. Having seemingly stopped growing at six feet, I was taken on a trip to Pall Mall to acquire the latest fashion and the most accurate fit. Oakes dressed me for the occasion, being more accustomed to the precise rituals and requirements of London's high society. Mrs Robson looked ready to burst into tears at the sight of me as I departed with Sir Godfrey for the club. 'He's a gentleman now, alright,' she said. And indeed I believed she was right: I had been well tutored and had applied myself diligently; I had learnt the fundamentals of business first-hand, and at times in spite of my patronage; I was now welcome on the Wrakeley hunt; I had acquitted myself with integrity when faced with a crisis at St Peter's Field. And now I was to attend my first society engagement.

The entrance to the building was unprepossessing, giving me no hint of the opulence within. The doorman greeted Sir Godfrey like an old friend, though he told me he had not visited the rooms since the death of his wife, almost twenty years previously. As we walked inside my mouth dropped open – swiftly spotted and rectified by Sir Godfrey. The entrance hall gave way to a grand staircase and, at its top, a splendid assembly room, one hundred feet long at least, and filled with people in the finest attire. I was relieved that we had gone to such trouble over my own appearance, so that I now did not feel conspicuous as we entered. A balcony protruding over the main dancefloor barely contained the orchestra, while their music spilled down onto the hundreds of revellers stepping, leaping and spinning below. At the sides, elegant ladies and gentlemen peered out at the movements of other elegant ladies and gentlemen. The windows, still allowing the last fingers of light into the room, were fully twenty feet high, and hung with the finest yellow silk curtains, replete with tassels and cords. Around these windows stood huge mirrors, elaborately framed in gold, amplifying the light and rendering unnecessary the ornate crystal chandeliers hanging down the middle of the dance floor. The room was a riot of colour and fine fabric, of taste with no expense spared. Silk dresses whirled to a waltz, their owners appearing to float as they moved around each other. Tailcoats and breeches stepped and spun. And everywhere, beneath the sound of the soaring music, there was the hum of conversation.

Sir Godfrey did not linger long in the entrance.

'Come, Victor. You must be introduced to the Patronesses. And I must find a drink.'

We negotiated the edge of the room, emerging into another hallway and thence to a doorway. The doorway was closed, and guarded by a polite but firm footman. Sir Godfrey spoke:

'Please inform the Patronesses that Sir Godfrey Ramsay wishes to pay them his respects, and to introduce his ward, Mr Victor Winter, making his debut.'

At this the footman slipped behind the door, returning moments later to inform us that Lady Sefton and Lady Cowper would receive us. We were ushered through into a small but handsomely decorated salon, which looked out from an elevated position down the length of the dancefloor: all the better for ensuring that there was no small movement or suggestion of alliance which could go unnoticed.

The two ladies to whom I was now introduced were very different in appearance, although it was instantly clear from their deportment and finery that they were both of the highest breeding and character. They wore kindly expressions which did much to calm my nerves, painfully aware that I was here to be assessed. I did not know what this assessment would entail, but I had already seen enough to know that I wished to be part of this society. Led by my patron, we bowed low and long to our hosts. The elder lady spoke first.

'Sir Godfrey. It gladdens my soul to see you again.'

'Returned to your company, I instantly wonder why I have stayed away so long, Lady Sefton.'

This elegant flattery received a warm smile and knowing eyes from its subject.

'Sir Godfrey, I do not believe you have been introduced to Lady Cowper, my colleague and confidante here at Almack's.'

Sir Godfrey bowed again as he took the offered hand of Lady Cowper.

'Lady Cowper, I am honoured to make your acquaintance. Thank you for inviting me to your ball. Might I take this opportunity to introduce you both to my ward, Victor Winter?'

Uncertain of the etiquette, and uncomfortable to be the centre of attention, I defaulted to bowing again, which drew a simpering laugh from Lady Cowper.

'My dear Mr Winter. Please do not be nervous in our company. Almack's is a temple of levity and refinement – we wish you to enjoy yourself.'

I smiled apologetically and straightened.

'A ward of Sir Godfrey's is always welcome here at Almack's,' offered Lady Sefton. 'Your patron was once quite the dancer here, you know.'

I attempted to show no surprise at this revelation – but evidently failed.

'We are all of us shaped by events, Mr Winter,' she chided, 'and Sir Godfrey has had just cause for his absence.'

'You are too kind, my Lady,' he interjected. 'I hope that I may regain some of my former poise.'

'I am sure you will, Sir Godfrey. And Lady Cowper can advise on who is best placed to partner you and your ward. Enjoy yourselves gentlemen! Welcome to Almack's.'

As I danced with Lady Cowper's suggested partners that night, I did my best to forget that I was still being assessed from the salon, and that every movement I made would either cement my good standing at the club, or undermine it. The issue became suddenly of the greatest importance to me – the difference between a life of dour and meaningless apprenticeships and one of elegance and pleasure, in the company of the finest people in society. I was finally grateful for the hours of dancing lessons which I had lately endured, and which I had found faintly ridiculous with my tutor. Sir Godfrey largely remained seated – although from time to time I spied him engaging in some of the less boisterous dances. I suppose I should not have been surprised, remembering his speed of movement on the ice of the Thames all those years ago, but Lady Sefton had been quite right. It was plain that he was a fine dancer – and it left me to consider, as we walked home that evening, what a change must have come over him with the death of his wife.

It was a question which Oakes was loath to offer his insight into, when I created a pretext to find him alone in his quarters.

'Sir Godfrey is indeed a fine dancer, Master Winter.'

'Undoubtedly, Oakes – but it sometimes seems to me like there are two different people inside that body.'

A look darkened his face, and I could not decide if it was confusion or anguish.

'I can't profess to understand, sir.'

'Nor can I, Oakes. I sometimes see flashes of the kindly, hopeful man of action who chose to help an abandoned child – when even his own housekeeper doubted the wisdom of the decision. This man is an adventurer – a buccaneer who dances, and defeats malefactors armed with only his fists. But these flashes are few, and far between. The man I am used to seeing is at odds with the world. An introvert who chooses cynicism over zeal, and punishes independent thought. I cannot reconcile them – nor do I know which is the real man.'

I had spoken without restraint. It was a complaint born of all the frustration and confusion of my teenage years – of striving to satisfy a patron whose true nature seemed utterly impenetrable.

Oakes' face twitched and winced. Anguish then, not confusion. Sighs and head-shakes gathered in strength. It was as if he hosted a private debate within his head, with me a silent onlooker. When he eventually spoke, his words came slowly and quietly. It seemed almost cathartic.

'Sir Godfrey is both those men, Master Winter. The Sir Godfrey you know has been shaped by the dreadful loss of his wife. It has turned him into the cynic, as you call it. The careful man. But the extrovert still hides within. And you may not see it, but the more he is with you, the more he becomes his old self. You are good for him, Master Winter. He may not even see it himself – but deep down, buried within himself, the best part of him knows it.'

'So what does he want from me, Oakes? How can I be the man he needs me to be?'

'I think you have two questions there, Master Winter. And they may have different answers.'

'What?' I exclaimed, exasperated.

'But at least you can now face the challenge head-on.'

Oakes said no more, but simply returned his attention to the household accounts on the desk before him. I stood for a moment, trying to make sense of it all, before deciding that a clear head was required for these riddles, and taking myself off to bed.

The letter I wrote the next morning, describing the evening to Miss McNeil, prompted a barrage of questions by return. To whom had I been presented? What music was played? How did I acquit myself on my first dances? What did the ladies wear? I answered these as best I could, flattered by her interest in my world. She offered no insight into my patron's character, however, and I judged that I could not in good faith press her, or indeed Oakes, on such a matter.

I returned weekly to the club and, with Sir Godfrey rarely again in attendance, revelled in my new-found freedom. Before long I found myself part of a small crowd of like-minded bucks, and was very quickly made aware that beyond Almack's there was a whole world of entertainment and opportunity to which I had yet to be introduced.

Chief among my new-found friends were Edward Ball-Hughes (though the papers named him Golden Ball on account of his fortune), and William Lord Alvanley. Being several years my senior, William was the natural leader of our set, and took me under his wing, teaching me the finer points of appearance and behaviour known only to a very select few. Whilst William set all his store by his appearance and reputation, Edward could not have been more different. If truth be told, William displayed something of a coldness to him, but seemed to tolerate him on account of his easy way with money. Edward was a devilishly handsome fellow, but dressed only as instructed, rather than with flair. His chief talent was that there was not a pursuit, game, distraction or dispute in which he did not have an interest – and against which he would not place a bet.

Both these friends were adamant that studies and apprenticeships were not suitable past-times for a society gentleman, and they proposed instead that I join their club, White's. As Sir Godfrey was also a member, his name together with theirs ensured a swift enrolment – though his countenance was grim as he heard my appeal.

'Almack's is a relatively harmless place. I am not so sanguine concerning White's. This may sound like hypocrisy from a member, yet I know only too well the distractions and iniquity which dwell within. One may conduct serious business there, certainly. Our Association often avails itself of a room at White's. And yet a young man without sound judgement and strength of character may easily be led astray... There is a fashion amongst the younger set to fritter away fortunes which they have not yet acquired – and these clubs are at the centre of it.'

I had expected this. It was the old complaint. Despite my years of exile in Manchester, it seemed his faith in me would never be restored. My character and judgement would forever be questioned for that childhood transgression. I was reminded of Oakes' counsel. This cynicism was hard-learned, and would be hard to erode.

'Sir: you have raised me to be circumspect in all that I do. I shall always be mindful of the error I made when I was young - but I have learned from it. I have been diligent in my studies – both towards books and lessons, and in my apprenticeships with your operations. I do not look to leave all this behind me now. I mean to learn more from my contemporaries, and form alliances which may serve me well in the future. I hope I do not presume too much, sir, in considering that the alliances you yourself have formed are crucial to the success you enjoy?'

His brow furrowed further, and for a moment I feared I had let my frustration run too far. However, closing his eyes and drawing a full breath, he let out a sigh of grand proportions and shook his head, as if disbelieving his own decision.

'I cannot guide you all the way to your destiny, Victor. You have always been impetuous. Sooner or later you will see all that this city has to offer. I fear that with this membership I open Pandora's box. But if I don't open it, someone else will.'

I thought his words overly dramatic, but reasoned that he was for the first time allowing me to set foot in the world unchaperoned. In his eyes I was still the stray he had taken from the street, and he was afraid of what I might do when he opened my cage's door. The irony was all too clear to me. It was precisely because he did not trust me that I needed to form my own alliances. I could not rely on his patronage, much as I might wish to.

White's had a first-class reputation: a gentleman's club admitting only the quality of society. With Edward and William as my guides, I soon became familiar with its customs. Luncheon was to be taken fashionably late. If he were feeling indulgent, or judged that my appearance passed muster, William would invite me to sit with him in the bow window overlooking St James's Street, where the great sport was to look uninterested, whilst keenly observing and discussing each and every passer-by. Conversation of a serious nature, such as politics or business, was reserved for the rearmost rooms, which were in turn relatively quiet. Most members frequented White's for the society gossip, drinking, and gambling – and there was no curfew for these pursuits. It was not unusual to find a dozen or more members availing themselves of a drink at the bar before noon, discussing the previous night's most salacious rumours, and challenging one another to a game of chance.

The gambling took many varied forms. There were of course card games and dice games. But I also witnessed substantial bets placed on the outcome of the toss of a coin, or the colour of a gentleman's jacket, or indeed the favour of a lady. Ball-Hughes was invariably at the front of the queue to place such bets, so fierce was his instinct for gambling. On several occasions I returned to the club in the morning to find him still at the table where I had left him the night before. But the club also opened the door to other pursuits outside its walls.

Trips to the theatre with Sir Godfrey had been a rare treat in my adolescence, but as a member of White's, and in the company of my friends, they became a frequent fixture. It was almost irrelevant what production might be on. Indeed, we were known to attend the same one several times if the players were 'prime articles', as Ball-Hughes would call them. He in particular found nothing more entertaining than the company of a beautiful woman – and one maudlin early morning he recounted to me rather dolefully the tale of the various women he had loved and lost. If the production were utterly forgettable, the evening might nonetheless be a roaring success if we spied in the audience some rare beauties to flatter and flirt with at the interval. We also found entertainment at the Castle Tavern in Holborn. Though there was little chance here of engaging with the gentler sex, the high-spirited knavery and free-flowing drink more than made up for it. It was here that we also learned of upcoming boxing matches, and gained the inside track on form from the sporting set who called it their home.

If there were a girl to be wooed, I was advised to take her to the pleasure gardens across the river in Vauxhall. Taking a boat through the water entrance, she would be enchanted by the thousands of lights hanging from every branch and column, the wandering minstrels and performers, the firework displays, the dancing, and the walkways and attractions en route. She would be wise to steer clear of the punch, however, as I discovered to my cost on my first visit. My friends at White's shared a laugh at my expense when I recounted the experience to them. They informed me that the punch was infamous, and that I should consider it a rite of passage. I thought it wise to write only in broad terms of these adventures to Miss McNeil.

White's swiftly became the centre of my universe – a feeling which was only strengthened when, upon entering the club one afternoon, I nearly walked straight into the dashing Lord Elsfield. Making my apologies, and not yet realising his identity, I sidestepped him and continued on my way, when he called out:

'Surely that cannot be the young Master Winter?!' His tone was incredulous, such that I wondered why my appearance in my own club should cause such surprise.

'Well I should say so!' I replied defiantly, turning on the spot and instantly recognising the peer, despite the years since our last encounter. I froze in body and mind, painfully aware of my disrespectfulness. Lord Elsfield, to his credit, brushed the affront aside with no more than a raised eyebrow.

'You have grown some several inches since we last met – and I see you have been accompanying Sir Godfrey to John Jackson's saloon.'

Embarrassed and now confused, I struggled for a response.

'Your footwork, Master Winter – or rather, I should say, Mr Winter. It was reminiscent of Sir Godfrey's that day on the ice!'

Despite my embarrassment I found my voice, and at his insistence we proceeded together to the bar and thence to luncheon. His conversation was enthralling. He told me of his activities of the past few years – of voyages to Africa and the Americas. Of the opportunities for a young gentleman of means and good judgement such as myself. There were canals to be built in North America. Mines to be opened in South America. Railroads in Europe. Exploration in Africa.

As he spoke it occurred to me that fate was handing me an opportunity. I was an orphan whose only prospects had once been to freeze to death, nameless, on an icy church porch in a forgotten village of rural England. Through some twist of fortune, I had come to be raised by a wealthy man with important connections. Yet it was increasingly clear that Sir Godfrey's aspirations for me were limited. If I showed no initiative, I seemed doomed to drift aimlessly from one apprenticeship to another, always the master's lapdog, never earning the trust to make my own mark. I would be tied to his favour forever, never more than a change of heart away from being returned to the street whence I came.

My patron's great hope had been that I would prove myself capable of continuing his family's work: to turn Ramsay's into the foremost operation in the British Empire. To do so meant being alive to each and every opportunity which presented itself; to weigh each one carefully, and make shrewd and sometimes bold decisions when needed. Yet he denied me the authority to make those decisions, and the opportunities to prove myself capable. Instead, fate was here offering me that opportunity.

My time spent with my society friends was not time wasted – Sir Godfrey himself had conceded that it was largely due to 'The Association' that he had prospered. However, there could be little more time frittered away on idle entertainments – on theatres, sporting, gossip and gambling. The greater game was to follow in the footsteps of Sir Godfrey and Lord Elsfield, and fully engage in the world of commerce. And to do that, I just needed a start. Emboldened, I questioned his lordship closely on the nature of his current investments and concerns.

'My dear Victor! You will surely bankrupt me if you extract all the details of my operations from me!' Yet he said this kindly, and with a smile. 'But your interest and energy do you great credit. I would be happy to advise you on your investments, lending you what information I have without perhaps revealing all of my own concerns. Tell me briefly: what are your current speculations?'

My heart sank. He clearly imagined that a gentleman of my years should already have some business interests. I wondered how to tell him that my career to date had been spent either apprenticed to my patron's lieutenants, learning from books and tutors or, more recently, indulging in the city's clubs, taverns and amusements. I had not even discussed with Sir Godfrey the possibility of an income with which to establish my own interests. What I currently received was sufficient only for my subsistence. I felt suddenly deflated – as if I had disappointed a second patron.

'Am I to understand, Victor, that you have yet to be given licence to forge your own career?'

'I regret that my advancement has not been at the pace I had hoped.'

'Indeed not, my friend. Yet your ambition is boundless. I wonder if Sir Godfrey is fully aware of your drive to succeed, or of your abilities. He may not be inclined to press his own agenda onto you, waiting rather for you to reveal your desires to him.'

There was some sense in what he said and, relieved that my guilt was perhaps unfounded, I began to plan my approach.

'How much did you say, my boy?!'

Sir Godfrey's voice wavered somewhere between incredulity and anger.

'Five thousand as a lump sum, sir, and two thousand a year. Having accounted for normal expenses, I believe that that will allow me sufficient...'

'Seven thousand! Well at least I know that my ears do not yet deceive me. I thought for a moment I must be in the grip of a seizure which had damaged my hearing. But no. You did say seven thousand. Seven thousand pounds to put my ward into business. Seven thousand to keep him in the manner to which he has grown accustomed.'

'Sir. I assure you that I shall secure a substantial return on this investment...'

I was quietened by a wave of his hand.

He sat behind the walnut desk in his study at the back of the London house, an instinctive thumb and ring finger now pinching his temples, while I stood before him, feeling increasingly like an estate worker begging for charity to cover some unseemly debt. He had agreed to the meeting in full knowledge that I was come to request an income, and now he seemed determined to make me suffer for it. It was June and the season in London would soon be drawing to a close. I had limited time to exploit information gleaned from my associates before we dispersed for the country, and the opportunities for swift windfalls disappeared.

'Seven thousand is too much, Victor.' Again a raised hand prevented my protestation.

'I have high hopes for you. Do not think otherwise. You are a willing and able apprentice, and you have applied yourself with vigour. But you are still young, and at times headstrong. The intricacies of a business such as mine are manifold. It is my intention that you will come into Ramsay's incrementally, as shrewd management dictates.' These fine words did not disguise from me that his tone remained negative. 'However, I cannot perceive the value of allowing you to establish your own private venture. Even if your optimism bears fruit, and you achieve some small success, this will only distract from the running of an international operation, which *I* assure *you* requires nothing less than one's total attention.'

He paused, and fixed me with eyes that brooked no further discussion.

'I warned you only a few months ago that London society would be a distraction – that it would suggest to you myriad ways in which to fritter away a fortune you do not yet possess. I do you the honour now of presuming that this application is not, in fact, to cover some swiftly-amassed debt...'

My cheeks burned at the insult. I issued a cry of protest – but Sir Godfrey would not be interrupted.

'Yet presuming you now to be solvent does not guarantee that wealth easily acquired will not be equally easily disposed of... I *will* grant you an increase. Yet it will not be so grand a figure as you desire. I ask that you reward my trust in you by remaining careful in its investment and expenditure.' At this he drew his writing paper towards him, dipped a pen in ink, and began to write an instruction to his bank. 'I have several schemes afoot, Victor, which will soon require your assistance. Enjoy London these last few months. I ask only that you remain circumspect. You and I are planning for the long-term.'

As he wrote, I perceived the figure he intended for me. I forced myself to remain dignified and silent as he finished the instruction and signed and sealed it. The insult complete, he handed it to me for execution. Five hundred pounds would keep me entirely at his service, allowing me no freedom to set myself up independently. It was the final confirmation that I had no future in this house. I left his study resolute that I would find another source of credit. He had brought me up preaching hard work and self-reliance. I would prove myself a better student than he realised.

VII

I could not approach Lord Elsfield for credit. He had already offered to take me into his confidence, and had presumed that I was resourceful enough to secure my own finances. To return to him empty-handed, asking for both his advice and his backing, seemed certain to undermine his confidence in me.

Yet he was not the only man of means in my circle. I could not directly ask for money from my friends without causing some considerable discomfort, and certainly not without damaging my own reputation. But if Ball-Hughes would wager thousands of pounds on the toss of a coin, perhaps he might be coaxed into a game of chance where I could stack the odds in my favour. There existed a prevalence of confidence tricksters around him, who would gull him into unwinnable wagers with cogged dice or duplicate cards. As urgent as my need might be, I would not take that route. Instead, one night as I attended the theatre, the solution presented herself to me – a solution which I believed would suit Edward as much as me.

Maria Mercandotti had enjoyed some success before she came to England, in the theatres of Spain. Nonetheless, she arrived in London still something of an enigma. Quite by chance, I happened to be at the theatre to witness her first performance. The ripple of astonishment which passed through the audience on her first dance was entirely justified. She was mesmerising. She had been billed as 'The Andalusian Venus', and the sobriquet would stick. Proceeding to the stage door at the end of the performance, I was one of a score of young men who were eager to make her acquaintance. As entranced as I myself was by this beauty, I was more astonished at the effect she had on others – men turning into wet geese in her presence. Her lack of English only added to her mystique, and I heard one suitor declare passionately that he would forsake all his titles to make her his own.

The theatre manager was quite aware of the value of his star, and allowed only brief interviews with her, passing all further enquiries on to her patron. It was therefore to him that I applied the very next morning, agreeing that for a price, I might gain a private audience with the matchless Mercandotti that night. I then removed myself to White's to await Ball-Hughes. My plan relied on encountering him before the word spread.

I did not have to wait long. After luncheon, he strolled into the club in a fine mood, apparently having had some success at the tables the night before, and eager for some new entertainment. Spying me he enquired what sport there might be about town. I could not have hoped for a better introduction to my scheme.

'Funny thing, old friend. I think I have something that will tickle your fancy!' I attempted to sound nonchalant, when in fact I felt anything but.

'Is that right, young Victor?' Being his junior, he inevitably referred to me as 'young'.

'In fact, I'd wager I've found something the like of which you've never seen before.'

The *mot juste* did not escape his attention.

'Oh yes? A sporting bet, is it? Go on. I'm all ears.'

'Tell me: did you enjoy any female company last night at the tables?'

A rather self-satisfied smile appeared on his face, and my question already had its answer.

'Indeed I did. A fine specimen indeed. A prime article and no mistake.'

'But would you say your company last night was the finest you've *ever* had?'

The smile remained as he parried me deftly.

'Young Victor: women of this sort cannot be compared. They are unique. One of a kind. Diamonds each.'

'Of course my friend, of course. I meant not to suggest otherwise. But what if I told you – nay, wagered you – that I could engage you this very night with the most radiant beauty you had ever set eyes upon?'

His eyes narrowed.

'What are you up to, you rogue?'

'Exactly as I say, old friend: no more, no less. A sporting bet.'

The smile dissolved. Edward had two great weaknesses: a love of gambling, and a love of women. I fancied he could not resist the combination. For a moment longer he looked at me quizzically, as one might view a painting when judging its fairness. Despite my confidence in my friend, my heart still thudded in anticipation. And then the fish was hooked.

'Alright. Let's see what you've got. I should warn you though, I've known some rare specimens.'

Indeed, it was true and well known. My enterprise was not without risk – but I believed it was as close as I could get to a sure thing without cheating a friend.

'I will take your judgement on the matter, Edward.'

'What are you playing for then, young Victor? What's in your pocket?'

'Shall we say a thousand? Make it interesting?' I said, focusing all my energies on keeping my voice level. If I lost, I was ruined, and would be forced to seek Sir Godfrey's help to settle. He would rescue me, probably, but it would only confirm his poor opinion of me – and I would be condemned to slowly bury myself in his clerk's office until my end, one close-lined sheaf of accounting paper at a time. If Ball-Hughes got a sense of my fragility, he might not accept the wager. Yet if I wagered too little, I could not profit sufficiently to change my circumstances. I had considered and reconsidered my course. I did not have an alternative.

'A thousand? I think we can do a little better than that, young Victor! If this thing you've found really is the modern Venus, then we should honour her properly. Two thousand at least!'

His smile returned. Ball-Hughes spent all his waking hours gambling, whilst I had only watched, afraid to enter with my paltry income. If I refused his bet, the deal was off. He would know I was at a standstill. If I agreed, I was committed to a bet far beyond my means. I would be ruined utterly, and cast out from society. I was not even sure that Sir Godfrey would forgive me. I wondered now who was the fish, and who had done the hooking. I looked uncertainly at Edward. He simply smiled back.

'Do we have a deal, young Victor?' He asked, stretching out his hand.

I swallowed hard. The long case clock ticked in its cabinet. The drone of the club faded away around me. My chest tightened.

'We do, Edward.' I shook his hand.

A strange bond formed between us at that moment. I felt both in his power, and also to have power over him. Perhaps it was the knowledge that I could not honour my debt that made me feel in thrall to him – or perhaps he felt the same in spite of his plentiful resources. With our sparring complete, we retired to the bar, where he stood me a drink and had me explain my terms.

'I have two tickets to the theatre tonight, Edward. If you accompany me, I guarantee you will see on the stage a beauty without equal.'

'So that's your game, is it? Well I should warn you, young Victor: many appear tantalising from a box. That is their art. But up close they rarely hold up to scrutiny.'

I suspected he did not truly value the ladies of the stage so little – but he certainly enjoyed toying with me now I had committed my fortune – and my very future – to him.

'Well, you will have ample opportunity to decide for yourself tonight, my friend,' I replied. I would not give him the satisfaction of seeing me panic. To him this was just a gentle amusement – a distraction. To me it was a matter of life and death.

My carriage called at his residence at six, and from there it was a short drive to the King's Theatre. We sat in our usual box, from where we were guaranteed a good view of the dancer's entrance. Edward had maintained a bemused yet affable demeanour throughout the escapade, and now as the moment approached I watched him closely out of the corner of my eye – desperate not to miss any sign of his emotions, but cognisant that he should not perceive my desperation.

As with the previous night, a ripple ran through the audience as she appeared. Everything came down to this moment. I could not breathe, so focused was I on the reaction from my friend. My hands shook in anticipation, and I clasped them together in my lap to hold them steady. My heart pounded so loudly in my chest I thought Edward himself must hear it. But his attentions were well and truly elsewhere. He rose from his seat the better to stare at this vision before him, suddenly ignorant of my company, and indeed of all else around him. Relieved beyond measure, I sank down in my seat and drew breath once more.

Edward did not return to his seat until the dance was done. His eyes did not leave Mercandotti. His hands gripped tightly around the box balustrade, and I could not decide whether it held him back from leaping onto the stage itself, or served to support him from otherwise falling to the floor. He bore an intensity of expression which I had never seen before. Normally resolutely languid, his eyes seemed wild with passion now as he turned to me.

'She is magnificent, Victor. Magnificent! I *must* meet her. How can it be done?!'

'It is already arranged, dear friend,' I replied, feeling at last that I had the upper hand in our little sport. 'You may go down behind the stage and await her. Tell her patron that I have sent you.'

He looked puzzled at this, but asked no further questions, leaving me immediately and proceeding to his rendezvous. I remained in my seat, mind whirring and my constitution recovering from the tension of the moment. He had not yet conceded, but he was a man of honour. It would be a small scandal now if he were to deny his immediate reaction or indeed his words to me later. The rest of the performance passed in something of a blur. I did not wish to retire home nor to the club, but rather welcomed the general distraction. Finally, the performance at an end, I rose to leave, only to be intercepted by a footman carrying an envelope from Mr Edward Ball-Hughes, and addressed to me.

To his distinct credit, the enclosed note read:

My dearest Victor.

Two thousand does not begin to do honour to the Lady Mercandotti. I have never been so soundly beaten in all my days.

Yours etc, Edward.

Despite having sensed that the bet was already won, my relief now was palpable. I walked home with a spring in my step, and it was all I could manage not to reveal any hint of the enterprise to Sir Godfrey. He would without doubt not have looked kindly on such reckless behaviour, regardless of its outcome.

A further surprise awaited me upon my arrival at White's the next day, when another footman delivered me another envelope, this one containing no message but a banker's draft for not two, but four thousand pounds. I sat agog in the morning room and read and reread the draft. Golden Ball was known for being free and easy with his fortune, but this seemed extravagant even for him. Yet there was no mistake, and later that day, when he made his appearance at the club, he seemed barely able to contain his exuberance. He bounded towards me and put both his hands on my shoulders, looking me squarely in the eyes.

'Victor, my friend: it was a rotten trick. A rotten trick!' I was dumbstruck. I had hoped he would be pleased with the outcome – at least to a degree. I searched for words with which to defend myself, but he continued:

'You could have bet your entire fortune last night, and I still would have been honour-bound to pay. It was an unwinnable bet for me and you knew it! Yet a sweeter loss I have never encountered. Oh the Lady Mercandotti is beguiling. Utterly beguiling! I felt cheap to pay you the sum we agreed. It did her a disservice. Any amount would! Please consider this not the settling of a wager, nor a payment of any kind, but a gift – a gift of thanks for my introduction to my future wife.'

Once again he had me at a loss – though this time I did not fear for my honour.

'Your wife, Edward?'

'Why not?! She is quite wonderful. A diamond of the first water! Who else could match her?'

'Well... I am pleased for you, I am sure. Very pleased. Glad to have been able to effect an introduction.'

'You rogue, Victor. You made a tidy profit out of me and no mistake. But I don't begrudge it. Not in the least. Now then. Let me buy you luncheon.'

Still rather shocked at the pace of events, I dumbly took my exuberant friend up on his offer, and listened to him wax lyrical about his new love while I enjoyed my food. Presently, once he had rehearsed the finer points of his story with me, he sought out new ears to spread his happy news to. He was not yet engaged, of course – and knowing his history of engagements, it was likely he never would be. But he was full of the joys of spring, and I felt somewhat vindicated in my tipping of the scales for the wager.

With my friend now occupied elsewhere, I sent a note to Lord Elsfield, requesting to meet with him and take him up on his kind offer. I received an invitation to dine with him at the club the very next day.

VIII

'So you got the funds, eh?'

Once again Lord Elsfield was immaculately dressed, exuding an air of superiority and wearing what I now took to be his characteristic smile of easy confidence. He gestured for me to sit.

'I did. As you suggested, Sir Godfrey was waiting only for me to approach him. He encouraged me to follow my interests in business.' I had debated whether to tell the truth, or to tell this lie. The truth would reveal my resourcefulness. Yet it would also show that I had not yet won the trust of my patron. I wanted Lord Elsfield to respect me, and to see me as a good investment. I took a forkful of roast beef to my mouth and chewed, the better to conceal my nerves. His response was swift.

'Excellent! Of course, of course. Sir Godfrey is no fool! He knows a good investment when he sees one. I had no doubt he would support you just as soon as you made the case. But did he not seek to guide your hand himself? Was he happy that you would take advice from me?'

Having begun the lie, it seemed prudent to extend it.

'He did offer, sir, but I suggested that I already had some strategies I wished to pursue. I made the case that it would be better for me to develop my own sense of a shrewd investment - of good and bad information.' I surprised myself by how easily the falsehood was maintained and embellished. Dishonourable as it might be, this lie at least protected my patron from his lack of judgement, and did no harm to me.

'Well then. We should begin to talk business, Mr Winter. What do you know of the securities markets?'

I knew nothing and, over the ensuing hour, did my best to sound intelligent whilst revealing gap after gap in my understanding of modern investments. Lord Elsfield explained that his advice years ago in Dover had been accurate. He had reduced his shipping and trading operations significantly, and now relied heavily on information from agents around Europe and further afield to make profitable investments in shares and bonds, spreading his investments so as to balance his risk. Having explained to me the basic mechanics of stock trading, he declared that the United States was embarking on a programme of infrastructure projects which would revolutionise its economic power. He advised me to invest a substantial amount into the Erie Canal concern, being certain that it would prove hugely profitable, and that a little invested now would be returned several-fold in a short time.

About government bonds he was more conspiratorial. We spoke in generalities until dinner was finished and we had retired to a private room where, over port and cigars, he spoke to me in a low voice.

'Everything I have told you so far is true, Victor – and you should take this information as your grounding principles in the markets. However, anomalies arise. And anomalies are extremely profitable. Do you remember the episode I recounted to you when we met in Dover?'

I cast my mind back. Whilst I remembered the encounter vividly, the details of his story escaped me. He perceived that a reminder was required.

'News reached London that the war had ended, and the markets reacted predictably. To someone who had prior information such as me, this was an opportunity to buy government bonds cheaply before the news broke, and sell them soon after when the price peaked. The more unexpected the news, the more favourable the profit.

'In this case, the news turned out to be false. But it did not matter. All that matters is that people behave in a predictable manner. If we can predict their behaviour, we can profit from it. Do you see?'

My head spun. I understood – but it was not simple. This was an art which I knew to be beyond Sir Godfrey. If a venture looked unsound, he would simply not invest. He would not see the potential for others to be less circumspect, and hence he would not see the opportunity to profit from their lack of judgement. A new world of possibilities was revealing itself to me, and I was eager to learn all I could.

'I believe I do see, my Lord.'

'Excellent! This is not for the faint-hearted, Victor. If investing wisely were simple, it would not be so profitable. There are innumerable opportunities which will only lose money. The trick is to discover those that will be successful before others do.' He paused, and leant forward. His voice lowered further. 'I have received information about another such anomaly. If you are willing to be bold, there is a significant opportunity.'

For the second time in as many days, I felt the anxiety that accompanied a momentous gamble. Decisions taken now might reverberate throughout my life. This was the path I had chosen. If I did not act boldly now, then for what had I so recently risked everything in hoodwinking Ball-Hughes? I knew there was only one reply I could give, yet still I felt my heart racing as I gave it.

'I am, my Lord. I am willing to be bold.'

'Of course you are!' he replied, delighted. 'You haven't come this far to back down now! The opportunity relates to the recent coup in Spain[1]. Let me explain. Their government of bickering liberal housewives claims to be freeing the people.' The expression of scorn on his face communicated his own opinion on the matter. 'In reality, they are paralysing enterprise and destroying their own economy. There is concern across Europe that the example could spread. A strong message must be sent that revolutionaries will be defeated. Our systems of law and order will not be at the mercy of the mob.

'Yet no such message has been forthcoming. In Verona the Powers mimic the Spanish government, bickering amongst themselves and achieving precious little. European bonds should be risk-free.

Well here is the anomaly: the threat of war will ruin a bond, just as surely as the promise of peace will send it up. Values are falling across Europe.'

At this he paused, and took a long drag on his cigar, allowing me to reflect on the prospect of turmoil and war in Europe once again. 'The French and Russians are spoiling for a fight. They will mobilise troops soon, and bonds will tumble. And then – the Congress will declare its decision. And it will be the obvious one. It will sanction the restoration of the king. It may not even come to a fight. The Spanish know their experiment is failing. A French army knocking at the door of the Pyrenees, with the blessing of all the Powers, may be all they require to throw in the towel.'

I began to understand. 'So values will dip, and then recover?'

'Exactly!' His conspiratorial demeanour morphed into the familiar confident smile. 'You certainly don't wait around, do you Victor? While the frightened investors of the world seek to sell bonds they fear will default, we can swoop in, knowing that law and order will prevail. Debts will be honoured, taxes will be collected, crops will be harvested. In short, the status quo will be maintained – and the only people to lose out will be those who were too cowardly to support the stability they crave.'

I leaned forward now, keen to show that I was allied to him. 'Lord Elsfield – how may I join you in this venture?'

Throughout the remainder of that year Lord Elsfield and I worked together to great effect. I remained uncertain of the sources of his information, but time and again they proved correct. In the course of the six months to November my fortune doubled. This was gambling I understood. Not over the fall of dice, or the turn of a card – but over governments, over national enterprises, and over the globe. My cabin-bound view of Calais in 1814 remained the closest I had come to foreign soil, and yet now I stood astride the world with my interests. Miss McNeil wrote to tell me that she was to travel with her parents to London in the new year, and hoped to stay for the season. Emboldened by my new-found success as a businessman, our correspondence gathered pace once more. I told her of the investments I had made, and of their rewards – but was careful to withhold the identity of my new business partner. Her letters to me could not hide her admiration. She had known when we had met at St Peter's Field that I was courageous. Now she saw that I was judicious also. She asked if I might call on her as soon as she reached London, and I promised that I would.

My fortune remained for the most part invested, and thus it was not difficult to conceal my wealth from Sir Godfrey. I regretted that it was necessary to do so, but reflected that it was he who had forced my deception, when he had refused to trust in my maturity and judgement as an investor. Left to him, I would still be a prisoner of Mr Crisp and the clerk's office.

Ball-Hughes remained besotted with Madame Mercandotti. Though he explained that it was impolitic to flaunt their affections in public (her professional success being dependent in part on her eligibility), there was a deep understanding between them. I feared my friend was once again about to be disappointed, but nonetheless heard his eulogies when he offered them.

It was therefore with some wariness that I spied Edward entering the club one December day, assuming that I was to receive another such monologue. Instead, I received something altogether different.

'Victor, old friend! How are you?' He did not pause for a response, continuing straight on. 'I would very much like you to meet a new acquaintance of mine. His name is Sir Gregor MacGregor, Grand Cazique of Poyais.'

Somewhat alarmingly, and on mention of this name, out from behind Edward now stepped a man dressed in a velvet black tail coat and breeches, with golden epaulettes and golden flashings on his collar and wrists. Across his chest was a crimson panel with more golden embroidery overlaid, while across his waist was tied a crimson sash. I had not met a Cazique before, but could well believe that one now stood before me. Unsure of the etiquette appropriate for receiving one however, I stood and offered my hand. The Cazique instead offered me a short bow and, somewhat embarrassed by my presumption, I reciprocated.

'Pleased to meet you, Your Highness,' I ventured. It seemed wise to err towards royalty in my address, not knowing what rank a Cazique might be.

The Cazique seemed satisfied with my greeting, and replied in a broad Scottish brogue: 'Pleased to meet you too, Mr Winter.'

To say the accent took me by surprise would be an understatement. I automatically looked to Edward for guidance, who could not resist a smile at my expense as he explained:

'Sir Gregor is a Scotsman, Victor. He was made Grand Cazique of Poyais by the King of the Mosquito Shore, while visiting him there. He is in London at the moment to recruit settlers to return with him, and to invite selected gentlemen to invest in his expanding nation.' Edward now looked at Sir Gregor to elaborate.

'As you say, Mr Ball-Hughes. I presume you have heard of the Principality of Poyais, Mr Winter?'

I had to confess that I had not. I hoped I had not offended his highness. Edward stepped in to smooth the ground.

'Mr Winter has swiftly gained a reputation here as a keen-eyed investor, Your Highness. He seems to *smell* what the markets are going to do. Isn't that right, Victor?!'

I lowered my eyes to the ground in unfeigned humility. The confidential nature of my alliance with Lord Elsfield meant that I now received more credit than I was due.

'I have made some fortunate predictions, Your Highness, and hope to continue with some modest success.'

'Then perhaps you would be interested in investing in my country, Mr Winter. The first boat of settlers will have arrived by now and they will already be developing the lands they have purchased from me. I have a second boat leaving in January. The prospects are perhaps matched only by our ambition.'

From what I had learned in the past six months, the offer seemed an attractive one. Bonds were safe investments, and here was an opportunity to jump to the front of the queue on an emerging prospect. It was also an opportunity to impress Lord Elsfield: showing him that I too was privy to closely-guarded secrets, and could be as useful to him as he had been to me. But to do this I must first ensure my information was correct.

'I would be delighted to make an investment, Your Highness,' I replied. 'However, if I may understand a little of your country's situation first? Please excuse my ignorance. I'm afraid London society can be terribly suffocating.' I risked offending him, but I required a level of assurance before parting with my money.

'Of course,' he smiled. 'You are not the only investor to have little knowledge of our corner of the world. You will find all the information you need in the recently published 'Sketch of the Mosquito Shore' – an encyclopaedic survey of my country. But, if I may, I would urge haste. The number of bonds I can sell is limited, and the demand has been quite extraordinary.'

I thanked the Cazique for his indulgence, took his card, and left him to be escorted by Edward to luncheon. I then set about acquiring the book of which he had spoken, eager to waste as little time as possible in my decision.

By January that decision was made. Having spent Christmas at Wrakeley, enduring the seemingly timeless contempt of the staff, and the measured wariness of my patron, I approached him on my birthday in his study. I had not often had cause to be in this room, and as I stood at his desk it brought to mind the occasion – nineteen years ago to the day – that I had been presented to him. On that day he had taken a chance – a leap of faith – on an unknown proposition. I urged him to do so again.

'...I had the good fortune last month to be introduced to the Cazique of Poyais, sir.' I paused, hopeful that this would stir some recognition, or even admiration. He remained unmoved. 'The Cazique is currently raising funds for the development of his country, in Central America.' Still Sir Godfrey's expression remained inscrutable. 'I have taken the time to learn about this country's situation in some detail, sir. I consider it to be most advantageous. On the anniversary of my being welcomed by you into this house, I wished to offer you the opportunity to invest in the Principality of Poyais, and to send goods to that country in order to profit directly from its certain advancement.'

It had not been an easy speech for me to give. It seemed almost as if Sir Godfrey had made it intentionally difficult with his silence. Even now I had finished he remained silent. I wondered what he waited for. Finally he spoke.

'Victor. I am glad to have you as my trusted apprentice. I hope I treat you well. I hope I have kept you in good health, and equipped you with the tools to succeed in this world. I would reiterate what I said to you last year – that there are schemes afoot in which I would involve you. Those schemes are sure to come to fruition soon. I refrain from detailing them now only for fear that you will form an attachment to one which fails.' It was as if he had not heard me. My heart sank. I already knew what his response would be. 'I am pleased that you continue to take an active interest in the world of commerce. But this Poyais business... It's very unsound...'

'Sir!' I protested, 'investment in a government is a low-risk venture...'

'It is unsound, I say! No one knows anything about this country. The stocks have already slid....'

'...they have now stabilised, sir.'

'They have *indeed* now stabilised. And I shall watch with interest to see whether they remain so.'

'My view is that it would be wise to act ahead of the masses, sir. In a matter of months more settlers will arrive in the country. The stocks are bound to rise as news comes back.'

Our voices were both now raised. I had wanted to avoid a confrontation, but had found my patron as obstinate as ever.

'And where does this view come from, Victor? From years of experience as a businessman? From a deep understanding of the world of commerce? From insights into the inner motivations of men – men who are often not what they appear?'

It was a breath-taking ad hominem, delivered by the very man who had proscribed the experience he now mocked me for. I had never in my life wrestled so hard with my anger – anger that urged me to tell him of my successes of the past six months. Of my alliance with men within his own Association. That I was valued by everyone – even his own friends – more than I was by him. No doubt he could see the turmoil writ large on my face, for his next words were softer.

'I am sorry, Victor. It was unworthy of me to speak that way to you. It is a difficult time for you and me. You have ambition and energy – and I could not be more pleased that this is so. You are eager to test yourself. Yet there are no test grounds outside Wrakeley. No risk-free ventures. No forgivenesses. You must be cautious in your approaches. You must trust that I have your best interests at heart. That I...' I stopped listening. He belittled me one moment, then patronised me the next. He still spoke to me at nineteen as he had at ten. I realised with some sadness that in his eyes I would always be the village boy who fell on his charity. I would always be the apprentice, never the partner. His voice faded out in my ears, and I imagined myself flying far away from this place – far from his stolid and stubborn study, with its arrogant old-world illusion of safety and sensibility. Far from the slow-ticking clock and even slower-moving servants, carts, and labourers down in the grounds and village below. It was clear now that I could never change Wrakeley, slowly suffocating in its airless stasis. Instead, I would escape it.

IX

Miss McNeil arrived in London in mid-January. After delaying my visit by what I hoped to be an appropriate length of time, I called on her at her father's Berkeley Square house – a large and impressive edifice, with a footman present at all times outside the door.

I was ushered into the drawing room to await her. Her mother, an elegant lady in a cream dress with carefully pinned and ringletted hair, received me first. Having provided tea, she then fired a full broadside of questions at me.

'Mr Winter. It is a pleasure to meet you at last. I was sorry to miss your short stay at our Manchester home. The tales of your bravery that day have become rather famous in our household.'

I was grateful for the compliment, but blushed nonetheless. My actions had, after all, been largely impulsive, motivated by an animal instinct to survive.

'I am sure there are elements which have eluded her over the intervening years. I would be most grateful for a retelling of the story – from its author, as it were.'

She smiled politely, but with something of her daughter's sparkle in the eye. I duly did my best to retell the story of four years ago, pausing where my memory demanded. Mrs McNeil maintained her interest throughout, smiling where I gave her the opportunity, gasping when I told her of the press in the crowd and of the woman and child underneath Mr Trenchard's horse. Upon finishing, she proclaimed that her daughter's version of the tale had if anything underplayed my part, and once again I found myself blushing.

'I understand also that, having come with your father to London last year, you have established yourself in London society *and* in business?'

The mention of Sir Godfrey darkened my mood. 'He is my patron, Mrs McNeil.'

'I'm sorry, Mr Winter?'

'Sir Godfrey Ramsay is my patron. He is not my father. I have not been adopted by him. As you say, *I* have established myself in society and business.'

Even as I spoke I regretted my indiscretion. The conversation in Sir Godfrey's study was still raw in my mind, and I could not bring myself to portray our relationship as harmonious. Mrs McNeil's reaction, despite her elegance and poise, was not well-masked. She was shocked and perhaps even disappointed.

'I see.' She reached for her tea and took a long sip. An uncomfortable silence settled between us. Replacing the cup, she continued. 'And tell me of your time in London. My daughter tells me you are a member of White's.'

Relieved to have found a new topic of conversation, away from the open wound of Sir Godfrey, I spoke avidly of my activities in London: of the dances at Almack's, of evenings at the opera, and of my high-society friends. I was discreet enough to omit those escapades which were not for genteel discussion. Sporting, gambling, revel-routs – these were things which were known to go on, but which were better left unsaid. Mrs McNeil listened politely, no doubt equally glad to have moved the conversation away from the indelicate matter of my parentage. Her questions seemed to echo those of Miss McNeil's letters, and were easier to answer for it. She also asked after my friends, and I told her what I could of their characters and interests.

I lost track of time answering these enquiries, but was exceedingly glad when, at last, Miss McNeil entered the room. As I stood to greet her my foremost thought, cutting through all of the conversation that had passed whilst waiting, was that I had forgotten quite how beautiful she was. Her golden hair was ringletted like her mother's, and she wore a simple, silver dress which hung gracefully from her shoulders and accentuated her tall, slender frame. Her lips were full and parted slightly in a smile which I unconsciously found myself imitating, but which drew my gaze upward to those eyes which I had surely never forgotten. They were as piercing and blue as ever, and they looked directly at me so that for that moment I felt as though I might be the only other person in the world. I was guilty once again of allowing a silence to endure in the room. Miss McNeil rescued it.

'Mr Winter!' she exclaimed, her voice echoing her smile. 'How delightful to see you once again. And how tall you have grown since we last met!' A polite curtsey accompanied her words.

I bowed in response. 'The delight is entirely mine, Miss McNeil. I regret the years I have spent without returning to Manchester.'

'Nonsense!' exclaimed Mrs McNeil. 'Manchester is but a dour, provincial outpost. Some people are progressive, but it is not the seat of power in this world. You cannot be faulted for choosing to remain in the Empire's capital – at the heart of modern affairs. I rather regret that, due to Mr McNeil's work, and his rather old-fashioned sensibilities, it is only now that Annabel has been allowed to travel – to see society at its finest, and see more of the world than mills, factories and fields.'

I was unsure how to respond to the criticism, but Miss McNeil artfully guided the conversation, moving to her mother's side and taking her tea as she did so.

'I will admit, dear Mr Winter, that Manchester society no longer holds my attention. As mother has said – whilst there were some people there with whom I could converse, I am most glad now to be here. There is so much more occurring in London. So much more to be involved in. I look forward to seeing all that it has to offer. I do hope you will join me in my adventures.'

For the third time now I found myself blushing to be the object of such a rare beauty's affection.

'Of course,' continued Mrs McNeil, 'now that we are here, we intend to announce our arrival in the grandest style, Mr Winter. There will be a ball for Annabel. And we will be honoured if you will attend.'

'Of course,' I echoed. 'The honour will be all mine, Mrs McNeil.'

'There is the business of etiquette, however, mother.'

'Quite so, Annabel. Quite so.' Mrs McNeil composed herself, before fixing me quite intently with her eyes. 'Mr Winter: we require an introduction.' I remained attentive, unsure of the nature of the request. 'We would be most grateful if you could effect an introduction to your friends at Almack's...'

'...It is only proper, you see Mr Winter, that before we host a ball to announce my debut, I am presented at court.'

'And to be presented at court, Mr Winter, Annabel requires an introduction to a lady of the court. You yourself were presented to Lady Sefton and Lady Cowper, I recall?'

I had thought the earlier topic little more than polite conversation, but now realised that Mrs McNeil had listened quite carefully throughout.

'Indeed,' I replied, adopting a chivalrous tone. 'Lady Cowper and Lady Sefton are both friends of mine. I should be delighted to introduce you, Miss McNeil.' I was not at all sure that these ladies would in fact remember me, but I hoped they might remember my introduction alongside Sir Godfrey, whom Lady Sefton had known.

'Splendid, Mr Winter. Splendid. You are most kind. It can be so difficult for a young girl such as Annabel, you see. Such excellent character; full of poise and beauty. But without patronage, she is like a flower kept in a book. Unseen and unappreciated.'

The simile struck me as rather clumsy, but I could not deny its truth. Miss McNeil was a lady to be appreciated, and if I could win her favour by helping her, I would.

I penned a note that afternoon to Lady Sefton, though I doubted my ability to write eloquently and persuasively, and how best to jog her memory without appearing indelicate. I hesitated over using Sir Godfrey's name to curry favour with her. However I judged that, if a patron would not provide his ward with reasonable means and opportunity for advancement, the very least he could offer was introductions and a position in society.

Remarkably, I received a response the very next day. Lady Sefton was pleased to hear from the ward of Sir Godfrey, and would gladly be introduced to some 'new blood' in London society. She warned however that as a patroness of Almack's, she had particular standards to maintain, and she could not promise the outcome I sought. Britain was a progressive society, she wrote, at the head of the modern world. But means – particularly recently established means – did not always marry with manners and delicacy.

I awaited news of the interview therefore with some anxiety. I had found my affection for Miss McNeil rekindled, and had promised to assist her in entering society. Yet this entry was by no means a given. If I failed, it would call into question my connections and influence, and hinder the progression of our acquaintance.

I resolved to occupy myself with other concerns – chief of which was the time-limited opportunity presented by the Cazique of Poyais. Having failed once again to persuade Sir Godfrey to put his faith in me, I would now offer my information to Lord Elsfield. I might not make a profit directly, the majority of my money being tied up in other investments, but I would at least earn his gratitude and respect for such a valuable tip.

The meeting however, in our room at the back of White's, did not go as I had expected. Having exchanged the usual New Year pleasantries, I carefully laid out the opportunity as it had come to me. The difference in its reception was immeasurable. Lord Elsfield remained silent for a time after I had finished. Indeed, even his posture did not change, and he continued to look at me through narrowed dark eyes as if he were still listening to my account. Eventually he lifted his gaze and spoke.

'And you say you had the opportunity to meet this man, this Cazique of Poyais, Victor?'

'Yes, my Lord. A Scotsman – albeit a finely dressed and mannered Scotsman.'

'And would you say he was forceful in his sale of bonds to you?'

I paused to consider this.

'No, my Lord... I expressed a sensible degree of caution for an investment in unknown stock, and he accepted this, adding only that the stock was limited, that events were in train which would doubtless shortly increase the stock price, and that I could obtain a third-party account of the country's situation from a Strand bookseller. This last I have done, and have now related to you the information I found within. Information which, I must say, I believe to be compelling, my Lord.'

'And where is the stock trading at now, Victor?'

'Around sixty-eight pounds, my Lord.'

'Down from a start of eighty, correct?' I felt my stomach suddenly churn as I realised Lord Elsfield knew more about this venture than me. He was testing me and I had embarrassed myself. Neither he nor Sir Godfrey would back me now. Reluctantly, I confirmed his statement.

'Ah but Victor – I do believe that the stock has stabilised, has it not?'

My heart now leaped. He had fixed upon the same information as Sir Godfrey, yet it was clear he took a very different view of it.

'It has, my Lord. I believe that it will now only increase in value, as good news filters back from the settlers who even now are on their way to Poyais.' I hesitated to speak of my failed transactions, but having just been embarrassed for withholding information, I felt that now was the time for full disclosure: 'Sir Godfrey did not view the situation as auspicious, my Lord. He declined to invest when invited.' I watched Lord Elsfield closely for his response.

'Did he now?' he mused, as he sat back in his chair, grasping his port, with the characteristic smile spreading across his face. 'Did he? Well. I dare say you had hoped for a rather better response than that.' He spoke slowly now, as if he were solving a mathematical problem, and his right hand rubbed his chin. I presumed to give him the silence to complete his thoughts, aware that his question had been a rhetorical one. After a few moments, and to my surprise, he stood and walked to the window overlooking the garden at the back of the building. I wondered if I should now interject, when suddenly he turned to face me, his right hand with a single digit raised and wagging at the ceiling in emphasis as he spoke:

'I think we *can* do better than that. I think we can.' He approached the table once more, and placed both his hands, palms down, upon it. 'Has Ball-Hughes bought shares in Poyais?'

'Many, my Lord. As have others. Sir Gregor seems to have sought out the wealthy for his backers. Yet it may not be too late...'

'...excellent. It is not at all too late, Victor. In fact, I believe your timing is just right. You say a second boat of settlers is already on its way to Poyais?'

'Yes, my Lord. It left two weeks ago.'

'Perfect. Perfect. We are going to make money out of Poyais. A lot of money. And we are going to do it swiftly. But if you are going to assist me here, I must have your complete trust.'

I wondered what could prompt such a demand. We had been in business together now for some eight months, and had relied utterly on each other's discretion in that time.

'Of course, my Lord. It has never been in question...'

'Absolutely. You have been the very soul of discretion – and that discretion will be needed more than ever. The enterprise we are about to embark on is the reversal of the system you have until now been familiar with. In short, we will profit from the devaluation of the market.'

I could not hide my confusion. I felt my brow contract and my eyes narrow as I tried to make sense of his words.

'The bonds will fall again. Of that I am certain. Yet this does not mean we cannot profit. Your case to me today is ample evidence that there remain plenty of investors who do not share in my certainty. Even Sir Godfrey, whilst he may have shunned your invitation out of his customary caution, is still not certain enough to invest in the loss.'

'I must apologise, my Lord. How does one invest in a loss?'

At this, Lord Elsfield took his seat once more and adopted his former relaxed pose.

'It is called 'shorting'. It is frowned upon by those who do not understand it. In its simplest form, I agree a contract with another party to sell them a number of shares at a fixed price. I promise to deliver those shares in seven days' time. At this time I have received the money for the sale, but do not yet possess shares to deliver. I now wait for six days, during which the price of the shares plummets. On the seventh day I buy the shares from a disillusioned investor for a fraction of the price in the contract. I then deliver these shares as promised to my purchaser.'

'But... your purchaser has already made a loss on the shares.'

'Indeed. For someone to win, someone else has to lose. Surely you realise this?'

I feared I was at risk of disappointing him with my naïveté. I searched for a similar truism to demonstrate my alignment to his philosophy.

'Of course, my Lord. And those who play know this when they enter.'

'Precisely.'

'But – forgive me once again, my Lord – why would your purchaser agree to the delay in supply? This prevents them from selling the shares the moment the value starts to drop. They are trapped.'

'They are most definitely trapped. And this is their risk. Perhaps I make the sale attractive by offering the shares to them at below-market rates on that day. Perhaps I simply make them believe that the shares are currently undervalued, and difficult to obtain. They can only increase in price, and hence a week's delay is a small inconvenience in order to obtain such rare commodities. This is known as naked shorting, and whilst it is simple and effective, it is now banned in this country. We can discuss the rights and wrongs of it at a later date. The fact is that I will not engage in activities which are illegal. But there are other methods.'

He paused, his eyes never leaving me, and I sensed he was assessing my capabilities. Perhaps he was now concerned he had overestimated me.

'I would be keen to learn all I can about this business, my Lord. I would like to employ this stratagem with your help.'

He nodded. 'You do yourself and your patron credit with your adventure. I sometimes worry that I have driven you very hard down this road. It is an intricate and at times treacherous business. But your application and endeavour never fail to impress me. Very well. Let me explain the part you will play in this scheme. I shall borrow a quantity of Poyais bonds. There are those who will lend me such things for a small sum. I will require you to find buyers. Your friends are keen to invest, you say.'

'They are, my Lord.' I thought of Ball-Hughes's eagerness to introduce me to the Cazique.

'I will offer you twenty percent of the profits for your efforts. The more you sell, the more we make.'

Everything he had said was logical. And yet somewhere within me I felt an unease. We would be deceiving people. I would be deceiving friends. Their loss would be my gain.

'My Lord...' I began, unsure how to broach the subject. 'I wonder if I might cast the net a little further. I would prefer not to involve friends in this plan.'

He nodded once more. 'Your compassion does you credit also. But it does not sit well with an incisive business mind. Compassion is a weakness in business. You cannot depend on others to exercise it towards you. Consider your friend Ball-Hughes. Did he not approach you, recommending that you buy these stocks?'

'Yes, my Lord, but he did it innocently...'

'Did he?!'

'Well, I...'

'Victor – you have been hoodwinked. It is more than likely that Mr Ball-Hughes has already recognised the fate of his investment, and is attempting to convince pliable young men such as you to bolster the price so he can sell.'

The possibility of what he said was inescapable – and I realised I had indeed been naïve.

'You say he introduced you to Sir Gregor himself?'

'Indeed, my Lord.'

'Then it is possible that he has the same information that I have. I have known Sir Gregor a little while, and have him in my debt. As a result he has admitted to me his great secret.'

He paused again, and again I felt that I was being assessed. It struck me that on moments such as these hinged fortunes. Lord Elsfield leant forward across the table, and spoke in a low voice which beckoned me closer to him.

'I may be sure that the bonds will fall again, because Poyais is a fiction. The whole country has been invented by Sir Gregor to induce people to invest in him.'

My mouth dropped open. It was impossible, surely.

'But... my Lord – the book...'

'...Is a first-class work of fiction, penned by Sir Gregor himself.'

He was smiling again, but this was not his usual smile. This smile seemed to convey *admiration* for Sir Gregor's fraud. Fraud on an incredible scale. Fraud which would cause the ruin of countless men – not least those men, women and children who even now made the crossing to settle a land which they would not find. My head was spinning. Once again my eyes had been opened to a world beyond my imagination. My heart told me that the fraud must be revealed, before more damage was done. But my head bade me pause, and consider the circle into which Lord Elsfield had just admitted me. If I wished to move in this circle, I had to learn how its members behaved. I had to grow up. To prove Sir Godfrey wrong. Lord Elsfield spoke again.

'Mr Ball-Hughes likes to gamble, does he not?'

'He does, my Lord.'

'Then what is Poyais but his latest wager. Wagers are voluntary. He chose to enter into this one. Just as he chose to enter into your wager over that lovely Spanish girl...'

I felt my stomach churn. He knew of my wager. He knew how I had obtained funds to begin my investments with him last year. Yet he had feigned ignorance. He had allowed me to sustain the lie that Sir Godfrey backed me.

'It was admirable that you chose to defend your patron's honour. He is a cautious man. Too cautious for some. You and I are cut from a different cloth. We understand the nature of risk. We understand its potential for ruin and reward. And that understanding allows us to play the game.

'You understood the risk when you offered that wager to Ball-Hughes. And you judged it wisely. He is a man who enjoys to play as much as to win. That is his formula, and good luck to him with it.

We play to win, Victor, and only to win. And if we are to win, others must lose. You won money from him before, stacking the odds in your favour. This plan is no different. He has introduced you to the game. You have accepted to play. But you are the better player – and that is no fault of yours. He will lose some money – but he loses money every night at the tables. Better he loses it to you than to a Seven Dials card sharp.'

Everything he said was true. I had been naïve. Ball-Hughes often played cards with his friends – and for vast sums. Whether he won or lost, debts were honoured, and friendships sustained. This was no different. Knowing that I had the winning hand did not preclude my playing. Indeed, others were already playing from this position. Having never had a fortune to manage, I had not built an understanding of this etiquette. This was hardly my fault. Had I not applied to my patron several times for the opportunity to learn? To be entrusted with responsibility? Without Lord Elsfield's guidance and encouragement I would still be a witless ingénu. I was indebted to him for taking me into his trust, and I would repay that debt by following his instruction.

X

As it turned out, Edward was only too keen to invest more heavily in Poyais. Whilst this behaviour exonerated him from being part of Sir Gregor's deception, I could not risk warning him, and thereby destroying the market. I reminded myself that he still bore responsibility for introducing the scheme to me.

Lord Elsfield swiftly obtained a quantity of Poyais stock, and was forced to obtain more when my qualities as a salesman surprised even myself. As he had predicted, far from being viewed with suspicion, I was heralded as quite the goose that laid the golden egg, one sale leading almost inevitably to a further introduction and sale.

At the end of February sales came to 'an abrupt stop, as the value of the bonds began to decline. Rumours began to circulate that the settlers had not found the land as bountiful as promised. Fact was, however, difficult to distinguish from fiction from the other side of the world, and some bold investors argued that the value would return. But as the days passed, the decline became a rout, and soon everyone was trying to sell Poyais. Lord Elsfield sent word, congratulating me for my part in the scheme, and counselling me to be proud of our success. It took courage to bet against the market, and was no different in principle to backing an enterprise in which no one else would invest. The bonds had halved in a month, and we had made a small fortune.

I accepted his counsel, not simply because I had become considerably richer, but also because other events came to pass which proved a very welcome distraction for all who had lost out to the Poyais affair. Happily, Ball-Hughes himself was foremost in this distraction. Never being one to shun the public gaze, his actions were quickly the talk of the whole town. I was not present at the great reveal, nor was I given prior warning – but I was swiftly able to piece the evidence together.

On the evening of March 8th, as even the most optimistic investors began to acknowledge the failure of the Poyais stock, a full house in the King's Theatre settled down to the ballet. Whilst some in that audience may have claimed that they were there to enjoy the show, it was widely understood that once again the main attraction was in fact Maria Mercandotti, who continued to send hearts racing and young gentlemen into raptures. However, on this particular evening the audience was to be disappointed – for when the moment for her entrance arrived, there was none. Whispers scudded round the stalls and circle, and turned swiftly into outcry. The manager was compelled to appear onstage and declare to all present that Miss Mercandotti *could not be found*. The outcry turned into a riot, and gossip spread like wildfire.

I happened that evening to be engaged with friends at the club. Upon hearing the story, I searched for the man most likely to be able to give an explanation. However, he too could not be found – neither in the club, nor at his home, nor at any one of the gambling hells and haunts he was wont to frequent. Edward also, it seemed, had vanished – and I judged that too much of a coincidence.

Indeed, within days, the rumours were confirmed in the press. Ball-Hughes and Mercandotti had eloped to Gretna Green, and were there married in the presence of God, the dancer's mother, and none other than her patron and the manager himself. Clearly the scheme had been some time in the making, and I thought it charmingly typical of Edward's flair for the dramatic that it had been carried out in this manner. Perhaps, a victim of his own reputation, even he could not contemplate the scale of the wedding celebrations which society would expect of its most eligible (and lavish) bachelor.

As a result I did not see Edward throughout March, between his nuptials and their subsequent honeymoon. Knowing him as I did, it was certain that the vagaries of the Poyaisian New Three Percent Consolidated Stock value mattered not a jot to him.

At the same time, I also received happy news from Miss McNeil. Her interview had been an unqualified success. Lady Sefton had seen, in her own words, 'great potential' in Miss McNeil – and whilst acknowledging that she was not of traditional stock, believed she would be a welcome addition to society. Several further meetings had since taken place, the better for Lady Sefton to assess where Miss McNeil's strengths and wants might be.

Invited once more to the McNeil residence, I was excitedly told of her new prospects. Lady Sefton had proved a most resourceful ally, and plans for the coming-out ball were proceeding rapidly under her sage stewardship. Miss McNeil had been advised in no uncertain terms that whilst an interest in politics and diplomacy were not to be sniffed at, they were not fitting subjects for society. Her love of reading was to be encouraged, but to be redirected away from the polemics of Mary Wollstonecraft[2], and focused instead on the great works of literature and the latest novels. These were but peccadilloes however, and to her credit Miss McNeil was an accomplished linguist, a superb musician and dancer, and had a fine hand for detail in watercolours. Her conversation, whilst it could be improved, was informed and well-poised, and her company generally delightful.

This, I was told, was Lady Sefton's overall view, and I was only too happy to agree. So it was that at the end of March I stood squeezed amongst a mass of other courtiers to watch the delightful Miss McNeil charm the King himself upon her presentation at St James's Palace. More corpulent than ever, he made no attempt to disguise his interest, inviting Lady Sefton and her charge to step closer and exchange a few hushed words with the monarch. It was over in a moment, but its significance would endure for a lifetime. Around me, I could sense the stirring of interest in the eligible gentlemen of the court, craning their necks to identify and mark this debutante who received special favour from the King. The moment was not lost on Miss McNeil either who, her interview complete, seemed to glide back across the floor in a state of effortless elegance with her chin raised high, and her smile somehow aimed at each and every one of her many admirers.

I found myself grinning at her success, and considered that it reflected well on me and my introduction. She was indeed a beautiful and elegant prospect, and I dared to think that as her friend and favourite, I was now well-placed to begin to court her.

I left St James's Palace with a spring in my step, reflecting that I was a self-made man, in both business and society, who had survived and thrived due to an ability to seize the moment. I called on Miss McNeil the very next day, set on declaring my intentions. On my arrival, however, I was informed that the ladies of the house were occupied with another gentleman in the drawing room. The footman who showed me to the library to wait was easily convinced to surrender his name as one Lord John Russell. I had a passing knowledge of the man. Though he was a member of Brook's rather than White's, I had been introduced to him once or twice at various functions. An ambitious and zealous politician, he struck me as a little too dry and serious a gentleman, and I felt confident that Miss McNeil would also find him so.

I did not have to wait for long, and took this as a good omen as I entered the drawing room. I congratulated Miss McNeil on being the talk of society after her debut at court, at which she smiled, and pretended not to acknowledge the fact. My attempts, however, to discuss my eligibility as a suitor were utterly thwarted by Mrs McNeil. Regardless of the topic I might introduce, within five minutes I would find it morphed into a conversation about decorations, invitations, or music. It quickly became clear that she would entertain no thought of a private audience with her daughter while her ball was still to be planned. I therefore deemed it wise to submit to her will, to bring about a swifter conclusion to the arrangements.

Mrs McNeil explained that she wished the ball to host only the very finest of London society, now that the king had picked her daughter out for special greeting. She asked that I sit with her to assist in the drawing up of invitations, and once again I adopted the role of the charming and considerate young gentleman. I took comfort in the knowledge that time spent ingratiating myself with Miss McNeil's family would pay dividends later. I felt certain that at her debut at Almack's I would have the opportunity to dance with her, and there to speak my mind. This made the day's disappointment easier to bear.

The invitations were completed and runners sent in all directions to deliver them to the great houses of society. Within days the clubs were filled with speculation. Some had seen Miss McNeil presented to the king at court, and these lucky few were full of praise for the debutante, encouraging those who had not to mark their calendars for the evening ordained. Others made their own enquiries, either in person or by return. Some enterprising fellows asked colleagues or even servants for information. Those who asked me received an equivocal response. I was keen to have Miss McNeil be a success, and be fêted in society, but I did not want all the Lord John Russells of this world to ingratiate themselves with her. I gave enough praise to warrant attendance, but tried not to pique any interest such that a young buck might pay Miss McNeil a visit prior to the ball.

Lord Alvanley claimed to see straight through me, declaring: 'I do believe you find Miss McNeil to be captivating, young Victor. You may deny it, but I believe you intend to keep her for yourself! Beware my friend. You face some competition.'

His warning, jovial as it was, alarmed me, and he read the concern on my face.

'Oh you need not worry about me,' he continued, holding up his hands in mock-surrender, 'I shall not attempt to come between you. But one hears things, you know. Particularly when one makes it one's business to hear things. Miss McNeil has not long been in town, but she has already made some powerful friends. Lady Sefton presented her at court – but of course you know that. So you will also know that she has since been welcomed at Carlton House, and been seen with that Whig upstart Lord John Russell. There are even rumours she's paid a visit to Lord Melbourne – though I could not vouch for their truth. In any case, she is certainly no retiring mopsey. If she continues at this rate she'll be running the country before the year is out! And if this lady is to be the future Mrs Winter, you will have to attend this soiree properly attired for once.'

I sensed a joke at my expense from the best-dressed man in society and, happy to move the conversation on, I raised an eyebrow accordingly. Alvanley needed no further encouragement. 'Come now, young Victor. Surely if this young belle is even half as attractive as your evasive answers suggest, you would not dream of wearing those dreary old clothes from last summer.' He placed a brotherly arm round me, continuing 'I shall consider it my duty to ensure that you are the most spectacular of bucks at the ball, my friend. You will be eclipsed only by me.'

Lord Elsfield was rather less superficial in his enquiries. Having discussed the latest opportunities for investment in our room at the back of White's, he produced his invitation from an inside pocket and, turning it over in his hands, appeared to be judging its merits based solely on the card itself. He remained in silent contemplation for so long that eventually I felt moved to speak.

'Are you minded to attend, my Lord?'

'Oh. Yes. The ball.' He seemed utterly distracted by some other purpose, and I wondered if I should press further. I was keen for both Sir Godfrey and Lord Elsfield to attend, so that they might speak in my support, albeit separately, to Mrs McNeil. 'I am not familiar with the host. Are you, Victor?'

'Indeed I am my Lord. I happened to meet Miss McNeil, in whose honour the ball is being held, in Manchester four years ago.'

'And have you any more recent information on the family?'

'Yes my Lord. Miss McNeil and I exchanged letters when we were younger. None since she came of age, of course. But it was I who introduced her to Lady Sefton when she first arrived in London.'

Lord Elsfield had stopped turning the card. He looked at me a moment longer, then asked pointedly: 'And what do we *know* of Mr McNeil, Mrs McNeil, and Miss McNeil?'

'I am sorry my Lord, I'm not sure I understand your meaning.'

'My meaning is simple enough, Victor. What do we know about the family who have invited us to their daughter's coming-out ball. What do we know about the family who is attempting to cause a stir in London society, and make room for itself here?'

'Mr McNeil is a factory owner in Lancashire, my Lord. I understand that he runs a highly successful operation and is well respected in the North. Mrs McNeil I have only met once or twice. She seems ambitious for her daughter, and has interviewed me closely about my London friends... Miss McNeil is certainly a rare beauty. She has elegance and poise, and won particular praise at court only a fortnight ago from the king.'

'And this is the sum of your knowledge?'

I did not know what more I could add. Despite being far more information than that which had satisfied others, he seemed unimpressed. I nodded apologetically.

'We will see what we can find. What is your interest in the family?'

I should not have been surprised by his directness – it was no different to his normal way of conducting business. Except that I did not consider the matter of Miss McNeil to be business. It made me nervous to be assessing it in this way.

'Well, my Lord,' I hesitated, unsure of where or how the matter of love fitted into a business proposal. 'I have a particular interest in Miss McNeil...'

'You mean to marry her, yes?'

Again I hesitated.

'If such a match is acceptable to all parties... There is certainly money in her family. And Lady Sefton thinks highly of her.'

'Very well. The likes of Byron and Shelley would have young people believe that one should follow one's instincts in these matters, to the subjugation of all else. But they are fools and rakes. A marriage is a business proposal like any other, and must be properly considered, with the advantages and the risks clearly set out and understood. Your patron himself could have benefited from a little more perspicacity in his own marriage, as I dare say you know.'

I had not expected this turn in conversation, and my interest was immediately piqued.

'My Lord?'

'Surely you have heard of dear Catherine's fate? It is one of my chief regrets that I could not rescue her from your patron's pull. I introduced them, Victor. Her family and I were close friends from my business in Portugal – but when Godfrey met her, I am afraid there was no halting them. The cautious man you know today was not always so. Their engagement was a whirlwind of society balls, and they were the talk of the town for a season. But they were too eager to believe in their own invincibility. When Godfrey could not avoid attending to his work any longer, she insisted on accompanying him. They travelled to the West Indies against my advice, full of romantic notions of adventure, but she returned to us a sickly shadow of her former self. Within a year she had passed – and all who had known her felt her loss.'

There was a maudlin quality to his words now which intrigued me, being so at odds with the man I knew. Another silence ensued which I dared not interrupt. When he spoke again, he was himself once more.

'Godfrey was reckless in both his pursuit and his treatment of Catherine. But if conducted properly, a manoeuvre of this nature can bring great success to a young man such as yourself. I will look into this young lady, and if her prospects are good, I shall do what I can to help you.'

He paused, turning the card once more in his hands and then looking up at me.

'I presume you have not yet made your intentions known to her, given the paucity of your knowledge?'

'I have not, my Lord.'

'Good. The ball is not for three weeks. Indulge me not to do so until then. In the meantime I shall make enquiries.'

The conversation had been a decidedly strange one, but the outcome was everything that I could have hoped for. I would delay my conversation with Miss McNeil by a few weeks, but now with the support and favour of Lord Elsfield, I surely stood alone as the most eligible suitor for her hand.

And then, just a week before the ball, everything changed.

XI

It was a crisp, cool April day and I had enjoyed my afternoon walk to the club, greeting those I knew, and scrutinising those I did not on my way. On arrival the doorman passed me a note – and so began a day of many intrigues. It was from Lord Elsfield, and in uncharacteristically cryptic style, it simply advised me that:

> *Our alliance should not be revealed today. The time will come when it will be to our advantage to do so – but that time is not yet upon us. I know I can rely on your discretion.*
>
> *E.*

I considered the note for only a moment, reflecting that I had previously had no intention to make public the extent of my collaboration with Lord Elsfield. He and I had generally been discreet without being secretive. A particularly interested servant might have pieced together the nature of our association, but at White's there was nothing remarkable about two members meeting from time to time in private. Indeed, we might have attracted more comment by taking more extraordinary measures.

The second intrigue followed hard on the heels of the first. Sir Godfrey entered the dining room as I was finishing luncheon and, scanning the room and seeing me, joined me at my table. This in itself was strange enough, as he rarely appeared at the club, and very rarely indeed associated with me whilst there. Our relationship had been decidedly cool since his refusal to assist me with the Poyais stock several months earlier – though he had probably not noticed the change. It prompted me to ask the question.

'A pleasure, sir, to share the table with you, but I am afraid I was just finishing my meal. Was there something in particular you wished to speak with me about?'

'As a matter of fact, yes. Something *very* particular.' His tone caused me to look again at the man I had known so well. There was something different about him today. He seemed distracted. There was a frantic energy to his speech and actions which unsettled me. Sir Godfrey had never been distracted. He had never been frantic. Even when fighting the footpads on the ice, he had remained calm and collected – both during the danger and after it. Yet now he struggled to hold my gaze, and his hands fidgeted, clasping and reclasping each other. It occurred to me that he was nervous – and now his nervousness infected me, wondering what it could be that could unsettle a man as unflappable as Sir Godfrey Ramsay.

'Should we perhaps go somewhere more private, sir?' I suggested, while my mind conjured all manner of scenarios which I would not want played out in this room.

'No, no. No need for that, Victor – just a word of warning, really.'

He paused, his face working through myriad expressions before he spoke again. It was almost painful to observe.

'We have been invited to see Lord Elsfield this very afternoon, Victor.'

Relief swept through me. I struggled to control my mirth at his revelation, my jaw clenching and brow contracting severely. It must have looked very much as if I was sharing his concern.

'You will recall that this is a man with whom I endeavour to have only the most formal of relationships,' he continued.

'I recall your business colleague, sir.'

I had aimed my words carefully, and they struck their target.

'I would not describe our relationship in those terms, Victor,' he snapped back.

'I meant nothing by it, sir. I merely recall that he forms part of your Association, and that you and he have in the past collaborated. I believe this is what you told me after I first encountered him – the day you were attacked on the ice.'

'Indeed,' he allowed, regaining some of his poise. 'Indeed. That would have been your first encounter with him. And I suppose he seemed something akin to a hero to you with that introduction. But remember all of what I told you, Victor. He is not to be trusted, much less trifled with. If you are finished with luncheon we should go at once.'

'As you say, sir.' Feeling I had scored a point with my jab, I left the matter at the table, and together we stood. Sir Godfrey declined the doorman's offer of a carriage, indicating that he had more to say, and that the walk would give him the opportunity to say it. We had only taken a few steps along St James's when I asked the obvious question.

'What do you think is of such pressing importance that Lord Elsfield wished to see us immediately, sir?'

'I cannot be certain – but I have an inkling. There is a business opportunity of which Lord Elsfield made me aware some months ago. He approached me as he requires a ship. In the past few years he has disinvested quite aggressively in his mercantile interests, choosing rather to involve himself in stocks and bonds. I understand this has brought him some success – his contacts in Westminster and the City have doubtless played a part in keeping him one step ahead of his colleagues. But the opportunity we have discussed goes beyond the reach of those contacts, and he requires my assistance to make a success of it.'

Again I found myself having to contain a sense of mirth that I knew more of Lord Elsfield's activities than my patron. As he did his best to describe the business which his associate now conducted, I realised that I understood it better. Sir Godfrey had apprenticed me to various arms of his operation, the better to understand his trade business. But he had never exposed me to the stock market: it was a gap in his understanding. My apprenticeship for stock trading had been with Lord Elsfield – and now I possessed a unique combination of knowledge from both men. I remembered Lord Elsfield's note to me, and an idea started to form.

'Why do you think Lord Elsfield wishes me to accompany you, sir? I don't see what role I have to play in this opportunity.'

'I'm afraid Lord Elsfield may see you as collateral, Victor. I have long been aware of your desire to find adventure. I recall when I first took you to the head office. You were more interested in the paintings of ships battling storms than the books! And the look on your face on first seeing the London Docks: your eyes have never been wider. I have been attempting to create a position for you to find that adventure. I had hoped that it might be possible without exposing you to danger. I fear that Lord Elsfield is not so concerned with your wellbeing. We will see. But I would exhort you, when we hear what he has to say, that you consider your position very carefully. There will be no need for an immediate response. We may retire and consider what is best for us. If he is to make the proposal I suspect, then it is a dangerous one, and whilst I have every faith in your ambition and energy, I worry that it may ask too much. You know that I would not risk putting you in harm's way for the sake of profit. But nor do I wish to stand in the way of your advancement.'

These last words were rich, given how stoically he had blocked my advancement to date. He continued to underestimate my capabilities. Lord Elsfield knew me better, and if he were about to present an opportunity, I was confident it would be one that I could succeed at.

Despite our interactions, I had not yet been invited to Lord Elsfield's home. Meeting on neutral ground had better served our need for discretion. I was of course fully aware of his success in business, but nonetheless I found myself standing in awe at the front of his magnificent London residence. Built in the classical style from smooth white stone, four giant columns rose at the centre of the building from the doorway, past the high-ceilinged first floor, up to the second, and ended in a huge temple pediment at least thirty feet across. The architrave tracing the roof of the building was a stonework tapestry of classical figures, intertwined with laurels and the stylised lettering 'AHE'. Whilst the main building must have been one hundred feet across, two-storied pavilions at either end doubled this frontage, so that only by standing in Hyde Park, some hundred feet away, could one take in its full scale. Sir Godfrey observed my first impression.

'Yes. Subtle, isn't it? That is entirely the reaction his father wanted people to have when they saw it. Puts you in his thrall even before you've begun negotiating. Try not to be distracted, Victor. It is exactly what he would want.'

I accepted the wisdom of this advice even as I wondered at the power the building projected. Yet once in the entrance hall I struggled to remain objective. Here again was a lavish projection of the power of the dynasty which had created it. A grand, sweeping double staircase uncoiled majestically around both sides of the hall, spilling out a rich crimson carpet into its centre. More columns adorned the marble walls, which were decorated with giant friezes of Old Testament scenes. Above us the sun threw light through an ornate cupola onto various tasteful objets d'art, strewn carefully about the floor.

As the footman led us through the house, each room we passed revealed a new example of exquisite extravagance. In one, a priceless Old Master hung over a fireplace. In another, a chandelier dripping with crystal stood suspended above a table laid for thirty. I reflected that I had the privilege to be the apprentice to not one, but two wealthy and successful businessmen. Yet I now realised that they were not the same order of businessman. Lord Elsfield's power and wealth was something beyond imagination.

We were ushered into the study, where the master of the house sat behind a great mahogany desk. It reminded me of Sir Godfrey's study at Wrakeley – but once again, Lord Elsfield's was larger and more opulent. Two busts stood either side of the double entrance doors. The fireplace and mantelpiece were larger and grander. It was more subtle than elsewhere in the house, but here too was the unmistakeable taste of power at its most refined.

Our host sprang to his feet as we entered, crossing the floor with long strides and thrusting out his hand to shake Sir Godfrey's. His usual knowing smile was absent however, replaced with an expression of brooding seriousness. Much as Sir Godfrey had unsettled me earlier with his nervousness, Lord Elsfield now did the same. Whatever was to be discussed was not a subject with which either man was comfortable.

'Thank you for coming so swiftly, old friend.' Without so much as a glance at me, he ushered us both into seats opposite his. As I sat, my eye was caught by a small portrait that sat on his desk. It faced away from me and was only partially visible, but there could be no doubting its subject. I had seen the same face every day of my life, at Wrakeley and St James's Square. It was Sir Godfrey's beloved wife, Catherine. He could not see it from where he sat, but still I shifted uncomfortably at the recognition. Regardless of Lord Elsfield's connection to her, it did not seem altogether proper for him to keep such a thing on his desk.

'I came as soon as I was able, Andrew. What is it that requires our attention?' Sir Godfrey's voice stirred me from my introspection.

Lord Elsfield retrieved his brandy decanter and glasses from their table and brought them to the desk, pouring as he spoke.

'Events on the Gold Coast appear to be gathering pace. Sir Charles MacCarthy has sent word that, having hosted delegations from both tribes, he sides with the Fanti and intends to muster a force to subdue the Ashanti. I do not know how long his preparations will go unchallenged, but the War Office will certainly wish to dispatch a consignment to support him.'

He passed a glass to Sir Godfrey and, as he passed a second to me, caught my eye with an icy stare. I tried to find solace in his attention, but could not.

'I see,' Sir Godfrey replied. 'Sir Charles has not acted as we expected – nonetheless the outcome is much the same, if a little sooner. I can have a ship available by August, I should think. That should enable sailing for West Africa by October, provided the War Office has everything in hand by then.'

'I will make sure it is in hand. And I will make sure your name is at the head of the list for the contract.'

It seemed that Lord Elsfield's news was indeed on the subject Sir Godfrey had expected. However, I still failed to see the role I might play in supplying a colonial war. I turned towards my patron to indicate my confusion, and he perceived my plight.

'You asked me to bring Victor with me. I must ask what you have in mind.'

At this, Lord Elsfield's familiar smile reappeared – a sight which gave me comfort that matters were in hand.

'I think you have a good idea what I have in mind, Godfrey. You and I have long spoken about the need for this mission to be led by a trusted and capable deputy.'

'Yes, of course. Yet neither of us quite imagined this deputy would be called upon so soon.'

'Events have gathered pace,' he repeated.

He did not move to expand upon this. He simply sat at his desk, brandy in hand, and looked intently at Sir Godfrey, who looked with exasperation right back at him.

'Andrew, I...'

'...Why don't we see what Victor makes of all this, hmmm?'

A strange moment passed between the two men, its only clue being the absence of sound or movement from either. Sir Godfrey broke its spell, turning slowly in his chair to face me.

'Victor. Lord Elsfield and I have previously discussed a scheme which we believe would be to our mutual advantage. It relates to the British colonies in West Africa – specifically, to the Gold Coast colony, recently created by parliament.

'Its previous rulers, the African Company of Merchants, proved incapable of resolving the historic disputes which keep the tribes in that area in a perpetual state of war. With the creation of the colony last year, that task now falls to the governor, Sir Charles MacCarthy. Sir Charles is a good man, instrumental in realising and protecting the free state of Sierra Leone. His task must, we believe, involve force against at least some of the antagonists. They have not to date been shown the full might of the British military, and a firm hand now should swiftly serve to subdue the native warmongers and solidify the order of things.'

He paused to sip his brandy, and Lord Elsfield took the opportunity to continue.

'In short, Victor, Sir Charles will need supplies. He already has a small force of regulars, and will even now be training up local volunteers to form a militia. These men will need food, uniforms, weapons and ammunition. The War Office has too many concerns to predict each and every possible dispute of this sort. It reacts slowly to requests for support. Godfrey and I perceived with Sir Charles' appointment that supplies would be necessary. We have been observing developments for some months. As you have heard, Godfrey can have a ship ready to transport those supplies by October. He can also see to the supply of food and uniforms, while I take care of the military equipment through other connections. We can make an offer to the War Office months before any other syndicate might be ready to depart. Speed is of the essence in these colonial disturbances. A swift response now will save many lives and a great deal of the public purse later. We will be able to command a high price in exchange for our readiness. What we lack, however, is an officer to represent our interests faithfully from London to the Gold Coast, and to see that the operation is executed as planned.'

It was Lord Elsfield's turn to pause, the smile still etched on his face, his eyes fixed on me and his eyebrows slightly raised. It was a silent question. A challenge.

'We had thought that the opportunity might arise towards the end of next year, or even the year after. I had in mind your desire to spread your wings, and to see a little of the world. I thought that perhaps after some missions around Europe finding your feet, you might make a good candidate for this role. However, the timing we now face gives me cause for concern.'

'We cannot afford to wait, Victor. Our advantage now is our ability to react swiftly. Our requirements for this officer are stringent. We must both have complete confidence in their loyalties and their abilities. They will doubtless be forced in the course of the mission to be flexible, and to execute their judgement. It may turn out to be an uneventful trip. However...'

'However,' continued Sir Godfrey, 'it may well be the most difficult thing you will ever do. There is no knowing, once you leave these shores, what twists of fate may befall you. You will need to be a shrewd judge of character, and to lead with presence and conviction. Victor – I do not in all honesty think we can ask you to give us an answer here today.'

Lord Elsfield looked for a moment as if he would rise from his seat. 'Godfrey!' Another silence passed between them. 'I would be grateful for a private audience with you, sir. Victor – would you excuse us a moment?'

The tension in the room was palpable. I felt dwarfed by the scale of the two men. They seemed to stand astride the globe, sending ships and soldiers to its corners – and now they wished to send me there also. I rose to my feet, feeling strangely unsteady, and left the room, closing the door behind me.

My thoughts immediately turned to Annabel. Fate seemed to be conspiring against my plans for our future. My chance meeting with Lord John Russell had served as a warning that I could no longer expect to be her only suitor. Yet I did believe I was her favourite. Our history and correspondence had drawn us close, and having helped her find patronage in society, she and her mother could not help but look on me favourably. Nonetheless, I recalled the murmur when she was presented at court. Even the king had picked her out for particular attention. It was inevitable that others would soon be pressing their cases. I could not hope to remain her favourite *in absentia*, and even while I remained in London I feared that others such as Lord John Russell or even my own circle of friends would prove rivals for her affections. The mission could well ruin my prospects with Annabel. Except that the architect of all that I had become had requested it – and I feared that without Lord Elsfield's continued stewardship, I might yet be sucked back into Sir Godfrey's suffocating sphere.

And then, was it not also true that for years I had yearned for the adventure and independence of an assignment such as this? For as long as I could remember, I had dreamed of being given the opportunity to show Sir Godfrey – and indeed the world – that I was a capable and resourceful young man. I thought back to the hushed conversation I had shared with Mr Crawshaw, on the eve of my infamous voyage to Calais. I had dreamed of travelling the world, and creating an empire... I caught my breath as another vivid memory came flooding back to me: the elephant on the ice. Africa. Adventure. Those were the words I had written on its living skin: a wide-eyed boy's wish for a future version of himself. And *yet*... the very name still conjured magical, mysterious images. Perhaps I was mistaken – perhaps fate now conspired in my favour, to fulfil that wish.

I could not reason my way through the proposition. It seemed foolish to refuse and just as foolish to accept. I needed more information – and already behind me I could hear the muffled sounds of animated debate issuing forth from the study. Feeling suddenly very conspicuous, I glanced around the empty corridor to ensure I was alone. The servants had retreated to other posts throughout the house – and yet I still did not feel comfortable as I stepped gingerly back towards the doors and placed my ear against them.

'The enterprise is *inherently* dangerous. You have always known this. That alone is no reason to refuse it to young Victor.' Lord Elsfield's voice boomed against the door.

'As a man who has never lost anyone he cared for, your reckless optimism is not in the least convincing, thank you.'

'Surely you are not suggesting Victor be kept under close observation in Hertfordshire for the rest of his days!'

'Absolutely not. Having successfully cared for his needs these past nineteen years, you will forgive me if I consider myself a better judge of his capabilities and limitations than a complete stranger. Victor has great potential and, given the correct opportunities and guidance, will become a credit to the company. Throwing him to Charybdis to see if he can swim may resonate with your philosophy, but it does not resonate with mine.'

'Godfrey, old friend – I apologise if I have offended your sensibilities. You have safely guided him through nineteen years of life. The fact that he is so well-liked and well-turned out is a credit to you. All I am counselling is that he needs to become his own man. He needs to make his own decisions and his own mistakes, out from under your shadow. There can be no reward without any risk. You know this.'

Silence. I imagined Sir Godfrey sighing in his chair. It was strange to hear him spoken to on level terms. Sir Godfrey had always been at the head of any conversation.

'What are you planning?'

Another silence.

'I'm sorry?'

'For God's sake, Andrew: I wasn't born yesterday. You have fixated on Victor for this role. What are you planning?'

'I admit I have taken a keen interest in your protégé of late. I cannot pretend to know him or his capabilities as well as you. But he has impressed me. I have spoken to people with whom he associates at the club. I have heard of some shrewd investments he has made which indicate fine judgement...'

'...and you have not heard of those which I had to dissuade, of course.'

'Of course, Godfrey. Nonetheless, I have a good impression of the man. And for this enterprise to succeed, you and I must trust each other once more. I believe he has a good head, and I know that you hold him in high regard. This means that we may both feel comfortable that he will represent our joint interest fairly. In short, if we can both agree to put our trust in Victor, then perhaps we might learn to trust each other again.'

I pulled myself away from the doors. Sir Godfrey had always been at pains to distance himself from Lord Elsfield – but this was an open admission that there was distrust between them. And now I was to be the focal point of their reconciliation. I felt the weight of responsibility grow heavier on my shoulders. If I declined the assignment, I would remain safely in London, and would be free to court Miss McNeil and propose. However, in doing so I would also be endorsing Sir Godfrey's trudging approach to my future, and infuriating my closest ally, Lord Elsfield. I settled into a chair a few feet from the doors and awaited my invitation to return. I gazed up at portraits of Lord Elsfield's ancestors - proud military men staring icily out of their frames at me from the scenes of their triumphs in the Indies, North America, and the battlefields of Europe. They dared me to be bold – to take the opportunity of the unknown. And then I thought of all I had achieved so far, away from any battlefields. Sir Godfrey was right. This was not a decision I could make without deliberation.

The doors opened. Lord Elsfield and Sir Godfrey stood together before me.

'A week, Godfrey. Ten days at most. Then I must have an answer.'

'Victor and I shall speak, Andrew. You will have your answer.'

They shook hands, and I perceived that a reconciliation had already begun.

XII

'I shall warn you once more, Victor. The rules which govern decent conduct in this world do not apply to the likes of Lord Elsfield. He knows them well enough. He simply scorns them.'

Sir Godfrey passed me his cigar box and bade me select one. We were now comfortably reinstalled in his own study in St James's Square. The fire crackled and spat, and the clock ticked loudly in the corner. The deep wingback chair enclosed me in its arms like an old friend. Leather tomes lined the walls, recounting the tales of other young men who had stepped out into the unknown, and Lady Ramsay's portrait watched serenely over us. As I looked around the room I felt that I was only now appreciating what these sights and sounds signified to me.

'He would think nothing of employing a spy to play the part of a coachman – to listen to a conversation and to report every word back to him. It is not that he is immoral. It is rather that he does not believe in morality – its necessity, or even its existence. Lord Elsfield believes in egoism. He believes we are no better than base animals, and that we all are motivated only by self-interest. The world must be a very dark and ugly place to him.'

I had not yet been invited to offer my own view on the events of the day, nor on the proposition with which I had been presented. I began to wonder whether Sir Godfrey was even fearful of me speaking my mind. I supposed that to a cautious and meticulous man, events outside one's own control must be the most difficult to contemplate. Sir Godfrey had always appeared to be the master of his world – but now for the first time events were in motion which he could not stop. Whatever else Lord Elsfield had said to him in my absence, it had clearly given him pause for thought. He still seemed minded to counsel against the assignment, but he would only go as far as warning me of the character of his associate – unaware that I already knew him intimately.

'Do you recall the occasion of our meeting in Dover, in 1814?'

Sir Godfrey now stood by the fireplace, seemingly too agitated to settle in his chair.

'I do, sir. The night before you sailed for France.' The night before my exile, I did not add.

'Quite so, quite so. And do you recall, he regaled us with the manner of his profiting from the Stock Exchange Fraud?'

I nodded. I had now been reminded of this event by both gentlemen.

'Well this piece of subtlety was typical of the man. And it will not have bothered him at all that his 'friend', Lord Cochrane, was stripped of his title, removed from his position, imprisoned, and then banished to the other side of the world.'

This revelation caught me unawares and I was unable to hide my reaction. Sir Godfrey perceived it instantly.

'Oh yes. He was only too happy to crow at us with his successes – and he has had many. But there is always someone who suffers from Lord Elsfield's successes. There is always some damage. His great skill is ensuring he is always far enough removed from that damage that his reputation remains spotless. Lord Cochrane took the fall for Lord Elsfield's manipulation. It will never be proved, and Lord Cochrane is certainly too stubborn and principled to bear witness to it, but that is the truth of it.'

The decision before me grew no easier. It forced me to ask difficult questions of my patron.

'If Lord Elsfield is so treacherous sir, why do you associate with him? Why risk becoming the next Lord Cochrane?'

Sir Godfrey looked back at me with tired eyes.

'Because he has connections. He has connections that other men do not. Whether legitimate or otherwise, whether indentured or free, he has people who open doors. It is perhaps to my discredit that I continue to associate with him. Perhaps if I were not so ambitious, I would be content to cede opportunities to competitors, safe in the knowledge that I had maintained my honour. As it is, I continue to accept the information and opportunities he offers. Not always – some are too risky, or too vague. But I do knowingly accept his assistance from time to time.

'We cannot deal only with honest men in this world, Victor. If we did, we would surely come to ruin, for they make up by far the minority. But this does not mean that we must place our trust in dishonest men – for we may work with them without ever trusting them. This is what I counsel. But I cannot in good faith recommend this assignment. It would be risk enough to send you to West Africa on your first voyage, to deal with the natives and the myriad shifting allegiances there. But to do so at the request of Lord Elsfield? It makes me uncomfortable. He has met you only twice – and not for almost ten years – yet he expressly requests your leadership?'

His words well conveyed his disapproval of the scheme – and yet there was something else in his manner which left the matter open. He remained uncomfortable, nervous. I waited.

'I will allow that I may have been cautious in your development: I have perhaps not accelerated your fortunes as swiftly as I might have done. Above all, I have looked to ensure stability and safety for you – and perhaps this has come at a price. This assignment could be the making of you. I am clear on that. And for the company there would be value beyond the contract. It is difficult for either of us to turn down. There's even significant risk to the company if we refuse Lord Elsfield's terms. He has ways and means to damage us if we anger him.' He placed his cigar in his mouth and took a long drag, holding the smoke in and chewing it round as if it were the problem itself, before exhaling.

'You are at an age now where you must make your own decisions. I have done my best to show you the world as I have found it, and it is now up to you to make of it what you will. I will of course support you however I can, whatever you now choose.'

I looked carefully up at him at this unexpected remark. He was relinquishing his hold over me, granting me the power to make my own decisions. It meant I could approach Miss McNeil for her hand even without his approval. It also meant I did not have to convince him of the trustworthiness of Lord Elsfield – which surely would have been impossible. I myself had had my doubts in this regard – but it did not matter: I was a part of Lord Elsfield's scheme. I was on the inside.

'I am honoured, sir, that you afford me such respect.' I was as surprised as I was humbled. 'I do not yet know my mind on the matter. I too harbour doubts. Not least of which relates to a lady here in London.'

Sir Godfrey's face altered markedly. I did not know why I had said it – except that in response to his candidness, it was difficult to offer anything different in return.

'My dear Victor – I was unaware...'

'There has been no discussion between us, sir. At least not yet. I had meant to make my feelings clear to her only last week, but... the moment was... unpropitious.'

'I see.' He was suddenly a changed man. The nervousness and hesitancy were gone. He stepped swiftly across the room and placed himself in a seat opposite me. 'But who is this lady? How did you meet? What are her circumstances? Has she given you any indication of her favour?' His questions were spontaneous, without agenda, and I carefully began to describe the relationship between me and Miss McNeil.

Sir Godfrey's interest in Miss McNeil was gratifying. She was the daughter of a business rival but, he declared, it was a tradition as old as civilisation itself for rivals to be united by marriage. There was an excitement and even a youthfulness I had not seen in him since he had first accompanied me to Almack's a year ago. He listened intently to my descriptions of her beauty and poise, and of her reception at court, leaning forward on the edge of his seat with his head propped in his hand like Michaelangelo's Thinker. He smiled and nodded encouragement, and when I was finished, he seemed almost to have forgotten that there was a larger issue at hand. I retired to bed that night still none the wiser as to whether I should accept the assignment or reject it – and the next day, the decision became yet more difficult.

It was not unusual for Lord Elsfield to request to see me. It was not even unusual for his request to give me little notice. But it was unusual to meet somewhere other than White's. If there were rumours circulating about our alliance then they were yet to reach my ears. Nonetheless, I dutifully took a carriage down Fleet Street and arrived at the Cheshire Cheese Tavern at the appointed hour in the evening. Not knowing the venue, I was forced to peer tentatively into successive dark rooms and alcoves, unsure of where I might find my quarry. The tavern was a honeycomb of small rooms and bars, each different to the previous and the next, but united in their windowless gloom. It made my task all the more frustrating, and as I interrupted a second and then a third surly customer, only to ascertain that they were not the man I sought, I began to wonder if this were not some elaborate practical joke. However, as I approached the point of capitulation, a voice behind me rasped: 'Over here, lad.'

I spun on my heels and approached the rascal in order to take issue with his over-familiarity. He sat in a murky corner of a vaulted room, with no one for company and a dark cloak over his head and shoulders.

'Now look here...'

'Take a seat,' he responded, taking down his hood to reveal the heavy brow and piercing dark eyes of Lord Elsfield. His appearance was so unfamiliar that I looked twice at my friend before being assured of his identity. His smile was noticeable by its absence; his clothing drab and non-descript and encased in his black cloak. It was a far cry from the dashing figure who had introduced himself on the ice nine years ago, and indeed from the elegant and refined man whom I had visited in his mansion only yesterday. No sooner had I sat down than he replaced his hood.

'No names here, my friend,' he muttered. My amusement at the theatricality of the charade was tempered only by an instinct which told me that there was more to this rendezvous than our usual discussion of investments.

He pushed a pot of dark liquid towards me and bade me join him in a drink. Leaning forward over our small square table, he then began to explain his purpose in hushed tones, his eyes fixing on me as a sailor fixes a sextant on a star.

'Apologies for the rather vague note, and the unfamiliarity of our meeting place. What I mean to discuss with you tonight is more delicate and more dangerous than anything we have previously undertaken. It would be better for both of us if we remained anonymous.'

Having spent the past year profiting from this man's schemes, I was intrigued by what was to come – and yet his caution concerned me. I felt the hairs rise on the back of my neck, and could not honestly discern whether it was from excitement or fear.

'You have now heard from me and from your patron the details of our scheme. You have no doubt gauged our differing appetites for risk – but this will not come as a surprise to you. Your patron is a skilful and successful businessman, but you and I both know that he is cautious where we have been bold. You may also understand better than him why I wish for you to lead this expedition. He remains unaware of our bond, and to have revealed it to him yesterday would not, I fear, have allayed his concerns, but rather increased them.

'He does not trust me. He does not agree with some of my business decisions, and he considers me at times reckless. Well that is all very well. I do not agree with some of his decisions, and I consider him over-cautious. The difference is that I continue to respect and trust him.'

I saw his eyes flick behind me, and turned to see the tavern-keeper pass by, collecting pots. Lord Elsfield waited until he had moved away before continuing.

'There is something else. An additional opportunity on this expedition. One which, given the state of distrust between us, I cannot share with your patron. But one which I can share with you. You must understand: this opportunity is not for the shy or retiring. It is an opportunity similar to others we have taken – but it requires a stout-hearted Englishman to execute it properly. It is for *this* reason I have insisted on your captaincy – on your courage and judgement. Do you understand me?'

I answered without hesitation: 'I understand.'

'Good lad. Good. Then I shall explain. Governor MacCarthy is an able administrator, but he's no solider. He's bound to underestimate his native adversaries. He has taken some sensible diplomatic steps, cutting off their supply of arms and ammunition. But the Ashanti are not without friends in the region. They will establish a new supply route, and they will pay their new allies well, with gold.

'The war will ultimately go the way of the Empire, make no mistake. We will not see African chieftains sailing their armies down the Thames, laying waste to our cities, raping our women and selling our children into slavery. But there is little profit in a short campaign – and no profit whatsoever in allowing the French to resupply our enemies from their neighbouring territories. If we control the supply, we may judge when to halt it. The economics are complex – but what I require of you in this enterprise is simple. You must ensure that our consignment is met by my agent and no-one else. The rest you may leave to me.'

I frowned, turning the words over in my mind. What he had said was simple enough – but it was what he had not said which troubled me. Beneath the euphemisms lurked something more significant. To meddle with His Majesty's imperial interests. I forced myself to take that thought no further. I was not being given all the information – yet his countenance, eyes fixed on mine, did not invite further questions. Yesterday I had been presented with a scheme fraught with danger, balanced against the lure of adventure and a long-held desire which somehow still held its appeal. I had struggled to agree to that scheme, and now it had become more opaque – and more dangerous.

I suddenly realised that my heart was pounding and my hands were sweating. The feeling brought to mind the day I had been kidnapped on the ice. Lord Elsfield had saved my life that day. And then he had freed me from the slow suffocation of Sir Godfrey's apprenticeships, becoming a close ally and business partner. He was indeed more bold than my patron. He was also wildly more successful. I thought of the extravagance of his Grosvenor Square house, and of Sir Godfrey's own words: 'He has connections that other men do not... He has ways and means to damage us if we anger him.' If Lord Elsfield chose to reveal the extent of our alliance to Sir Godfrey, or the knowing part I had played in the sale of the Poyais bonds, my reputation would be finished. And still there was the issue of Miss McNeil. The line between excitement and fear was a thin one. I looked into the dark eyes across the table, and they looked right back at me, until I was not sure who was examining whom.

'My L...'

'...Friend,' he interrupted, quick as a flash.

I blushed at my error, and began again.

'My friend.' Even when bidden, the form of address did not sit well. 'I am sure that the opportunity is a fine one. I am sure it is the right one. However, I fear I still require more time to understand my position and truly commit to the scheme.'

Lord Elsfield did not flinch. His eyes continued to bore into me. I wondered what decisions were being made and what plans were being formed behind his impenetrable exterior. His eyes flicked behind me once again, just for a moment, and once again I turned to see the same tavern-keeper lingering in the shadows. I turned back to my colleague and was suddenly very aware that no one knew I was here. I had never visited this tavern before. I could disappear tonight and there would be no trail of breadcrumbs which might lead an investigator to the scene of my doom. Why had he chosen this dark, labyrinthine meeting place? Was he here alone? Was I naïve to be? I found the sense of excitement rapidly draining from me, as fear bloomed like a fog in its place.

And then, without warning, the spell was broken.

Lord Elsfield released me from his gaze, and swayed back from the table, his arms crossing in front of him and the familiar smile returning to his face. He closed his eyes and nodded gently in a gesture of silent approval.

'You test my patience, my friend. Let me be clear.'

'I regret my indecisiveness, sir...'

'Yet I see much of my former self in you – and perhaps this makes me indulgent.' And then, in a change of subject so sweeping I had no ready defence, he asked: 'This woman you told me of – I shall not speak her name here. Has any further discussion passed between you since we last spoke of her?'

'No, sir. You bade me not to...'

'Indeed I did. Well I may inform you now that my enquiries have met with only positive news. Her family, although not of aristocratic roots, is of strong stock, and her fortune is indeed great. She would make a fine and obliging wife... Might I suggest, given the concatenation of circumstances with which we are faced, that you seek *her* approval of the expedition? As your intended future wife, it seems logical to broach the two matters in unison. If she is sceptical of the proposal, I shall not hold it against you to withdraw. A man must be mindful of his obligations to his wife, and be wary of the representations of others to her.'

A sharp stab of fear. In the course of his enquiries, he must have discovered that other suitors had an interest in Annabel, and he now counselled me to ensure they were disappointed. He knew my mind, and whence my doubts emanated. I realised with a start: he knew me better than Sir Godfrey.

A hand uncrossed itself from his chest and extended towards me, inviting mine to join it.

'I know I can trust you to disclose no part of what we have discussed here tonight – to her or anyone else. Do we have an accord, my friend?' he smiled at me.

I took his hand.

XIII

The day of the ball promised fine weather and warmth right through the evening. Mindful of my position as a guest of honour and old friend of the family, I arrived in good time at the house, attired in a fine new black kerseymere tail coat, white waistcoat and stockings, and black satin breeches and shoes, matched with a new chapeau bras and cane, all picked out by Lord Alvanley who had insisted on accompanying me to the tailor. He had taken particular trouble over my neckcloth, insisting to the valet that he make the final adjustments himself – and on looking in the mirror I believed I sported the finest cravat I had ever seen.

Mrs McNeil was particularly attentive to me on my arrival, taking me on a tour of the house to show me the decorative efforts she had instructed. From every fireplace, white and pink lilies burst forth like fireworks from fine Chinese porcelain vases, filling the whole house with their heady perfume. The dining room, already generous in its proportions, had been thoughtfully rearranged to maximise the seating for hungry and weary guests. In the centre of the room, the long dining table stood dressed in starched white linen, awaiting the feast. Elegant silver candelabras splayed out down its middle like branches, interspersed with budding flowers that seemed to grow out of the table itself. It was a masterful display of taste, for all society to appreciate. My host waved towards the kitchens, and began reciting a long list of the dishes she had instructed, which would soon cover the table.

But as she led me into the ballroom, I could not prevent a great smile breaking over my face – which satisfied her hugely. It was clear she had left her piece de resistance for last. What had been a cold, empty and rather unwelcoming room was now transformed. The walls had been re-decorated in the latest and most expensive magnolia wallpaper, and while I gazed in appreciation, a man atop a stepladder applied the finishing touches to a huge chandelier hanging coruscating from the ceiling.

'I commissioned it especially from Baccarat', she told me, the note of pride clear in her voice. 'Though it was supposed to be fitted yesterday.'

The man half-turned from his work, her raised voice making her frustration known. But he thought better of making a reply.

'It is a masterpiece, Mrs McNeil.'

And indeed it was. Each crystal perfectly captured and amplified the early evening sun which streamed through the high windows, turning the empty floor into a patchwork of dappled light, while the walls seem to glow with colour. Once guests arrived and the music started, I could well imagine the scene as that same light floated over ball-gowns and tiaras, rebounding off sequins and crystals and being sent on further again.

The house was a triumph. The ballroom in particular was bright and well-appointed, showcasing the host's good taste and understanding of the latest fashions. It occurred to me that the ball was as much to announce Mrs McNeil's new place in society as it was her daughter's. Lady Sefton had assumed the role of co-host at the ball, and had used her considerable influence to elevate the family. Now the family was determined to justify that good faith.

However, Mrs McNeil's attentiveness detained me from being introduced to Miss McNeil upon her entrance to the ball, and by the time my tour was complete she was fully occupied alongside Lady Sefton, welcoming other guests to their home. My planned discussion with her would have to wait until the dancing commenced. I consoled myself that both Sir Godfrey and Lord Elsfield would speak with Mrs McNeil upon their arrival, and that my suit would be strengthened through my association with them. In the meantime, I was happy to be reacquainted with Edward and his new wife, Mrs Ball-Hughes, who were recently returned from honeymoon and full of the joys of spring at their union – and no doubt at the scandal they had generated in society. Lord Alvanley soon joined us, and gave good sport in judging each guest on the elegance of their dress. His eye had already been caught by Miss McNeil who, if possible, looked even more captivating than at her presentation at Court. She wore elbow-length gloves and a long pink silk gown, tightened to scarcely a hand-span across her waist with a wide pink sash. A surely priceless diamond necklace hung down between her golden ringlets, which were festooned with ribbons. She was, in Alvanley's authoritative view, 'the belle of the ball'.

Whilst enjoying Alvanley's assessment of my intended, and the admiration it invited from the group, I was careful to remind him:

'I trust, Lord Alvanley, that you will keep your word and not take your interest in our host's daughter any further.'

He turned to me with a look of bemusement on his face. 'Of course, young Victor – of course! I simply do her the same honour I do everyone. Indeed – I could also adjudge your attire, excepting that it would be hopeless vanity, as anyone who knows you can see that it is I who have clothed you in the first place! However, I could not offer kind words on the styling of the young gentleman whom she currently greets. Observe his shabby neckcloth, and ill-cut tails! Why, I do believe that is young John Russell. No one quite misfits a coat like him!'

I looked round in horror, and while my group of friends laughed, and Alvanley continued his disparagement of my rival, I could not help but wonder what words they exchanged, and whether he might already have prised her affections away from me. Despite Alvanley's comic portrayal, Lord John Russell to my mind looked too much the kind of suitor that a parent would welcome. He was a small man, admittedly, and his clothes rather hung from him, but his appearance in all other regards was closely attended to, and his posture and manner befitted the son of a duke. He might be only the third son, but even Lord Elsfield could not contend with the power and wealth of his father, the Duke of Bedford.

The moments I stood there, oblivious to Alvanley's witticisms, seemed like hours. I winced as I saw her mouth broaden into a beautiful smile, or her head incline in what appeared to be affection. It was with great relief that I watched him eventually move on to greet Lady Sefton and Mrs McNeil, to be replaced by none other than Sir Godfrey Ramsay. My whole world tonight seemed condensed into one room, as rivals and sponsors made their impressions upon my intended and her mother. I might awake tomorrow engaged to the darling of London, endowed with a fortune by Sir Godfrey, and set to make my name leading an expedition to Africa. Or... all my hopes might be dashed at once. It was impossible to wrench my attention away – to avoid analysing and interpreting every subtle movement or raised voice, each laugh or gasp, as a signal of abject failure or final triumph. I knew that my patron could be charming. I had observed his effect on Lady Sefton and was glad that she stood between Miss McNeil and her mother, the better to intercede on my behalf at the opportune moment.

Having made his greeting to his hosts, Sir Godfrey sought me out, standing now apart from my friends. As he approached I heard the first strained sounds of a violin and then a cello waft across to me on the still summer air, as the band tuned up.

'Capital evening, wouldn't you say?!'

I looked at my patron rather curiously, and detected that same note of exuberance that I had first seen at Almack's, where again he had been in the company of Lady Sefton.

'It is certainly a handsome house, sir, with decorations befitting a fine lady such as Miss McNeil.'

It was his turn to look at me with curiosity.

'Handsome house?! Decorations?! What are you speaking of, my boy? There is a lively atmosphere at this gathering, with the very finest people present and the promise of the rarest dancing. Your Miss McNeil, for a start, is a rare beauty indeed.'

I was taken aback by the forcefulness of his convictions, though admittedly pleased.

'What did you make of our hosts, sir?'

'Capital people, Victor. Capital. Lady Sefton has always been an excellent judge of character. Introduced me to Lady Ramsay, you know. I do believe she has unearthed a true diamond in Miss McNeil. She was most attentive in her greeting. As was her mother. Knew all about me, of course. No doubt Mr McNeil has told them many times of our competition!'

Something jarred as he spoke. Lord Elsfield had told me *he* had introduced my patron to his wife. I wondered who would lie, and why.

'Miss McNeil was eager to recount the circumstances of your meeting, Victor,' he continued. 'It seems the version you gave me of events at Peterloo rather downplayed your own role. Her version casts you as quite the hero.'

He paused, but I did not respond.

'Perhaps you were wise to do so. I may not have taken well to my boy of only fifteen being thrust into the heart of such a massacre. Mr Trenchard's list of crimes grows ever longer. Mrs McNeil was particular to praise my swift action following his shameful behaviour. Other murderers received no such censure. It is a strange world indeed when the King congratulates the slaughterers of his own loyal subjects[3].'

'I do not believe I acted wisely that day, sir. Looking back, I rather think I acted only on instinct.'

'Perhaps that is my point, Victor,' he said, all trace of gaiety now gone from his voice. 'Perhaps I have been guilty of stifling your instincts, when they in fact do you great credit.'

He stood beside me a moment longer, appearing to consider his own statement. Then, without a further word, he walked away, leaving me utterly bemused. Sir Godfrey had discouraged and underestimated me my entire life, and had forced me to seek alternative alliances. Now, belatedly, it seemed he might be perceiving this error. I wondered if it might not be too late to reconcile our differences.

However, the news that Miss McNeil was portraying me as a hero did not escape my attention either. My hopes soared. This was not mere fancy: I was eligible, successful, and she was fond of me.

I turned to find my friends, but they had vanished, doubtless seeking out a suitable partner for the first dance. I turned back to the reception line, to see Lord Elsfield now approaching Miss McNeil. He was dressed smartly but austerely – an impression only amplified by his expression. Lord Alvanley would have said that he was more ready for a funeral than a dance. There was a pretty curtsey and a stately bow, and I imagined the usual exchange of pleasantries – but I was troubled by his sombre demeanour. I had hoped that he would take the opportunity tonight to vouch for me, having given his blessing to our engagement. But the easy smile was nowhere to be seen as, with Lady Sefton now overseeing the commencement of the dancing, he spoke alone with both mother and daughter. There was a short word to a footman, and then the two ladies turned and led him away to a private room. Concern became alarm.

There was no set of circumstances I could construct which might explain this behaviour. The guests had all arrived and been ushered into the lavishly decorated ballroom, ready for the commencement of the ball. I followed the footman to its door, where I was greeted by the grand sight of the cream of London society, arrayed in a formation the Duke of Wellington would have been proud of, awaiting his signal to commence battle.

Lady Sefton had assumed the role of the Duke, even now martialling the last of her troops into position, matching dance partners and hopeful brides alike. Looking through their assembled ranks, I could see the midnight blue cravats of Alvanley's entourage, strategically positioned amongst the most eligible of the Ton's ladies. The rich pale silks of their dresses contrasted sharply with the dark colours of the men around them, highlighting what was fair and fine, drawing my eye to them. A shock of orange feathers, rising above its surroundings near the centre of the line, announced the presence of Queen Anna of the Netherlands, alongside Slender Billy, her husband, bedecked in gold lace and medals. Behind them, I caught a glimpse of the Duchess of Clarence, a wide burgundy dress and elegant tiara beside a sailor's dress uniform. On either side, splashes of aquamarine and azure, emerald and pale gold rippled and glistened, as their bearers turned to offer a whispered compliment or cutting criticism to a neighbour. Whilst Almack's was absolutely the high command of fashion in society, the McNeil ball had seemingly brought out another level of refinement from its regiments.

Everyone now waited to welcome Miss McNeil for her first dance. The band had finished tuning and stood-to expectantly, arms at the ready. The excitement was palpable. The footman did his professional best to remain invisible as he made his way around the edge of the room to Lady Sefton. From my position I could see her expression quite clearly as he delivered Mrs McNeil's message – and it required no great skill to interpret. Even for a woman of her impeccable manners, the outrage was writ large on her face. Heads around her began to turn and take notice: the undercurrent of excited murmurs changed key, and grew – but already she was on the move, marching towards me and the door, with the footman now rushing to soothe and slow her down, all thought of professional protocol banished. His efforts were largely in vain, however: Lady Sefton was not a woman to be trifled with. My mind racing, I followed them back to the room into which Lord Elsfield had disappeared with Mrs and Miss McNeil.

As she prepared to knock on the door in question, it opened, and out hurried a flustered Mrs McNeil. She nearly collided with Lady Sefton as she smoothed her clothes and composed herself. More hurried words were exchanged, and in spite of my sense of propriety I found myself edging nearer, desperate to understand what had occurred. Lady Sefton was clearly battling to maintain a graceful aspect in the face of adversity. Before I could overhear anything however, she turned smartly and retraced her steps to her guests in the ballroom. Mrs McNeil now addressed her daughter as she emerged from the room – and now I was close enough to hear.

'Annabel my dear, you will please do Lord Elsfield the honour of the first dance, as he requests.'

'What shall I say to others when asked, mother?'

'You will say what you must, my dear. Lord Elsfield is an important guest. He is powerful and wealthy and his good opinion of us, much like Lady Sefton's, counts for a great deal. It is a small price to pay for his favour.'

'And if he makes further requests?'

Mrs McNeil drew herself up to her full height and let out a long breath, smoothing down her clothes once more before replying: 'Then we shall have to consider each request upon its merits, Annabel. We are in London now, and the stakes are raised.'

She turned to the footman, and instructed him to attend directly to Lord Elsfield, ensuring his every need was catered for. At the mention of his name he appeared through the doorway to stand alongside Miss McNeil, and together they proceeded towards the ballroom, the familiar smile now returned to his face. Suddenly it seemed less reassuring.

I was not sure what game was afoot, but I was decidedly uncomfortable with it. Taking the best possible view of events, I hoped that perhaps Lord Elsfield had wished to vouch for me in private, explaining the high regard in which he held me, and his view of my prospects. I recalled with horror that I had corrected Mrs McNeil over my inheritance, and I now hoped that both Sir Godfrey and Lord Elsfield might have repaired some of that damage with their kind words.

The sound of music roused me from my introspection, and I hurried back to join the fray in the ballroom. Where only minutes before there had been well-martialled order, there was now the general melee of a ball finally in full swing. The delay to its commencement had only heightened the excitement, and the combatants now whirled and stepped to a quadrille with the nervous energy of a warhorse given its head. The floor was a riot of colours and fabric and elaborate hairstyles, all jostling to find their rhythms with their new partners. Yellow spun and blurred alongside azure, turning to green before a black and navy canvas. Feathers and ribbons flew across the room in great circles, as if a platoon of cats had been released into an aviary. The music rose and rose in volume, desperately competing with the noise of conversation and dancing for supremacy. The strings soared urgently up to the sparkling chandelier, showering the cream of society below with a thousand beams of light, which played and rebounded from the finest silks and silvers, glittering gowns and golds.

Everywhere I looked, majesty flirted with chaos, yet everywhere majesty triumphed. It was truly a scene befitting of the gods – but having hoped to share the first dance with Miss McNeil, I now found myself without a partner, stood by the fireplace, watching a strange drama unfold. While my feet remained still, instead my mind whirred, taking in all that it saw. For all his ability in business, Lord Elsfield had none of the fluency or gaiety of Sir Godfrey in his dancing. He and Miss McNeil moved stiffly around the room. The movements were accurate and timely, but there seemed to be no connection with the music. I found this heartening: try as I might to convince myself that this first dance was only a gesture of respect, I could not entirely shake the notion that Lord Elsfield might be attempting to win Miss McNeil for himself. I watched their faces closely as they moved, and fancied I saw distaste on hers, in spite of her attempts to conceal it. Whatever he was saying to her, it did not seem to be working. He retained his confident smile, and she her strained expression throughout the dance.

At its end there was a general applause for the debutante and her partner, and a brief moment of stillness to catch one's breath and exchange partners if desired. Many couples remained attached, having learnt something about each other (terpsichorean or not) and keen to learn more. I was gratified to see Miss McNeil move smartly but graciously away from Lord Elsfield, who retired to the edge of the room, his eyes not leaving her, until with a sudden movement I realised they were fixed upon me. His smile broadened and his head inclined in deference, and I wondered what he could mean, until I realised almost with a gasp that Miss McNeil now stood before me, eyes abashed and the corners of her mouth just suggesting a smile.

'I am so sorry, Mr Winter. I had very much hoped to share my first dance with you. Alas, being a new family with no ancestry to rely upon, we must be sensitive to the whims of those who would patronise us, and who might take offence at our snubs.'

I muttered reassurances, knowing all the while that my entire body gave the lie to them. Nonetheless, she took them in the spirit they were intended. Then she surprised me again, by asking for my hand for the second dance. Almost struck dumb with joy, we moved together into the middle of the floor. I allowed myself to savour the moment, knowing that all around me the finest people in society were taking note as I, an orphan of no prospects, left to freeze outside a nameless village church, stepped out with the most eligible lady in London. Whatever aid I had had in reaching this moment had been more than matched by my own endeavour. My first meeting with

Miss McNeil, the fortune I had amassed and continued to grow –
were these not my achievements and mine alone?

Barely had the music started than she began to speak freely. She
described the frustrations of living away from society in Manchester,
and her excitement at being able to move in the circles of great men
here in London. I took the opportunity to question her friendship
with Lord John Russell.

'Oh yes. Dear John. He is a thoughtful man. But that is all that
he is, Victor. Do you remember when we first met, in that room overlooking St Peter's Field?'

'How could I forget? It was the happiest chance of my life.'

'I recall how brave you were. How indignant you were at the
pompous magistrates, all self-interest and cowardice. You were a man
of action. You may think me fanciful, but Shelley and Lord Byron
move me with their poetry. These are men who follow their hearts;
who act with passion; who fight and risk their lives for their beliefs.
You are such a man.'

'Then perhaps London is not for you or me after all, Annabel.
There is little fighting to be found here.'

'You may be correct – but I do believe a man's character is fixed.
You are a man of action. John speaks a great deal, and thinks a great
deal. But he does not act. He gives hope with his words, but dashes
it with inaction. If you had an opportunity to act, to adventure like
Shelley or Byron, I know that you would take it.'

She could not know the power of her words at that moment.
Fate seemed to propel me onward.

'It may please you to know then, that just such an adventure is
currently laid out before me.'

A captivatingly coy smile came across her face.

'Lord Elsfield did inform me that there was some great decision
on your mind at present. He said it was for you to describe, but that
I was to forgive you for your distraction tonight.'

My heart lurched. I had been the subject of their conversation. His behaviour tonight had been unsettling, but once again it seemed there was no one over whom Lord Elsfield could not wield influence. I felt a surge of optimism.

'Annabel, I have been asked to lead a convoy to Africa's Gold Coast; to meet with the governor of the colony, and perhaps even to play my part in protecting the local tribes and suppressing a rebellion there. It will be a great adventure – but the risks too are great.'

Her response was writ large on her face before she could speak a word. Her blue eyes widened and the full red lips parted in surprise. I tightened my grip on her, guiding her through the dance steps.

'My dear Victor! This is indeed exciting news! When do you sail? I presume you have accepted this opportunity?'

I hesitated.

'As long as I have known you – as long as we have exchanged letters – we have told each other of our desire for adventure. To do something that makes an impact in this world. Escaping the confines of my existence in Manchester was the first step for me. You succeeded sooner. Surely this is the next step? To strike a blow for the freedom of all men. What is stopping you from seizing this opportunity?'

My moment had arrived, and I suddenly found myself woefully unprepared. I looked into her eyes, searching for the courage to speak, or perhaps for an indication that my words would meet with approval.

'Do you doubt that you will return? Or do you doubt that I shall be here upon your return? How could I speak this way of the romance of adventure, and then choose to love another? The boy I met when I was a girl threw himself into harm's way with no thought for his own security – only to defend his beliefs. You defended *me* when you defended those people, Victor. You showed me that we can all make a difference through our action. You must take this opportunity. You must. And when you return with tales of far-off lands and daring deeds, I shall find you more captivating than ever.'

She spoke as passionately as she had that day at St Peter's Field, and once again it gave me courage.

'Then I shall go. You are my strength, Annabel, and I shall think of you daily until my return.'

We passed the remainder of the dance in a daze, smiling knowingly at each other over our shared affection. At its end, having bid each other adieu, I left the floor to find Lord Elsfield and tell him of my decision. However, it was he who found me first, accosting me within a matter of moments.

'Mr Winter! A pleasure to see you here! I trust you are enjoying the delights of a fine society ball?'

'Indeed I am, my Lord. For as you know, this is the coming out ball of the object of my affection.'

'And have you yet had a chance to speak to your lady? To offer her your compliments, and perhaps to tell her of your intentions?'

I was growing accustomed to his direct questions. 'I have spoken to her, my Lord. As I believe have you also.' We shared a conspiratorial smile.

'Victor, I said only what was fair and true to our hosts. It was incumbent on me as your friend and ally to commend you to them. Anything they have done or said thereafter is entirely your own affair.'

'Well there has been much said, my Lord, but the salient news for you is that I have decided to accept the proposition. I shall be your man on the Gold Coast.'

'This is excellent news, Victor – excellent news! You have made a bold and wise decision. This will be the making of you, I do believe. Do I take it Miss McNeil was agreeable to the proposition then?'

It occurred to me that it would not do me credit to appear entirely in the thrall of my intended, and so I couched my answer carefully: 'I explained to Miss McNeil that I was minded to accept the assignment, my Lord, and that I hoped it did not cause her too great a disappointment to have to await my return. She was good enough to commend my desire for adventure, and to make my mark on the world.'

'Excellent, excellent. She is as I advised – a fine and obliging lady. Well. I am glad we have reached an agreement. Perhaps you and Sir Godfrey will pay me a visit on Monday to set the wheels in motion. We have a busy few months ahead!'

He offered his hand and, after a firm shake, melted into the throng, leaving me alone with my thoughts. I wandered through the house for a time, still not quite able to believe how swiftly events had moved forward to my advantage. Not only would Annabel await my return, but she even encouraged my adventure, seeing it as a kind of Romantic odyssey. I would return more eligible than when I departed, while rivals might bluster and bicker over her in my absence. The spectre of Lord John Russell and his like still hovered over me, but it was a spectre much diminished in power. These men would not steal my lady's heart with words alone.

It was as I picked over the lavish dinner our host had prepared that I encountered Sir Godfrey once more. He seemed genuinely delighted with my record of the conversation with Annabel, reiterating that he believed her to be a 'rare beauty', and adding that 'a fine woman such as her could be the making of you, my boy!' On the matter of the expedition he was more cautious, continuing to voice concerns over the dangers and my lack of experience. But he accepted my decision, and we spent the remaining hours of the ball together in a spirit of harmony the equal of which I could not recall having passed with him.

XIV

In the wake of the ball, Annabel swiftly became the darling of Almack's and a subject of much discussion at White's – one which I could do precious little to change. My meetings with Lord Elsfield continued, but now focused on our clandestine arrangements for the Gold Coast expedition. These were in addition to the regular planning meetings with Sir Godfrey and Lord Elsfield, where they would often argue about commitments, deadlines, profit-share and risk. It was bizarre to witness them so unable to agree, when separately I managed to reach agreement with each of them. I had long known that I was more capable than Sir Godfrey gave me credit for. However, for the first time now, I wondered if Lord Elsfield too might underestimate my value.

Sir Godfrey and I had seemed to reach a new understanding in the wake of my decision, and I found myself increasingly brought into his confidence. Much of his offered wisdom, late as it was, I had already discovered for myself or through Lord Elsfield – yet the atmosphere in our St James's Square house became distinctly more civil as a result.

My visits to Annabel at Berkeley Square remained as frequent as decorum would allow, and I even began to believe that her mother might now encourage our connection. Our polite discussions would range over the fashionable topics of the day, and would inevitably include any great scandal which a public figure might have created. However, when we were alone together on the floor of Almack's, Annabel would enquire hungrily for information about my forthcoming adventure. I became certain that she imagined me standing alongside her revered poets, battling elemental forces and raging against the injustices of slavery. I did not entirely discourage such an image, painting heroic portraits with my words, with me as the protector of the noble savages on the Gold Coast from the wicked and corrupt Ashanti. Yet in my darker moments, I considered the premature end which seemed to be such men's fate, and hoped that I might survive as a Byron and not drown as a Shelley[4]. She too would always temper each enquiry with an earnest plea for my continued wariness throughout the voyage. As a result I grew increasingly restless with a mixture of concern and excitement as the day of my departure grew closer, and the gossip and trappings of my usual society entertainments somehow lost their former lustre.

Sir Godfrey expedited the manufacture of British Army uniforms from his factories. Lord Elsfield was equally true to his word in arranging the provision of arms and ammunition from the Royal Naval Armaments Depot at Devonport. Other supplies were organised by Sir Godfrey and his web of connections, including belts, buckles, buttons, blacking, saddles, stoves, tents, canteens, knapsacks, salted and dried foods, and all manner of other items necessary for an army in the field. Most important of all, Sir Godfrey extricated an Indiaman from its other commitments so that, by the start of October, I stood on the quayside at the London Docks alongside Mr Crawshaw and Sir Godfrey, overseeing the loading of the supplies. The captain of the ship was none other than Captain Horwell – a man I had not encountered since our visit to the 'City of Moscow' tent on the Thames nine years earlier. In the intervening years, Captain Horwell had made the London to Archangel route his own, fulfilling scores of contracts for Sir Godfrey and earning an unparalleled reputation (and fortune) amongst his fellow sailors. He greeted Sir Godfrey like an old friend, striding down the gangplank and clasping a large hand around my patron's with a laugh which reverberated throughout his body. I thought Sir Godfrey might have his hand wrenched off before it was safely returned, such was its vigour and duration.

'Sir Godfrey! A pleasure to see you again. A pleasure!' The captain's voice pounded against the walls of the nearby warehouses and came back upon us even stronger. A life at sea, barking commands above the arctic winds, had clearly developed his lungs.

'A pleasure to see you too, Captain Horwell. The company is indebted to you as ever for your great service.'

'Gammon, Sir Godfrey! Indebted indeed! It's no secret I've done very well out of the company, and may say there's not a single debt outstanding – I'm most particular about such matters! Mr Danvers sends his regards from Archangel, sir, where he too prospers. But I shan't deny that the *White Star* and I are looking forward to some warmer climes on this voyage.'

'Well said, Captain Horwell – well said. I shall leave the provisioning of the ship in your own capable hands. I should like to introduce you to my ward – Mr Winter.'

Captain Horwell turned smartly to face me, his familiarity banished, and inclined his head in a bow.

'Mr Winter, sir. A ward of Sir Godfrey's is an honoured guest upon my vessel. I look forward to having you aboard.' As he said this he extended his hand once more and, recalling the vigour of his last action, I tentatively met it with my own. His skin was hard as leather and his grip vicelike. I focused my mind to prevent the involuntary gasp which begged to be released. Yet his shake was gentle – a concession to a stranger he respected.

'We have in fact met before, Captain Horwell,' I ventured, 'though I would not expect you to remember it. Nine years ago, in a tent on the Thames. I was with my patron that day.'

I saw recognition wash over Captain Horwell, and his face brightened. I was glad that I had released myself from his grasp at this moment, as his whole body became more animated and the stiffness of formality ebbed from him. 'Aye, Mr Winter. Now you mention it, I do see a resemblance to a young face I saw at the table that day. A day that changed my fortunes, sir, as you may bear witness! I am happy to be entrusted with such precious cargo by Sir Godfrey.'

'You may find this cargo to be quite a handful, Captain Horwell,' interjected Sir Godfrey.

We both turned to face my patron at this strange remark. Visibly amused with his quip, he continued:

'Through nineteen years, I have found myself constantly surprised, out-thought and out-manoeuvred by Mr Winter. He will be a valuable counsel, Captain, and, in all non-nautical matters, he will represent me directly on board.'

My mouth dropped open momentarily. Sir Godfrey and I had discussed many details over the intervening months, and I felt thoroughly prepared for the expedition. However, we had both tip-toed around the matter of ultimate authority at sea. Normal practice gave the running of the ship to the captain, and as a 'landlubber' all my life, I had no wish to run the *White Star* myself. The question of who would take responsibility for the safe delivery of the cargo, and who would make key decisions on-board, had lain before us unasked. It had now been answered. A strange glow suffused me. It felt very much like pride.

'Very good sir,' chimed Captain Horwell amiably, nodding first to my patron and then to me. 'Perhaps then, if I might be permitted to take Mr Winter through the charts, and agree a course with him?'

'By all means, Captain. Please, use Mr Crawshaw's office.'

Captain Horwell gestured for me to lead, and together we walked away to agree the detail of the voyage. I supposed, on reflection, that the confirmation of my position on the boat was something of a formality. Lord Elsfield had specifically requested my leadership as the glue which would hold his alliance with Sir Godfrey together. Nonetheless Sir Godfrey had given the order in front of me, and in glowing terms. Captain Horwell would report to me. It was a vote of confidence from a man who had never been free with such things.

My report back to Lord Elsfield the next day gave further reason for satisfaction. Though he did not care for Captain Horwell as a man, he conceded that his record, his ship and his crew were first-rate. Furthermore, my confirmed seniority would make the supply of the cargo to his agent considerably easier.

'Of course, it will make your ultimate mission somewhat more challenging, in the midst of such competent crew,' he reflected. He had taken to referring to our planned treachery as my 'ultimate mission' – a phrase which protected us both from any would-be eavesdroppers, and also made the scheme somehow more palatable. 'But you will find a way. I have absolute faith in your abilities, Victor. You must be ever alert to opportunities, vigilant against discovery, and ruthless in your execution. These are all qualities I know you to have.'

The scheme still did not sit well with me – but between my two patrons' plans, events were long past the point where I could withdraw. I questioned, as I reflected for the thousandth time on the conspiracy I was now part of, whether I had ever really had a choice. Lord Elsfield had been careful to reveal details to me slowly, drawing me in one reluctant nod at a time. What had seemed like a harmless detail - *to ensure the consignment is met by my agent and no-one else* – had morphed into something beyond my darkest imaginings. His 'agent' was not an unscrupulous Gold Coast trader, as I had perhaps imagined. He was a Portuguese mercenary. And he would intercept the *White Star* in the Gulf of Guinea, before we reached land. I knew what that made him, but once again Lord Elsfield's gift for euphemisms was a welcome dressing around the naked truth. We could not be sure what resistance the *White Star* might offer to the mercenary, but the responsibility was now mine to ensure it was minimal, and to prevent loss of life.

That last element was not something Lord Elsfield once discussed, and I increasingly wondered whether it was for fear of being indelicate, or simply because he did not care. It was the task which weighed heaviest on me. The mercenary was already engaged – nothing could prevent his intervention now: how he would be received was up to me.

It was not long before the cargo was loaded, the manifests checked and copied by Mr Crawshaw, and the crew returned from shore leave. The morning tide would bring with it our departure, and I thought to call one last time upon my Annabel, to bid her adieu.

My visit however was not successful. Upon enquiring at her door, I was told by the footman that Miss McNeil was not at home. I hurriedly scribbled a note, giving her my compliments and hoping that she might instead be able to visit the docks tomorrow to bid me farewell and good fortune. My return was not anticipated within six months, and I could not mask my disappointment as I walked back across the square. An apple-seller on the opposite corner bade me stop and make a purchase, and I reasoned that anything that might take my mind from the image of my beloved would at this moment be welcome. Observing my mood, the vendor enquired as to my predicament and, being now unengaged in any matter of great urgency, I shared my situation with the woman. Having received the customary platitudes in response, I completed my purchase and looked over my shoulder for one last look at the square. The trees were in full leaf, and a couple walked happily through the manicured garden, looking up and around at the birds and the flowers. An elegant coach sporting the coat of arms of its owner clattered into the square and rolled to a sedate stop outside the McNeil home. Before I could consider what this might signify, the door of the house opened and a tall, hooded figure emerged. I could not discern the figure's features, but its gait and stature were clearly male. Annabel herself now emerged, clothed in a large, hooded olive cloak with a white dress visible underneath. As I watched, the stranger took her hand and led her to the coach, and the very footman who had misinformed me of her whereabouts bowed stiffly to the couple, and opened the door of the carriage for their hurried ascent.

I felt the blood rise to my face. I did not yet understand what I had witnessed, but I knew I had been duped, and I acted upon instinct. I ran to the street and summoned a hackney carriage, instructing the driver to follow them at a discreet distance.

My heart thumped heavily as we traversed London's streets. I had not had time to think at first, but now we were in motion, I asked myself what I hoped to achieve in my pursuit – but also what reason Annabel could have for deceiving me. I replayed the scene in my mind. There was something about the coat of arms, with laurels wound around it, which seemed vaguely familiar. For a time I felt certain that we were bound for the Bedford Estate, and the home of Lord John Russell himself, and I tortured myself with notions of his secret continued liaison with my beloved. However, though we passed within a street of his abode, we continued, and as it disappeared behind us I felt that whatever might now be revealed could not be worse than what I had imagined. Eventually her coach drew to a halt, at an unfamiliar and nondescript address close by Cripplegate church. Instructing my driver to stop a good way off, I watched Miss McNeil alight and enter the building adjacent, at which her coach and its mysterious occupant set off again at a canter. I wavered for a moment, wondering which miscreant to confront. Then I exited my carriage, and proceeded on foot.

The building before me was three storeys high, with a plain façade of brickwork punctuated with two large windows either side of a single large door. I searched in vain for any sort of marking which might give away its purpose. I lingered a few minutes longer, hoping to discover some clue to this new mystery. As I waited, three further visitors approached and entered the building, and it struck me that none were male. I began to wonder if this might be some form of 'ladies' club', to mirror White's or Brook's, and my indignation grew with that notion. Were the situation reversed I could not imagine a lunch or game of cards with my coterie which might take priority over a conversation with Annabel, and certainly not when we were destined to be parted the very next day.

My indignation gave me resolve, and I strode purposefully across the street and pushed open the door. Inside I saw the same plain design, with function taking precedence over form. I was in a small double-height lobby, with three doors of equal size leading off the room in different directions. Engraved in stone above the door opposite the entrance were the letters 'LFPU'. No explanation of their meaning was evident around them, but to my right was a desk where a female clerk eyed me with exaggerated bemusement. Suddenly self-conscious and aware that I did not have a good reason to be here, I approached the desk and struck up a conversation.

'Good afternoon, madam. I would be most grateful for your assistance. I have a friend whom I have arranged to meet here. I wonder if you could tell me where to find her.'

'I'm afraid I cannot help you, sir.'

'I am sorry. You must have misheard me. I said that I wished to meet an acquaintance of mine here. I require your assistance.'

'Yes, sir, I understood your meaning. However, the rules here are quite clear that there are to be no gentlemen allowed on the premises.'

I took this to be some reciprocal form of the gentleman's club ban on female members, and took little offence.

'Of course, of course. But you will understand, I wish to speak with my friend, and I would be grateful if you could send for her.'

'I'm sorry sir,' continued this Cerberus, 'but that will also not be possible. There are no gentlemen permitted to call on our members here, nor to be made privy to our membership register.'

'What the devil for?' I burst out.

'Well, sir. Not all gentlemen are supportive of the work of the London Female Political Union, and anonymity is therefore a key founding principal. If you are a friend of a member here, I would encourage you to speak with the lady in the comfort of her own home.'

I could not find words to spar further with the gatekeeper. Mustering no more than a surly 'thank you for your time', I turned and exited the building.

Making my way home in the carriage, I felt suddenly very low. I wondered who Annabel's furtive companion could be, and what the nature of her involvement with a 'political union' was. I recalled that upon our meeting at St Peter's Field, and subsequently when I had stayed with her in Manchester, she had expressed an interest in politics. However, I had not understood that interest to have endured in the face of the myriad distractions of London society, nor to take such a tangible form in her life. Could her connection to this stranger be purely political? Or was that wishful thinking on my part? I racked my brains for the house of the coat of arms. This rogue was not even attempting to hide his identity, yet still it eluded my grasp. Perhaps that at least was a blessing. If there were no serious attempt at secrecy, should their connection merit concern? I was not at all certain what course of action to take, and I reminded myself that the greatest challenge of my life was set to begin in the morning. I could not afford to be distracted at this stage, and so I endeavoured to bury my concerns until they could be properly addressed – face to face with Annabel.

XV

The dawn brought fine weather, and as I exited the carriage with Sir Godfrey, a cheerful Captain Horwell hailed me from the quarter-deck:

'Ahoy there Mr Winter! You've brought with you a brisk nor'wester this morning! Timing couldn't be finer to blow us right past Margate and out to the Channel. I'll thank you to keep bringing us good luck!'

However, even at the hour of my departure I could think of little else but my happiness to see Annabel on the quay, alongside Lord Elsfield. Her smile seemed somewhat tempered by the early hour, but for one who had thought he might not see her face again, it remained the smile of an angel. Lord Elsfield stepped aside to grant us a moment alone.

'Annabel... Miss McNeil,' I corrected myself, though I could not correct the foolish smile which spread involuntarily across my face. 'My heart is heavy at the thought of leaving you, but gladdened that you came to bid me farewell – even at this ungodly hour.'

'I received your note, Mr Winter, and nothing on this earth could have prevented me from being here, to see you one last time and wish you well. Lord Elsfield kindly offered to chaperone me here, when mama baulked at the hour.'

For a moment we stood silent, wishing for nothing more than to extend this moment in each other's company.

'You must promise me that you will return unharmed, Mr Winter. I shall not pass a day while you are abroad without thinking of you.'

Her words were balm to my anxious mind, and all thought of the strange occurrences of the previous day was washed away. Caught up in the moment, I took her hand, kissed it, and looked into those sapphire eyes.

'Miss McNeil: never was a man more determined to return than I to you. And when I do, I shall have something most particular to ask you.'

We both smiled, and out of the corner of my eye I saw Lord Elsfield move back towards me, hand outstretched.

'Good luck, Mr Winter.' His grip seemed firmer than ever around my hand. 'Remember: all the resources you need for your mission are within you.'

My stomach churned at the mention of my 'mission', and I knew it had not been a carelessly chosen word.

'I will reward your faith in me, my Lord.'

Turning lastly to Sir Godfrey, I offered my hand and, as he grasped it, he quietly reiterated his warning of the past few days, months and even years:

'Be careful, my boy. Be *vigilant*. We are allied to Lord Elsfield now and, all being well, we will profit from the alliance. But I do not trust him, and nor should you. He would not think twice about sacrificing the whole enterprise, or indeed us, if necessary to protect himself. We know less of this scheme than we have been led to believe. Observe keenly, and give your trust sparingly. You may rely upon Captain Horwell – I can vouch for him. Others you must sound out yourself. Trust your instincts. Above all, dear Victor, return home safely. You are my only son. It is to my shame that I have not yet made our bond legal, though I have long intended it. Upon your return it shall be done. You have my word. A fine man such as you should have a fine endowment for a fine wife."

He said these last words with a smile, but through that smile I saw tears in his eyes and, to my surprise, felt the same gather in mine. He released my hand and we stood silent for a moment. Then, with a small nod, I turned and took my leave of those people I cared for most in the world – and who cared most for me – and boarded the *White Star*.

The lines were let go, and the pilot began to steer the ship out towards the Thames. I stood at the rail on the quarterdeck beside Captain Horwell, returning the farewell waves of my closest ally, my intended, and my future father. I considered all of what had been said in those short few moments. Promises to keep to a lady; a mission to fulfil for a partner and for profit; advice to weigh from a father figure. Sir Godfrey's declaration had taken me completely by surprise. I had not perceived any change in him which might have given me forewarning. I did not know how to feel, after so many years of frustration and doubt over his intentions for me. As we passed out of view of the docks, it occurred to me that I was waving goodbye to the only parent I had ever had. The sense of loss that swept over me in that moment was almost overpowering, and I grasped the rail with both hands to steady myself.

'There'll be a fair amount more of that before you find your legs, Mr Winter. We're not even in the Thames yet!' remarked the captain. I preferred to let it stand than tell him the truth. I suspected only one who had been raised their whole life as an orphan would understand.

As we reached the river, the promised breeze gathered in our sails, and I found welcome distraction in the view that greeted me. London was already wide awake with the sights, sounds and smells of commerce. Our pilot guided us skilfully down the bustling waterway, and I moved to the helm beside him to watch the comings and goings of this – the centre of the greatest empire the world had ever seen.

On either side of us, ships of every size criss-crossed the river. Lightermen transported goods in their river barges from the tall, ocean going vessels anchored in the river to the jetties and piers that stuck into the shoreline like quills from a porcupine. The cries of dockland porters filled the air, vying with each other for receipt of the latest cargoes. Coal barges carried the currency of the new age to the factories on the banks and to the steamships in the stream. The smell of their fires hung above us, mixed in the wind with that other familiar London smell: the sewers. Nightsoil men too plied their trade on barges below us, and could be smelled before they were seen. It seemed a fitting picture. From the most basic functions to the most advanced and lucrative, the Thames bore all through the heart of this great city.

Looking back over our stern, I watched the familiar landmarks of my home slide out of view. St Paul's Cathedral, the Monument, Southwark Cathedral, the Tower of London. One by one, these footholds of my world receded to the west, and I began to consider the journey before me.

With the wind on our beam we would reach the channel tomorrow evening. Another two days of good weather would take us to the Solent. We would continue our march along the south coast until Devonport, where we were to rendezvous with a detachment of Royal Marines and the remainder of our cargo. After taking on-board the arms and ammunition, which would remain under Marine guard for the duration of the journey, we would wave farewell to England, and make our way into the Atlantic and towards Africa.

The excitement of adventure filled my thoughts, but my patron's words of warning echoed amongst them. He remained suspicious of Lord Elsfield and I felt a pang of guilt, now he had declared his intention to name me as his heir, that I was keeping information from him. His suspicions were, on this occasion, well-founded, but I myself was privy to Lord Elsfield's secret scheme. That gave me an advantage over every other soul on the vessel, and I was certain that I would rather be involved in such schemes than be an unwitting victim of them. The person to beware of was, in fact, me. The scheme that was to be feared was in fact my scheme – and I would plan my actions safe in this knowledge.

Such a scheme was simply not within the purview of Sir Godfrey. Lord Elsfield conducted his business according to different rules –

and Sir Godfrey viewed his operations with a mixture of suspicion and condescension. If he did fully understand their breadth (and I suspected he did not), then he did not have the skill or perhaps the determination to match them. But I, with the advantage of my apprenticeship under Lord Elsfield, could help, and together we could build Sir Godfrey's empire until it had no equal. A happy thought struck me, and I allowed it to grow and take root. I pictured the dour office building near St Paul's which housed Sir Godfrey's company clerks. I recalled the featureless brick exterior. I imagined the sign above the white door of the main office. I imagined the lettering. And I imagined it reading 'Ramsay and Son'.

XVI

The hierarchy on the ship was simple. Captain Horwell was lord and master of the vessel. His word was law. Beneath him the first mate, Mr Daniels, ran the ship like a sergeant-major, taking commands from the captain and translating them into a stream of orders for different groups of crewmen to execute. The second mate, Mr Pritchard was in theory third in command, but in reality seemed to be somewhere around fifth in command, with no one occupying third or fourth. His orders were followed, but with a discernibly less proper level of respect. These three men constituted the officers of the vessel.

The crew of sailors numbered seventy, and was split into two equal teams or 'watches', which worked four-hour shifts between 4pm until noon the following day, so that one watch was employed above deck at all times. This rhythm of life aboard was meticulously marked out by the half-hourly cumulative ringing of the ship's bell through each shift. It began with a single chime after thirty minutes, acting almost as a countdown for that watch until their moment of release, when the bell would ring eight times. The mates each commanded a watch, with the first mate having the larboard watch and the second mate the starboard. From noon until 4pm all hands were employed on deck, and the ship was a hive of industry. Indeed, at times it seemed as though tasks were created for the crew, in order to keep them busy and out of mischief. Rigging was endlessly inspected, tested, fixed or replaced, the decks were scrubbed, metal polished, and oakum picked. This was in addition to the tasks I had known of already – servicing the sails and masts, manning the pumps, and weighing the anchor.

There was also a handful of supernumeraries on-board, excluded from the watches. These were the cook, the carpenter, and the steward: the captain's personal servant. This then was to be the total of my company for the next few days and, but for the addition of a handful of surly Marines, for the next few months. My status on-board was somewhere between unwelcome baggage and honoured guest – and seemed to oscillate, depending on the weather and the mood of the crew. Captain Horwell set the example by treating me at all times with respect, and deigning to discuss sailing matters with me, as if inviting me to offer an alternative opinion. However, even if I had been knowledgeable enough to do so, it was abundantly clear that this was merely a courtesy. From mate to second mate and then to the crew, this respect towards me dwindled, so that I chose to spend my time engaged only in conversation with the captain and his officers – a situation which seemed entirely sensible in any case.

I needed to learn the skills of the sea swiftly, in order to effect the plan which Lord Elsfield and I had concocted. With this in mind, I resolved to take First Mate Daniels into my close company, to learn from an experienced sailor. Captain Horwell struck me as too high a rank, and too closely connected to Sir Godfrey to approach. He would no doubt continue to be amiable towards me, but I did not feel I could exert authority over him as I hoped to over Mr Daniels. I could not divulge my true purpose, but I would tap the reserves of his knowledge, whilst revealing as little as possible of my own agenda.

On the morning of the fourth day, with Hastings behind us, and a capricious wind blowing us in gusts along the Channel, I made my approach. Mr Daniels stood on watch at the helm, while Captain Horwell and Mr Pritchard were engaged elsewhere. I seized the opportunity to address him alone.

'Mr Daniels,' I began, moving to his side and mimicking the stance I had seen the captain adopt beside the mate of the watch. 'As you know, I have not yet learned the crafts of the sea. This is in fact only my second voyage. However, I trust it is sufficient assurance for you to know that Sir Godfrey Ramsay placed his faith in me, and me alone to oversee this expedition.'

A muttered 'Aye, sir' escaped the seaman's lips. It was not easy to read this weather-beaten sailor's mannerisms, and I needed to be sure of him. I continued.

'Nonetheless, I do not intend to allow my seniority to outweigh your wealth of sea-going experience.'

I received the same inscrutable expression.

'In short, Mr Daniels, I should very much like to learn all I can regarding the sailing of an ocean-going vessel such as the *White Star.*'

Did I perceive a softening in his countenance? Perhaps I was making headway after all.

'For our enterprise to succeed I must know that I have the confidence of the officers on-board. The captain is in charge of the vessel, of course. However, as Sir Godfrey and Lord Elsfield's chosen officer on-board, I am entrusted with the safe delivery of the cargo to Cape Coast. I shall not presume to intercede on nautical matters, nor to abuse my position in any way: this vessel, your captain and crew come to me on the highest recommendation. But I like to view every experience as an opportunity to learn. If you are agreeable, you will become my tutor on all things maritime. I, in turn, will support you both aboard this ship and afterwards, when we return to England and I am asked for my report on the voyage. My word will go a long way, you will find – both with Captain Horwell here, and with Sir Godfrey and Lord Elsfield.'

I felt the full intensity of his gaze now. The look of disinterest had been chased away, and it was as if he was seeing me for the first time. The silence seemed to stretch beyond bearing – and I realised that I could not afford to be drawn into his game. For my authority to persist, I had to rise above these petty psychological plays.

'Do we have an accord?' I stuck out my hand for him to take. He hesitated only a fraction of a second more before clasping it in his own, leather-bound grip.

'I'll teach you what I can, Mr Winter sir.'

'Excellent. I shall apply myself wholeheartedly to your lessons, Mr Daniels. You will find me a model student.'

'Aye, sir.'

'Please,' I gestured, 'continue at the wheel. Consider this my first lesson.'

And so Mr Daniels took me into his tutelage, and I applied myself as promised. We started simply, practising knots in my quarters, and reciting the terminologies he described to me: the mainsail, the foresail, the staysails; the bowsprit, the backstay and forestay, the points of the compass, the types of sail to set, and myriad other terms which could be used to command the crew. These terms were picked up easily enough, once I could watch the crew respond to them. However, the art of sailing, he explained, was not in naming the parts of a ship: it was in knowing how to use those parts. This was what separated the landlubber from the seadog. And it was not easily taught or learned. A sailor could read the sea as a pupil might read a book, and know how to handle their ship accordingly. The slightest change in the wind might signal a mighty change in weather. Tides and currents might overpower even the most perfectly rigged vessel. A sailor must learn to read warnings in everything around him. The depth of the waves, their colour and direction, the movement of clouds. All these things were harbingers of the sea's mood.

If I wished to learn, I must observe carefully his every adjustment, and understand its cause. After the swift early lessons, this would be the slow assimilation of knowledge. If I was a good student, the full length of the return voyage might furnish me with a basic understanding, he told me.

As a result, my skills had not progressed far before we reached Devonport. It did not have the commercial bustle of London, but the naval dockyards teemed with activity. Ships of every size, from lowly gunboats to mighty men-of-war filled the space behind the breakwater, with rowboats skimming like pond skaters between them, carrying uniformed men about their business. Along the hulls sailors hung on swing-seats from the rails, scraping off barnacles and repairing below the waterline while the ships lay empty. Barrels of powder and crates of ammunition stood stacked beside warehouses, and cordage of every size lay coiled on the quayside. The air was filled with the calls of gulls, circling and scavenging around the newly-provisioned vessels. Their cries seemed to mimic those of the sailors, exchanging greetings with their brethren, bartering for supplies or sharing jokes. The ships themselves, not to be left out of the symphony, played their creaking basses as their hulls twisted and flexed in the water.

We had not long secured our mooring at the edge of the yard, when I spied our troop of Royal Marines marching smartly towards us along the harbour front. At their head, leading them through the melee, was their officer, Lieutenant Newton. This man would be my gravest challenge: a man charged solely with the safe delivery of this cargo to his counterpart in Cape Coast. A professional soldier and, on first impression, a good one. He stood around six foot tall but, due to his breadth, did not have the appearance of great height. Wide shoulders bore the epaulettes of his rank, and there was a sense of great power barely contained within his gait. I reasoned that I must watch, listen, and learn whatever I could from this man, the better to take any opportunity that might present itself.

I stood alongside Captain Horwell and his officers at the top of the gangplank as Lieutenant Newton arrived.

'Permission to come aboard, Captain?'

'Ahoy, Lieutenant Newton. Permission granted.'

Captain Horwell stood back to grant them passage as the troop followed their commander up and on to the *White Star*. Without more than a muttered order, they filed neatly onto the weather deck and stood to attention, facing the lieutenant and our welcoming party.

He stepped towards Captain Horwell, removed a white gauntlet from his right hand, and thrust it forward.

'Lieutenant Newton, His Majesty's Royal Marines, at your service, sir.' The clipped, military tone was as sharp as the sabre he held with his left hand in its scabbard by his waist.

'Captain Horwell, of the Indiaman *White Star*. A pleasure, Lieutenant Newton.'

'Captain Horwell: may I present to you Bravo Troop, 1st Company, of the 3rd Regiment, His Majesty's Royal Marines. My men and I are to provide close protection for your ship and its cargo until such time as we reach Cape Coast or, in adverse circumstances, another mutually acceptable harbour. I would request billets for each of them, and an equal share of the ship's rations. While they are onboard they are answerable to me and me alone, sir. However, I will of course look to command in our joint interests. I trust this meets with your approval?'

'Absolutely, Lieutenant. Second Mate Pritchard here will see to the needs of your men. I should also like to introduce First Mate Daniels and Mr Winter, my personal guest aboard, and the company representative.' As he spoke Captain Horwell gestured to each of us, and Lieutenant Newton stepped along our line, shaking each of us by the hand. 'I should be honoured if you would dine with us tonight, sir,' he concluded.

It was difficult not to be impressed by the military precision of Lieutenant Newton and his troop, and the sense of order and purpose they brought to the ship. In a strange way I felt comforted by their presence – as if it demonstrated to the crew how discipline and hierarchy should be observed, already assuring our safe passage. But I knew it was a false assurance. Our purposes were not aligned. I was soon to be leading these men into harm's way - and I felt my treachery keenly as I met Lieutenant Newton's earnest gaze and shook his hand.

'Certainly, Captain Horwell. The honour will be mine. I also bring a message from the Admiralty.'

'Oh yes?' enquired Captain Horwell, making no attempt to hide his curiosity.

Lieutenant Newton reached into his dispatch pouch and produced a sealed letter. Captain Horwell, caring nothing for ceremony, opened the letter immediately and, after a brief scan of its contents, exclaimed 'We're to have company on our voyage! Very well. Mr Pritchard! After billeting these men, please find me in my cabin. We'll be extending our hospitality to the captain of HMS *Cherwell* also.'

My face momentarily betrayed my horror – however, I swiftly recovered my poise, and queried in the most nonchalant tone I could muster: 'Am I to understand, Captain Horwell, that we will have the pleasure of an escort for our voyage?'

'Aye, Mr Winter. It appears HMS *Cherwell* has been assigned to bolster the West Africa Squadron, and will be making the journey alongside us.'

My mind raced. This was an unexpected and unwelcome development. My plan for ensuring a peaceful transfer of the cargo to the Portuguese allowed for our small detachment of marines, but would not stand up to a warship of the Royal Navy. As the marines were led below, and I was left alone with my thoughts, the problem swiftly crystallised. It was simple: if the escort could not be disposed of before we reached Cape Coast, the plan would fail. That gave me ten weeks to study and understand our combined operations, and to devise and implement a new plan.

It seemed an impossible task, and I considered instead the possibility of reverting to the original, sanctioned mission of simply delivering the cargo to Sir Charles MacCarthy. The option was an attractive one, requiring none of the subtlety or intrigue of Lord Elsfield's plan. Yet it also promised none of the reward. The contract would be completed, Sir Godfrey would make a healthy profit, of which I would see a small proportion; but Lord Elsfield would seethe.

At the very least it would mark the end of our association. He had brought me into the very core of his confidence, and entrusted me with a daring and difficult mission – a mark of the esteem in which he held me. There would be no question of his consolation with a job half done. He would view it as a failure, and worse: a betrayal.

My thoughts returned to the night of our rendezvous in the dark recesses of the Cheshire Cheese, and the creeping sense of fear I had felt. There was more to my motivation than a desire to demonstrate my capabilities and earn personal reward: there was also the spectre of ruin – for me and for Sir Godfrey – if I failed. We would be the next Lord Cochrane, penniless, titleless, disgraced, banished.

And so, in spite of my growing concerns, I resolved to find a way to succeed as planned. It seemed likely that my only chance would be to find a way to separate the vessels, and I turned all my efforts to understanding how this might be effected.

We loosed our mooring that evening with the tide, and put into the roads with the myriad other vessels. There we remained for the night, awaiting first light and fresh winds to set sail, and I took the opportunity over dinner to study the men whom I would need to outwit. Captain Horwell sat at the head of the table in his finest clothing, eager to show his position in society. His cravat was a poor imitation of something Lord Alvanley might have created, but more than acceptable for a ship's cabin. The steward served his best wine, and the cook his best food. The sense of occasion had not been lost on me either, and I had judged my attire to show that I was a man of both action and refinement. I wore Hussar boots – a detail which I felt would not be lost on Lieutenant Newton – and fine buckskin breeches, while my shirt was an elegant but simple white silk under my black coat. The two mates did not appear able to muster much in the way of finery, and I reflected that this might be no bad thing, as Mr Daniels would here see further confirmation that I was cut from the same cloth as Captain Horwell and his guests, and hence a man of some influence. Mr Russell, the ship's surgeon and a man of few words, sat quietly and dourly down the table. Lieutenant Newton sat to Captain Horwell's left and my right, unmistakeable in his bright red jacket, with dark blue facings overlaid with gold insignia, and the golden epaulette on his right shoulder denoting his rank. He wore a fetching red sash high on his waist and a golden gorget around his neck.

To the right of the captain sat Captain Parfitt, of HMS *Cherwell*. The naval captain held senior rank at the table, a fact immediately evident even to the uninitiated from his own splendid appearance in his dark blue uniform jacket, edged with lavish gold trim, gold buttons and large golden epaulettes. He exuded a confidence which, in the circumstances, I found disturbing. He had long, grey hair tied back with a ribbon and a clean-shaven face revealing a complexion formed in the Atlantic wind and rain. His pale blue eyes scanned back and forth constantly between his fellow diners, as if daring someone to disagree with him as he chose the topic for discussion. As we began our main course, the topic he selected was the growing British involvement in Africa.

'The attachment of the *Cherwell* to the West Africa Squadron will bring the total force up to ten vessels, Captain Horwell. As you can see, this now represents a significant establishment. The question on all our lips in the Service, however, is what is the nation's *intent*?'

'Surely the intent is most clear, sir,' responded Captain Horwell. 'The law is long passed, the squadron not only founded but expanded, and the mandate to clear the waters of slavers enshrined in Admiralty orders.'

'Is that your reading, sir?' There was a tone not unlike a tutor's in Captain Parfitt's sneer. 'Perhaps Lieutenant Newton here might offer an alternative?'

I did not envy the lieutenant his position, caught between his allegiance to a fellow naval officer and to the captain and commander of his current vessel. He himself seemed acutely aware of this position, answering rather cryptically:

'I believe that Captain Horwell's view is most likely to be shared by our government, sir – and indeed by all gentlemen in London who work to impress order and security upon our world. However, London is a long way from Sierra Leone and the Gold Coast, and perhaps no office understands the difficulty of instilling British values upon distant regions better than the Admiralty.'

Whilst I had no wish to cause the gentlemen round the table to squirm, I was both impressed and intrigued by Lieutenant Newton's answer, and found myself querying his response almost before I knew what I was doing. To his credit, he was both illuminating and again diplomatic.

'With your leave, sirs...' he began, casting a deferential glance at the two captains. 'The law is clear, and has been with us now some fifteen years; the Squadron also. However, it has not dared to abolish slavery, but rather the slave *trade*. As such, it has left all countries of the world free to continue such practices. Our island remains something of a beacon against it, but even in many British colonies, the practice continues - and where the practice continues, the demand will continue. Until that demand is addressed, we can only hope to wound the trade – not kill it. Cowper's[5] great call to arms remains mired in diplomacy.'

'But surely, sir, you cannot doubt the *intention*?' offered Captain Horwell. 'Why, the government's dissolution of the African Company of Merchants alone is a clear sign. The installation of Sir Charles, who has done so much for the free people of Sierra Leone, is another.

The abolitionists in London and abroad continue to agitate for stronger legislation against slavery, and the *Cherwell*'s posting is evidence of the Admiralty's growing commitment to that intention. The writing is on the wall for slavery under British rule.'

Captain Parfitt scoffed.

'The government may dabble in abolitionist sentiment if it wishes. It may pass further laws. It may dissolve irresponsible companies which do not do its bidding. But if it truly wishes to reach across the globe and halt the slave trade, it must do more. Even with ten ships at its disposal, the Squadron cannot hope to police a coast of three thousand miles. And when it *does* intercept a vessel, it does so with one hand tied behind itself. You see, we may credit our navy with ruling the waves, but our diplomats rule the navy. The ships of the Squadron have been forced on many an occasion to release slavers who belong to a nation which still supports the trade. Our diplomats do not dare let us upset our neighbours by policing their dark deeds.

'Our government is like a strict mother who brooks no dissent from her own children but who, on finding fault with another's child, would petition the parent, rather than take the discipline into her own hands. And so our diplomats work to have the Squadron's authority recognised by others. And they do so slowly. A few have agreed to our terms... Portugal, the United States, France and Spain... I dare say not without some coercion. But still I hear stories of ships throwing their slaves overboard rather than be taken with an illegal cargo. And if they fly a non-treaty flag, they know we cannot hold them.'

I fancied I had learnt much in my years in London – particularly of the human condition – but I shuddered at the notion of human beings jettisoned overboard like unwanted ballast. To my naïve mind, Britain had outlawed slavery, and it enforced that decision with the mightiest navy the world had ever seen. I could well imagine the indignation my beloved Annabel would express had she heard Captain Parfitt.

'If what you say is true, sir, then your mission is indeed a difficult one. It is no good bringing a prize dog to a fight, only to keep it on its lead. Remove the lead, and it will maul its opponent. Restrain it and the opponent will grow bolder.'

Captain Parfitt, who until now had focused his attentions towards the head of the table, shifted his gaze to me.

'Aye, Mr Winter – my very view. This petty diplomacy advantages no one but the slavers – and they become increasingly piratical with every passing year. Give the Royal Navy a free rein, and give Sir Charles the means to stamp his authority on the tribes slaving along the coast, and we'll have civilisation taking hold in short order.'

'God willing, Captain Parfitt, our two ships can help both those causes.'

'I believe I will drink to that, Mr Winter,' said Lieutenant Newton – and there was the sound of scraping chairs as the table rose to its feet. 'Gentlemen: to the success of our missions, and to the eradication of slavery from West Africa!'

We raised our glasses, and toasted the lieutenant's causes. I had intended only to observe my company over dinner, but it now occurred to me that my conversations with Annabel had influenced me more deeply than I had realised. As we retook our seats, and the steward refilled our glasses, Captain Horwell enquired after his two guests' recent service. I sat forward, taking great interest in their responses.

Lieutenant Newton was a veteran of the American war of 1812. He had fought in Quebec and at Bladensburg, and was mentioned in dispatches at the crossing of the Potomac. He admitted he had remained a lieutenant for longer than planned, but he hoped that in the coming engagements with the Ashanti he might find opportunity for advancement, and perhaps even to make some small profit from the gold trade whilst in Cape Coast.

Captain Parfitt was a veteran of the French Revolutionary and Napoleonic wars, and had seen action across the globe. He spoke of meeting Admiral Jervis at the Battle of Cape St Vincent, but spoke more glowingly of serving in Admiral Nelson's pursuit of the French across the Mediterranean and defeating their fleet at the Battle of the Nile. I was unable to resist the romance of these recollections, my earliest memories being similar stories from the lips of Old Jack in the scullery at Wrakeley. I pressed Captain Parfitt for details and he happily obliged, painting a picture of Nelson as the indefatigable warrior, ever daring and ever triumphant. He had been aboard *Goliath* at Cape St Vincent – an onlooker when Nelson had famously leapt from his crippled *Captain* to first board and capture *San Nicolas*, before continuing over the deck of that first prize to capture *San Jose* – but he recounted the tale with great gusto nonetheless.

'The thing about Nelson, you see my friends, is that he commanded such loyalty from his men. Who else, in all honesty, could have led his crew into the very jaws of the Spanish fleet – unsupported, mind – and still have inspired them to fight as only English sailors know how?'

A murmur of approval rippled round the table.

'There must have been six hundred guns laid against his seventy-four. Yet he did not hesitate. He knew in an instant what needed to be done, and he acted without thought for personal safety. He acted for king and country, gentlemen. Jervis said afterwards that the fate of the entire battle was decided by Nelson's manoeuvre. Perhaps he did him a disservice however.' The captain paused, and I wondered if he were about to dampen the eulogy. 'Indeed, I believe the fate of the entire war may have been decided in that moment.'

A roar of approval rose from the table. The captain had stirred his audience quite marvellously, and we each nodded and banged our fists, and perhaps credited ourselves with a little reflected glory from the triumphs of our most famous sailor.

Emboldened by the mood, I ventured to ask the captain a further question, hoping for a similar story from Trafalgar:

'And what of the later wars, sir? What action did you see after Amiens?'

His face darkened instantly. He let out a sigh, and his eyes lost all their vigour. I realised I had touched on a memory he did not care to recollect. For a long moment he said nothing at all, simply staring past me to the stern windows and out to darkness. When he finally gathered the resolve to speak, his voice was low and joyless. He paused between each sentence, almost as if the very uttering pained him.

'I was posted to *Ramillies* in the West Indies when the treaty was signed. I remained there for ten years, circling islands, avoiding gales and arresting petty thieves. It was a poor way to see out the war.'

After the brio of the previous stories, the silence that followed his words was even more pronounced. The creak of the ship's timbers, and the sloshing of waves on the hull seemed only to underscore it, and I stayed my fork as it carried a piece of beef to my mouth, not wishing to draw attention to myself. It was Mr Daniels who rescued me from the agony.

'I served in the West Indies myself, sir. A miserable posting. I sometimes wonder if we went to war with the Americans just to pull the Red Squadron from that infernal place.'

Mr Daniels had perfectly matched the tone of Captain Parfitt's lament, and found his reward as the captain turned and seemed to see him for the first time.

'Indeed, Mr Daniels? I did not know you were in the service.'

'Aye, sir. Twenty years in the service. Ninety-five to fifteen. Paid off at Port Royal, with a pat on the back and a boot in the rump. Not much for a lifelong tar to do after that but find another posting.

Me and scores like me signed up to serve in the Pacific with Lord Cochrane. I never fought with Nelson, but the Sea Wolf deserves every word of his reputation. A great leader, and just mad enough to do the thing his enemy believes to be impossible.'

'Aye,' agreed Captain Parfitt, seemingly distracted from his depression. 'Cochrane is one of the best. The sooner the Admiralty reinstates him the better. They can't abide his tone, you know. He's not so different from Nelson – except Nelson was better at biting his tongue.'

Once more I found myself drawn into the conversation. I had known Cochrane only as the unfortunate victim of Lord Elsfield's scheme. Yet here he was hailed a hero. I had managed to reconcile the notion that for a speculation to succeed and profit to be made, another had to fail. This may not have sat comfortably, but it was certainly logical. But to understand something of the individual – to find reason to admire and revere him alongside the great Lord Nelson – this made it harder to stomach the collateral damage of my ally's actions. I tried to push these thoughts from my mind as the dinner and conversation progressed, considering instead what I had learned of my fellow gentlemen. I reflected that there might be a chink in Captain Parfitt's armour.

XVII

Our nor'wester reappeared the following morning, and with full sail we set out on a broad reach for a point off the tip of Brittany.

HMS *Cherwell* took up position ahead and to our windward, the better to screen any passing traffic – though no one imagined we might encounter any of interest. The crew were again put to work on deck, and I resumed my studies under the watchful eye of Mr Daniels. My respect for him had grown since the dinner, now I knew him to be a veteran of fighting ships. I considered his reserve towards me to be no more than his rough sailor's manner, and applied myself to the letter of his teachings. Though he became no more conversational, I did during the following week gain some insight into his character, and even some praise where I had exceeded his expectations for a 'lifelong gentleman landlubber'. For a man who disliked authority almost as much as his Lord Cochrane, it was ironic that both should choose for themselves careers governed by the very strictest codes.

Captain Horwell had none of Mr Daniels' reserve, and I could not decide whether this made me more or less comfortable. My lengthy apprenticeships at Ramsay's Importers and Exporters had taught me little besides how to waste an existence through drudgery, but I had observed that those few who gave their friendships too freely often did so with ulterior motives. Had I not needed his confidence, I might have given him a cool reception. He was almost overfamiliar, and seemed at times to be seeking my approval. However, as the ultimate authority on-board, it was him whom I needed to influence above all others. Thus despite my reservations I looked to match his cordiality, and to volunteer my opinion, unqualified as it was, when invited.

Lieutenant Newton conducted a parade of arms at eight bells on the first morning before we weighed anchor and, repeating this display on the second morning, I began to understand something of the man. His marines were the epitome of military discipline, immaculately turned out in uniform, equipment and formation. I took this as a reflection on the lieutenant and the force of character with which he led. His men were well drilled and proud of attaining the high standards set for them. They seemed to understand that the peccadilloes which he identified were just that, and that the smile etched on his face as he inspected them was the true barometer of their achievement. Their officer instilled confidence in them, and they instilled confidence in each other, and even somehow in the crew of the *White Star* – who took a clear interest in the performance of their on-board protectors. Their live-firing drill off the quarterdeck was, to an untrained eye, smooth and swift; the melee exercises were both savage and controlled – and they gave me an idea.

Lieutenant Newton sought me out on our second day, as we cleared the Brittany peninsula and headed into the autumn gales of the Bay of Biscay. Whether by accident or design, he therefore found me at my most vulnerable, battling to come to terms with the unnatural pitch and roll of a boat at the mercy of a distemperate ocean. I had long fancied myself a maritime adventurer in the making, trapped on land, and had allowed myself to believe that my easy adaptation to our smooth passage along the channel was proof of my 'sea legs'. My introduction to the autumn swells of the Atlantic put paid to that fantasy – and as it turned out, I would earn my sea legs the same as every other sailor, over the course of three full days of my body resisting, and eventually resigning itself to the motion.

However, as the lieutenant entered my cabin that morning, it was immediately obvious, despite my half-hearted attempt to receive him with studied nonchalance, that I was at the beginning of this particular apprenticeship.

'Please do forgive my intrusion, Mr Winter,' he said, stooping under the doorway and standing to face me with an ease of which I was instantly envious, hat tucked under his arm and sword pommel in his hand. 'Only, I could not help but understand from some of the conversation at the captain's dinner that you have accrued a... a substantial fortune, sir, if you'll forgive the indelicacy, by trading in the London stock market.'

Through my suffering, I had failed to note the lieutenant's awkward manner and recognise his likely intent. However, having spoken these words, I began to comprehend. I murmured a suitably self-deprecating platitude, and motioned for him to sit in the seat across from mine. He continued.

'As you may have understood, I have no great fortune, but have nonetheless been careful with what little I have accrued.' A nervous smile appeared from the corner of his mouth. 'A Royal Marine lieutenant's wage is not Croesus' hoard, and the better part of it goes directly to my wife in Plymouth, so that she and our son are able to live in a *respectable* manner – no more than that.' I nodded politely, while my stomach churned and my head pounded.

'I hope to take the opportunity afforded by this mission to grow some little wealth for myself, if I am able. The gold trade continues to thrive around Cape Coast, and I intend to acquire as much as my current means can afford, and transport it back to London for some small profit. I would be most grateful, Mr Winter, if you were able to advise me on the negotiation and transactions when we make landfall.'

Throughout this speech, the lieutenant had continued to paw nervously at the hat in his lap. Affecting a smile under my sickness-induced frown, I pointed at the hat now and croaked: 'My dear Lieutenant. Lesson number one is simple. Project confidence – particularly when you feel none. Your hat merits better treatment, I am sure!'

He looked down, as if unaware of his hands' activities, and exclaimed as he saw my meaning. Placing both offending articles now squarely on the chair arms, he raised his head back to me and saw the humour in my eyes. We both laughed and the tension seemed to dissipate.

'You have me at a distinct disadvantage, Mr Winter,' he offered.

'And you me, Lieutenant Newton! Let us reach an understanding. I do not intend to remain a prisoner to Neptune's whims for our entire voyage. I shall soon resume my lessons with Mr Daniels, teaching me the fundamentals of sailing. I have noticed your exercises on deck, and they've given me an idea. I am as able a sailor as I am a swordsman – and now I find myself upon this vessel with experts from whom I might learn a great deal. In exchange for my tutelage in the nuances of commerce, I propose that you teach me some basic skills with a sword and a musket. What do you say, Lieutenant? Would this be an acceptable agreement?'

Lieutenant Newton made to paw at his hat once more, but caught himself in the act and stopped short. Looking sheepishly up at me, he replied: 'It would be most unusual, sir. There is a need for an officer to retain an air of dignity – particularly on deck, where he is on display.'

'Of course. I suggest we effect what lessons we can in the confines of my cabin, away from prying eyes. I dare say there is some theory or solo practice which can be accommodated in here. We are fortunate in having such a large vessel that our quarters are commodious. Yet I would also say that, while I am sensible of the need to project authority, the crew on this vessel is already accustomed to my tuition with Mr Daniels. It is not unusual, I understand, for seamen-in-training to receive some practical tuition. Indeed, I have read that Wellington himself attributed his success to the army training with live ammunition. Well then – my training might never be so effective as in a cramped cabin or on a swaying deck.'

I paused, not wishing to overpower my guest with my conviction. Despite his square frame, there was a fragility to Lieutenant Newton in private. His previous words – the need to retain an air of dignity – resonated in particular. My first impression had been precisely as he would have wished – of a man in perfect control of his environment. A man respected to the very point of fear. A man who might be equally at home on the floor of Almack's, or on the deck of a French man-of-war, holding off a gun crew whilst directing his men onward. For them to follow him unquestioningly into battle, this was vital, and to be maintained whenever he was in the company of subordinates. Yet in private, with equals or superiors, he allowed his true nature to surface. There were doubts. There were weaknesses – just like any other man. I realised that I could learn much from the lieutenant besides how to wield a blade.

'Forgive my reticence, Mr Winter,' he replied. 'I am certain that we can come to an arrangement.' However, it was clear that considerable doubt remained in his mind, so I continued:

'Good. Perhaps it would also give you heart to consider that merchantmen make their profits from low running-costs and large holds. Every crewman we *can* go without, we *do* go without. The *White Star* is a vessel of some one hundred and thirty feet, built for service in an age of conflict. Half of her gunports now stand empty, and the crew that would have manned them was not recruited for this voyage. This allows her to carry more cargo at less cost to Cape Coast – and will, by the by, allow you to carry more gold back. Of the skeleton crew we assembled in London, eighteen were taken by the *Cherwell* yesterday to fill her complement. That has left us with fewer than sixty all told, to handle the sails, maintain the hull, rigging, masts and yards, and keep us fed and watered. The *White Star* was not built for speed, I will admit – but with this small crew it is no wonder we make such slow progress. Mr Daniels intends to approach you to employ some of your men on the deck, such is our need, and if he were here in person he could certainly tell you more of our disposition. But the upshot is that there will at any time be precious few on deck to observe our sparring, and those who are present are likely to be fully engaged in their own business.'

I inwardly thanked Captain Horwell for keeping me in his cabin while he had received Captain Parfitt the day before. The usually affable Captain Horwell had turned quite red as his guest had made his demands through a thin veil of niceties. Still being a novice in the business of sailing, much of the terminology had been lost on me – yet I was by now something of an expert in the human condition, and there was no mistaking the tension between the two men. I had closely marked the conversation, thinking that it might prove of future use. Lieutenant Newton was not to know that I had just employed Captain Horwell's very words to persuade him – nor that I had chosen to omit his further assertion: that the *White Star* would now be quite unable to defend itself if attacked. Captain Parfitt had scoffed that with the *Cherwell* alongside, there could be no need for Horwell to 'play the buccaneer', as he put it, and he had then added insult to injury by drafting the *White Star*'s gunner, on the premise that if there were insufficient crew to man the guns, there was no need for a gunner either. Whilst I pitied Captain Horwell for this blatant undermining, I was swift to appreciate the advantage it gave me in my mission. If I could separate the *White Star* from the *Cherwell*, the merchant ship would now be more defenceless than ever.

'You make a good case, Mr Winter,' responded Lieutenant Newton, with more conviction than before. 'I am more used to serving upon men-of-war, where sailors are crammed into every space, and there is no privacy to be found on-board.'

'Well then, Lieutenant – enjoy your current luxury! What the *White Star* may lack in martial efficiency she makes up for in comfort. The *Cherwell* may have taken our sailors, but she did not take our cook, nor our stores. Let her patrol our horizon, while we make our stately way.'

It was no mean feat to eulogise in this way – not least about food – while my insides squirmed in time to the infernal rolling and tipping. Lieutenant Newton, however, was convinced. He stood to leave and I, with some effort, rose also, and offered my hand. He accepted it with a smile. Once again, face to face it troubled me to think that I was to betray this man – a good man, and a man of integrity – but I pushed such thoughts swiftly from my mind, and focused instead on regaining the ability to appear on deck.

By the end of our third day at sea I felt my appetite returning – or perhaps the need for sustenance now simply overpowered the dread of the ship's motion. In either case, I found myself with enough strength to stomach some salt beef, bread and soup. Captain Horwell, on hearing that his guest was eating again, came to visit me and convey his happiness that he would soon have my learned company once more. As was to become the norm for our voyage, he could not resist a small comment on the conduct of his counterpart, Captain Parfitt, wedged nonchalantly in-between his description of our planned sailing route and progress to date. I was grateful for it, as it confirmed my impression of a man with a desire to prove himself a great wartime captain, and faced with peace. The following days, as I ventured above decks once more, bore out Captain Horwell's comment, with the *Cherwell* busying itself around us to all points of the compass. It was exhausting just to watch, and in my privileged status as neither officer nor crew, I overheard several sailors giving thanks that they themselves had not been drafted onto the endless drill-vessel that the *Cherwell* had become. On the occasion that a sail was spotted on the horizon, the frigate would immediately come about, bend all sails, and strain all stays and shrouds to intercept them as if they were the *Santisima Trinidad*[6] herself. Throughout this endless scurrying, the *White Star* maintained its steady heading and pace. If we had accompanied our escort to investigate each sail, we should never have reached Cape Coast.

As the days turned to weeks at sea, I busied myself with my studies, both theoretical and practical, and concerning both seafaring and combat. Lieutenant Newton had pressed into my possession a copy of 'Rules and Regulations for the Infantry Sword Exercise', and bade me study it closely, while Mr Daniels had found a text entitled 'The Elements and Practice of Rigging and Seamanship'. I was for a time therefore swamped with unfamiliar expressions and, most infuriatingly, the presentation of illogical conclusions as established fact. Yet when I questioned the need for this learning, I was firmly rebuffed:

'If you wave a sword at me without knowing its parts, Mr Winter, how am I to describe to you your errors, or where I shall attack? When you know your foible from your forte, you will know at least where to guard my cuts as I call them.'

And Mr Daniels was no less scathing:

'If you send a man up to furl a staysail, only to find you have misnamed a topgallant, you had better be prepared to climb the masts and make it right yourself.'

I had thought my days of scholarship well behind me, and was reminded of difficult hours spent reading and rereading my Latin primer in the schoolroom at Wrakeley Park. The association was not a pleasant one, and instead I allowed my thoughts at times to drift back to the world I had left behind in London.

I wondered what Miss McNeil might now be doing, with the season finished. Would she return to Manchester and be reunited with her oft-absent father? Or would she remain in London, with a string of engagements to keep her occupied in spite of the exodus? I wondered if she was still visiting that strange building in Cripplegate, and regretted not having had the time or the fortitude to ask her about it. I hoped that she continued to remember me fondly, and lamented that we were unlikely to hear word from London until we reached Cape Coast – particularly with our overzealous escort chasing away any sails which might cross our path bringing news or mail. These thoughts were of course self-indulgent and sentimental – but on a long voyage with little to occupy one's mind save the study of impenetrable texts, or the practice of the day's learning, they were impossible to repress entirely. I also thought of Sir Godfrey and Lord Elsfield, and hoped I would continue to make them both proud. At my most optimistic, I considered that the successful execution of the enterprise, despite the loss of the cargo to Sir Godfrey and the subsequent insurance claim, might somehow serve to bring the two men closer together through their shared experience.

The practical element of my education was at least better for my health than remaining below, peering through the salted gloom at poorly reproduced pages. Lieutenant Newton began by teaching me the basic guard positions of the sword-drill, in the privacy and confinement of my cabin. I swiftly learnt that the key to swordsmanship was balance, and for a time my tuition consisted of little more than mimicking or reacting to my teacher's movements. This was no straightforward task for two men of six feet, where the beams of the ceiling vied at every turn to catch us on our foreheads. After one too many such incidents, the lieutenant's concern for his own skull overcame his sense of propriety, and we made our transition onto the deck where, as predicted, barely a head was turned by the spectacle of our routines. I credited him with being an able teacher, as I could not in good faith call myself a natural student, but I surprised myself with the speed of my progress. Even Captain Horwell, clapping me on the back with an overly-familiar hand after a successful practice, remarked: 'You may yet get the better of our sword master here, if you continue at this pace.'

He said it with a smile and a mischievous look in his eye, and at a volume intended for Lieutenant Newton to hear – but I took heart from it nonetheless. The lieutenant, too, gave me encouragement, and the accumulated hours spent in one another's company began to form a friendship between us, such that our sparring would now be punctuated with phrases such as 'A fine hit, sir!', or 'Well met!', or simply 'Bravo!'. The handshake at the end of each session grew warmer and more heartfelt, and I caught myself wondering, in spite of myself, if ours was a friendship which might endure the ordeal yet to come.

My tuition with Mr Daniels, by contrast, remained more formal – and in some ways I respected him for this. He was a reserved man by nature, and his praise and affection were hard won. As with my sword-craft, my sailing lessons progressed from theory, learned and tested in my cabin, to practical application on the quarterdeck and beyond.

Having learned an entirely new vocabulary to describe the parts of the ship, I found the setting and directing of them relatively straightforward, compared to the terror that first accompanied me when I was sent aloft onto the tops and thence onto the yards. Indeed, Captain Horwell had himself questioned Mr Daniels when I was directed to join the hands on the mainsail yard, suggesting it was too dangerous for a passenger (by which I was certain he meant 'landlubber'). Mr Daniels, to his credit, had deferred the decision to me, stating that he would not wish to place me in any situation with which I was not comfortable. I was determined to learn all I could about the business of sailing, however, and reasoned that not everything could be learnt from the safety of the quarterdeck. In truth, I believe I was also determined to disprove Captain Horwell's slight.

Whatever served as my motivation, I conquered my fear and, taking close note of the movements and points of contact of the sailors in front of me, ventured out onto the yard. Even though the winds were light and the sea calm, I struggled to do anything more than hold on with all my might on that first occasion, such was my body's dismay at being so high above so solid a deck. Yet I found the courage to return a second and a third time, and slowly began to take part in the duties as they were called out by Mr Daniels. I suspect that my colleagues aloft considered me by turns both bizarre and a hindrance as I laboured to play my part – yet I learned far more from the successful deploying of the sail than ever I could have done from the cold theory of the textbook. I also gained some compliments from the crew, a few of whom muttered that they had not seen a gentleman on a yard before, and that it was to my credit that I returned to deck via the shrouds rather than the direct aerial route. I took this as good-natured jesting from one sailor to another, with the implication that I was now one of them, more or less.

In time, I even received a compliment from Mr Daniels. We were running south south-west, and were well into our second week at sea. I was standing at the larboard rail, looking through my spyglass towards the horizon in the knowledge that somewhere out there lay Portugal – another land of which I had read, and longed to see. HMS *Cherwell* was once again on manoeuvres, this time to our leeward quarter, and Mr Daniels and Captain Horwell were consulting each other at the con. Hearing my name called, I turned from my fruitless scan to face them.

'Mr Winter! Captain Horwell and I were just discussing your apprenticeship as a tar. We believe it may be time for you to take the helm.'

I looked incredulously at the captain, who simply nodded his agreement, his hearty smile filling his face almost to the breadth of his hat above it. This was a moment to savour: the control, if not the command, of a ship – and what a ship! The *White Star* was a full 750 tons, and now I was to take the wheel and steer her with my own two hands. I thought back to the paintings in the dreary clerk's office in London, and saw myself as the helmsman of those ships, steering them safely through tumultuous seas. It was the daydream of a second, no more, but it added to the thrill as my hands closed around the weathered wood of the wheel.

'Very good, Mr Daniels,' said the captain, stepping away from the wheel. 'You have the con. Carry on, Mr Winter.'

He left the quarterdeck, leaving Mr Daniels to instruct me. I knew the theory well enough from the book, and from observing the helmsmen as they had taken their turns steering the *White Star*. In front of me, the binnacle contained the ship's compasses, and either one would give me our current course. On a calm sea such as we sailed today, it was a trifling matter to keep the bows pointed in the right direction, with only small adjustments needed. However, on rougher seas, such as we had encountered in the Bay of Biscay, there was far more skill and strength to maintaining a course, as the waves buffeted the bows and beam of the ship, and lifted and pushed it off course at every moment. My sole responsibility now was to maintain the course as set by the officer in charge – in the present case Mr Daniels, stood behind me, observing my every adjustment. In terms of the difficulty of the task, this was as nothing when compared to my ordeals on the yards. But in terms of responsibility, this was the pinnacle, short of becoming the captain. I chanced a sideways look at Mr Daniels, hoping to share my moment of pure, child-like joy with him. Inscrutable as ever, he stared straight ahead over my shoulder, and without moving even his eyes he saw me and said:

'Eyes front now, Mr Winter. That's a lot of vessel you're responsible for.'

Yet as I returned my gaze to the bows, I saw out of the corner of *my* eye a wry smile appear on his face, and shortly after heard him mutter:

'You're not doing too badly at all. For a lubber.'

In our third week at sea we passed Gibraltar and so left Europe behind. There was no change to our routine to mark the occasion. Somewhere over the horizon one piece of land ended and another began – but to us on our ocean voyage, it was a matter for charts, compasses and dividers. The prevailing winds slowly shifted, and whether imagined or real, I sensed that we were entering warmer climes. My swordsmanship was improving with my seamanship, and whilst I no longer followed the sailors into the shrouds, I understood all of what Mr Daniels or Mr Pritchard now commanded them to do, and why they did so. My turns at the helm had become something of a fixture, and though I had no wish to be drafted into the crew, I was now comfortable at sea, and occasionally allowed myself to imagine that I might yet become the captain of a vessel such as this. I hoped that Old Jack would be proud of me, no doubt sipping his tea in the scullery at Wrakeley Park at this very moment, to know that he had planted the seed of adventure in me that was now sprouting. The wish I had made on the hide of an elephant all those years ago seemed to be coming true.

On the morning of our twentieth day at sea there was a cry from the masthead of 'Land ahoy!' It is perhaps a reflection on the drudgery which can swiftly take hold on a ship that such a simple cry inspired such an excitable reaction from me. Yet I was not alone: Captain Horwell and also Mr Daniels made their way to the forecastle, and stared out through their glasses in the direction the lookout had indicated. My glass was also trained on the horizon and, sure enough, we all spied the promised land, looming out of the dark sea.

'The Canary Islands, gentlemen,' declared Captain Horwell. 'We will make port at Tenerife by evening tomorrow and take on fresh supplies. No dawdling, though. I have no wish to have such a volatile cargo on-board a day longer than necessary. Besides: I suspect our valiant escort might simply abandon us if we delayed him further. Let us pray he doesn't board every single vessel in the harbour in search of a pirate or slaver.'

XVIII

We dawdled. A mixture of bad luck and bad planning kept us in the Canaries for five days, and it was my misfortune to observe what effect day after day of inaction can have on a ship's crew.

At first Captain Horwell was determined to keep them all onboard, allowing only the ship's officers and a small working party onto shore. However, with the Tenerifan authorities infuriatingly slow in their bureaucracy, and in particular in their supply of fresh comestibles, discipline became a genuine concern. What should have taken no more than twenty-four hours took forty-eight and then seventy-two, and in the interim, simmering spats between crewmates boiled over into brawls, into which Lieutenant Newton's marines were forced to intervene.

It was an exasperated Lieutenant who greeted the captain, Mr Daniels, and myself as we returned on the second day from the shore – once again with some, but not all, of the necessary provisions. He would not break protocol and speak it openly, but it was writ large on his face, and the moment we were in Captain Horwell's cabin, he fairly exploded.

'I must entreat you in the strongest terms, Captain Horwell, that the crew be allowed some shore leave. The situation on this vessel grows more combustible by the day – and knowing the nature of our cargo I do not use that word lightly.'

Captain Horwell's normally jovial character had been worn thin by his exposure to the port's officials, and this confirmation of a situation he already sensed innately was as unwelcome as it was expected.

'Aye, Lieutenant Newton.' He spoke softly, with a severe countenance that did not at all suit him. 'I had hoped to be away from this wretched island by now. Do you see, Mr Winter, why we hesitate before making port in this business? A long voyage settles everyone down into a routine, and the miles slip by peacefully. Then we make landfall, and people itch for a change – for a chance to go and raise some hell ashore. If these damned Spaniards had not quibbled and queried so we would be away by now. Instead I must now form shore parties and attempt to keep the less sensible of my men from mischief.' Turning his glare towards the lieutenant and raising his voice, he continued: 'Lieutenant Newton. With your agreement I should like to detach a squad of marines to accompany the shore party. I shall leave it to your judgement what portion should remain aboard. Mr Pritchard!'

The care-worn second mate snapped to his best approximation of attention.

'You will please ready the jolly boat. I shall have to visit Captain Parfitt and attempt to calm his tempers. I fear it will take all of my powers.'

Lieutenant Newton confided to me that some of his marines were just as restless as the crew, and he was more than happy to send them ashore in rotation. Captain Horwell returned from the *Cherwell* some hours later, a look like thunder on his face. Conscious that the enmity between the two captains was crucial to my plans, I invited myself into his cabin to gauge the situation, and see if my encouragement were needed. The captain looked up from his pacing as I entered.

'Mr Winter! Good. Pour yourself a glass, man. Pour me one, too. Captain Parfitt is driving me to the bottle more surely than a harridan wife.'

Clearly no encouragement was needed. 'I presume your afternoon has been a difficult one, sir?'

'You presume correctly, sir! Damned correctly!'

He paused after this outburst however, and took the glass I offered him.

'I apologise, Mr Winter. You did not come here to face my wrath. That is mine, and mine alone, to bear. Though Captain Parfitt has much to answer for in its regard! Since you are here though, perhaps you might provide some pleasant company to wash away the memory of the past few hours in the company of a fool. There. I've said it and I hope you will not hold it against me.'

'Dare I ask, sir, what the outcome of your interview was?'

'Outcome? Oh the outcome remains the same. He's all sound and fury, that man, but he signifies very little. Very little indeed, apart from the command of a frigate of His Majesty's navy. He sounded off about the inconvenience of extending our stay here. Took great pleasure in insinuating we were intentionally delaying – that we were on a pleasure cruise to warmer climes, with no inclination to complete our mission. The nerve of the man!'

His glass danced toward and away from his lips as each new indignity was related, never quite reaching the safe haven of his mouth before being tossed alarmingly back out in another expansive gesture.

'Reminded me frequently of the singular importance of his own mission to rid the coast of piracy and slavery. Made it quite clear that he considers his escort duty little more than an addendum to his orders. The pompous oaf. No wonder he waited until we were out of port before pressing our men into his service. He already had a full complement, but intends to take more prizes in his first season in West Africa than Nelson took at Trafalgar! He'll not last three months – I'd stake this ship on it. He'll overstep his authority and be court-martialled before the London season begins!'

'But he will remain with us here, sir?'

'He will remain. He has to remain! He merely wishes me to know how little he cares for his duty. He made a fatuous threat to leave tomorrow, with us or without us – but I do not believe even he would be so foolish. Nonetheless, I shall not give him any reason whatsoever to abandon us. These are not the most dangerous waters in the world, but I should still not like to pass through them with our depleted crew and a cargo which makes us little more than a floating tinderbox. Do you happen to know how we have fared today with our Spanish antagonists?'

I had not truly believed that Captain Parfitt would abandon his post, much as I may have wished it. He was reckless, but recklessly *ambitious*, and that would prevent him directly disobeying any part of the King's orders. Nonetheless, Captain Horwell's report gave me further heart. The *Cherwell* would need only the slightest excuse to detach itself from its convoy duties and follow its captain's favoured course to fortune and glory or, far more likely, disgrace and ruin. On the matter of provisioning, I was at least able to offer Captain Horwell some solace.

'I believe Mr Daniels has managed to agree an acceptable price for the final provisions, sir, and that we should be able to complete the business in the morning.'

This unexpected news brightened his face considerably, and he replied with something approaching his more usual tone.

'Excellent! This is good news indeed! Let's see what Captain Parfitt finds to rail about now!' He strode to the cabin door and bade Mr Pritchard and Mr Daniels join him to prepare the ship for departure by the following afternoon.

But we did not depart the following afternoon. A great still came over the island, and all flags and sails dropped lifelessly down against their masts. Captain Horwell was sanguine about the situation: calms befell every voyage sooner or later, and there was no point expending energy railing at the winds. However, the glint in his eye suggested strongly that his counterpart upon the *Cherwell* would be doing just that.

The calm did not lift the following day, nor indeed the day after, and the tensions amongst the men could be felt by all, simmering just beneath the surface. Lieutenant Newton took the opportunity while his men were occupied ashore to advance my swordsmanship and musketry, and I reciprocated, teaching him all I knew on the business of importing and exporting. I was happy to be able to instruct him, feeling that I had gained far more from his lessons than he had from me. But when I arrived onto deck later that evening, I found myself once again the pupil. The lieutenant was in the act of re-boarding the ship from the jolly boat, and behind him came a marine closely escorted on each arm by another. Their steely-eyed expressions were enough to inform me of a crime, even before their commander spoke.

'Take him to the brig! I don't want to see his face again until we leave this blasted island!'

I had not witnessed his ire before and, my curiosity overcoming my sense of propriety, I invited him to join me for a drink in my cabin – an invitation he readily accepted.

'I'm afraid I rather lost my temper on deck earlier, Victor.'

'I should imagine it is good for discipline for the men to see that temper.'

'Oh, quite the contrary, my friend. I think you misconstrue my meaning. I am angry with myself. If one of my men is injured, it is my fault: I have not trained him sufficiently to carry out his duty. If he is poorly turned out, that is my fault. If he acts incorrectly, that too is my fault. My men are my family, and a reflection of me. I have a duty to them as much as they have a duty to me.'

'These are admirable sentiments, Robert, certainly. But no commander can answer for every act of his men.'

'And yet they will answer with their lives when I command?' He looked up from his glass and fixed his eyes on mine. His words were calm but unequivocal, and I found myself incapable of a riposte. 'You may yet best me with a sword, Victor. But a man who can command an army of swords need never wield one himself. Discipline has its place; fear may drive a man to do terrible things. But love and loyalty alone will make him do great things.'

He held my gaze a moment longer, before returning to his wine and to lighter conversation. But his words had found their mark. This man was far more than a master-at-arms.

The following morning I awoke to the familiar sounds of activity on deck – of creaking oak, billowing sails, and of gainfully employed sailors. Our journey had resumed and there would be no more interruptions until I fulfilled my mission for Lord Elsfield. My guilty conscience had turned the plan over and over in my mind, but could not find another way which ensured the safety of the *White Star* and its crew, and left Sir Godfrey and myself unthreatened by Lord Elsfield's ire at home. To do nothing now would put everyone at risk once the Portuguese appeared. With the heart of one who knows he must do something unconscionable to prevent something awful, I now awaited my opportunity.

XIX

It came soon after we sighted the Cape Verde islands to the west. With storm clouds gathering ominously off our larboard bow, *Cherwell* signalled that she had spotted a sail to our north and would come about to our starboard to investigate. Captain Horwell passed a comment that it was 'damned foolish, with the sky set as it is, and nightfall not far off', but made no attempt to stop her, knowing only too well what little effect it would have.

Even Lieutenant Newton, bound to Captain Parfitt through the service, could not summon up the zeal to defend his colleague. As they beat their way up past us into the wind, he shot me a look as dark as the sky.

'Do you see over yonder, friend Sancho, thirty or forty hulking giants? I intend to do battle with them and slay them,' he muttered.

It took me by surprise, but in a moment I had it, and smirked at the observation. 'With their spoils we shall begin to be rich...', I replied.

'Our very own Don Quixote, Mr Winter, tilting at another windmill.' He gave me a weary smile and turned away. 'Captain Horwell! With your permission I shall detail my men below decks.'

Captain Horwell nodded, and instructed Mr Daniels to prepare for the incoming weather. 'All hands' were called up onto the deck, lifelines were set, topgallant masts struck, and storm staysails set and reefed. I took a position alongside the officers on the quarterdeck, and stared hard at my oncoming moment.

The sea was beginning to rise in anticipation, and in the distance I could see the white tops of waves where they were whipped up by the wind. The sun was off our starboard beam and seemed to be plummeting headlong towards the horizon. It cast an eerie glow onto the storm clouds, which appeared almost orange in the twilight. I could feel the wind changing as we came towards it, turning from our stern to our larboard quarter, blowing now at my cheek and lifting the sea spray onto my face.

Not for the first time, I found myself in a state somewhere between excitement and terror. A storm at sea is an awe-inspiring sight. On a ship one is constantly reminded of one's insignificance in a vast ocean and unbroken sky. Yet when presented with the full might of nature's fury, that calculation is redoubled, and I watched the sailors working on the yards with something approaching envy: they were occupied body and mind with their duties, and had no time to ponder the coming ordeal. I was sadly not so preoccupied, and instead free to contemplate my fate at the hands of the approaching storm which now covered the whole horizon in front of us.

We would be drenched both from above and below, and we would be pummelled – tossed about by the wind and the towering waves as a naturalist tosses a beetle he has captured in his jar. The ship would roll and dip, and its timbers would creak and moan with the stresses, testing any man's resolve as it threatened to break apart. But the worst fear was of lightning. We should be desperately unlucky, but there remained a chance that we would be struck by lightning as we crested a wave. There would be no surviving such a strike. Our cargo would see to that. All we could do was pray for deliverance.

Yet amongst this rational fear, there was also excitement. This was the opportunity I had waited for these past weeks. The *Cherwell* had once again rashly deserted her post in the vain hope of a prize, and was even now working away from us aft. Meanwhile the sky darkened, partly from the sun, now cut in half by the horizon, and partly from the mass of storm clouds that reared up to our bow, blotting out any light which the rising moon or stars might have offered. As we pushed underneath those clouds we would be enveloped by the peaks and troughs of the sea, becoming invisible to the *Cherwell* for lengths of time. Even without my intervention, it would be difficult for the two ships to remain in close contact. My task was to lengthen those odds further. The thrill of anticipation ran through me as Captain Horwell explained his orders to Mr Daniels for the night watches. I listened closely, better to understand where my moment might arise.

I had thought I had experienced storms in the Bay of Biscay. However, nothing had quite prepared me for the ferocity with which this one broke over us. It was as sudden as the sun's disappearance, which made no spectacle at all of its departure, leaving us in total darkness. The wind rose to a howl across my swiftly sodden face. Soon after, a cacophony of rain, sheeting down with enough force to make a man's head bleed. The *White Star* was set for the onslaught, yet still we were sucked with terrifying speed into the teeth of the gale. Sheer walls of water reared up above us. Becalmed in their lee, we scaled them slowly, teetering on the angry crests, plunging down into their wakes, burying the whole forecastle into the base of the following peak. It took all of my nerve to remain on deck, one hand firmly gripping the rail while I waited for the captain to go below. Finally, satisfied that there was no more to be done, he nodded in grim approval, and handed the con to Mr Daniels. Turning to me, he revealed an expression of genuine surprise. In the roar of the storm I believe he had quite forgotten my presence.

'Mr Winter!', he bellowed, putting an arm around me and bringing his face in close so as to be heard, 'You are still on deck! Whatever for, sir?! No good will come of this storm! You should head below with me and weather it in your cabin.'

'Thank you, Captain, but there's a peculiar thrill in being up here. I should like to remain a while longer.'

His features morphed in confusion and then acceptance – the whole effect made almost comic by our enforced closeness.

'As you wish, Mr Winter. But have a care and clap onto the lifelines. I could not bear to break Sir Godfrey's heart anew with news of a second snatched away from him.'

He turned to go below, leaving his words to linger with me despite the raging storm. It was not the first time I had been told of my patron's loss, but with each reminder its significance seemed to increase. The effect upon him must have been truly profound, for all who knew him to remark on it. Was it really possible that he might feel my loss as keenly as his beloved wife's? I had never before believed that I was anything more than a charitable project to him. He had invested in my advancement, certainly, but he had not invested in *me* – in who I was, or who I might want to be. But with his behaviour since Annabel's ball, and his words at the dock, I found myself questioning what I thought I knew.

The ship's bell stirred me from my introspection. Mr Daniels had called for eight bells, signalling the beginning of the first night watch, and the *White Star's* deck emptied like the water which poured over our bows and down through the scuppers. He detailed several crew to duties about the ship, but was careful to station as many as could be spared below decks, the better to preserve their energies and health through the night. Able Seaman Jones, a gnarled and serious character, was briefed and put at the helm – no simple task on a sea as violent as ours – and I steeled myself for my task. The *White Star* wore only one ship's light this night: the storm having broken before the main topmast lantern was due to be lit. In this weather, Mr Daniels would not risk sending a sailor up to the topmast – particularly with our complement already being so scant. We relied solely upon the lantern alight at the rear of the quarterdeck to guide the *Cherwell* to our position. In normal weather even this would barely have been necessary, as with only starlight and the merest sliver of a moon we had been able to see and follow each other at a distance of perhaps two cables. However, Captain Parfitt's impetuousness in spite of the coming of night and the storm had now put at least two miles between us, and had played into my hands perfectly.

I was now alone on the quarterdeck but for Jones and Mr Daniels – and their eyes were fixed on the bows of the *White Star* and the path in front of her. I nevertheless waited until Mr Daniels made his round of the deck before making my move. As soon as he began on his path away from us, I reached for a boarding pike, secured against the taffrail and, steadying myself with one hand still on the rail against the pitch of the boat, swung with all the force I could muster at the lantern. It was no good for me simply to extinguish it, for it would be seen and it would be relit. My task was to decommission it beyond repair. The casing was stubbornly tough, as perhaps I should have expected, but the glass panels yielded far more easily, and with the roar of the storm to mask my exertions I made quick work of it, pausing between each swing to ensure I remained unseen in my treachery. It was not an elegant plan, I knew, but I took solace that the simpler plans were the ones less likely to unravel.

My work complete, I threw the now damaged boarding pike overboard, the better to conceal the true cause of the lantern's destruction. It would inevitably be attributed to the storm when discovered, and with the task of sailing the ship safely through the night paramount in the officers' minds, I did not expect that it would be repaired or replaced before the morning. My heart racing from the exertion and the thrill of having succeeded, I stumbled with the roll and pitch of the deck towards Mr Daniels, who had halted his patrol by the forward lookout, a miserable and dangerous posting on a night such as this. Bracing myself for the drenching I was sure to receive, I approached the pair and did my best to engage them in any manner of conversation I could – for while I had convinced myself that the lantern was beyond immediate repair, I did not intend to leave it to chance. Every minute I could keep Mr Daniels distracted and unaware of the lantern's demise was a minute longer that the *Cherwell* would search fruitlessly in the dark for us. When his patrol resumed, I was particularly careful to engage him whilst he regained the quarterdeck, hoping against hope that my naïve questions of sea-manship would distract him. Sure enough, he slowly turned upon reaching the con and resumed his position behind Jones, none the wiser to the sabotage that stood only fifteen feet aft.

Around four bells the exhaustion from the mental strain of my subterfuge, combined with the physical strains of remaining on deck in such apocalyptic weather forced me to go below and seek shelter and rest. I had done what I could to compound Captain Parfitt's in-competence. The morning would reveal its effect.

I was awoken by the thudding of an army of feet on the deck above me, and by the accompanying shouts and continual ringing of the ship's bell. Even though the seas still buffeted the ship, the clam-our of the crew seemed to overpower them. My immediate thought was that the *White Star* had been broken by the storm: perhaps dismasted, perhaps worse. Taking the sword I had been learning to wield, I steadied myself against the rolling and battled up onto the quarterdeck, fighting all the while the rising terror in my gullet as I contemplated abandoning ship in the midst of a churning sea. As I emerged however I was relieved to see that, to my landsman's eye, all looked as well as could be expected, given the situation. The sky was lightening to the east, though the sun had not yet appeared, giving hope of a better day ahead. The sea had in fact lost much of its anger, but the ship still bucked and rolled with the wind. The whole crew appeared to be on deck, and made little concession to the weather as they rushed about tightening lines, gathering sheets, and shouting and pointing at something off the larboard quarter. Still gathering my senses from my sudden awakening, I crossed to where Lieutenant Newton, Captain Horwell, and his officers stood, hard against the larboard rail of the quarterdeck.

'Gentlemen!' I hailed, doing my best to show that I was at ease with the conditions, in keeping with everyone else on deck. 'Might I ask what this commotion concerns? Is all well?'

Mr Pritchard shot me a look that could have done murders. Mr Daniels replied, without taking his eyes from the sea.

'All is not well, Mr Winter. A man has fallen overboard, and a brave lad...'

'...Millette. Benjamin Millette,' interjected Mr Pritchard, staring at me as if it were my doing.

'...has gone in after him.'

'It is a terribly brave thing to have done,' declared Captain Horwell, who like Mr Daniels refused to face me as he spoke. 'I fear we may have lost two men instead of one in these seas.'

I joined the officers at the rail and, gripping it tightly against the sway of the vessel, peered over. A shout from the maintop caused me to look up, where a lookout pointed out past us into the water. Following his direction, I saw a head bobbing in the swell and, not far from him, another, with a rope trailing back from him all the way to the *White Star*. The shouting from the crew rose as one, urging Seaman Millette towards their crewmate. It did indeed seem a doomed mission, even now that he was so close to success. The sea was rising and falling all around him, pushing him away from his quarry as if it were a sentient and malevolent entity, toying with him as he toiled in vain. In that moment, absorbed in the struggle playing out before me, the existence of Neptune and Triton seemed certain. The sea could not be just a liquid mass of minerals, to be whipped, scolded or flattened by other natural forces. It had a will of its own. It demanded a sacrifice, and it would not be denied.

And yet Seaman Millette was determined. I remembered my studies at Wrakeley, and the men who resisted the will of the gods. Hercules, Ulysses, Jason. It was *possible*. We all sensed it on-board. Millette closed on the stricken sailor. Even as a wave came to crash over them, his arms locked around his shipmate, and a cheer arose from the deck.

'Dear God,' said Lieutenant Newton, almost too quietly to be heard. 'I think he's got him.'

'Dear God,' echoed Captain Horwell.

Mr Daniels and Mr Pritchard said nothing, but both hurried down to the waist. Mr Daniels stationed himself at the rail, while Mr Pritchard took command of a team of sailors. As one, all heaved on their rope, and slowly the two swimmers were pulled, despite the raging seas, back to the ship.

'Make way there,' cried Mr Daniels. 'Gibbs! Free the main cargo boom! Webb! Lend a hand there! Rig a sling. Make haste now – make haste!'

The change was remarkable. From a gaggle of unruly men, crying out to sea in desperation, to well-drilled sailors, acting as vital cogs in a machine. Millette approached the *White Star* and the boom swung out a sling into the swell for him. He tied it around the rescued sailor, released him from his grasp, and the crew lifted him up out of the water and onto the deck. A pair of men immediately released him from the sling and carried him below to the surgeon, while the boom was swung out again for Millette. He was received on deck with a hero's welcome, the officers allowing their crew this moment of undisciplined release from the drama of the morning. Captain Horwell walked slowly down to the sailor and, as the crew quietened for him, spoke to the deck:

'Seaman Millette. That was an uncommon brave thing you did. Uncommon brave. There is a man below who owes you his life, and a ship who owes you a debt of gratitude. We are all brothers at sea – and this morning you have worked admirably in trying conditions. Mr Daniels!'

'Sir!'

'A double ration of grog for each man, if you please. Mr Pritchard?'

'Sir!'

'Please be so good as to lend this man your berth for the day, and relieve him of his duties if he can be spared. We must keep such men fit and well. They are a credit to the ship. Have him taken below to the surgeon. When he is discharged, he is to report to me in my cabin. Mr Daniels – please join me on the quarterdeck when you are ready. I believe the worst of this storm is behind us and it is time to assess the damage and find our errant escort once more.'

The captain was correct – the storm continued to lose its force even while we stood on the deck. The lookouts were doubled in the tops, the better to peer out to the horizons, and I hoped against hope that my small act had been enough. Taking a liberty with my status, I followed the two men and, remaining a respectful distance behind them, listened attentively to their conversation.

Mr Daniels and Captain Horwell made a complete circuit of the ship, noting rigging that had loosened, stays that needed tightening or replacing, and bolts and other fastenings that warranted further investigation. The damage was remarkably light, considering the ferocity of the storm, and the captain was quick to complement the First Mate on his handling of the ship overnight. The smashed lantern on the taffrail was acknowledged without a hint of suspicion, and a course of action to fix it agreed. The two men then steadied themselves at the rear of the quarterdeck and set about taking readings to determine our position. It was only then I realised that the sun had still not risen despite the colour of the sky. I reached into my coat pocket and examined my timepiece. It read seven thirty, and I was certain that at this latitude we should be past sunrise.

'Damn!' Came the muted exclamation from in front of me. 'There's no joy with this fog. Can't see a damned thing. Can't see the sun in the sky, let alone that fool of a captain aboard the *Cherwell*. What do you have, Mr Daniels?'

'Nothing here, Captain. It's the *harmattan* that's done it, for certain. Won't be able to make any observations until it's cleared.'

'Damn, damn, DAMN!' The captain was silent a moment and lowered his head, brow furrowed in thought. 'You had the first and third night watches, Mr Daniels.'

'Aye, sir.'

'Who was at the helm for you?'

'Seaman Jones, sir.'

'For both watches?'

'Aye, sir. He's our best helmsman, and he don't scare easy from a storm.'

'Please ask him to join us on deck right away. I should like to know how we held course and speed through the night.'

Mr Daniels paused. 'Seaman Jones was the man overboard, sir.'

A look of disbelief passed over the captain's face.

'Good God.' His voice dropped to a murmur before recovering. 'Then it falls to you – until we can get some sense out of Jones. What were your observations of our sailing over the night?'

'As I observed in-between my rounds, sir, all was well and as you commanded. The *White Star* pitched and rolled, but I saw no great yaw. The waves came straight onto us: we didn't need to alter course over them. It was hard to take a log of our speed in the conditions, but with reefed and furled sails we could not have pushed more than four knots, even in that blow.'

'The *Cherwell* was directly abaft us when the storm hit. She should have come alongside us in the night. With the seas the way they were, and with just a binnacle lighting the ship, she could have gone straight past us without knowing.'

'What should we do, sir? With the wind died down we can make sail in any direction.'

'Either way, sitting here won't do us any good,' the captain concluded, raising his voice to assume its customary authoritative air. 'Nor will it get us clear of this infernal fog. Continue our course south, and spread as much sail as she'll bear. Let me know when we have sky enough for observations. The con is yours, Mr Daniels.'

'Aye, sir.'

'Ah – Mr Winter,' said Captain Horwell, turning and pretending to notice me for the first time. 'I trust you managed some sleep last night? The ship has held up very well to her battering – but alas, until we are able to see the sun and confirm our position I'm afraid all we can do is continue our planned course to Cape Coast. If Captain Parfitt knows his business, he will find us. Perhaps you will accompany me in paying my respects to the surgeon, to see how our two seamen fare.'

'It would be my pleasure, sir.'

As we made our way below deck, the captain explained:

'It ain't really a fog, of course. No fog looks that colour. The *harmattan* is the local name for it. The wind whips up sand from the Sahara, hundreds of miles inland, and blows it out to sea. Puts the fear of God into simple folk. We'll have that eerie orange glow for a sky until we're past it. But if we can speak to Jones and Mr Pritchard's helmsman, we should have a decent idea of our position all the same. Provided Jones is up and speaking.'

We reached the surgeon's cabin, and after a knock, entered.

Mr Russell, the ship's surgeon, turned to look gravely at us, and I knew immediately that the news was bad. Millette sat wrapped in blankets on a chair in the corner, huddled over a mug of tea, staring blankly past me at the wall of the cabin. Jones lay still on the table.

'I'm afraid Seaman Millette's efforts were for naught, Captain,' he declared coolly.

'You mean...'

'I'm afraid so, sir.'

It was the first corpse I had seen, and I found it strangely difficult to take my eyes from it. The 'it' that had only moments before been a 'him'. The him who had been the subject of such a titanic human effort only minutes before. The silence surrounding him was as still and final as his fate.

Captain Horwell stared at the body of Jones a moment longer, then nodded good day to the surgeon, and retired, with me in his wake. He would not get the information he sought after all.

The sky did not clear all day, and that night the stars too were obscured, so that for fully twenty-four hours we sailed blindly on, lookouts searching in vain for a light or sail on our much-reduced horizon. I began to believe that I may have succeeded in separating our vessels. The morning of the following day brought clearer skies, however, and by noon the captain gathered the two mates, Lieutenant Newton and me into his cabin.

'Gentlemen. I have bad news. It will affect us all in one way or another. I have checked and double-checked my calculations, and I am in no doubt. We are off course. Some forty miles off course.'

Disquiet filled the room. We looked around at each other, incredulous. I worked to compute what this would mean for our chances of encountering our escort, and indeed, for fulfilling my mission. Mr Pritchard spoke first.

'Seems an awfully long way to be off, sir.'

'Indeed it does, Mr Pritchard. Given what information I have from you and Mr Daniels, it seems impossible. But there it is. I regret that no one around this table is able to suggest when or how this has occurred – and that perhaps the only man who might have shed some light on it is now in his final resting place on the seafloor.'

The looks continued between us, but there was an edge to them now. An unspoken accusation.

'I have spoken to the surviving helmsmen, and I have tested our navigational equipment for accuracy myself. It will remain a mystery, it seems,' continued the captain. 'I must therefore assume that the *Cherwell* has passed us during our forty-hour wandering to leeward, and is currently somewhere off our larboard bow. We will therefore set a course east-southeast, so as to rejoin our intended route. I need hardly remind you all of the sensitive nature of the cargo we carry, nor of our current paucity of crew. Our escort may have been skittish, but it was an escort nonetheless, and a King's ship will have been a damn sight better at warding off curious captains than we will be. Suffice to say I shall be taking a much keener interest in our course for the remainder of the journey! That is all, gentlemen. Good day.'

For a captain who normally invited comment and conversation, the silence he had commanded hung awkwardly in the air, and as we filtered out of his cabin the sombre atmosphere followed us. Lieutenant Newton suggested I join him for sword exercise on the quarterdeck, now that the storm had abated. After the captain's scolding, however, my conscience was not in the mood for such frivolities. I was about to refuse, when something in his whispered tone struck me as strange. I had, I realised, only known this man for six weeks – and yet such was the nature of the confined life at sea, even upon a large vessel, that one swiftly formed understandings, and even friendships. My dealings with Mr Daniels had led to a mutual understanding and respect, but it dawned on me in that moment that I now considered Lieutenant Newton a friend. I turned to look at him, already knowing that I would see an expression of the most earnest sincerity.

'Do you think now is the best time?'

'Indeed, Mr Winter, there is no better time.'

'Then, as in all matters, I shall readily accept your counsel.'

We made first for my cabin, to retrieve my sword. As I turned to leave, sword in hand, I was surprised to see that he had hurried in behind me, closing the door with great care. He held up a hand to quieten my question, and I caught the words in my throat, offering instead only an interrogative frown.

'I hope you will forgive the presumption,' he whispered, drawing close to me, 'but I have something most singular to impart that I would not wish others to hear.'

'Very well, Lieutenant,' I replied, as cautious now as I was confused. 'Please. Go on.'

'The death of Seaman Jones may not have been an accident. When I visited the surgeon's quarters yesterday the unfortunate sailor was still on his table, and as a man who has seen such injuries before, it was apparent to me that his neck was broken. The surgeon was loath to discuss the matter with me, but being plain I had already reached my conclusion, he inclined to confirm it.'

I felt my heart quickening. I did not yet know what this news meant, but foul play of any sort aboard this ship was a cause of alarm to me.

'It is possible Jones broke his neck as he fell. Perfectly possible.' The repetition served only to convey his doubt however, and he could not find any other words to add credence to the suggestion. A silence drew out between us as we both considered a more sinister cause.

'And Jones was the helmsman during the storm?'

'The majority of it – yes.'

'And when we emerged from the storm, *Cherwell* was nowhere to be seen.'

'I believe your thoughts pursue a similar course to mine, Victor.'

'As you say, it's possible that we have simply been unfortunate. However, it is also possible that there has been foul play – and foul play towards a nefarious purpose. Have you shared this information with anyone else?'

'No. Though it must be assumed that Captain Horwell has been informed.'

It had not occurred to my racing mind, but he was right, and that raised a new set of alarming possibilities. I could not at that moment find anything more incisive to say. I was acutely aware of my own secret agenda on the *White Star*, and that I had already taken steps towards its fulfilment. Added to that, I now considered the possibility that someone else on-board – perhaps more than one person – had another, equally secret agenda. Whilst it ran parallel to my own I could consider myself fortunate – yet it could diverge at any moment and undermine me or, worse by far, expose me.

The realisation hit me like a blow to the belly. I hastily thanked Robert for confiding in me, and asked that he leave me to contemplate what this might mean. I needed to be alone to control the rising terror in my throat.

Foremost in my thoughts was the captain. If he knew of the circumstances surrounding Jones' death, why had he not shared this knowledge – or at least pursued it by questioning the crew? But then – whom would he question? Who was under suspicion? I was reminded of Sir Godfrey's parting words: 'We know less of this scheme than we have been led to believe. Observe keenly, and give your trust sparingly.' I had flattered myself that I was privy to Lord Elsfield's plans, and knew the whole of it. I had been careless, and had not considered that there might be others beside myself with hidden agendas. I hoped that it was not too late to discover them, and prevent them from damaging my cause.

I was glad to now be alone. My hands were shaking and my eyes staring wildly. I knew that I had to find a way to conceal my anxiety, or it would betray me as surely as any man's denouncement. Yet it was not easily done. If Jones had been killed, he had been killed to conceal something. Something he had seen, or something he knew. And that meant that whoever was behind it was prepared to commit murder to achieve their goal. If the aim had indeed been the same as mine – to shake off HMS *Cherwell* in the storm, and then to conceal that aim – then it was possible that this agent was tasked with the same goal as me. I tried to find some consolation in this possibility, but could not. I had stepped on-board this vessel in London confident that I could complete my task. I had raised myself from modest means, despite the unwarranted reticence of Sir Godfrey. I had raised capital, built a small fortune of my own, and laid plans to double the return on this assignment. I was resourceful. But I had not dreamt of harming anyone through my actions. I was not a killer.

Was this what was expected of me? Was this what Lord Elsfield thought me capable of? Surely not. Had I given him reason to believe it? I searched my conscience. *Had* I harmed people? No one had died through my actions. I had justified my involvement in the Poyais affair to my satisfaction at the time. There was little doubt that many – most even – would have invested in the scheme whether through me or through another agent. Yet they *had* invested through me. I was the face of that deception. I thought of Ball-Hughes: good-natured, trusting Edward. I had taken advantage of his trust. Certainly many others had done the same – and no doubt some of them had been as close to him as me. But despite this knowledge, I found little solace. The misdeeds of others did not justify my own: they coalesced together in a morass of low morality. The same morality that lied to the faces of friends, and to the innocent. To the face of Sir Godfrey.

The thought stopped my mind dead. Was I not even now planning harm against him? Against my own patron? And against Robert Newton? To place this *entire vessel* in danger? The nausea grew. I felt it rippling through my stomach, tugging at my gullet. I had justified my plans to myself, reasoning that there was a course of events possible where Sir Godfrey would experience no loss. The same might even be possible for Robert Newton, Mr Daniels, and the whole crew. Yet it might not. I was putting lives in jeopardy, and flattering myself that I would be able to control the inevitable chaos. And now there was a new, unexpected element to contend with. Now there was an unknown force working to an unknown end somewhere aboard. I could not make my hands stop shaking. The realisation that I was no longer in control of the situation rocked me with all the force of the earlier storm. The nausea broke through me. I felt my stomach heave, and my legs folded underneath me. Crouched on the floor like an animal, I retched and retched again, the acid bile burning my throat as it passed. Another realisation: I had never been in control. Another wave. I had wanted so desperately to believe I had mastered my fate. The fate that judged me worthless, and left me to freeze to death, nameless, outside Wrakeley Church. I had needed to believe that I would never be at another's mercy again. I had rebelled against Sir Godfrey – the closest I had come to a father – because he refused to recognise my independence, even as he supported me.

I had convinced myself that I had fought my way up through sheer determination, earning my opportunities as they came. But it was all delusion: that I could control so many independent forces, so many unknowns. I had been chaperoned throughout. Now I had walked, wide-eyed, into a situation beyond the reach of Sir Godfrey or Lord Elsfield to help. Now I had to find a way to extricate myself, and those around me, from it.

The responsibility weighed heavy. Even after the retching subsided, my legs struggled to lift me. I reached my desk, and sat there, trying to form a plan. Slowly the fog of panic ebbed, and logic took over. I had one more task to fulfil for Lord Elsfield's mission, and I realised then that I could not go through with it. I could not incapacitate the crew and convince myself that it was for their own safety. I had been deluded. The risks were too great. I could not be responsible for the fate of so many souls. If Robert Newton was responsible for an injury to just one of his men, then to risk the whole ship and its crew in a confrontation with *pirates* (I forced myself to acknowledge the word) was not an equation I could balance.

I longed for someone to confide in. In London, Lord Elsfield would hear my most base instincts and not criticise them. Miss McNeil would hear my deepest fears without judgement. Even as I considered this, I felt ashamed, realising that Sir Godfrey should have been the first name to come to mind. And yet our dealings over the past few years had slowly moved us apart. I would turn over a new leaf upon my return. If I could extricate myself from this situation, I would work more closely with him, and eschew Lord Elsfield's labyrinthine schemes. But here, I was alone. My regard for Robert both tempted me to speak to him, and also prevented me, knowing that he would not be able to forgive my involvement in such a plan. It would ruin me, Sir Godfrey, and Lord Elsfield to confess all now. And perhaps I could not even be certain that he was not the killer. I forced myself to think it, though I could not in truth believe it.

I moved to my cot, if only to change my perspective on the room and perhaps also my dilemma. I felt the eyes of the murderer boring into the back of my skull, yet every time I turned my head, he was gone. I saw the faces of the men on the vessel. Unwitting victims of another man's scheme. Moths dancing blindly around a fire. Millette, Jones, Pritchard, Daniels. Russell, Horwell, Newton. Marines, sailors, murderers. As I passed by each man he raised a hand, but with my eyes firmly fixed on their faces I could not tell whether the hand was open in greeting or closed around a dagger. The faces spun around me, with others now joining them. Alvanley, Ball-Hughes, Gregor McGregor, Sir Godfrey, Elsfield...

I awoke with a start, and shot out a hand to steady myself where I lay. The nausea was back, clawing its way up from the pit of my stomach. I sat up, the better to fight it, and considered what had woken me. Sir Godfrey had vouched for Captain Horwell above anyone else. Yet it was he and only he who had once worked for Lord Elsfield. Could the captain be once again in his employment? This time my legs responded. I stumbled from my cot and thrust my head from the window. In between convulsions, I could hear Robert above me, instructing his men on parade. Men he was drilling to protect the ship, and us – me – from the very danger I would place us in. I had made up my mind. I would abandon Lord Elsfield's scheme. Without my further action we might yet evade the waiting Portuguese pirates, and mine and Sir Godfrey's good name would be secured. Whatever consequences were to be faced with Lord Elsfield, I would face them. They were preferable to the abandonment of morality, and the betrayal of a friend. And I would keep a very close eye on Captain Horwell.

XX

'...It is a most troubling situation, Lieutenant. One which, with no disrespect to you or your troop's professionalism, we are ill-equipped to manage.'

'Of course, Captain. I quite agree.'

'Any attack on the *White Star* cannot be allowed to provoke cannon fire. That leaves only your men and the fighting spirit of the crew to defend the ship.'

Mr Daniels, Mr Pritchard and Mr Russell sat silent and glum in Captain Horwell's cabin whilst he lamented the situation of which we were all painfully aware. The atmosphere was not helped by the stifling heat and humidity, the like of which I had never imagined, let alone experienced. It dampened appetites, and made me long for the frozen Thames of yesteryear. We each picked at our food despondently, though whether more from the heat or the exhaustion of nerves it was hard to tell.

We had proceeded now without an escort for four weeks, through fickle and contrary winds. Christmas and New Year were celebrated with all the cheer of a seemingly cursed ship – thought no one would speak that superstition aloud. We had held to the southerly edge of our planned course, staying as clear of the coast and local craft as we dared. However, as a result we had seen almost no sails during our long journey, and when we did Captain Horwell proved loath to investigate. There was a genuine dilemma aboard the *White Star*. Were a ship a democracy, we might have oscillated wildly between chasing every sail in the hope of finding our wayward escort, and running out to sea at every whale or shark fin we saw on the horizon. As the captain himself had observed, that policy would have left us still several weeks from the Gold Coast, instead of now lying some three hundred miles to its south west, and a few of us daring to hope that we might yet discharge our mission without further incident.

I was not one of the hopeful. I knew what waited for us in these waters – yet I could not raise an alarm without exposing my involvement in the scheme. Even if I could tell someone, I no longer knew who to trust, nor how to direct them any better than our current course. Whilst Captain Horwell continued to arouse my suspicions, I increasingly perceived guilt in every crewmate's behaviour. The *White Star* had become a lonely, joyless place for me, and the tension of weeks at sea without an escort, and with a murderer lurking in our midst, had worn on all of us who knew.

Our supper was interrupted by a sailor from the starboard watch, who appeared at the door in a state of some agitation.

'Begging your pardon, Captain, but Mr Russell's presence is requested in sick bay.'

'My apologies gentlemen,' said the surgeon without a moment's hesitation. 'I hope you will excuse me.' He wiped his mouth and hands with his napkin and stood, asking our visitor as he approached him: 'What poor soul has come to harm now?'

'Fletcher and Webb, sir, from the starboard watch. Complaining of fearful agony in their bellies.'

'If they're drunk spare them no sympathy, Mr Russell!' cried Captain Horwell from the table. 'I'll not have drunkards on my ship. Nor layabouts!'

The surgeon did not reply, but nodded a swift adieu and ducked under the doorway, following the sailor.

An hour later another two men from the starboard watch were in sick bay, plus one of Robert's marines. By four bells of the first watch I knew beyond a doubt. Someone had taken my plan and applied it themselves.

There was only one thing, Lord Elsfield had told me with his usual confidence, which could be guaranteed to bring a ship to its knees. It did not matter whether it were merchantman or man-of-war. From the largest three-decker ship of the line to the lowliest lugger, every ship needed a functional crew, and every crew needed sustenance. Thus with just a small amount of the right chemical, applied to the cook's evening meal, the *White Star*, *Cherwell*, or even HMS *Victory* herself could be rendered utterly defenceless. After the realisation of my folly, I had thrown my vial overboard, ridding myself of any temptation to reconsider. But here, unmistakably, were the hallmarks of that same intervention by another's hand. Mr Russell's sick bay swiftly filled and then overflowed and the surgeon, mystified and increasingly panicked by the outbreak, advised those unaffected to remain above decks, the better to avoid any miasma. Before the morning watch had begun, that contingent comprised only those of us who had dined at the captain's table the previous evening.

There was little the captain could do in the circumstances but hoist the yellow pennant, warning other ships not to approach for fear of infection, reduce sail, and attempt to handle the vessel slowly and clumsily with his makeshift crew of four. Even with the wind now directly behind us, blowing us toward Cape Coast, the going was difficult. Captain Horwell attempted to raise our spirits by noting that there was now no great hurry – even when we reached port we would be required to sit in quarantine until we were declared no longer infectious.

Yet this was scant consolation to us as we worked through the long night, accompanied only by the ghoulish moans from a company of unseen souls suffering below our feet, and the smell. The smell of a ship's crew, poisoned to the point of immobility. Some attempted to reach the heads – but it was a token effort. We each attempted to keep our minds from these things by busying ourselves on deck – and indeed there was much to be done, taking observations, working the shrouds and stays looser or tighter, and making what small adjustments we could to the sails.

I felt like a leaf tossed in a gale – utterly unable to control my own direction, driven by the whim of a malignant force which acted unseen around me. In London I had sat proudly in the sunlit canopy, basking in my own ignorance, only too happy to believe I had mastered my own destiny. I had built a small fortune from my ability to understand and anticipate the world around me. But here at sea I had no such advantage. Once again I sensed the eyes boring into my back – the unknown hand on my shoulder and the furtive movements in the shadows. I worked to keep this panic under control, aware that even while I hauled on a backstay or stood at the helm, I might be under observation from my tormentor – from a man who must now know that I had reneged on Lord Elsfield's plan. For them to have shown their hand a second time, they must have determined that I had missed my opportunity to act. I caught myself staring at Captain Horwell's back, considering the case against him. He had certainly had no love for Captain Parfitt. He had plenty of opportunity, as captain of the ship, to roam where he pleased, poisoning a pot in the galley, or murdering a sailor while alone on the quarterdeck. He had once been in the employ of Lord Elsfield – why not now?

Yet for all this, Sir Godfrey had vouched for him above all others. Mr Daniels remained sullen, but dutiful and diligent, and had taught me a great deal through the voyage. He too could be my nemesis, but it did not seem likely. Even Mr Pritchard, second in everything, dogsbody to the officers, fell under suspicion. I could not forget the murderous look he had given me the morning Seaman Jones was lost. He seemed a man driven by anger and choked with envy. I could only fully discount Lieutenant Newton. Perhaps this was a weakness in me: a need to feel that there was at least one man above suspicion – one man I could call friend.

As I dwelt on Robert's exoneration, I realised that I had convinced myself I was pitiable – yet I was advantaged more than almost all on-board. The sickness that had struck down a whole crew must even now, with its cause unknown, be terrifying to all but the instigator. Equally, what was to come next, as I was now sure it would,

would also cause panic. But my knowledge removed that terror for me, and perhaps gave me power after all. I was not yet certain how, but I reasoned that, much as in London, knowing what was to occur in advance must allow me to manipulate events to my advantage.

XXI

They came that same morning, emerging wraith-like from the mist. They might have been tracking us for some time, waiting for the yellow pennant to invite them in. Not having a man to spare for lookout duty, they must have seen us long before we saw them off our starboard beam. Even had we seen them sooner, there would have been precious little to do in our handicapped state to avoid or repulse them.

Captain Horwell gathered his pitiful remaining crew around him on the quarterdeck - even Mr Russell, excused his duties below.

'Any craft not showing an ensign on this coast to a yellow pennant can only be one thing. We do not have the crew to enter into a chase, and even if we did, she would surely outrun us. The *White Star* is built to stand and fight, not to run. But with our escort vanished, and an entire crew taken ill, we cannot hope to win.'

'We still have time to load several cannon, sir! We could give them a rolling broadside that would make them think twice!'

'No, Mr Pritchard. I applaud your spirit, but as I have said before, our cargo is too volatile to invite a duel with the great guns. Lieutenant Newton – you are charged with the close protection of the *White Star* and her cargo. What is your assessment of the situation?'

Robert tensed his jaw, drew in a deep breath and, having exhaled forcibly, replied.

'It's no good, Captain. I wish I could advise otherwise. I could issue pistols and muskets to every man below, but lying in their cots they'd still be slaughtered like rats in a barrel. We six here on deck could stop the first handful of boarders, but I fear that would only get their blood up. They'd give us no quarter after that, and we'd be signing the death-warrant of fifty more souls.'

'Who's to say they'll give any quarter anyway, Captain?' cried Mr Pritchard. 'They're pirates! They follow no code!'

'As you say, Mr Pritchard,' cut in the captain, keeping his voice low and steady. 'But I agree with the lieutenant. To offer any sort of contest would be futile, and would only invite harsher treatment. What little mercy we may hope for is best ensured by our timidity. We will hold our course, remain in plain sight, and keep our weapons sheathed. If we are fortunate, they will see how few crew we are able to muster, and understand that our contagion is real. They may choose to stand off.'

Mr Pritchard said no more, but retained the same look he had worn the day Seaman Jones died. He wanted all to know that this was not his chosen path.

As if on cue, the mystery vessel broke out a red flag from its mainmast, with a skull's profile and crossed bones underneath. No one spoke on the quarterdeck, but even I felt my heart sink – and I had known as soon as the sail had been sighted. The sense of failure gnawed at me. The strength of my allegiance to Lieutenant Newton and his King's mission had grown with my admiration for him and his values. It was now total. Perverse as this emotion was, I could not change it. I despaired that my own plan had come to pass. These were the mercenaries whom Lord Elsfield and I had employed in order to stage the transfer of the cargo – though I increasingly wondered how much we had agreed, and how much I had allowed myself to be drawn in to his already-formed plan.

There was a puff of smoke from the larboard bow of the pirate ship, followed shortly after by the boom of a gun, and the sight of a cannonball skipping past us some distance off our bow. We were being told to stop in the unmistakeable language of the sea. Something within me snapped. I could not stand by and allow events to take their predetermined cause. I turned to Robert and begged him join me on the forecastle, away from other ears.

'These pirates will surely take our cargo, Robert.'

'They will – though it pains me to admit it even now.'

'And we are agreed that to attempt to prevent them will only lead to bloodshed?'

'I cannot see how it can do otherwise. My first duty is to my King and my country. My second is to my men. If I cannot protect the cargo, I must protect them. I will not sacrifice them to satisfy my honour.'

I had already resolved to intervene in events – but even so his words stirred me. Honour was a term I had rarely encountered with Lord Elsfield. He had labelled it a troublesome concept which paralysed great schemes, too often valuing method over outcome. Robert had taught me differently. Honour was his very essence. It flowed in his veins. And here he was, sacrificing his honour for his men.

'Then we must find a way to sabotage their prize. If we cannot prevent them taking it, then can we not reduce its value to our enemies?'

My eyes bored into his, hoping that I might have sparked some possibility into flame.

'It would have to be subtle. The sabotage would have to go unnoticed until the *White Star* were safe beyond the horizon.'

'Agreed. Longer, if possible.'

He broke my gaze, and looked out to sea with narrowed eyes.

'I cannot think that they will concern themselves with uniforms or more food than they themselves need.'

'As you say. Their hold is too small to take all our cargo.'

'Having no gold, their likely prize will be our muskets, swords, bayonets and powder. We cannot easily render a blade inoperable. A single musket might be possible, but not the hundreds we have in the hold – and certainly not before that ship of criminals is upon us.'

'Which leaves the powder.'

'Which leaves the powder,' he repeated. His eyes returned to meet mine as he spoke, and now I could see the fire in them.

Begging the captain's pardon, Robert and I raced below decks to the main hold, and began levering the barrels of powder open. I was ready with a sack of sand from the stores, and watched as he carefully poured and mixed in the contaminant. British powder was really Indian powder, he explained, and free-poured fine powder was its apogee. It gave a man perhaps twenty extra yards range over his enemy. But it had to be measured and packed down correctly. Too little powder would make the bullet drop short, while if it was not packed down it would only fizz, and not fire at all. If too much was packed down, the pressure in the barrel would make the musket explode. Consistency in the powder was therefore key to a consistent shot – and our sand would prevent that. We did not need to affect all the barrels – simply enough that there would be no consistency. Any man who had seen a musket explode would quickly pour less powder – or throw the weapon aside.

However, we had only worked sand into three barrels before a cry came down the hatch. All able-bodied men to present themselves on deck or be murdered where they stood. We had run out of time, and we had not done enough. Looking anxiously at each other, fixing the lid back on the third barrel, I said what needed to be said.

'I will go with them.'

Incomprehension passed over my friend's face.

'I will go with the pirates. I'm a rich man's son. I'm a ransom just asking to be claimed. My chance will come and I'll finish the job.'

His expression changed. He understood, but now he looked at me as if I were mad.

'Victor: they are *pirates*! We'll be lucky if they don't scuttle the *White Star* and leave us all to the mercy of the seas. You would be mad to entrust your safety to them – let alone think that you will be able to escape and finish this.'

'If they think there's money in me, they'll not dare harm me. As you say: they're pirates!'

I flashed him my best approximation of Lord Elsfield's confident smile. I needed him convinced. What he could not know, and what burdened me with guilt, was that these pirates were mine and Lord Elsfield's mercenaries. I found little joy in my proposal, but reasoned I should be welcome enough on-board their ship as their employer. It was not the plan we had agreed, but they should have no reason to demur. Once away from the *White Star,* I would find a way to gain access to the gunpowder. But Robert was right: the loyalty of a pirate was not something upon which I could rely – particularly not if they caught me tampering with their cargo – and I fought to stave off the fear which threatened to overwhelm me as the reality dawned. I was to be alone on a ship of pirates, and lives depended upon me deceiving them all. I wondered how I had ever convinced myself to undertake this enterprise. I had been younger then, I supposed. Young and naïve.

We climbed back up to the weather deck. On the final stairway, I turned to Robert and extended my hand. 'This may be the last time we meet, Robert.' He looked at me with surprise. 'It has been my honour to know you, sir.'

Grasping my hand, he replied: 'It has been *my* honour, Victor.'

'We must assume this powder will find its way to the Ashanti. But I will not fail you, Robert: it will be spoiled. You *must* get word to our army to stay at range.'

He held my hand a second longer, and then we proceeded up the stairs.

As we emerged through the hatchway, speaking slowly and loudly so as not to surprise anyone, we were set upon by rough hands which lifted us almost bodily upwards, and thrust us towards our companions. The pirates were exactly as I had imagined – a rag-tag crew in an assortment of colours and clothes, but all armed to the teeth and lean, hungry-looking African men. Captain Horwell, his two mates, and Mr Russell were stood straight as ramrods against the rail on the quarterdeck, guarded by four men with pistols in their hands and swords in their sashes. There was a strange air somewhere between indignity and terror among them, as their captors harangued them in an alien tongue. More and more boarders were pouring over the side behind us, swiftly taking control of the ship.

'I'm afraid your little ruse will not work with us, *meus amigos.*'

The words, in a foreign and yet distinctly European accent, made us all turn, to see a short man in an elegant purple frock coat, buff-coloured nankeen trousers and black half-boots striding nonchalantly onto the *White Star's* gangway with his right hand tucked behind his back and his left resting on the hilt of his sword. As the wind clawed at the lapels of his jacket, I could see black facings over a clean white shirt running down into a bright crimson sash.

'Where is the rest of your crew *por favor*?' He mounted the quarterdeck steps as he spoke, coming to a halt directly opposite us. He had a swarthy complexion which spoke of years beneath a tropical sun, and long, dark hair tied back in a ponytail and hidden under a surprisingly well-kept black bicorne. From its top, as if to add inches to his stature, sprouted five long, bright feathers segmented into blue then yellow then black. He wore a wicked smile which reached impossibly broadly across his face, and even when his satisfaction with himself seemed to ebb, one side of the smile remained, morphed into a deep sneer.

'Please.' he emphasised, inclining his head to Captain Horwell.

'The crew of the *White Star* are confined below decks, quarantined. This is no ruse. We here are the only survivors.'

'Convenient, no, that your officers are spared this... *contagio*?' The smile conveyed supreme confidence – which he could quite justify, knowing as he did how the ship had been disarmed.

'It is customary in his Brittanic Majesty's Navy – even his merchant navy, *sir*, for an officer to introduce himself.' Captain Horwell gave the honourific all the sarcasm he could.

'Of course! Where are my manners? My name is *Capitao* Carvalho, of the *Kraken*. I see you have already met my crew. Whom do I have the honour of capturing?'

Captain Horwell bristled at Carvalho's easy insolence, but had no advantage to hold over him, other than an innate sense of superiority.

'Captain Thomas Horwell, of the *White Star*. I offer you my sword, *Captain*,' he said, presenting the weapon in its scabbard.

'Yes, yes,' replied Carvalho, dismissing the gesture with a wave of his hand. 'And I say something about honour, and insist you may keep it, under oath not to do anything stupid.'

We were stunned into silence by the manner of the man. If Captain Horwell were indeed the secret agent of Lord Elsfield, he was acting the part of the insulted commander to perfection. Captain Carvalho however appeared to take no notice, continuing with his sneer: 'You know, it strikes me, *Capitao*, that what I see here bears all the signs of a mutiny. All officers on deck, hopelessly incapable of sailing their ship. All sailors locked down below, and perhaps your men,' he pointed at Robert, 'keeping them there under close guard. I wonder, if I were to go below myself, how many new recruits I might find.'

Captain Horwell turned crimson. His eyes bulged with rage. 'If that is the low opinion you have of an English captain and his crew, sir, then I entreat you to go below and breathe deeply. The sooner you are struck down and I have my vessel back the better.'

'No, no!' cried Carvalho – and now the full smile returned. 'I have no desire to go below. No, I can smell quite clearly from here what is indeed *down there*.' He gestured to the deck beneath his feet. 'But I do enjoy a little sport – and there is no greater sport in life than to rile an Englishman. No, I prefer the fresh, sea air. I was raised on the coast, you know – in the Algarve. We *Algarvios* say we have the sea in our blood.' He paused, seemingly lost in his own reverie. I could not decide what to make of this strange man. He was an enigma. Eccentric yet pragmatic. Flamboyant yet sinister. He was the first Portuguese I had met, and I wondered if this was their general character.

'Now tell me, *Capitao*,' he resumed. 'Exactly what sort of cargo do you carry – and where to?'

'Ballast, Captain Carvalho. We carry ballast and are bound for Accra.'

The smile broadened. 'Is that so, *Capitao*? Well – then you are riding low with all your ballast – perhaps you have need of lightening. We wouldn't want you to ground on a shoal on your way in.' He turned to address a group of his crew, many of whom were now glaring spitefully at us. He spoke quickly, in an alien language which I took to be a local patois. The group headed down the stairs to the forecastle. Turning back to us, he said: 'Of course, should my men find anything other than ballast below, that would indeed be a surprise. It would make me wonder, in fact, whether you could be trusted, *Capitao* Horwell: you and your precious honour. At present, I am undecided what to do with my prize and her crew. Any little thing might make my mind up. I have the good of my men to think of as well, of course. They do love a spectacle. Where I am from we have the sea in our blood – but where my *men* are from – well. They like to put men's blood into the sea. Brings the fish swarming, you know. And especially the *tubaroes*.'

'What on earth are the *tubaroes*?' I whispered urgently to Mr Daniels.

'If my Spanish is to be relied upon, he means sharks, Mr Winter. Man-eaters.'

Horror ran down my spine. 'Gunpowder!' I blurted out, almost without thinking. Captain Horwell and the two mates looked at me with utter disgust – but I could not care. The time for deception had passed. The captain knew well enough what we carried. His performance was purely for the benefit of any report which reached London. This was to be a random act of piracy – not a prearranged act of subterfuge. Yet I did not know how far he was willing to take his deception. He was, after all, a mercenary – a man for whom killing was employment. He was currently in the pay of Lord Elsfield – but we had not specified how he should treat the crew or the boat. Wrapped up in the all-knowing confidence of Lord Elsfield's scheming, it had not even crossed my mind that human lives were at stake. From the comfort of our leather seats, in the wood-panelled safety of White's, it had simply been a game – another clever plan which proved my merit. But now that I knew them, somehow all that mattered was ensuring the safety of these men.

Captain Carvalho, smile seemingly permanent on his face, turned to face me.

'And to whom do I now have the pleasure of speaking, *senhor*?'

I straightened myself, the better to convey my importance as head of this expedition.

'My name is Mr Winter. Mr Victor Winter, representing Sir Godfrey Ramsay and Lord Elsfield. I am empowered to conduct all negotiations on their behalf on this expedition.'

'Well then, *senhor* Winter, my apologies for not addressing you sooner. So I am in the presence of a knight *and* a lord of the British Empire?!' He removed his hat and bowed extravagantly to me. 'Tell me: how would Sir Godfrey and Lord Elsfield suggest you *negotiate* with a man who has taken control of your vessel, and who has your crew held at gunpoint on their own deck?' Sarcasm oozed from his every word and gesture, but this only stiffened my resolve.

'I would tell him that there was still a tidy profit more to be made or lost, if he had the vision.'

Captain Carvalho's smile melted into his sneer with the mention of profit. I had his attention.

'I am a rich man's son. If you take me with you, there is a ransom to be made. If I choose not to come with you, you get nothing.'

'I think, *senhor*, that we may take what we want here,' his smile had returned, and he gestured around the ship, master of all he surveyed.

'Your crew may go down into the hold. If they mask their faces and stay away from our men, they may not die. No one here is equipped to stop you stealing our cargo. But if I do not wish to be your prisoner, I need only press a pistol to my head, jump into the sea, or simply run at one of your crewmen with my blade. Or perhaps I will refuse to sign my name to your letter. It is hard to threaten a man who is prepared to die.'

I even surprised myself with the audacity of my words. I felt my determination to fulfil them waver, but found it reinforced by the reactions they drew from my shipmates.

'The gunpowder is mine, *senhor* – and anything else I find of interest. So what is it *you* want?' He spoke slowly now, and with eyes narrowed. He had enjoyed playing out a little drama on the deck – perhaps for his own gratification, perhaps for the morale of his crew. He had not anticipated this turn of events. He did not yet know what game I was playing.

'I will come with you, and sign your ransom letter, if you leave this ship and this crew unharmed.'

I saw the eyes of my shipmates widen. I focused on controlling my trembling hands by my sides.

Captain Carvalho stared at me another moment. He looked left, to his crew even now heading down warily into the forecastle hatches. He cast his gaze over and around the *White Star*, as if assessing its value to him. He looked back to his own ship, with perhaps only ten men still aboard. At last he returned to face me, and once more his whole face broke into a broad, wicked smile.

'*Senhor* Winter – your masters chose their man wisely: you have a talent for negotiation. I do believe your shipmates owe you their lives!' He followed this declaration with a string of further instructions to his crew, who pressed into our group and extracted me from it.

With a man on both arms, I was pulled over to where a gangplank now stood lashed between the two vessels, the better to transfer the loot down to the *Kraken*. I realised I was leaving my colleagues forever. At that moment, despite knowing that within their number lurked a murderer and a traitor, I felt more attached to them than ever before. Once again I was leaving behind people I had grown to care about and, in Robert Newton, a friend who also cared for me. I turned to give my shipmates one last look, and then I was manhandled along the gangplank and aboard my new home.

XXII

'You are not what I had expected, *senhor* Winter – I must confess.' Captain Carvalho neither smiled nor sneered now, as we sat in his cabin aboard the *Kraken*, its hold heavy with muskets and gunpowder from the *White Star*. '*Senhor* Elsfield's man was clear on some details, less clear with others. But you will now conduct the talks with the Ashanti yourself?'

'And you have arranged the meeting?'

He nodded. 'As agreed.'

'Good.'

For all our fine manners, I remained wary of him. From the comfort and safety of the drawing rooms of London, the proposal to rendezvous with a pirate ship had seemed full of romantic adventure. Now that I faced the grim reality of a ship full of mercenaries – men who built their fortunes through savagery – there was nothing in the least romantic about it. The pirate's life was brutal, and a world away from the leadership espoused by Robert Newton. The only discipline was that enforced through the lash. The prospect of profit was all that held the men together. That, and the energy and charisma of their captain. I would not trust him – but I nevertheless perceived and respected his ability to control the crew.

He too must have been aware of the delicate balance – for he berthed me in his own cabin. This both sent a strong message to the crew, and prevented any hotheads taking the law into their own hands. For on any ship, pirate or otherwise, a captain's word was law – this much I knew.

The *White Star* had long since disappeared off our starboard quarter, creeping timidly away on its course like a whipped pup. I had felt my jaw clench and a lump form in my throat as I watched it go. It felt as if my pride had somehow been tied to her, and lost with the ship and her crew. Yet there was no time for sentimentality. Despite being granted passage on the *Kraken*, I was not safe. Indeed, I wondered when I might once again encounter that sensation. I had succeeded in assuring the lives of the crew, and in minimising the loss to Sir Godfrey. It now remained for me to minimise the damage to king and country – and to do that I needed to earn and maintain the captain's trust, and to reach an understanding.

'I am grateful to you, Captain, for maintaining the charade of my capture for the benefit of the ship's company.'

'Not at all, *senhor*. A little theatre is good for the soul. I presume there can be no ransom note in truth?' He even looked a little disappointed as he spoke. Nonetheless I was glad to re-establish the inviolability of my position.

'I am afraid not, Captain. The sale of the goods to the Ashanti must go ahead, and I must conduct the talks. If you were to hold me ransom, I fear you would only attract the further interest of his Lordship – not to mention Sir Godfrey and His Majesty's Navy.'

'And I would rather maintain an alliance with this man. It is a good line of work,' he said somewhat glumly. 'I thought this would be the case, and I applaud you on a fine show of bravado – but it really was unnecessary. Much as I should like to add such a fine ship as the *White Star* to my fleet, she is not at all suited to my line of work. The Royal Navy patrols these waters with ever increasing zeal, and one tends to run rather than fight against His Majesty's men-of-war. The *White Star* is not a runner.'

For all his faults, I imagined that Captain Parfitt's *Cherwell* could indeed make short work of the *White Star* if necessary.

'And, whilst my crew have many fine qualities – chief of which, you will have noticed, is intimidation of *Europeus* – they are not first-class sailors. It would require all my time and all my crew to manage such a vessel – and I am very attached to my *Kraken*. Not that they would ever have stayed aboard anyway,' he added, straightening in his seat and reaching for his glass of Porto, recently liberated from the

White Star. 'They are very suspicious of disease – particularly *branco* disease.'

'Even so, Captain, it had occurred to me that you might choose to make a "spectacle" of the crew and the vessel... I believe that is what you suggested. I was anxious to prevent it.'

In the blink of an eye, my host leapt to his feet, banging his fist with all his force on the table, sending the half-full glass over onto its side. His eyes glared as he spat:

'Is this what you make of me? Because I fly this flag, you presume to know me? Do you assume all soldiers to be murderers? Or all Africans savages? This is what a London education will do. Fill a head with simple stereotypes, so a man need not observe for himself, think for himself, judge for himself. Easy to condemn me when you do not know my story. Well *Capitao* Carvalho is no slaver! He is no murderer of the defenceless. I have *honra.*'

I shrank back from the heat of his anger. I had enraged where I had hoped to charm. It had not occurred to me that there might be such a thing as a pirate with a conscience. I had assumed the occupation to be a broad one, enveloping its practitioners in all manner of maritime crime. But now I considered it, his reproof was entirely logical. A man engaged in robbery might yet baulk at cold-blooded murder, even if it promised to line his pockets.

'I apologise, sir.' I held up my hands in a gesture of supplication. 'You are entirely correct to take me to task. I spoke without thought. I have judged a situation – a man – without knowing him. I ask your pardon.'

'Yes, well. You see what you have made me do, *senhor* Winter? A waste of particularly fine Porto. Mindlessness and mindless loss. And we are poorer for it.' He was returned to his former, eccentric character – yet I perceived that my offence had been real, and my apology was genuine. A man's honour was a curious, private thing, I realised. It might allow him to do things considered vile by another, whilst proscribing the slightest of peccadilloes. Having claimed worldliness for so long it was only now, in realising my innocence, that I felt I was seeing the world as it truly was. I had much to learn, and often from the most unexpected sources.

'If you will allow me, Captain, I should like to earn my passage – and, I hope, your respect.'

He looked at me with pure incomprehension.

'I am sorry, *senhor* Winter?'

'No, Captain Carvalho. It is *I* who am sorry – I presumed to know you purely from the flag you fly. I should like to know you better. And I imagine there is no better way to do that than to be one of your crew.'

Once again, I spoke with more courage than I felt, but found in its very speaking some strength. If I was to gain the trust of all onboard the ship, and access to its cargo, I could not remain in the captain's cabin. And I had learned that I could not rely on my preconceptions of these men to understand their minds.

Despite his reservations, the captain was glad to have another pair of hands, and put me to work with Kwabene, his bosun and most trusted crewman, inspecting and replacing rigging. Our lack of a common tongue was no barrier to understanding when a rope was frayed, a stay slack, or a spar rotten. There was an honesty and pride to his work which he shared with the sailors on the *White Star*, in spite of the very different roles of their vessels. I began to consider that the world might not be quite so straightforward a place after all, and that people – be they English, Portuguese or indeed West African – might be both savage *and* skilled, simple *and* cerebral. People were not absolutes, to be judged dependent on their grasp of English, or their numeracy – though it might be far simpler to consider them so. Grace walked hand in hand with ugliness, and strength with weakness.

Perhaps it was this dawning realisation which softened my view of my shipmates, and lowered my guard. The next day I received a timely reminder. I had become somewhat immune to the glowering and muttering of my crewmates as I went about the ship with Kwabene. Perhaps I had convinced myself that as the captain's guest, I would be respected. When the mutters turned to outbursts I shot a glance or two at Kwabene, but when he remained unmoved I presumed these were either not directed at me, or not signalling malcontent.

It was only when a big, bruising specimen of a man stepped between my chaperone and me on the forecastle that I realised I would have to defend myself. Despite my height I had always been slender. John Jackson had taught me to rely on movement during the sparring sessions in his gymnasium. My challenger was my equal in height and reach, but had the bulk of a grenadier guard sergeant-major. He was stripped to the waist and his chest and arms bulged huge before me. I would have to avoid his main assault altogether, or I would be knocked down in an instant. My best hope was to manoeuvre around him, keeping him off-balance and swatting at my shadow. All this consideration took place in a moment, as he issued what I presumed to be his challenge. His gesticulations brought cheering from his shipmates, who clearly still relished the promise of a spectacle – particularly one which might see the captain's pet taught a lesson. I looked for Kwabene, hoping at least for a moderating voice, but he was already absorbed into the ring of onlookers around us. There was no time for panic – only for action, and I duly dropped down into my pugilist's crouch, guard up in front of me. My pose drew a roar of derision from my audience, who perhaps expected me to simply stand and take what was coming. Happy to confound them, I focused on assessing my opponent's abilities as he moved slowly forward, a malevolent smile drawn on his face.

I took a step to my left – not too swiftly, as I did not yet wish to reveal my hand, but far enough that I forced him to adjust. His turn was slow, as I had hoped, and I began to circle just fast enough to stay out of reach of his striking zone. It was already apparent this was not the type of fight he or the crew were used to, and it took less than a minute for his frustration to show. He began by throwing hopeful punches, though I kept diligently ahead of his left swing or his right jab. Then he attempted an impossible right hook which, flying past me, left his entire back exposed. I flew in with both fists to his kidneys. His back arched up in anguish, and he staggered momentarily to regain his balance before coming roaring back, leading with his right elbow. I had been expecting something suitably ungainly, but nonetheless remarked to myself that an elbow was not within the rules. Stepping backwards, I stumbled over a rope which should have been coiled away. His eyes lit up, and he closed on me, right fist pulled back in anticipation. I had time only to duck as the massive bludgeon came flying over my head, but took the opportunity to throw a quick left jab into his ribs as it went past. I did not anticipate the knee which rose up and caught me a glancing blow between my chin and right shoulder. Again I stumbled, and this time he was on me much more quickly. Twisting to regain my balance, I saw a left hook come thundering towards me and raised an arm to meet it. Even blocked, its force was quite extraordinary, and pushed me back further. I was dimly aware of the onlooking crew cheering as I staggered and then, with a flailing jab into thin air, I tumbled to the deck.

I now knew there was more to this fight than Broughton's rules, and was hurrying to regain my feet when I felt a blow like a sledgehammer connect with my back. At first I thought he had swung a tackle block at me, but realised as I sprawled in pain that it had simply been his enormous boot. He stood above me now, grinning again, and in no rush to take his next swing. I feinted to roll one way, and he swayed with me, his boot taking aim. I reversed my motion and jumped rather groggily to my feet, to see another left hook bound for me. Remembering the previous one, I chose to duck rather than block, and again attacked his midriff with two jabs which I now feared might be only token resistance against this Goliath. Mindful of his knee also, I stepped back in time to see the very trick repeated into thin air. An idea occurred to me as it reached its zenith, and I charged at the single-legged man with all my might. The impact was utterly jarring. I had imagined that he would be thrown back in disarray – but he was not. His big arms wrapped around me and together we slowly toppled down like the colossus struck by the earthquake, gathering speed until we came to the deck with a crash which seemed to shake the ship's very timbers.

I knew he could not be impervious to my blows, yet he gave no sign of their having registered. Instead, he started to squeeze, and I felt the breath slowly being pushed from me. My chest was being crushed, and I tried to cry for mercy but found there was no air to make the sound. The world began to close in around me. The shouts, the colours, the smells, even the sensation of being crushed – everything tended to numbness. And then, suddenly, it stopped. I had a moment of lucidity where I wondered whether I had fallen unconscious – but the ship still creaked and the wind still blew. The arms around me had released their hold and I stumbled to my feet and turned, to see Captain Carvalho standing in the ring that the crew had formed. In his hand, pointed at the sky, was a smoking pistol, and on his face was a vision of fury – an expression I had not seen at any time during his raid on the *White Star*.

His brow worked up and down, his eyes switching between glaring and almost disappearing under the scowl, while his mouth remained contorted tight with rage. For a moment he seemed unable even to speak. When he did, it was with a roar that I had not imagined he could produce. His words were in the local tongue and meant nothing to me in themselves, but there was no mistaking their mood, nor to whom they were directed. The effect on the crew was remarkable. Having bayed for my blood only moments before, to a man they now hung their heads in shame. My assailant still laid where we had grappled on the deck, not daring to move, and now the captain extended his spent pistol towards him in a gesture which could mean only one thing.

I could not say what strange sentiment made me act at that point. Something from Robert resonated within me. Had our roles been reversed, I do not imagine that I would have benefitted from the same charity. Yet I walked back to my prostrate opponent and, still shaking from the exertion and shock, extended my hand to help him to his feet. He looked back at me with dumbstruck confusion – but he took my hand nevertheless, and then he was standing next to me, facing the captain's empty pistol.

Captain Carvalho shared the puzzlement of his crew – but he addressed me cordially.

'*Senhor* Winter. This man has assaulted you – a guest of the *capitao*. An assault on you is an assault on me. He must be made an example of. I shall allow you to carry out the sentence, if you wish.'

I did not know why, but I knew that I could not let Captain Carvalho kill this man. Perhaps it was the memory of seeing Jones' body on the surgeon's table, with Millette's crestfallen face behind. Perhaps it was a sense of honour that Robert had awoken. Whatever it was, I gave the captain the only response I could think of.

'I am afraid that that will not serve, Captain. For you see, it is I who first struck this man. Were it not for my short temper, you would not have found us here in such a state.'

The captain slowly lowered his pistol, control returning to his face, which now fastened into an expression of doubt: head raised, eyes narrowed and looking from their corners.

'You, *senhor* Winter? You assaulted Bekoe here?' The cynicism was rich in his voice, but he could not directly decry his own guest.

'I did, Captain – foolish as it may sound. I believe I have been away from land for so long that I am not quite in my right mind. Your man here did little more than defend himself – I fear I could not live with myself if he were punished for my madness.'

A hush drifted over the forecastle. African, English or Portuguese, we all understood what had passed – and no one quite knew what should happen next. Eventually Captain Carvalho took it upon himself, inviting me for a drink in his cabin, and dismissing his crew to their labours. Curiously however, our drink appeared more for his benefit than for mine, as we discussed only frivolities, and things utterly unconnected with the chaos he had just interrupted on his deck.

It was not until that evening that we returned to the matter, after dinner, once his mates had departed his cabin and we sat once again at his table with a glass of Porto each.

'I do not take kindly to being lied to, *senhor* Winter – much less being made a fool of in front of my men. Please.' He halted my protest with a wave of his hand. 'Do not continue this game. It is very good – very noble of you to have acted as you did. I respect your sense of *honra*. *Honra* among thieves, no?' He chuckled to himself at his observation, and lifted his glass in recognition of it.

'Bekoe is a very useful member of my crew,' he resumed. 'It would have been a great shame to have killed him.'

I nodded politely. It did not take great imagination to construe what Bekoe's chief skill as a pirate might be.

'And the crew would not have liked it either. As you see, I have no marines here to protect me – so I must act always to maintain discipline, but also as my crew would wish me to. It is a delicate balance of trust. I must suggest now – request, even – that you end this charade of assisting on deck. We will make the coast in two days, perhaps. I would hate for Lord Elsfield's representative to be battered, broken, or dead when he meets with the Ashanti.'

This time there was no chuckle, and I was left to judge for myself how serious a consideration my very survival on this ship was. Nonetheless, I knew I could not now waver in my purpose. Robert was depending on me to complete what we had begun on the *White Star*, and I was desperate to sabotage the remaining barrels before they were passed to the Ashanti – for if I failed to complete my task at sea, I knew I would have to pursue it on land, under the noses of the enemy. As fierce as the pirates had proved to be, I preferred my chances on-board to those ashore, amongst the tribal warriors.

I wished it was a noble courage which drove me, but I knew that it was not. Fear of failure drove me onward. To a mind tormented with the guilt of what I had set in motion, this was now my only route to absolution. The thought of carrying this guilt forever more pressed down on me. It seemed to actually *crush* me, outweighing the fear of my enemies. If by some miracle I was successful, there would be no hero's welcome – no mention in dispatches from a grateful governor. My reward – and it was all I longed for – would be the erasure of my shameful plot from history, and my ability to stand straight and look a man in the eye again. Until I had met Robert, I had not realised how highly I prized that right. A man's honour was indeed a curious and private thing.

'I am afraid I cannot accept, Captain. I must insist on being allowed to continue to work my passage. Perhaps your crew will view me differently now.' I was not at all sure if this was the case, but I would certainly be more careful around them.

The captain sighed, leant back in his chair, and drained his glass. He contemplated me for a long moment before speaking.

'You are not at all as I expected, *senhor* Winter. Not at all. You make your own mistakes, but you make your own way out of them. Tell me: why would *senhor* Daniels want you dead?'

I stared at him.

'I'm sorry, Captain. I think I must have misheard you...'

'The first mate, on the *White Star*. *Senhor* Daniels. Why would he ask me to kill you?'

'There must be some mistake...'

'There is no mistake, *senhor*. Unless a man can hand a pirate a bag of gold, ask in return for a murder, and mean something else.'

There was no smile now on either of our faces. Captain Carvalho scrutinised my expression closely – and now I saw that one of his hands remained out of sight, below the table.

'So there is no cause? No great wrong you have done him or his family? Nothing?'

'I barely know the man. He was cordial, but we cannot have exchanged more than a dozen words in two months that were not professional in nature.'

'Then I must advise you, *senhor*, to become a better judge of character – and quickly. For there are people in your midst who wish you harm.'

We looked at each other across the table in the flickering lamplight and for a moment, I wondered if this was to be my end. His words hung, laced with menace, between us. The darkness obscured all but his unsmiling face. Then he spoke again.

'But I am not one of those. Not even for this blood money. This Daniels: whatever feud he has with you, he will have to resolve himself. I do not kill without good reason *senhor*. This bag of gold: it was a good reason when I took it. Now, I think it is not good enough for a man of *honra* such as you. You have saved Bekoe's life today. In return I shall spare yours. A life for a life.'

I could not find the words to convey my thoughts. Horror, relief, confusion and gratitude all vied for voice inside my skull. Amongst their noise, it struck me Robert's friendship, and what he had taught me, had just saved my life.

Carvalho closed our conversation with another chuckle, as he stood and opened the door of the lamp.

'In any case, I think I may keep the money. If *Senhor* Daniels takes issue with it, he must come and find me – and I have made a career out of disappearing. Goodnight!'

XXIII

I did not sleep that night. First Mate Daniels had been the spy in the camp. The man who had pushed the *White Star* off course – or rather, the man who had ordered poor Jones to steer off course, and then killed him to hide the truth. I pictured his face in my mind – stern, guiltless – as he worked with the crew to rescue Jones and Millette from the churning sea, and as he lied to his captain about our course through the storm. Daniels.

He had poisoned the crew, presumably when he decided I had failed – perhaps even when he saw the *Kraken* on the horizon, in the pre-arranged location. And he wanted me dead. I shuddered again to think that I had been in close company for so long with a man who bore me such ill will. I could only assume that he had been hired by Lord Elsfield to watch over me. But he had surely now exceeded his remit. With me eliminated there would be no one to question his version of events when he returned to London. I would doubtless become the official scapegoat, responsible for nullifying the *White Star's* defences, in league with the pirates from the beginning. And he would command a bigger cut of the deal from Lord Elsfield now, as the sole survivor of the operation. In the end, it always came down to money.

Despite my reservations, a change came over the crew of the *Kraken*. It was most evident in Bekoe, whose deference was almost alarming. Upon encountering me he would smile, saying no more than 'Senhor', and bow his head – often maintaining the pose until I had passed out of sight. If I had not been assured otherwise, I might have thought it was done in mockery. I in turn endeavoured to show that I was a valuable addition to the crew, climbing the rat lines as swiftly as any, handling the sails, and attending to any maintenance that might be required on deck. My opportunities to stray below decks were few, however, between lodging in the captain's cabin, and being apprenticed to Kwabene. I felt my debt of honour weighing ever more heavily upon me. With every passing day I looked back on my life in London with greater horror. I had been selfish, arrogant, and hopelessly naïve. The need to undo the damage I had done here had become all-consuming. It was a promise to myself that I would change. That I *had* changed.

On the evening of my third day aboard the *Kraken* we sighted land and, to the east, a town which Captain Carvalho informed me was Axim.

'A Dutch outpost. They are old friends. I do them no harm, and they do me none. Even so, I think it best on our current *missao* that we arouse as little suspicion as possible, no? The fewer who know of our passage, the fewer may require paying or killing for their silence. Either way, the bill is best kept short.'

Despite growing fond of his eccentricity, the captain had an off-hand way of speaking about death which I found decidedly unsettling.

'Where do we make the trade with the Ashanti, then?' I asked, understanding that he meant to avoid the town.

'We head for an inlet to the west. You will see it soon. Or maybe you will not! That is, after all, the idea!'

Understanding only a little more, I resigned myself to waiting to see what unfolded.

As night fell, I perceived that we had approached the mouth of a river. Once within close reach of the shore, boats were loaded and launched, and teams of men began to lighten the *Kraken* of its ballast, whilst others climbed into the canopy around the river. Their endeavours, obscured by the dark, must have continued for a little over two hours, after which they made camp for the night on the shore by their boats. With the first rays of dawn appearing over the horizon, the *Kraken* sprang to life once more, and I looked to the shore. Where last night the jungle had seemed to consume the river, now there was a gaping space in the treeline, wide enough for a sailing ship. The crews on land returned to their boats and with ropes attached to the ship, hauled her slowly towards the river. A hush descended over the ship. The sound of the surf breaking on the shore around us filled my ears. With the captain himself at the helm, and men on either side of him with plumb lines reading out our depth, I barely dared breathe as we sailed serenely over the area cleared in the night, and into the river itself.

I was not the only one who, once the moment had passed, emitted a great sigh of relief. A grinning Captain Carvalho witnessed my reaction.

'Here in West Africa there is no writing,' he explained. 'No books. Certainly no rutters. What is known is passed down by word of mouth. This does not suit the *Europeus*, who send new governors as often as the seasons change. Each new governor is then doomed to spend his time here learning only as much as his predecessor. The result is that after two hundred years on this coast, the Dutch, the French and the English still know precious little about it. However,' he added with evident pride, 'we are not Dutch. We are not French. We are not English, *senhor*. We have been here for *four* hundred years. And we have learnt to keep our knowledge to ourselves!

'My father sailed this coast, and his father before him. There was once a French trading post on this river, fifty miles inland. But that was two hundred years ago, and it too was forgotten. Certainly the French are a curious people – yet even they would not establish a settlement for no reason. This river is the Ankobra, and it is deep – deep enough even for the *Kraken* all the way to our rendezvous. The only challenge is the entry, which must be completed at high tide. But with a little help from an old smuggler's trick, we have made that challenge seem impossible. So now you see we are quite safe from any navy, and may travel far faster and more comfortably than by land. I only hope your constitution does not mind the climate!'

Hardly had he finished speaking, turning to attend to the crew and the navigation of the river, than the first raindrops began to fall heavy and plump onto the deck. Despite the oppressive heat, the rain was little solace, being as warm as the air around it, and of such a weight that a man felt physically battered by its falling. I remained on deck long enough to stare momentarily at the river bank. After long months at sea the sight of any land up close was a great tonic to my spirits. Then, accepting that little could be seen through the deluge, I went below.

True to the captain's word, we reached our rendezvous point that evening, and anchored in the middle of the stream – 'a sensible precaution in uncharted lands,' he declared. The following morning, with the rains ceased, I was awoken by the oppressive humidity. I had grown accustomed to the heat as we had journeyed south and the quicksilver had slowly risen on the ship's thermometer. However, nothing had prepared me for the cloying closeness of the jungle, which made the very air I swallowed seem more liquid than gas. Wandering onto the deck, I saw great clouds of steam rising from the trees on either side of the river. There was a strange, echoing hissing sound abroad which, although not loud, invaded every corner of the ship, and extended out into the furthest reaches of the forest. It was punctuated with strange cries from what I assumed to be birds, or other arboreal creatures. Despite the ongoing peril of my situation, I found the collective sensation strangely gratifying. To have travelled so far and to have endured so much, only to have arrived at a landscape similar to my home, would have been difficult to bear. I had longed all my life for Africa, and for adventure. Africa and adventure had arrived.

After breakfast I prevailed upon the captain to allow me to go ashore with a small party to investigate the forest which enclosed the river thickly on both sides as far as could be seen. Leaving Kwabene in charge of the *Kraken*, he accompanied me ashore himself, reasoning that I 'would not obtain more than five words of sense from any of the rest of the crew.' To my surprise, my old adversary, Bekoe, was also amongst the shore party, as the captain told me he would not hear of being left behind.

The first thing that struck me upon gaining the riverbank was the atmosphere within the forest – for it was quite different to that on the river. Being now used to the wide expanses of the oceans, and at least being able to bring to mind the open reaches of the Thames, I had considered the Ankobra a narrow, enclosed watercourse. However, the Ankobra was a vast, airy plain compared to the suffocating confines of the forest. Here the canopies of hundreds of tightly-packed trees jostled for advantage, blotting out the tropical sun with their thick, overlapping leaves. The small relief from the heat, however, was countered by the increase in the humidity – something which I had scarcely believed possible. Water dripped lazily from every frond of vegetation, and the air, so thick as to be almost tangible, struggled to contain the moisture. For a full five minutes it was all I could do to focus on breathing, and to assure myself that I was not suffocating in this alien mixture. Slowly, I began to examine my new surroundings through the half-light which permeated the ceiling above me.

The forest floor was carpeted with leaves in various states of decay, punctuated everywhere by small plants, bamboos and mosses which, in spite of the privations enforced by their giant brethren, survived alongside them. The larger cousins were of all shapes and sizes, from thin, tall white-skinned trees which climbed elegantly into the canopy, to massive, buttressed strangler fig trees, spreading their corrugated bases three or four feet in every direction, meandering upward and outward and littering the ground with their fruit. Vines as thick as a man's leg wove an intricate web between the branches above my head. Mosses clung to these vines, and plants and flowers in turn to the mosses, so that in places there appeared to be terrace upon terrace of lush greenery, such as the gardeners at Kew would have envied. Throughout this scene, the trunks and roots of toppled trees criss-crossed with the living, blocking paths and lines of sight, offering more mulch to the ever-gluttonous soil.

Through this living, breathing tissue of vegetation, little noise penetrated. Despite the sense of being surrounded by all manner of life, there remained only the background hissing, accompanied now by the indistinct tweeting of a score of different insect species, and the occasional cry of a nearby monkey or bird. The mass of insulating matter prevented all but the loudest or the closest of calls from reaching our ears.

'It is a strange land, is it not, *senhor*? It is peculiarly enjoyable to watch a *branco* experience it for the first time.'

'It is unlike anything I could have imagined, Captain,' I replied, rotating slowly and taking in my surroundings.

Somewhere beneath the hiss of the forest, a new noise began. At first I questioned whether I imagined it as it faded in and out of hearing. But slowly it grew louder and more defined. A booming bass which crept under the forest's soft blanket of sound, pulsing regularly. Soon we could all hear it, inducing the captain to answer my silent question:

'Our buyers have arrived. We must prepare our stock.'

I realised with a start that my time was up. I would not have another chance to sabotage the barrels on-board. The drums of the Ashanti now summoned me ominously, drawing me further into their strange and savage world. There was no turning back. I would walk into the lion's den.

With a forced calmness I told the captain of my intentions.

'I would like you to offer my services to the Ashanti, Captain, as a gesture of goodwill in our trade.'

He looked at me quizzically.

'In short – I intend to accompany them to their camp, and there to demonstrate the quality of our wares.'

The eyes which could not be surprised widened; his frown deepened. It was a response reserved for a madman.

'You do not take advice well, *senhor* Winter. You wish to embark on another of your mistakes?'

'My integrity demands it, Captain,' I replied, offering a steady gaze to his bemusement. He could not know how truthful those words were – nor how my insides rebelled at the proposition.

He contemplated my words in silence for a moment, his face unaltered. Then, slowly, he began to shake his head, ridding himself of his expression. When he spoke, he was his old self once more, smile and all:

'The integrity of an Englishman. It is a thing of legend! If the Ashanti do not kill you and turn your head into a cup, then you will probably die of fever in the jungle. And if not – you are thousands of miles from home, and walking into a war. Yet you cannot help but be an Englishman, *senhor* Winter. I thank God I was born an *Algarvio.*'

The ship's boats were busied once more, transporting samples of our wares to the shore. Captain Carvalho left the logistics to his trusted bosun, and bade me follow him through the forest. I wondered where in this tangled maze of flora we might find space for more than four men to stand in a circle and converse – and then, suddenly, the answer was before me. The jungle, it seemed, had more wonders for me to behold.

We stood at the edge of a clearing. So thick was the undergrowth here that there was no sign of its existence almost until one emerged into it. Yet this clearing was not all that it seemed. For while it abounded in the same luminescent greenery as the forest, here, in a square perhaps three hundred feet across, were the crumbling remains of a colonial outpost. Mosses covered much of the broken stonework, and plants thrust up from every conceivable fissure. In places there remained the outline of a compound wall, three or four feet high at times, but for the most part the forest had reclaimed its home, roots undermining and shoots tearing at the foundations until they rose, cracked and shattered. The ground inside the compound was littered with toppled stones, yet the outlines of the paths and internal buildings were still visible beneath the vegetation. A handful of the most tenacious trees had managed to force their way through the foundations and grow to some forty feet, while one or two even appeared to be growing *on top* of the rubble. There was an eerie, still quality to the place: a glimpse of how nature might one day cover over all traces of human endeavour, wiping the earth clean of our legacy, as it had tried to do at Naples.

At the centre of the compound Kwabene placed a makeshift table, formed from planks and two empty barrels. Above it was erected a canvas sheet to protect us from the sun which, now the canopy had given way, beat down upon us with unrelenting ferocity. At one end of the table were placed our samples of muskets, pistols, powder, and ball. Captain Carvalho regarded the temporary trading post with a critical eye and nodded his approval. Half of the *Kraken's* crew – perhaps twenty-five men – joined the captain and myself in the compound, heavily armed and rather compressed under the canopy.

'The Ashanti are first among the Gold Coast tribes for their fairness and business-mindedness. Yet one would be foolish to confuse that position with any *Europeu* notions of *civilizacao*,' the captain explained. 'What you will witness when they arrive will at turns delight and disgust you, *senhor*. I strongly advise you not to allow your idea of morality to affect your judgement here, or indeed your countenance.'

I frowned at him, framing another silent question which he promptly answered.

'A display of your horror at any of their customs will be viewed here as a sign of weakness – or worse – an affront. Look around you!

Do you see streets and houses? Great institutions and factories? The landscape shaped and moulded to serve humanity? This is not London. It is not even Paris. Here, brutality is strength. Brutality keeps the people alive in a landscape that fights to kill them. Mercy is perceived as weakness. It is a luxury that most cannot afford.'

I pondered these concepts as the drums grew louder. I had always believed civilisation to be a liberating force for good – only resisted by those who were blind to its advantages, and to be impressed upon them for their own benefit. Yet here I witnessed for myself the undeniable 'otherness' of Africa, and I gave the captain enough credit to believe that, in this world, a different kind of character might be required.

XXIV

The Ashanti vanguard burst into the compound in a riot of noise and colour. To the rhythmic pounding of drums was now added the cacophony of horns, some sort of flute, and rattles. The overall effect was terrifying rather than triumphal or even martial – but perhaps this was their intention.

The warriors, forty or so in number, wore over their heads the skins of leopards and panthers as cloaks, and around their loins a white cloth wrapped into a girdle. Their bodies were otherwise exposed, but decorated with necklaces, arm and leg bracelets, and daubed across with bands of white and red paint. Their armaments followed no pattern, but were a mixture of musket, sword, spear, club, bow and arrow. All however carried a string of throwing knives secured over a shoulder and across their chests. They entered the compound in a running, crouched formation and, having assessed our group, formed into a line either side of the entrance.

Shortly behind them followed ten men of rank, carried in palanquins underneath a billowing sea of cloth. The cloths were carefully arranged over the tops of the carried, and bore ornate representations of strange and wonderful creatures. The carriers themselves appeared to be of low rank, wearing only loincloths, and with no markings or decorations upon them. Around them on either side came more warriors with weapons and warpaint, and a strange group of haranguers, running alongside the palanquins, shouting, squawking and brandishing their swords and spears in a fearsome manner. Through the din of their individual shouting, blended with that of the band, it was impossible to distinguish a single voice.

At the sight of this last group of screaming swordsmen I chanced a sideways glance at the captain, anxious to understand if this was the act of aggression it appeared. He caught my look immediately, and dismissed it with the slightest shake of his head. Softly, and still without turning his head to me, he muttered:

'Each herald competes to raise their *capitao* above the others by proclaiming tales of their superhuman feats, and by their fearsome appearance. The best is yet to come, though...'

And sure enough, these groups of captains and attendants also divided to either side of our position, and with a decline in their exertions which approximated standing at attention, the band seemed to grow yet more powerful and discordant, until it too finally entered the compound. It was now that I understood Carvalho's earlier warning. For hanging from the drums of this platoon were a score of human skulls and jaw-bones - some even gaudily painted gold, the better to catch the eye. Looking across their line, I saw that they too wore necklaces and bracelets – but now I perceived that amongst the beads, charms and feathers attached to these items were teeth: *human* teeth. A tingling sense of horror formed in my neck and swiftly radiated all through my body. If there had been any lingering belief that British sensibilities could prevail here, it was now dispelled. These people were quite apart from us. I had been prepared to witness a degree of savagery on the Gold Coast – but I was utterly unprepared for this.

I was still in this state of shock when a final palanquin, this one richly decorated with gold trim, and with a man inside seated on a throne of silver coins, entered the compound. Ahead of it came still more screaming warriors bedecked as their fore-runners, but with pheasant feathers arranged as headdresses, and with golden ornaments, swords and bells, and even golden muskets which they twirled and brandished. At a given signal, the music stopped, the warriors ceased their movements and their screaming, and the bethroned man leapt to the ground before us. He wore a fine cloth tunic, overlaid with the skin of a tiger, and studded with amulets and shining stones. On his arms, fingers and toes were more such beads and golden rings, and in his hand was now a beautiful sword, elegantly curved, and with a handle of bright gold studded with rubies.

For a moment he stood silent and still, facing our delegation, eyes blazing. And then, in a whirl of movement and colour, he was rushing towards us, sword flying, voice screaming. I could not help myself – I recoiled in my seat, but a hand from the captain steadied me. Our aggressor halted his advance just feet away from us – would no doubt have come closer had our table not prevented him – and proceeded to eclipse the efforts of his warriors with a display of terrifying anger, power and speed. At close range, the effect was all the more alarming – eyes bulged, sinews strained, his blade soared and glinted, foam sprayed from his mouth as he uttered blood-curdling words which were somehow all the more potent when unintelligible and left to my imagination to interpret.

And then, as suddenly as he had begun, he stopped, standing once again still and silent as a statue in front of us, though his chest heaved from his exertions, and the passion burnt fiercely in his eyes. I inferred from his appearance and the reverence he commanded that this must be the king – the man who challenged the might of the British Empire. It occurred to me that, just as awful and terrifying as this spectacle was – as utterly unlike anything I had ever seen or even imagined in England – so this king could not possibly have imagined the world from which his enemy came.

This man might well be the most fearsome warrior I had ever encountered – yet his enemy's world cared little for the ferocity of warriors. A brave man might be dismembered by a cannonball at a thousand yards just as easily as a cowering whelp. Nothing could prepare him for the tens of thousands of drilled infantrymen, for the cannon, the rockets, the grapeshot and the men-of-war which would prove the downfall of his people. Lord Elsfield might line his pockets from this exchange – but it would not save the Ashanti from the march of empire. They were doomed.

I realised that the guilt I carried with me now extended to them. With these instruments of war I gave them false hope – encouraged them into a fight they could not win. Horror and pity tangled within me. Undoubtedly there was raw savagery here – the barbarism that took the bodies of vanquished foes and paraded them about their persons like gaudy trinkets. Yet as Captain Carvalho had said, these people lived and died in a world so different to ours, so untamed and savage itself, that they could not be judged by our rules. I found myself vacillating, unable either to condemn or endorse it. I wondered what my dear Annabel would say were she beside me now. Would she condemn the warriors who enslaved and butchered their rival tribes? Or would she defend their misunderstood culture, and their enforced submission to our own, inflexible and unforgiving world?

My straying mind circled back to the matter in hand. This king was here for our cargo – and I now had no choice but to follow it onward. Having failed to access the powder on the *Kraken,* my only remaining option was to do so in the Ashanti camp, under the noses of these bloodthirsty warriors. My fate if discovered was certain – more certain even that it had been aboard a pirate ship – but my promise to Robert had become unbreakable. I must undo what I had done, or perish trying. My conscience would accept nothing less – and yet I knew, as I tore my eyes from the jaw bones adorning the side of a drum, that my courage hung by a thread.

The captain reeled off a series of phrases in the local language, and on a signal, an ornate tortoiseshell box inlaid with gold was produced by a crewman and placed on the table in front of the King. The captain opened it to reveal a pair of beautiful duelling pistols set in a velvet casing.

Turning to me while the King inspected his gift, he said:

'I have explained to Prince Sai who we are – a formality on my part as I have had dealings with the Ashanti before. I have suggested that I interpret for you, as Lord Elsfield's chosen agent and guarantor of the quality of these goods. I have also taken the liberty of making this gift on your behalf. The exchange of gifts is the cornerstone of any relationship with the Ashanti – and they will not trade with *brancos* if they do not have a relationship with them.'

As he spoke, the prince – whom I had mistaken for a king – gestured to a follower, who brought forward a long object wrapped in cloth and placed it on the table. Understanding this to be his return offering, I removed the cloth to see a scabbard of plain, gleaming gold, ending in an ornate golden hilt. Taking the hilt up, I removed the sword and swung it from side to side, as much to make a show of assessing its qualities as to actually do so. Its balance was remarkably fine, and having left my sword behind on the *White Star*, I offered my genuine gratitude to the prince, conveyed through the captain. Satisfied that honour had been served on both sides, we then sat down to begin the negotiations. The prince spoke first, and the captain explained:

'Prince Sai is glad we have met here, in a place where honest trade was always done between our ancestors. He advised we should meet here, as it avoids the trickery of the coastal people. The coastal people have long been the enemy of the Ashanti, claiming to act as brokers for their trade, whilst growing fat and lazy on the industry of others. When they have provoked the Ashanti to war, they then hide behind their *branco* overlords, and drag them into their infamy. Prince Sai is happy to be dealing with us – honest *brancos* who understand that men can be honest or dishonest whether they have black skin or *branco*.'

He paused here, to indicate to me that what followed was his own commentary.

'You are fortunate Prince Sai understands this, *senhor*. There are many in Africa who believe the colour of your skin must determine your loyalty, and your honesty.'

The prince looked at me, to see that I had understood his words, and then continued to the captain.

'Prince Sai is pleased you will accompany him, to guarantee the quality of the goods. He does not wish to suggest *your* dishonesty, but he has seen too many *brancos* slide into the ways of the coastal tribes, and cheat his people in trade. He is grateful that you will personally demonstrate the quality of what you sell.'

It felt as if an irresistible force was sucking me further and further into the abyss, and again I lamented the arrogance of my younger self that had driven me to this end. I had thought to win Annabel's undying admiration by travelling to the Gold Coast, and playing some small part in the defence of a helpless African people from oppression. I had thought to win a great fortune for myself, and a heroic reputation with Lord Elsfield and Sir Godfrey. I had longed for adventure. Now it was here, I longed only for the safety of home.

It became quickly apparent that Prince Sai would not enter into protracted negotiations. I had credited myself with having some experience in business – yet the business we conducted at that table was of a different nature to any I had undertaken in London. Indeed, his approach was edifying as a student of the discipline, removing any further possibility of driving the price higher, despite having precious little leverage to barter with. With his usual sources of armaments closed to him, I had anticipated a tense but rewarding interaction. However, as Captain Carvalho translated:

'His *excelencia* is grateful for our trade. He offers us a sum in excess of the value of our cargo, as a gesture of goodwill, in order to conclude the business swiftly, and without disagreement. He offers sixteen hundred ounces of gold...' The captain himself could not avoid hesitating over the words as he said them – though he managed to resist any further sign of surprise.

It would have been pointless to quibble with this generous offer, and I considered it better to conduct the trade on good terms, as the prince suggested, rather than stumble carelessly into a cross-cultural dispute. Allowing a moment of feigned consideration to pass, I turned to the captain to give my reply:

'Captain. Please inform the prince that we humbly accept his generous offer. We may begin to unload the *Kraken* as soon as you are ready.'

The business done, and done so swiftly, I once more felt the familiar sense of nausea creep up my insides. Though accompanying the Ashanti was the only way to fulfil my promise to Robert and redeem myself, I had taken some small solace in believing it was my *choice*. But with the deal concluded, I was now committed. There was no turning back.

The prince stood to shake my hand, and as I took it I felt the strength of his grip and saw the fire in his eyes, only feeding the fear within me that I had blindly followed a path to a place where I could not hope to succeed. Whilst a superstitious part of me warned against making plans for my survival, my rational mind bade that part be silent, and I turned one last time to the captain.

'Captain Carvalho. I believe this concludes your contract for our expedition. I am most grateful for the services you have rendered – and I wonder if you might be interested in a further engagement. Once I have fulfilled my role with Prince Sai, I will require return passage to England. If you will take me as far as Sierra Leone, I am in a position to offer you a good price.'

'Indeed you are, *senhor*. Though your new role threatens your return home...'

'That is my concern alone, Captain. I shall pay you now for fulfilling your contract. But if you will name a harbour where we might later rendezvous, I will add to that payment. You mentioned that you're on good terms with the Dutch?'

'Yes, *senhor*. I must first sail for Ajuda to honour another *contrato*, but I can return, and can anchor at the mouth of the Boutry river.

There is a Dutch settlement there. When should I look for you, in case you are still alive?'

'I intend to quit this country before February. I would ask that you await me from the 24th of January. If I have not arrived by the 31st, you may decide whether to remain or not.'

'I will do as you ask, *senhor*, and will hope that once again you find your own way out of your mistakes.'

'As will I, Captain. I have one further favour to ask. I require two good men to carry the proceeds of this sale, and to guide me back to your ship. If one of them can translate for me, so much the better.'

'My men are loyal to me, *senhor*,' he said, raising his chin in an unconscious display of pride. 'Loyalty is not bought with gold: it is earned.'

Despite my situation, a small smile crept across my face. I had grown fond of this man in the short time we had spent together. He had taught me to judge men by their actions, not their reputations or titles. 'I begin to understand this, Captain – hence I ask you to assign me men with your authority, rather than pretending to buy them from you. Consider it an investment: if your men lead me safely back, then it will be a wise one.'

It was his turn to smile now.

'You are quite right, *senhor*. And I see that already you work to find your way out of this mistake. I shall be sad to lose Bekoe and Kofi, but I shall be comforted to think that it gives you some small chance of bringing that gold back to me. They are both good men.'

The prince had retired to his own people, to make arrangements for the transfer of the cargo. Captain Carvalho sent Bekoe and Kofi to retrieve the gold, and I was afforded a moment to bid him farewell.

'Be careful, *senhor*. Remember what I said: the Ashanti are fair, and they are moral. But not always according to *branco* values. The talk on the coast is that a battle with your people is coming. Keep your *honra* and the Ashanti will respect you, and you may yet depart them with your life.'

His advice was sincere. Yet there was an inference which I could not fathom.

'Captain – do you believe the Ashanti may *prevail*?' I could not help my incredulous tone. 'You've been to Europe. You've witnessed the carnage of the cannon – of grape, shrapnel, and rockets. These men are *doomed*. Their savage looks and twirling blades cannot compete with the massed ranks. Wellington or Napoleon would despatch them in minutes from the battlefield.'

'You were beaten by Bekoe, were you not? And not because of his size: you chose to fight him in spite of his size, thinking you could win. You were beaten because you assumed he would fight to your rules. The way to win is to make the rules, *senhor*, not adhere to your opponent's. Wellington and Napoleon both knew this. They chose their battlefields to suit themselves. If the rumours are true, and Mac-Carthy brings his soldiers out here to face the Ashanti, then he will lose. If the Ashanti come to the coast, under the guns of the forts and the Royal Navy, *they* will lose. The difference is that MacCarthy should know this: he has seen how the Gold Coast people fight, while the Ashanti have no concept of how the *brancos* can wage war.' He issued his philosophy as a teacher of doctrine – it invited no contest. Instead, he put out his hand one last time for me.

'As I said, *senhor*: be careful.'

I took his hand and shook it, still wondering what he had seen in these people that I had not. As I turned to join Bekoe and Kofi, I still found myself pitying the Ashanti – proud warriors who could not hope to stand against the cold, disciplined march of an industrialised army.

XXV

We marched the rest of the day through the oppressive and alien jungle, reaching a small deserted village of wooden and clay huts at dusk, where we set up camp, and I collapsed exhausted in mind and body in a makeshift bed.

The next morning, I awoke with a start to the sound of screams and the heavy banging of war drums. I reached for my sword and rushed to the door, to find Kofi and Bekoe dutifully standing guard outside my hut.

'Kofi! What has happened? Where is the battle?'

Kofi barely dared raise his eyes to mine as he replied:

'I am afraid that you will be angry with what they do, *owura*.'

'Kofi. Please explain to me what the cause of this commotion is.'

He looked imploringly to Bekoe, who simply shrugged.

'It is our custom, *owura*. To thank our gods for bringing us the tools to fight. But Bekoe and I know the white man does not agree. *Capitao* Carvalho holds Sunday mass for us, and teaches us the bible. We are sorry, *owura*.'

'Agree? Agree with what? What are you sorry about?'

Another sideways look at his companion.

'They make the sacrifice. The prince makes it early, so that you will not see it.'

'I don't have to see it. You could hear it in London! What are they sacrificing...' my voice trailed off as I realised what the answer would be. My blood ran cold. I had heard of these rituals. I had perhaps intentionally blocked them from my mind. Human sacrifice. One look at Kofi's turmoil confirmed it.

Once again I wondered what I had drawn myself into, and why. I cursed that I had ever been so stupid as to undertake Lord Elsfield's treason, and then that I had not reneged on it sooner. The gunpowder had sat beneath my quarters for months upon the *White Star*, and yet, between blindly following the plan, and then naïvely believing I could prevent it, I had ignored my opportunity.

Daniels. Daniels was to blame for all this. He had forced the plan through despite my change of heart. And he had wanted me dead. No matter how many times I searched my conscience, however – no matter how many times I questioned why I continued, I always came back to the same answer. Lieutenant Newton. He had trusted me. He had instilled a sense of honour in me which I had not even realised was missing. And his life might well depend upon me. If I could save Robert, I could save myself.

I steadied myself and spoke again.

'Kofi. Please inform his highness that I wish to begin the demonstration of the goods as soon as possible today. The sooner we are done with this evil the better.'

'Yes *owura*. Prince Sai has asked that you visit him today, *owura*. Ten o'clock.'

'Well. Good then. No time to be wasted.' I did not relish another audience with the prince, but at least it moved my mission one step closer to completion, and might afford me the opportunity to express my distaste for his occult predilections.

My optimism was short-lived, however. The prince was not ready for a demonstration of the weapons. His priests had told him the omens from the sacrifice were not good. He would ask again tomorrow. Kofi explained that nothing of any import was done in Ashanti without consulting the gods. An army with the prince at its head would move only slowly, he said, as propitious days for encountering the enemy announced themselves in the dreams of the priests, or through the flight of birds, the paths of particular insects, or the howl of a monkey. Or indeed, through the death screams of a human sacrifice.

And while the prince spoke, and Kofi translated, I stood, my whole being focused on not staring at the ceremonial death stool be-

hind him, still spattered with the gore of its last victim. The prince
wore a dried mark of blood on his forehead, while at his feet stood a
chest filled with a bizarre assortment of charms, all soaking in blood.
The stench of decay was overpowering in the tropical heat. Flies
swarmed to the stool, while I fought back the urge to gag.

My efforts to appear unfazed were in vain, however, as Kofi began to translate:

'His Highness understands the white man's distaste for this rit-
ual. However, his gods demand more honouring than yours. He has
no choice. He would like you to know that the sacrifices are slaves.
People whose lives are already forfeited to the Ashanti through con-
quest. If another king is insolent, and the prince fights and kills him
for his insolence, it is only right that he should have his gold, his
slaves, and his people. He says surely the white kings do the same.'

I remained unmoved by his justification of slavery and cold-
blooded murder.

'In Europe, when a king wins a great victory, he becomes responsible for the fair treatment of the defeated warriors. He must feed
and house them until the conflict has ended.'

'His Highness says that this is no different. White men once
bought slaves from his people all down this coast. The Ashanti and
the white men grew rich. Now the white men pretend they do not
like slaves. They say that slaving is bad. But they still keep slaves,
across the sea.'

I decided that it would be impolitic to enter into an argument
on the nuances of international law and enforcement with my host.
Annabel might even have taken his part, feeling as she did that our
governments did the very least they could to appease the abolitionist
movement. All the while, the stool remained behind him as a grim
reminder of the precariousness of life here.

'It is true that we have encouraged and profited from slaving. It is
also true that in many places there are still slaves. I cannot therefore

pretend that his Highness is alone in his policies. Nor do I presume to advise him on them. However, I can assure him that Europe will never return to the practice.'

The prince seemed to accept my attempt at diplomacy, and moved on to what I presumed was the main cause of his wish to see me.

'His Highness believes that his people and the English are natural allies. He believes that they should work as they have done before for mutual gain along the Gold Coast. He would like to divide the country between himself and the King of England. But he fears that your king's man in Cape Coast is not a good man. When his Highness went out to fight against Dinkera[7], he sent to Cape Coast for fifty kegs of powder and some lead to make shot, because he liked Englishmen best. But the governor sent his messengers away, because he wanted more gold. They then went to Elmina, and the Dutch governor gave them the powder and shot, and sent his gold back. He asks, therefore, which was the best friend?'

I was given no opportunity to respond – not that I was at all equipped to act as the British Gold Coast's diplomatic mission. My host seemed to have requested my presence in order to justify his war to me. I was both flattered and bemused. The ceremonial butchery of unarmed men, women and children required only passing justification. But the official declaration of war was a matter for the record. I thought back to the massacre at Peterloo, and the king's response in the aftermath. There had been no attempt to justify the butchery there – only praise for the murderous yeomanry and the magistrates who directed them. I realised that for all our pomp, our behaviour was uncomfortably similar. Still my host continued, warming to his theme.

'Governor MacCarthy has been fooled, and has sided with the criminals who trick and murder the Ashanti when they come to the coast. They steal money from Ashanti and white traders, and hide behind MacCarthy's walls and guns when the prince challenges them. They know the Ashanti love the English, and do not want to fight them. But the King of the Ashanti is the rightful ruler of these people – and if they act to insult their king, and refuse the taxes they owe him – then they must be punished.'

With these words he had now worked himself into a rage, saliva flying from his mouth, fists shaking and pounding, and eyes glaring reminiscent of his war dance the previous day.

'The English know that with their own powder and shot the Ashanti drove these criminals of the coast under their forts, where the prince put them to the sword. The taxes from these people and from the forts now belong by law to the King of the Ashanti. But the English cheat him. They think to make fools of the Ashanti; they pretend to make friends with them, but join the coastal people to cheat the king – to put shame upon his face. This makes the blood come from his heart.'

There was a pause. The prince sat still once more, though his eyes still glared and his chest still heaved from his exertions. Raising an arm and pointing a finger ominously towards me, he now spoke quietly. Coldly.

'You are English, but you are not the governor. If you were Ashanti, he would have to kill you – for you betray your country. But if you did not do this, then he would not have his powder, his guns, his shot. So we understand: loyalty is complicated. He must reward you for your betrayal, but punish others if they did the same.'

My heart pounded. I had preferred the enraged prince. It had seemed more theatrical – more intended for the ears and eyes of all around him. His quiet, reflective persona carried far more menace. It suggested a man who would stab you in your sleep without a second thought, and I realised that he was both these men. He was the fierce warrior, at the head of a savage but small and undisciplined army, and he was the unscrupulous murderer of the defenceless.

The prince did not have more to relate to me that day. He thanked me for my audience, as if my mere presence had given the stamp of authority to his monologue, and dismissed me. He would consult the priests again tomorrow.

The following day the priests returned an equally unfavourable verdict from their grim work. I remained idle, with my two men, who were as much my bodyguard as my porters. But the prince's army did not remain idle. It grew. As if materialising from the murk of the forest itself, men arrived in groups and joined our camp. Three groups of perhaps forty each before noon; towards the evening, several companies' worth. More men to arm with British muskets. More grist for the mill.

Over several more days, the priests performed their macabre rituals, and shook their heads at the prince, while his army continued to grow. I remained more or less within my quarters, conscious of the fortune I guarded there, sweating as much from the climate as from the ever-present anxiety for the task I still had to perform. It would take only one sharp-eyed Ashanti warrior to catch me contaminating the powder, and every increase in their numbers therefore made the task more dangerous – and in my weaker moments, more hopeless.

At last, after I had become numb to the morning screams, and after several days of tropical rainstorms had precluded any effective use of gunpowder, the prince announced that the omens were fair, and I should now demonstrate his new firepower. The moment had come to fulfil my promise to Robert, and to earn my redemption.

With Kofi and Bekoe accompanying me, I was escorted out of the village with a party of warriors and slaves carrying a large part of the *Kraken*'s cargo. When we reached our destination – a great clearing close by, I stared in disbelief. The Ashanti army was no longer the small rabble I had pitied. Camp fires and men, hangers-on and supplies, stretched as far as I could see – men beyond number. Struggling to control my reaction, I asked Kofi how many.

'I have heard fifteen, perhaps twenty thousand, *owura*.'

In spite of the searing heat, a chill ran down my spine. Fifteen or twenty thousand men. I would not have thought it possible to gather such a force in such inhospitable terrain, and with no evidence of the necessary support. A British army of that number would have needed another two thousand in quartermasters, armourers, cooks, paymasters, provosts, and wagon masters – to say nothing of the armada of merchants and their wares and livestock, and the camp women. This army was of a different nature. It seemed self-sufficient. It had arrived silently, it rested easily, and it might fall just as suddenly upon an unsuspecting British Army.

My parting words to Captain Carvalho had been confident of a British victory. The Ashanti concept of warfare had seemed pitiably out of step with their adversary's. But now I understood the captain's doubts. These men would not offer battle in ordered ranks. They would not form square to fight off cavalry charges, nor would they stand stoically in the face of artillery fire. They did not need to. No army could bring cannon or horse into this jungle. An army which deployed in line here would be ravaged by hidden enemies firing from only yards away. And firing arrows with no sound or smoke, they would remain hidden. I was reminded of the natives of the North American forests, and their repeated successes against European armies invading their lands.

A cautious commander might draw these warriors out of their forests, onto a plain where they could be corralled and decimated by superior weight of fire. But a headstrong commander, eager to make a show of his superiority, might venture into this terrain and be destroyed. Fifteen or twenty thousand men could make short work of a thousand regulars in this jungle – and Sir Charles MacCarthy could not have amassed more than that number, even if local tribesmen might swell his ranks. My promise to Robert was now more than a debt of honour. It was all that stood between a British army and disaster.

The prince greeted me at the head of the column with a beaming face.

'You are ready, my friend?' I had become the prince's 'friend' over the course of my detention.

'I shall demonstrate the muskets' quality, as you requested, your Highness. And I shall explain their use to your men.'

'Excellent. This will make my men brave. They will see that they have the white man's tools of war. But why do you bring your gold here?' His expression turned to a frown and he pointed now at the locked chest which Kofi and Bekoe carried between them. 'Your gold is under my protection, *owura*. It is safe within your quarters.'

I could think of no response which would not offend his sense of majesty, so I offered none. His face darkened in disgust.

'You white people have no honour. No sense of tribe. You will betray each other for a handful of gold. What will you do when there is no more gold? How will you then project your power?'

I took no pleasure in displeasing him, but considered that I had escaped lightly. Nonetheless, his words found their mark. I had indeed been enticed by riches to betray the *White Star* – to betray Captain Horwell and Robert. And in doing so, I betrayed Sir Godfrey also. And before that, I had betrayed Ball-Hughes. My shame for these betrayals was sharp. Where my accounts profited, my honour had quietly suffered. But now I worked to redress that balance.

I had planned the demonstration meticulously: it would be vital to my success. It had to strike fear into the Ashanti warriors. Some of them would have handled muskets before, but if the ceremonial use of the weapons at the ruined fort was any indication, they would not have fired them in anger – and certainly not in a pitched battle where repeated loading and firing would be required.

I loaded three muskets: the first with too much powder, the second too little, and only the third with the correct amount.

I packed the powder for the first as tightly as I could, the better to make my point. With a line attached to the trigger, the musket was fired, and the result was spectacular. The musket exploded from its breech, with pieces of plating flying off like shrapnel in all directions. An over-filled musket would kill the firer more surely than the enemy. I did not need an interpreter to convey that lesson, nor to see the shock in the eyes of the nearest onlookers. They were too conscious of their prince's presence to show fear, but they understood what they had seen.

So much for my cautionary tale. The second musket I fired with my own hand, and demonstrated that with too little powder, the shot would not penetrate a target at full range. Yet I knew any man would consider an underpowered bullet preferable to an exploding breech. The third musket I also fired myself, and with Kofi's translation, showed that the bullet performed as desired.

And so the scene was set for my sabotage. The prince nodded his satisfaction to me, though I was certain he would have preferred my demonstration without the first musket, and captains and their men were brought in front of me to hear my instructions and handle the weapons. This procession continued unabated until darkness fell, and Kofi, Bekoe and I wearily accompanied the same party of slaves back to the village. Mingled in with the long line of barrels and cases in the gloom, we were not stopped by the guard at the door to the great hall which was packed tight with the army's military stores. Not wanting to jeopardise their task, I remained just inside the door while they moved deeper into the room, weaving in between barrels in the near-dark until they disappeared from sight completely. Satisfied that they had gone unnoticed, I then accompanied the returning party out of the hall and made for my own lodging, hoping that no one would remark this night on the absence of my guards.

Upon entering my room I saw the three packs loaded with gold dust where I had left them that morning. A part of me now felt redeemed. The prince had accused me of coveting gold to the detriment of all else – particularly honour. It had been a painful insight into my past, but as I looked at the packs, I knew it was not my future. I had left the gold here unguarded in order to take the chest, loaded instead with ash from the camp's fires, in plain sight to the store hall. There Bekoe and Kofi were even now busily mixing the ash with the powder barrels, to weaken the mixture. With my dramatic demonstration of an over-filled musket I hoped that in battle, the Ashanti would now under-fill their weapons, and that this combined with the weakened powder would render their volleys ineffective. It was still not likely to sway the outcome of a battle where twenty thousand challenged one, but it might allow time for a retreat. I had given my country – and my friend – a chance.

I endured a fitful sleep that night. I had expected as much, but the rainstorm which broke shortly after I lay down, and raged all night, ensured it. However, I comforted myself that the cacophony of noise, from rain on fat leaves, on thatches, on dry ground, and on stone, would serve all the better to mask my men in their work.

As the rains subsided and dawn broke I left my hut, eager to know if our plan had been successful. I found the whole village alive, with fires cooking breakfasts and horns sounding to rally men. It seemed that something was afoot, but without Kofi to translate, it was impossible to know what. I made my way to the store hall in time to see the guards unlocking the doors and waving in a long column of slaves and Ashanti tribesmen, daubed in paint and wearing belts with knives and quivers filled with arrows. My heart beat faster as it became clear – the Ashanti were readying for battle.

Kofi and Bekoe did not emerge with the first men carrying barrels and crates, and I told myself that this was sensible. But every minute seemed like an hour as I waited, my anxious mind considering how they might have been discovered, and how they might even now be being tortured. I was lifted from my gloom as I saw Kofi's grinning face emerge from the hall, carrying the chest. Behind him was Bekoe, more sombre. I moved to intercept them and engage in a small piece of theatre for the benefit of any nearby guards. Berating Kofi for disappearing, I told him to accompany me to my quarters, to pack my belongings into the chest which, throwing it open for all to see, I showed to be empty. Any interest any onlooker had taken was immediately lost once the contents were known. Guards were posted to prevent the theft of military hardware – not of empty boxes.

We returned to my hut with the nervous excitement of men who have been acquitted of a crime. Kofi reported in hushed tones that everything had gone smoothly. The clamour of the storm had masked any noise, and the ash in the chest had been spread between more than half of the gunpowder barrels. With what little I knew of the chemistry, I calculated this should significantly weaken its potency – perhaps by as much as a half. I commended my accomplices on a job well done, and suggested we attach ourselves to the prince's party, the better to understand his intentions.

The prince was returned to his enraged state, though I suspected this temperament was more for the benefit of his commanders than for himself. He railed and spat, receiving periodic cheers and affirmative shouts from his entourage. There was no map. No analysis of the terrain, no sudden intelligence of a fatal weakness to be exploited. Here there was only the whipping up of his army into a bloodthirsty state, ready for battle.

And yet, once his commanders were dismissed to their men, and the prince and his closest followers began their advance, Kofi was able to relate to me something of what had been said – and it seemed once again that I had underestimated the Ashanti.

'The scouts have reported on the enemy this past day. They are encamped across a river only four miles distant, by a village we call

Assamacow. They have endured a miserable night in the rain, without shelter. They are only five hundred in number – only a hundred redcoats – and the governor is amongst them.'

I halted mid-stride as Kofi said this, nearly tripping over myself as I did so. It could not be true. I had known that the Ashanti would have numerical superiority – and I feared that in this terrain they would have an advantage. But for Sir Charles himself to venture into the heart of enemy territory with so few seemed impossible. It would be suicide to oppose the Ashanti so weakly. I prayed that this were some trap which had been laid, but I feared the worst. I resumed my pace, and Kofi and Bekoe resumed alongside me, each of us carrying a part of the gold in our packs.

'The scouts are concealed around the flanks of the enemy. Prince Sai has ordered them to be reinforced without detection. He himself travels with the main body of his army, who advance as one towards the river to face the governor head-on.'

So this was it. Sir Charles, and presumably Robert and his men as well, were already surrounded, and they did not even know. If there were to be any hope of preventing the slaughter, there must be an immediate fighting retreat – before the Ashanti could cross the river in front of them. The sun had just reached its zenith. Battle would not be joined for several more hours. It was possible that an orderly retreat might survive until dark, at which point there could be no pursuit possible through the thick jungle.

Remaining within sight of the prince, we marched onwards for some time in silence. Between trees and roots and bushes I caught glimpses of countless columns of men moving alongside in single-file, so that the whole jungle seemed as if it were creeping forward with us. I presumed that the crackle of musketry would alert us to the beginning of the battle. Yet this strange country had one more surprise to bestow on me. Through the muffling walls of the jungle, I began to hear music. Not the toneless wailing of the Ashanti horns and flutes – but recognisable music. A melody. I could hardly credit my own ears, but with every minute the sound grew louder and more distinct, until I realised that I was listening to our very own 'God Save The King'. There cannot have been a more bizarre setting in the history of the British Empire for it – though it could only be a token act of defiance. In response, the Ashanti instruments struck up, each simultaneously playing their own melodies for their own commanders. The resulting maelstrom of noise was an impossible blend of farce and menace as it swept across the jungle in front of me, seemingly rising from half the compass.

And then, as the war drums receded, the sporadic crack of musketry began. Still accompanied on both sides by a moving mass of men, we pressed forward until we could hear the muskets firing around us. The gunfire was now incessant, and the steam of the jungle began to mix with the smoke of the gunpowder. Peering ahead through the trees, I could see a brown river flowing quickly and, beyond that, the bright red jackets of the British Army. It was an absurd notion, but it was impossible not to take some small comfort from the sight, or feel a slight sense of home. Having been so many months away from London, this small band was a reminder of everything I had left behind, and all I dearly wished to see again. They were pitifully few in number, strung out in a ragged line across the river, firing in no perceivable rhythm and with no perceivable effect into the wall of greenery in front of them. A thin veil of smoke hung across their positions, from their own gunfire. Taking care, I crept forward another fifty yards and now, with the river close at hand, I could see the British troops in detail: their officers barking instructions, and the smart actions of their loading drill. Around them buzzed irregulars, some dressed in the semi-uniform of militia, and some clearly local tribesmen opposed to the Ashanti. To my satisfaction, I noted that the British positions were well back from the river – perhaps fifty or even sixty yards. That would be maximum range for their muskets, as

I had urged Lieutenant Newton at our parting. For the Ashanti, with their weakened powder, it would be too far to be effective.

I scanned the scene for the distinctive Royal Marine hat and, sure enough, found Robert positioned with his troop on the British left flank. Once again I felt the absurd leap of excitement in seeing my friend, after the trials I had had to face alone. This emotion was immediately tempered by the knowledge of the peril he faced. I had to find a way to reach him. Even a disciplined force could only hope to hold off such impossible odds for a matter of hours. As soon as the Ashanti could effect a crossing of the river, which was only twenty yards wide, they would swiftly overwhelm my friend and his comrades.

Even as I took all this in, a group of Ashanti nearby began hacking with axes at a cotton tree. Groaning at first, then bowing with increasing speed, it fell to earth over the river, forming a narrow but serviceable bridge. Immediately, a detachment of redcoats moved to a position directly opposite and, arranging themselves into two ranks, poured three volleys into the first warriors to charge across. This blunted the attack, and the detachment remained on station, laying down a withering fire to discourage any further attempts to cross. However, it was surely only a matter of time before more commanders employed the tactic, and coordinated their attacks. Turning to Kofi, I instructed him and Bekoe to follow me along the river. We had to find a safe place to cross.

Time seemed to stretch out as my fear grew that we would be too late. Every minute that we progressed along the bank I heard renewed volleys of gunfire, and feared the British were being overwhelmed. We pressed on ever more urgently. Bekoe and Kofi went in front, carefully guiding me around the Ashanti lines. Slowly the jungle became quieter and emptier, the dense foliage oblivious to the struggle of its neighbours – until it seemed to have forgotten them altogether. The battle here was indistinguishable from the rustle of a leaf, or the snapping of a twig underfoot. Bekoe stopped, his head still scanning left and right as he spoke, and Kofi turned to me with a smile. We had found a gap in the enemy lines, and could proceed into the British lines. Between us we followed the example of the Ashanti and cut down a tree to form a bridge. Once across the river we worked our way around the battle, so as to approach from the rear, and avoid being shot by either side. As we proceeded, Bekoe periodically pointed into trees and thickets, where Ashanti scouts could be seen across the river, seemingly happy to let the battle rage for now. Their very presence made my heart sink. Far from leading the Ashanti into a trap as I had vainly hoped, Sir Charles had himself wandered headlong into Prince Sai's – and he had not required any great persuasion to do so.

As we drew closer to the besieged encampment, the sounds of war grew loud once again. The trees around us began to thin, and I could see the British position now from its rear. To our left the marines still held their line, though offering very little fire to the surrounding forest. I allowed myself a small smile. Somehow, against impossible odds, we had managed to reach Robert, and now I dared to believe we might yet make our escape together. Attaching a white cloth to the top of my sword, I led my two companions out from the forest and towards his position at a brisk walk. Every instinct urged me to run – but I knew that a British officer did not run, and nor did a man under a flag of truce. We crossed the open ground and then, suddenly, Robert was lifting his hat, hailing me.

'By God – if it isn't Victor Winter, back from the fires of hell itself! Make way there, open ranks!'

We walked safely into the midst of their formation, and then he was laughing and shaking my hand and shaking his head in equal measure.

'You have chosen the queerest place for a reunion, Victor, but I do declare it is good to see you nonetheless. I long to hear your story, but I fear we have a bit of a fight on our hands here. The governor appears to have brought us up against the whole Ashanti army – and we're just a few hundred in number.'

There was no time for niceties. 'I'm afraid your assessment is correct, Robert. These two men helped me escape, and they tell me the enemy numbers fifteen or even twenty thousand. There can be no victory against those odds. You must prevail upon Sir Charles to retreat as soon as possible.'

My friend's face went suddenly pale.

'But tell me, what of their powder? Did you manage to sabotage it?'

'I did – you will find their range much reduced. Provided they do not coordinate an attack over the river, you should be able to hold your position until dusk.'

There was something in the look he gave me which told me this was a forlorn hope, even before he spoke.

'I fear we will not be able to repel many more assaults, Victor. Much of our own powder was spoiled in the rains last night, and none of my men has more than four of their twenty rounds left. Mr Daniels was sent to bring up the baggage train with fresh ammunition this morning, but he has yet to arrive. All our hopes now rest on him.'

Now I felt the blood drain from my face. At times in the past weeks I had prayed for a reckoning with Daniels: a chance to balance my account – to balance Jones' account, and Millette's, whose face I could still see, huddled in the surgeon's cabin. But now he had returned, he threatened to condemn every man around me to death.

'Robert – Mr Daniels is in league with the enemy. During my time with the pirates, before I managed to escape, his name was mentioned. It was he who put the *White Star* off course. He who poisoned the ship's crew. If your only hope is with him, then there is no hope. We must effect a withdrawal immediately.'

He frowned, disbelieving.

'Surely you are mistaken. These are very serious accusations. I cannot imagine that an Englishman – a loyal subject to the crown – could betray his countrymen to a foreign army...'

'You cannot imagine it, because you could not consider it yourself. That is your great virtue, but also your weakness. Other men are more easily turned to evil. Daniels is one of those.'

It pained me to know that I spoke also of myself. I too had once colluded with the enemy. I knew what Daniels was capable of because I too had been capable of it. From the comfort of London clubs and studies, I had blithely weighed profit against men's lives – numbers against numbers, and seen only personal gain. I was ashamed to the bottom of my soul to see the consequences of my actions. Yet there was no time now for self-pity. My atonement would be to rescue these men – to lead them safely from their overpowering foe.

'They're making another thrust through the centre, sir!' cried an anxious private.

And so they were. The rains from the previous night had made the river impassable – yet the stream had now visibly decreased, and alongside the makeshift bridges, the Ashanti now began to ford it across a wide front, meeting only sporadic fire from the British troops opposite.

'Time to redeploy, I think,' said Robert, all debate quashed by the urgent need. 'Mr Simpson! Double time over to support the centre if you please!'

With admirable order, the small troop gathered their packs and we ran the short distance to lend support to the centre of the line, who were now engaged in hand-to-hand fighting to repel the Ashanti.

'Look sir!' came the cry from another marine. 'Porters!'

I followed his arm, and sure enough, emerging from the forest to our rear was a column of porters carrying kegs. They looked pitifully few in number, but they might be enough to effect our escape. At their head was Daniels himself, looking every bit the hero as he led them toward the battle. Utterly perplexed by the turn of events, I found myself unable to offer an explanation.

'Let us not wonder what gave you cause to doubt,' said Robert, relief washing over his face. 'Let us simply be glad. We may live to fight another day after all!'

The porters made their way to a point some fifty yards behind us, where we saw Governor MacCarthy, positioned with a major and a native commander.

'Let's retrieve some supplies, Victor. Mr Simpson!'

The burly marine sergeant snapped to attention, his pike blade bright with blood.

'I leave you in charge of the troop until my return. Lend supporting fire. Expend all ammunition. There will be more!'

With that, and leaving Bekoe and Kofi with the marines and our packs, Robert and I ran to the governor's position, all thought of etiquette banished in our desperation.

The major called to us as we approached. 'The natives on our right have deserted us, Lieutenant! You are to resupply your troops from here and organise an orderly withdrawal to our rear.'

Finally, it seemed, the governor and his commanders had seen sense. Rushing to a keg, Robert eased open the lid, and stopped dead. With a look of horror he flung his hand inside, and when it emerged, we all shared his expression. His hand grasped dried pasta.

'Wh... what is this?' came a voice from behind me. I turned to see Sir Charles himself, equally as horrified, looking from his major to Robert for some explanation.

'We have been betrayed, sir,' came the wavering response from the major.

'Daniels!' The name was uttered as an expletive by the governor. 'Where is Daniels, Major?'

'He was with the porters, sir... they retired to our rear just moments ago.'

'Lieutenant. You will pursue Mr Daniels and return him here to answer to me. I will have him hung! Major Ricketts. You will please organise the withdrawal.'

Even as he spoke, the small British force before us seemed to shudder under the weight of a renewed assault. I saw men in red jackets fall, and knew that the situation was already hopeless. Kofi and Bekoe were fighting valiantly at the edge of the fray, but I managed to catch their attention, and shouted for them to follow me. Turning, I saw Robert already forty yards away, running after the disappearing porters, and I set off after him through the jungle.

The sound of hand-to-hand fighting was now all around us. Sweat poured from my face and stung my eyes, and already my lungs screamed with each breath as I forced my legs on to catch both my friend and my foe. Time seemed elastic – I could not tell if I ran for seconds or minutes. I heard Robert shouting for Daniels to halt, clearly in vain, and followed the shouts blindly. Suddenly they were only twenty yards in front of me through the trees, both with their swords drawn, slowly circling, eyes fixed intently on each other, oblivious to the slaughter around them.

With a scream and a blur of movement, Daniels launched himself forwards, sword scything down at Robert from above. There was a quick step and a parry, and an immediate second attack from Daniels, hacking madly at his challenger, eyes wild. Another step, another parry. A third and a fourth attack met the same response, and Daniels withdrew, breathing heavily, to resume their circling. Again Daniels closed on Robert, with a savageness which made me wince - but try as he might, he could not penetrate Robert's defence – and slowly now Robert began to push back, learning his foe's style, countering the cuts and slicing neatly, efficiently in return. They now seemed evenly matched as they traded blows, Robert's science matched by Daniels' raw aggression.

Daniels licked his lips as they pulled apart once again, and I could almost see his vicious mind working, trying to find a way past Robert's sword. A tribal cry penetrated through the jungle to us, followed instantly by a response, and then the drums began to beat. Daniels cocked his head towards the noise, and lowered his sword.

'You hear that, bootneck?' His voice was loud – a challenge to Robert. 'That's the end of your men. You deserted them, didn't you? The niggers are coming for you now. You sure you want to waste time fighting me? You want to get running, bootneck.'

There was a twitch of movement from the point of Robert's sword, and Daniels leapt aside, seeing too late that it was only a feint. The faintest of smiles cracked over Robert's face – but still he remained silent, eyes fixed on his opponent.

Daniels' face meanwhile contorted with rage, and again he flew at Robert, shouting and cursing with each strike. A low cut from Daniels met a strong guard from Robert, who stepped to his side, and moved to cut inside Daniels' guard, right to left. Daniels narrowly avoided the stroke, jumping back and arching his back as the blade swept past him. He looked done for, but next moment was on the attack again, coming at Robert even as he recovered his balance.

Their attacks came fast and fluid: one moment one man seemed to have the upper hand, the next it was reversed as defence became attack. Robert parried a high cut and thrust forward, but Daniels reacted and parried in turn, stepping forwards across the thrust and delivering a blow with his left fist to Robert's face. Staggering back, he raised his guard to defend a wild slash from Daniels as he over-extended, offering only the tip of his blade to Robert's sword. Robert thrust again at his off-balance foe, who could only leap backwards with both feet to avoid the point, dropping his sword as he did so. His feet slipped as he landed, and he fell onto his back, defeated. Yet at that moment he reached to his belt, his hand emerging with a pistol which he levelled at Robert.

A cry erupted unbidden from my throat as I realised what was about to occur and both men, having been entirely oblivious to my presence, now turned to see me for the first time. Daniels' eyes widened as he recognised me – a man he believed he had killed. His pistol moved to follow his head, and I stared transfixed at the barrel of my fate. I saw a movement and a blur of red, and closed my eyes as I heard the final sentence of the gunshot.

When I opened them again I realised he had missed. I was unharmed. Daniels was already on his feet and running again into the jungle – but in front of me Robert lay motionless. My friend and, I now understood, my saviour. I ran to him, and knelt by his side. From his chest blossomed a dark red stain, blooming across his white shirt. I was lost for words. He lay dying before me, looking into my eyes.

'Why? Why did you do that?' was all I could think to ask. 'The bullet was meant for me.'

'For honour. For love. What else is there?' As he spoke, blood seeped from his mouth, and his eyes grew glassy. I felt tears running down my cheeks.

'Robert...'

'Take my letter. Give it to my wife. Tell her I love her. Tell her I am sorry.'

I was weeping now, my brow knitted with confusion that a good man should die to save my life, while a bad one escaped. I nodded. He raised a hand and placed it on mine. He forced a smile through his pain, exhaled, and was still.

'*Owura* – we must go. It is over. The Ashanti come now.'

Kofi and Bekoe had arrived by my side. They stood, looking down at my fallen friend.

I nodded once more, wiping my face with my sleeve. I reached into his jacket and retrieved his letter. Kofi knelt down by his head and closed his eyes.

'He saved your life, *owura.*'

All I seemed capable of was nodding. Bekoe unbuckled his belt with the scabbard attached, and replaced the sword inside it. Not knowing what to do, I crossed his arms over his middle and, taking Kofi's hand, rose unsteadily to my feet.

'We must go now, *owura,*' he repeated. 'The warrior's spirit goes to heaven. His sword to his wife.'

With Kofi in front and Bekoe behind me, we set off, away from the fading sounds of a battle lost. I felt numb. I did not ask where we went, or why. I could not think. I simply followed. Some small part of my mind observed that it grew dark rapidly. It did not seem to matter. We ran on.

XXVI

We travelled through the night. We ran to escape the jaws of the Ashanti army before they closed shut around us. I ran because it seemed like the right thing to do. Because Kofi and Bekoe urged me to. We stopped at daybreak, utterly spent. Bekoe disappeared into the jungle to ensure we had not been followed, while Kofi sank down next to me on a tree root.

'He was your friend, this man?'

I nodded.

'And why did this other man fight him?'

'Daniels sabotaged the ammunition. He was desperate to see the British slaughtered. I don't know why.'

'We did the same to the Ashanti. It is easy to call the white man enemy. He is different to me. But this does not mean the black man is always a friend. The Ashanti kill many of my people, so I help the white man to fight them. I have made friends with enemies, and found enemies amongst friends. The enemy is harder to see when he looks like a friend.'

'I have learnt my lesson, Kofi. And I will offer a reward for his head – for anyone who can find him.'

'Why did this Daniels fire at you, *owura*?'

'Because he wants me dead. Because I'm the only man alive who knows what he did. Because I can put a price on his head. Because I have the gold he wanted for himself.'

'Then perhaps you will not need this price, *owura*. Perhaps he will find you.'

He was right. Just as revenge drove me to find him, he still had cause to find me. I could not let my guard drop.

'Where are we heading, Kofi?'

'Boutry, *owura*. *Capitao* Carvalho is awaiting us there.'

The *Kraken*. I had forgotten the rendezvous in the panic and grief of our retreat. I had a way out. I might yet escape this disaster and see Sir Godfrey and dear Annabel again.

We reached Boutry the following morning, having made our way in stages, resting only for a few hours at a time to stay ahead of any pursuing Ashanti. It was no more than a handful of whitewashed clay huts, sitting low against the mouth of the river and beneath a hill upon which stood the Dutch fort. As we walked wearily towards it in the early dawn light, we could see a familiar ship sitting at anchor in the estuary, and Kofi confirmed it was the *Kraken*. After months at sea, I could not have imagined that I would be eager so soon to embark another vessel, yet the sight of it felt like a homecoming of sorts. Drawing closer, my footsteps felt lighter, despite the ordeal of the past few days.

The unmistakable report of a gunshot from the river shattered the tranquil scene, and I turned to see Daniels, my cursed shadow, stepping from a canoe to the shore before me.

'I thought I'd find you here, Winter,' he shouted across the dusty road between us. 'You're like a rat on a ship – you just keep reappearing. This time I'm going to stick the blade right through you till you stop squirming. Let's see if you can survive that.'

'You're murdering scum, Daniels. First Jones, now Newton. There's a debt for you to pay.'

'You still don't get it, do you, Winter?' He said, drawing his sword and approaching me with a swagger. 'It's me that's collecting today.'

Rage coursed through my veins. I fought to control it, knowing Robert would say it clouded my judgement. I drew my sword – the gift from Prince Sai.

'Bekoe, Kofi – please inform Captain Carvalho I'll be a little late. I have some business to attend to in town.'

Daniels tilted his head. 'Stealing my gold *and* my passage home, boy? Deserting me on this miserable coast? I don't think so.'

He took two more quick steps and flew into a furious attack, cutting left and right at my head and neck. His strokes were powerful, but the strength of my own anger matched them, and I guarded each one where I stood. He stepped back, both of us breathing heavily.

'What makes you think you've got any more chance than that pathetic whelp Newton? I watched him train you!'

Again he came at me, but this time I remembered my feet, stepping back and catching his foible easily with my guard. Attack followed attack, but I forced myself to be patient, guarding and stepping and blunting his efforts – waiting for a mistake.

He came to close with me, and did so clumsily, allowing me to step around him and cut at his cheek. He reacted late but with strength, swiping my cut away and swinging his body round towards me as he did so. In a split second I recalled the blow he dealt Robert, and ducked in time to see the left hook come sailing over me. As he twisted and overbalanced, I launched every ounce of my rage and grief up through my left fist into his midriff, and felt a dull crack from his rib. Staggering from my blow, I followed him into my own attack, cutting left and right. He guarded my attacks, but wildly now. He caught a cut late and we stood locked together, face to face for a moment. I looked in his eyes and saw they had changed. The arrogance was gone. He had seen me train with Robert, but he had not seen me fight Bekoe. Bekoe had taught me to streetfight.

I bent my arm and brought our faces closer in behind our blades. 'Where's your pistol to save you now, Daniels?'

As I said it, I raised my knee with all my force into his groin. He doubled over, but as I raised my hilt to strike him on the head, he charged at my midriff with his shoulder. My sword went tumbling from my grasp and I sprawled on the ground on my back. In a moment he was over me again, eyes streaming from my blows yet defiant once more. He drew back his sword to cut me in two, and in desperation I tore at my scabbard and held it out, catching the impact just as the blow landed. And there it stayed. His steel bit deep into the golden scabbard, and would not come out. He hauled at his blade, but I held on for dear life, and neither moved. In a flash he let go and instead dropped upon my scabbard, forcing it down onto my neck and choking me. I fought back with all my might, but his bodyweight was against me, and I felt myself slowly being suffocated. I could smell his vile breath on my face, and he spat as he retorted:

'I don't need pistols to kill off vermin, *rat*.'

Somewhere deep within me, something spoke – something primal. It was a thought, and yet not a thought. It did not emanate from my mind, but rather filled my whole body with one single resolve – a truth that seemed to take control of me.

I could not die here.

Not here – not at this man's hands. To heap more dishonour on Robert's grave. To make his sacrifice for nothing. I would find a way.

And then, I was looking at the answer. I released my right hand from the scabbard, and for a moment felt the pressure rise on my neck. The next moment, my hand was flying towards his belt. Another, and it closed on the hilt of his knife. Just one more, as my vision began to fade to black, and I plunged the knife with all my remaining strength into his heart.

There was a sudden intake of breath from my foe, and then a blood-curdling cry as he realised his fate. His face, just inches from mine, contorted into a grotesque expression of horror and pain, and he rose, hands around his own knife, staggering away from me.

Gasping for air, I instinctively placed a hand on my injured windpipe and pushed myself up with the other. Daniels stumbled a few feet further, before tripping and sinking finally to his knees in the dust, facing me across the road. With his face fixed in that same expression, eyes bulging and mouth curled, he rolled forward, and was still.

I remained sat opposite him, inhaling, exhaling, my mind frantically trying to put the past three minutes of life and death struggle into some sort of order. Slowly it dawned on me. Daniels was dead. The spectre hiding just beyond my sight these past months; the demon who caused those around me to suffer on my behalf – who robbed me of my free will, and forced events down their nightmarish path. Jones had died. Robert had died. But there would be no more. I had avenged them.

I saw movement out of the corner of my eye, and turned my head to see Bekoe, Kofi and Captain Carvalho running towards me. They stopped as they saw the prostrate Daniels. Gingerly now they walked forwards. Kofi spoke first.

'The *Capitao* says we are fools, *owura*. We must ask your forgiveness.'

I tried to speak, but found my voice only came as a whisper.

'Wh... What do you mean?'

'The *Capitao* says we should not have left you to this man. He says this man is a murderer. He says he is very fond of you, and will be very angry if you are dead.'

A smile came involuntarily to my face, and once again I felt the track of tears down my face. 'Well you may tell your captain that I am not dead, Kofi.'

'No *owura*. I see that. But this man is.'

'Yes. He is.'

XXVII

With some small cosmetic changes in appearance, the *Kraken*, temporarily restyled the *Leviathan*, sailed peacefully into Freetown harbour.

'I try to do as little as possible to upset the West Africa Squadron,' said Captain Carvalho, as we stood on the quarterdeck together, watching the bow cut through the water ahead. 'They fight to break a cycle which has made tyrants rich, and torn families apart. Some of the men on this boat were rescued by the Squadron. I stay out of their business, and I am able to come and go here.'

'I am grateful for your help, Captain. Were it not for you I would still be stranded on the Gold Coast, running from the Ashanti horde.'

'Oh, I think you would be safe behind the walls of the forts, *senhor* Winter. Remember what I told you before? If the Ashanti come to the coast, and try to take the forts, they will be defeated. If the British are wise they will stay on the coast, and let the Ashanti rule the interior. This is what the Dutch and the Portuguese do. We have no place in the jungle.'

'Nonetheless, I must thank you for awaiting my return.'

'You have seen enough now, *senhor* Winter, to know I did not wait just for you.'

I turned to look at him, but he stared stoically onward. There was something that still evaded my understanding. He relented and turned to me.

'Why do you think *senhor* Daniels found you at Boutry? Why was he there?'

My mind turned slowly.

'He... he was fleeing too. You took his money... you were meeting him too?!'

304

'I told you before to be careful who you trusted, *senhor* Winter. You have an alarming tendency to think the best of people. You and Daniels both planned to escape the conflict with the gold. Happily, I was able to extend my services to both of you. It did not matter who was successful. Either way I got paid. As it is, I do not even have to pay back Daniels for failing to kill you myself.'

The captain shrugged to underline his studied indifference, and a smile grew on my face.

'You would have me believe that you rushed to intervene at Boutry only for the sake of the money?'

Again I received the same studied expression.

'A wise man once told me you can't buy people's loyalty with gold, *Capitao* Carvalho.'

He could not resist his own smile now.

'You are a lost cause, *senhor* Winter. A true romantic.'

'As are you, Captain. But don't worry. I shan't tell anyone.'

Nonetheless, I was mindful of his warning. It was the second such advice I had received since embarking his ship. I would be more careful whom I trusted. I raised a hand to my left breast, and felt the letters contained in my pocket. One was a letter from a dead man – a good man, and a friend – to his widow. That would be my duty to deliver when I reached England. The other was a letter which had been tied together with it in Robert's pocket. It was a letter addressed to me at Cape Coast, from Annabel. In the panic of our flight from the battle and everything after, I had not even noticed it until I had sunk into my cot on the *Kraken*. I now knew the slant of every stroke by heart.

Dear Mr Winter

It has now been a month since you left London – a month which I have spent in a state of some distress. Yet this distress has been at least partially of my own making, and I pray that you will find it in your heart to forgive me.

We have long been friends, dear Mr Winter, and I recall with great fondness the passion in your eyes as you called out those frightened little men in their rooms at St Peter's Field. That was the occasion of our first meeting, but I regret that for a time our friendship remained silent or at least distant. Perhaps had we known each other better, I should not have felt compelled to take the course I have.

I too have passions, Mr Winter. It is not at all fashionable to admit this, and Lady Sefton has repeatedly entreated me to dispense with what she sees as childish fancies. However, a passion is not easily dissuaded, and I have found myself either unwilling or unable to give mine up. Indeed, it was our shared passion for social justice on that fateful day in Manchester which bound us together – so I find myself wondering if it should be so wrong for me to encourage such a force for good.

I will admit that your travel to Africa thrills and frightens me in equal measure. The selfish part of me did not wish to see you put in danger, though I know that the Victor who charged into the crowd at St Peter's Field would think little of that danger. However, the romantic part of me thrilled to think of you working for the equality of mankind – to defend African women, children, and men, who might otherwise be enslaved by their neighbours on the Gold Coast.

I sometimes wonder if I romanticise my friend Mr Winter too much, when I see him immersed in the frivolous pleasures of London society, or hear stories of his avid pursuit of wealth. Yet I have seen him risk his own life to save unknown innocents. And I have known him speak with such passion, and with such tenderness, that I know he has all this within him. I can conclude only that you, like me, are capable of being led astray from your natural goodness by those who would manipulate you to suit their own cause.

In this regard, dear Mr Winter, I am guilty, and I pray daily that you will not suffer because of my lapse of judgement. Whilst the romantic in me wished for your heroic involvement in the struggle against slavery, I was induced by another party to give you encouragement quite beyond that which I felt. That party believed that I, more than any other, might prevail upon you to undertake this endeavour – and whilst I believe he flattered me to think so, I must confess to my shame that I was easily coerced.

Lord Elsfield is undoubtedly a powerful man and a useful ally to us both. But what little I have observed of him leads me to question where his morality lies, and what he would not *do to further his own ends. One would be wise, I think, to trust such a man no more than was necessary.*

I do not wish to speak overly ill of a friend – as we have both profited from his patronage. But I do pray for your safe return, and I do hope that I have not led you astray.

Please destroy this letter, as I know you will.

Sincerely

A.

I was scarcely in control of my emotions upon boarding the *Kraken,* and the discovery of this letter had only caused further anguish. I realised that Robert must have taken it upon his departure from Cape Coast with Governor MacCarthy, never once doubting that I would be true to my word, and would find my way back to him. His trust in me, undeserving as I was, was truly humbling.

Its content left me equally distraught. There was fondness within it, certainly. But there was also regret. Regret that our friendship had not developed more swiftly into something more... Regret that she had placed me in danger... How much danger she could not have the slightest idea.

Her mention of Lord Elsfield's patronage slid a long-blurred memory into sharp focus. It had been *his* coat of arms on the carriage in Berkeley Square. *He* had accompanied her to the club in Cripplegate. I knew only too well how carefully he might have guided her these past months. I feared that we had both been manipulated by Lord Elsfield, and perhaps continued to be even now.

This was a fear which had consumed much of my energy during the voyage from Boutry to Freetown. I had been Lord Elsfield's pawn for so long, desperate for his approval, believing I could not win Sir Godfrey's. Now, bound for home with Sir Godfrey's promise still vivid in my memory, I wondered if I had been blind to Lord Elsfield – and if so, how much he might be capable of. I thought of Sir Gregor, and of Lord Cochrane, and now of myself. At the very least, he had sent me on a mission knowing that if I failed, I would join that illustrious list of scapegoats.

He had employed Daniels as his spy. But did this make Lord Elsfield responsible for his actions? He had been poorly chosen for his task, with a lust for gold which I now realised was evident from his history with Cochrane in South America. Somewhere between spying, embezzlement and murder, had Daniels followed his own path?

Yet I could not pretend, in my most candid moments, that I had not known the danger. I had accepted the mission, despite warnings from Sir Godfrey. Lord Elsfield had been determined to sway my decision. He had used my feelings for Annabel against me. I felt anger – outrage, even, at the betrayal by the two people I had trusted most in the world. But ultimately, it had been *my decision*. I had been younger then. I thought about what Captain Carvalho had said. What Annabel now said. I would be more careful in the future with that trust.

XXVIII

I left Kofi, Bekoe, Captain Carvalho and the *Kraken* with fond farewells and generous payment for their trouble, and arranged onward passage to England soon after. By the time I arrived at Plymouth the seasons had changed, and the air was mild and fresh. In the fields and front gardens of cottages daffodils greeted the coming of spring.

With some enquiries at a quayside tavern I found the location for the address on Robert's letter, and walked the short distance between them inhaling my native air with an appreciation I could not have imagined only seven months before. Yet my footsteps were heavy.

The door was answered by a smart but plainly-dressed lady whose clothes and demeanour belied eyes that could not have been older than twenty five. I had rehearsed this conversation many times on the voyage home, but still I hesitated with each new sentence, knowing that at any moment the truth would dawn upon this poor woman. It did not take long. At 'I recently served alongside your husband, Lieutenant Newton, on the Gold Coast of Africa...' I was invited inside, and I saw those young eyes suddenly age.

While she rocked their son in his cradle, I told her of a man who had become a friend, and taught me the meaning of honour. I told her of the battle, of her husband's unerring conduct, and of the overwhelming odds. News had already reached England, but few of the names of the fallen were yet known. Upon presenting her with his sword her grief overcame her, and rekindled my own. For a moment we sat encased in our solitude, unable to speak.

Finally, I told her how he had died, saving my life, and of his final words – words of love to her. I placed a satchel on the table before her, together with the letter he had bade me give her with his dying breath. I offered her and her son my deepest condolences, and gave her my St James's address, should she ever need for anything. Then, unable to bear the guilt any longer, I left. If Lord Elsfield even noticed the gold to be missing, I would answer for it. There were debts to be paid.

I took the stagecoach to London, and decided against sending word of my arrival ahead. Entering along the Bath Road, I found the great city just as I had left it, with soaring spires piercing the skyline as far as I could see, and St Paul's uppermost in the centre. The season was gathering momentum once more, and men and women on elegant mounts trotted gracefully along the paths of Hyde Park, while well-heeled bachelors wandered with a studied nonchalance towards their clubs in time for a fashionably late luncheon.

After the privations of the jungle, six months afloat, and four days in the stage, the poise and calm of my home town seemed almost dreamlike – but the unabashed lavishness of Lord Elsfield's London house remained altogether different, and quite extraordinary to behold. The King of Ashanti himself, with all his gold, had nothing so splendid with which to overawe his visitors. His Lordship received me in his study with the brandy, cigars and confident smile I had come to know so well. The fire flickered in the grate; Sir Godfrey's wife looked out from her picture; the books slowly rotted on their shelves, and I reflected that for half a year, half a world away, people had struggled, fought, and died, to secure an addition to his fortune whilst here, nothing changed. He took a careful lack of interest in the small fortune that I brought before him in gold. He took a polite interest in the recounting of my adventure. He nodded obligingly when I noted his spy.

'Of course, Daniels was a great help at first. Fine sailor. Not the talkative sort... but he was a poor choice of accomplice in the end, I fear.' I had had plenty of time on the voyage home to decide how to raise the matter. Lord Elsfield was nonchalant in his response.

'Oh really? Why's that?'

Did he struggle to contain an emotion? Suddenly, his confidence seemed slightly forced.

'He began to take liberties, my Lord. His greed got the better of him. I dare say he has an unsavoury past. He murdered a sailor in cold blood in a storm – and nearly caused the death of a second. He murdered a lieutenant of the King's Royal Marines, and then tried to kill me and make away with the gold.'

I felt my emotions welling up as I spoke. These people had names: Jones, Newton... They had *families*. Their blood was on his hands. If my name had been added to that list, would he have cared?

Concern passed over his face. He placed his cigar on its ashtray and leant forward across his desk.

'This is most disturbing, Victor. He came to me highly recommended. I hope you understand, I placed him with instructions to support you in any way possible.' He paused, searching my face. I was determined to give him no window into my mind. Annabel's advice circled round and round in my mind: *trust such a man no more than is necessary*. 'Where is Daniels now?'

I paused just long enough to judge his nerve.

'I left him by the side of the road, in a small town on the Gold Coast. He was face-down with a dagger in his heart. I shouldn't imagine there's anything left of him by now.'

It was my turn for nonchalance, façade though it may be. Daniels deserved no hyperbole, no sentiment. He deserved only to be wiped from the face of the earth and forgotten.

Lord Elsfield nodded thoughtfully, and leaned back in his chair, taking up his cigar once more.

'Then perhaps a sort of justice has been served. It is always a balance with these people. They must have the capacity to do harm, but must also have the wisdom to know when it is necessary. I fear Daniels lacked wisdom.'

He took a long drag on his cigar, blowing the smoke slowly from his mouth before continuing: 'On your next assignment you will be fully involved in the recruitment of any such accomplices.'

The familiar smile crept back onto his face – and my resolve buckled. In his mind, the matter was closed, and all was well once more. His ledger showed three more deaths against his name, and he smiled and turned the page. I could not maintain my show of indifference any longer.

'There will be no further assignments, my Lord.'

'What's that, Victor?' A look of condescension.

'I shan't be your stooge again. Perhaps you can no longer see it, but there's blood on our hands: on yours and on mine. It's all just a story here in London – but I saw their faces. I watched them die. No profit is worth that.'

I stood to leave, but he stood with me.

'You need some time. I can understand that. This was always going to be a big step for you – but look where you are now. You're shaping the *world*. Can you really go back to counting stores? To shipping grain?'

'I don't think the world needs shaping, my Lord. But it will always need grain.'

I walked to the door. For once he seemed to be speechless, and without his smile I could not read his reaction.

'What of Miss McNeil?'

I fought to contain my emotions at the mention of her name. So much had passed since our moment together at the ball: her association with the political club; her association with this very man; my promise at our parting at the London Docks; her letter, and all it contained. I did not know what I could expect from our reunion, and my mind battled my heart, hoping that however she had '*profited from his patronage*' would not affect us.

He smiled as he saw my hesitation.

'Will she be content to marry an office clerk? A man of no substance? Of no ambition?'

I shook my head.

'She will marry a man of integrity.'

I saw the smile reappear one last time, brimming with scorn, as I opened the door and left.

I knew that my duty was next to visit Sir Godfrey, but my heart prevailed, making the spurious argument that Annabel's home was a short stop along the route. It beat hard and fast as I informed the footman of my name and my business, and in spite of the cool spring weather I began to sweat as I awaited her arrival in the morning room. I soon forgot my interview with Lord Elsfield as I thought ahead to this next one. I had not dressed for elegant company. I thought of the fashionable set I had seen riding and promenading in Hyde Park, or meandering down Park Lane to their clubs, and worried that in my eagerness to see her I had overlooked common courtesies. Nor had I bathed since that morning – and that in a coaching inn outside London. After months in the tropics, or else surrounded by foul-smelling sailors and the fetid stench of airless ships, I doubted I could even tell a sweet scent from an abhorrent one. I had been foolish to succumb to my heart's will. I was on the point of making a hasty exit when the door opened, and there before me stood my Annabel, more beautiful than I had ever imagined. Quite unprepared and overcome, I stood still and mute for a disgracefully long time, until she came to my rescue with a smile.

'Mr Winter! Forgive me. I have prayed so long for this moment and now it is here I am quite overcome.' Her hands moved restlessly over her dress, smoothing it against herself. 'Please! Sit! I long to hear everything about your adventures. I have called for tea.'

We sat, and I talked until I had quite forgotten my nervousness. She asked endless questions about Africa, about its people, and their internecine warfare, and I did my best to answer, having been no more than a brief observer to so much of it. I blushed when forced to maintain the lie regarding the nature of my passage on the *Kraken* – I still felt the shame of deceiving Robert keenly, and supposed I always would. It was only when I paused at the end of my story that I realised we had still not been joined by a chaperone. This was my opportunity to say the words I had been planning since my departure, six months ago. Rising to my feet, I summoned my courage and began to speak:

'Miss McNeil. Annabel. I have something particular to ask...'

'Oh Victor. Please. Sit. There is so much that has happened. I must say *my* piece.'

And in that instant my hopes evaporated. She would not hear my suit. I sat with the heavy resignation of a man who knows that he has been denied the hand of a lady. Lord Elsfield's patronage had meant all that I had feared. I could see his scornful smile even now.

'You recall my letter, Victor. I have passions too. Ambitions. And Lord Elsfield promised to help me realise them, if I would help him convince you. I cannot tell you how many times I have regretted that agreement over the last six months, and the danger I placed you in. But agree I did, and he in turn has honoured his part. He has introduced me to powerful men – men who are in a position to influence the choices this country makes...'

Suddenly, somehow, I understood what she needed to tell me. Even as she continued to explain, I knew. I realised that she had always had this passion within her – it had been there that first fateful day – and that she had tried, in her own way, to tell me ever since. I listened, and with every word I found myself more reconciled to her path. I knew that the younger man I had been had pursued Annabel for himself. He had wanted her as a trophy, to increase his own worth.

'...I have always admired your ambition, Victor. I see myself reflected in it. But I have long known that *my* ambition goes beyond what society wants me to be. I cannot change it. It is my passion. We were not something I had planned for. What you want from me, I cannot give you. Not without sacrificing my passion. My other passion.'

'But do you want it too?'

The burning blue eyes looked at me, but where there had always been fire, I saw only water.

'I do.'

I hesitated. 'Then a promise between us and God is all I need.'

Her brow furrowed.

'The things I have seen, Annabel. The lessons I have learned... I have been foolish, and vain... I do not need the world to know. I need only know myself.'

I took her hand, and through the tears we shared a smile which penetrated my whole being. I was alive, and I had her love. Neither of these things had seemed possible when I had sat in a hut in the jungle, surrounded by Ashanti warriors preparing for battle against my countrymen. Annabel would pursue her own adventure, speaking for those who had no voice of their own, in Westminster, Carlton House, and beyond. It was the very same passion that had attracted me to her at St Peter's Field and ever since. But it was not an adventure she could pursue as a married woman. She must retain all of her allure. The Lord John Russells of this world did not stand a chance.

We parted more in love than we had ever been. There was a deep affection between us which would endure. But there was also sadness: the sadness of knowing that to fulfil some dreams, others must be sacrificed. The sadness that reason must prevail, and something so good must be hidden.

I walked onward to St James's Square in quiet contemplation, the sword and gold on my back the only reminders of all that had happened since I had last walked these streets. It seemed impossible.

By the time I came to knock on the door of Sir Godfrey's house, I had once again forgotten my appearance. For a moment I stood on the threshold, smiling while Oakes answered and gazed with curiosity at the bedraggled but familiar simpleton before him. Coming to my senses, and ignoring his attempted professionalism, I took his hand and pumped it vigorously, much to his surprise. Even he found himself lost for words for a moment.

'Is Sir Godfrey in, Oakes? I should very much like to see him.'

'Sir Godfrey is engaged in his study in a meeting with Mr McNeil, sir. He asked not to be disturbed...'

'I'm sure he did, Oakes,' I replied, undeterred, 'but I shall happily take all responsibility for your failure!'

And before he could say more, I was walking past him and towards the study.

The colour, grain and even the sound of the study door had a reassuring familiarity to it as I rapped once and entered without waiting to be denied. I took three steps inside the door and stopped, looking with serenity at my patron. He sat behind his desk with an expression of outrage on his face which befitted the breach of protocol. Yet even as I stood there, motionless, speechless, his expression changed and the frown lines were smoothed, his mouth broadening into a smile and his eyes widening in something akin to disbelief as he too stood.

'My God. Can it be? Victor?'

His joy was infectious, and I found myself smiling with him. He strode out from behind his desk and approached me. I extended my hand, but moving past it, he embraced me with both of his.

'My dear boy. When we heard the news, I feared the worst. The very worst! I cannot tell you how I have suffered – how all of us here have suffered.'

Almost forgotten by the desk, Mr McNeil now rose and joined us, face beaming to match ours.

'Mr Winter. A great pleasure, sir. I have not seen you since you stayed with us in Manchester. But I see you continue to do yourself credit. Pirates *and* an army of savages, I am told? Great credit.'

'As for that name, Victor. If you are amenable, I have a document in my desk which, with a signature from you, will make you my son and heir. I should have done it long ago. I should be honoured to have you a Ramsay.'

I looked from one to the other, attempting to take it all in. I should not have survived – but I was home. For the first time in my life, I was home.

Author's Note

Victor popped into my head, fully formed one morning: his full name, and a scene which I later realised was from the third book. It took me several years – and several conversations with patient friends – to track back and get to where it all began for him. That can happen when there's a day-job to do, and bills to pay. But the good news is that during that tracking process, there was plenty of good food and drink to turn it into an enjoyable experience in itself. Now that Victor has arrived in the world, I suspect he will be impatient to tell the rest of his story.

I have also greatly enjoyed the excuse to learn more about the early nineteenth century, and most of what happens around Victor is historical fact. The last 'Frost Fair' on the Thames in London took place in 1814, and records show an elephant walked the ice.

The Bank of England Fraud remains a mystery to this day. Whilst Lord Cochrane (and a handful of others) was blamed for it, many saw him as a scapegoat. His only crime was to have profited from the turmoil which ensued when, much as described, news of Napoleon's death and a French capitulation swept through London.

The Poyais Fraud was perhaps the most ambitious confidence trick in history, and Gregor McGregor a flamboyant proto-Charles Ponzi.

The battle of Assamacow (now styled Nsamankow), part of the First Anglo-Ashanti war, was a disaster for the British, and for Governor Charles MacCarthy in particular, who was killed there.

It would be another two and a half years before the British could inflict a telling defeat on the Ashanti, and use it to broker a settlement.

Researching the Ashanti was a particular challenge, and I was determined to portray them accurately, through a contemporary white European's eyes. I am therefore indebted to the accounts of William Hutton and Joseph Dupuis, real-life contemporaries of Victor who met the Ashanti and who wrote candidly of a culture alien to their own, fierce but with many remarkable and enlightened elements.

If you enjoyed reading Where Innocence Ends, you'll not want to miss The Eye of the Storm, an origin story set in the French Revolution.

I'd be thrilled if you joined my reader's club at www.WJStockdale.com/join, and you'll be the first to know when The Eye of the Storm goes to print if you do!!

Do also please leave a review (preferably positive, but all feedback is valid!) – they help me and help other readers too.

The Victor Winter Saga

The Eye of the Storm (A Victor Winter Saga prequel)
August 1792. The young Andrew Hardie, heir to the Earl of Elsfield, arrives at the court of Louis XVI in Paris determined to make his fortune from the turmoil engulfing France. Yet no-one could have foreseen how swiftly events would unravel, nor where they would end... *Coming soon.*

Where Innocence Ends (The Victor Winter Saga book 1)
As the industrial age dawns on London, an orphan is unwittingly caught in a deadly feud between two would-be-fathers. With enemies on all sides, he must learn who to trust, or perish on his mission to the jungles of West Africa.

An exploration of morality and self-deception, Where Innocence Ends follows its protagonist into the darkness and the light: from the ballrooms of Regency England to the rainforests of tribal Ghana, and leaves us questioning what we know.

The Student (The Victor Winter Saga book 2)
Coming soon.

The Master (The Victor Winter Saga book 3)

And don't forget – be the first to join Victor's further adventures: sign up to the Reader's Club at: www.WJStockdale.com/join

Notes

1. The Spanish Question was a crisis of government, known as the *Trienio Liberal* in Spain. It began when a military coup effectively overthrew the Bourbon monarch, Ferdinand VII, and enacted the liberal constitution of 1812, which Ferdinand himself had rescinded upon his restoration in 1814. The great powers of Europe convened at Verona in 1823 to agree an international resolution to the crisis.

2. Mary Wollstonecraft was a radical political writer, arguing in particular for the education and social equality of women. Her 1792 work 'A Vindication of the Rights of Woman' was well received at the time. However, revelations regarding her private life after her death turned public opinion against her and discredited her works for the next century. She was also the mother of Mary Shelley, author of 'Frankenstein'.

3. Following the events of Peterloo, the Home Secretary, Lord Sidmouth, wrote a public letter of thanks, stating that: 'The Prince Regent commands me to convey... his approbation and high commendation of the conduct of the magistrates and civil authorities at Manchester, as well as of the officers and troops, both regular, and yeomanry cavalry, whose firmness and effectual support of the civil power preserved the peace of the town upon that most critical occasion.' This letter was carefully aimed to demonstrate the firmness with which the government would put down threats to its authority.

4. Percy Bysshe Shelley drowned in mysterious circumstances off the coast of Italy in July 1822. Byron was in Italy until July 1823, when he departed for Greece to fight in their war of independence. He died there the following year of a fever, in April 1824. John Keats, another of the great British Romantic poets, died of tuberculosis in Rome in February 1821.

5. William Cowper, a prominent poet and abolitionist, published 'The Task' in 1785. A poem in blank verse over six books, book II considers slavery, and urges the enforcement of its abolition to be championed by the British Empire.

6. The *Santisima Trinidad* was a Spanish first-rate ship of the line, built in 1768 and captured by the British fleet at Trafalgar. It remains the most heavily armed sailing ship ever built, and one of the largest.

7. A tribal kingdom a little inland and west of Cape Coast

Printed in Great Britain
by Amazon

86173494R10187